"Dark suspense, sexy heroes, fiendish villains, and fantastic writing. Leslie Parrish is the hottest new name in edgy, exciting romantic thrillers."

—Award-winning author Roxanne St. Claire

## LOVE ME ... DEADLY

Though his immediate sensory reaction to the scent was a familiar jolt of tenderness and protectiveness, it didn't counteract his other senses. The scrape of her bare leg against his jeans ratcheted up the tension, as did the sound of each of her slow in-and-out breaths. Her hand, resting beside his on the table, was so damned slim, fragile, yet the arms revealed by the sleeveless tank top were toned and sculpted with muscle.

She was strong and soft, sweet and tough. The biggest distraction of his entire adult life.

*And you think she could be a killer?*

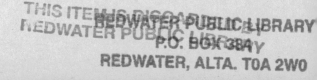

## ALSO BY LESLIE PARRISH

*Fade to Black*
*Pitch Black*

# Black at Heart

## A BLACK CATS NOVEL

## Leslie Parrish

A SIGNET ECLIPSE BOOK

SIGNET ECLIPSE
Published by New American Library, a division of
Penguin Group (USA) Inc., 375 Hudson Street,
New York, New York 10014, USA
Penguin Group (Canada), 90 Eglinton Avenue East, Suite 700, Toronto,
Ontario M4P 2Y3, Canada (a division of Pearson Penguin Canada Inc.)
Penguin Books Ltd., 80 Strand, London WC2R 0RL, England
Penguin Ireland, 25 St. Stephen's Green, Dublin 2,
Ireland (a division of Penguin Books Ltd.)
Penguin Group (Australia), 250 Camberwell Road, Camberwell, Victoria 3124,
Australia (a division of Pearson Australia Group Pty. Ltd.)
Penguin Books India Pvt. Ltd., 11 Community Centre, Panchsheel Park,
New Delhi - 110 017, India
Penguin Group (NZ), 67 Apollo Drive, Rosedale, North Shore 0632,
New Zealand (a division of Pearson New Zealand Ltd.)
Penguin Books (South Africa) (Pty.) Ltd., 24 Sturdee Avenue,
Rosebank, Johannesburg 2196, South Africa

Penguin Books Ltd., Registered Offices:
80 Strand, London WC2R 0RL, England

First published by Signet Eclipse, an imprint of New American Library,
a division of Penguin Group (USA) Inc.

First Printing, September 2009
10  9  8  7  6  5  4  3  2  1

*For Megan,*
*who reminds me every day of the wonders*
*of the world. I love seeing things through your*
*brilliant perspective, sweetheart.*

# Acknowledgments

To Caitlin—thank you so much for the fabulous job you did on the bible for this series. Keeping so many characters and stories straight throughout three novels would have been impossible without your terrific work.

To Bruce—you're my rock. And my everything else.

To my father, Ray Smith—thanks for passing on your love of the arts, which has served me so well. I might have gotten Mom's common sense, but I also got your creativity and I'm so thankful for both.

To Janelle Denison, Julie E. Leto, and Carly Phillips—the assistance you gave me in plotting this trilogy has been absolutely invaluable. I can't thank you enough. And Julie, that you took the time to read every word and bounce ideas in innumerable e-mails and phone calls is appreciated more than you can know.

Thanks to attorney Lee Smith for being my legal sounding board—as well as a great little brother.

To Trista Kruse, Karen Hawkins, and Jean Mason—thanks so much for being my unofficial beta readers. Your enthusiasm helps so much.

To my editor, Laura Cifelli—it's been a true pleasure working on this series with you. Hope we can do it again sometime.

Sincere thanks also to Leo A. Notenboom (www.ask-leo.com) for the technical advice and consultation. All the computer expertise is his; any errors are entirely my own.

# *Prologue*

Supervisory Special Agent Wyatt Blackstone had never had to attend the memorial service of one of his own team members before. After today, he hoped to God he never attended another one.

Especially since it was his fault Lily Fletcher was dead.

Against his better judgment, he had allowed a woman he knew shouldn't be in the field to participate in a sting operation with another FBI Cyber Action Team. She'd had no business being there. Lily had been an IT specialist, a computer nerd, young, untried, sweetly enthusiastic. But also haunted by her demons. Those demons had driven her to work a case she should never have been involved in. They had pushed her to be in on the takedown of a suspect whose twisted cyber fantasies of abusing children had haunted her dreams.

And there, everything had gone straight to hell. One agent dead on the ground. Lily wounded and trapped before bleeding to death in a vehicle driven by a desperate madman.

He was tormented by the thought of those awful, desperate hours she had endured.

The memorial service had been small and private. The FBI had not made it a media event, as they could have. Wyatt hadn't wanted it that way; none of the group had. Because of the screwups that had led to her death, and his team's recent successful capture of a serial killer known as the Professor, the bureau acceded to his demands.

Lily had had no surviving family and very few friends outside the bureau. Though many agents and FBI supervisors had attended the service in the nondenominational chapel, few had continued on to the cemetery. Not Arlington, though she had been entitled to that. Instead, Lily's thirty-year existence in this world was marked with a simple headstone in a small, private churchyard in Annapolis. Others nearby bore the names of her sister, her nephew, and her parents. He hadn't known her mother and father had died on the same day during Lily's childhood until he read the dates.

An entire family gone. Plucked off one tragedy at a time.

After the chaplain's final graveside prayer, only Wyatt and the other members of his team, who had formed a family of their own, had remained. Ignoring the bitterness of the January day, they'd talked quietly, said their good-byes. Then they'd all drifted away, lost in their own sadness, wondering how things might have turned out differently.

Wyatt didn't think he would ever stop wondering.

Even now, hours later, as he sat in the dark in his house, nursing a tumbler full of whiskey, he found it hard to believe. Sweet, quiet Lily, so eager to please despite being so visibly wounded by the horrors that had befallen her, was gone. Senselessly killed by someone who hadn't been fit to touch a single strand of her golden hair.

"I'm sorry," he murmured, lifting his glass to his mouth. "I should have protected you."

He sipped once. Then again. He needed the fire to spread through his body, burning out the anger, the helpless frustration. The grief.

Wyatt never allowed himself to grieve. He'd learned as a child how futile it was to wish someone back from the dead, to ask why horrible things happened, to give in to sorrow.

But Lily? He could grieve for Lily.

Realizing it was almost midnight, he finally rose, needing to go to bed. The past several nights had been sleepless ones. Tomorrow was another workday, another chance to keep moving forward, stopping whatever ugliness he possibly could.

Before he even reached the stairs, though, his cell phone rang. Wyatt pulled it from his pocket, slid it open, and lifted it to his ear.

"Blackstone."

No response at first, but a hollowness told him the line wasn't dead.

"Hello?"

Another long pause. Then a soft voice emerged from the silence like a specter appearing out of his own memories.

"Wyatt?"

He froze, haunted by the pain in that one whispered word. "Who is this?"

"Help me, Wyatt. Please help me."

# Chapter 1

*Seven months later*

As far as murder victims went, Dr. Todd Fuller didn't, on the surface, seem a likely candidate to be sliced to ribbons in a no-tell motel in the middle of nowhere. A respected dentist from Scranton, he had a wife, a pricey house, a nice car, a thriving practice, no criminal record. A charmed life, in fact.

There was nothing charming about him now.

Wyatt surveyed the scene from the doorway, wondering why he still had any capacity to be surprised by what man was capable of doing to his fellow man. After everything he had witnessed throughout his life, including some of his very earliest memories, he shouldn't be able to register dismay for the fact that such things were possible.

Yet he found himself having to close his eyes and take a moment to prepare before entering the room—because scenes like this one were usually reserved for twisted movies that delivered terror to the masses. Not the real world.

Steady now, calm and emotionless, he stepped inside. He skirted the wall, his shoes covered with plastic, and gave a nod to the crime scene investigators in acknowledgment of their work area. He didn't bend to examine any evidence, didn't focus on anything except the overall feeling that lingered in the room long after the crime had been committed.

He could only imagine the rage that had inspired it. In his years with the FBI, he had seen multiple homicides with less blood, inner-city gang-war battlefields without as much gore.

Todd Fuller had suffered greatly in his final hours.

Some murders were passionate and some impersonal. He had met killers who claimed to have merely lashed out in a moment they regretted one second too late and others who truly believed they had simply taken care of something that needed to be done. A few were remorseful, some soulless and happy with what they had achieved. Others calculated their crimes, meticulously planned them, with death the goal and the act of killing merely the means to achieving it.

This had been like all of those, and yet, like none of them.

Wielding a knife on a helpless victim, feeling the gush of warm blood spill from his veins, could never be an impersonal act. But the planning involved, and the time it had taken, would have required a level of removal, a dispassion. This killer hadn't lashed out; he had reined in. Inhaled his rage and his emotion. Controlled himself completely while also savoring every minute of it.

In this room, the killer had calmly and patiently accomplished the objective—a man's death—in the most vicious way possible.

Wyatt knew all that. Because it wasn't the first time he'd seen this unsub's handiwork.

Like the two that had preceded it, this murder had been carefully orchestrated by someone whose goal was not just death. Something deeper was at work here.

Pleasure? Insanity?

*Revenge? Are you wreaking vengeance on all of them because you can't get to the one you want?*

He thrust that thought away, not wanting to let any preconceptions color what he was about to learn regarding the murder of the dentist.

"You Blackstone?" a voice asked.

Nodding, he watched as a plainclothes officer stepped into the doorway. "Detective Schaefer?"

"Yeah. You made good time. Didn't think you'd show up until midmorning."

Considering how little he slept these days, it had been no great feat to leave his Alexandria home within thirty minutes of the detective's four a.m. phone call. And the desire to arrive before the body could be removed had prompted him to drive a little faster than normal. He'd pulled up outside the western Maryland hotel just as the automatic streetlights had clicked off, the hazy, gray morning chasing away the last remnants of dark night.

Wyatt extended his hand to the detective. "Thank you for contacting me about the case."

Schaefer, a middle-aged man with a strong grip and intelligent eyes that belied the crumpled suit and rumpled hair, nodded as they shook hands. "Not a problem."

"Have you learned anything more?"

The detective shook his head. "Just the basics I told

you about on the phone. Guy went missing two eve-
nings ago. Pennsylvania police were investigating. A local
cruiser spotted his car in the parking lot late last night
and ran the tag. When he noticed the smell coming from
inside, he got the manager up and they found the vic
like ..." He waved an expansive hand. "Well, like you
see."

Steeling himself against the smell of death, Wyatt
stepped farther inside and scanned the room. "What do
you know about him?"

"Not a lot. Missing persons report gave us the basics,
but I'm sure we'll learn more about him as the day goes
on." He shook his head and snapped his chewing gum.
"One thing I do know—his funeral ain't gonna have an
open casket."

"Indeed."

Wyatt already knew more about the victim than this
detective did, including the fact that Fuller's wife was a
thin blonde with a pixie haircut, freckles, and a childlike
figure. He had a picture of her on his BlackBerry, as well
as one of the pre-sliced-up dentist.

Handsome couple, although they'd looked more like
father and daughter than man and wife. Which came as
no great surprise.

As soon as he'd heard about the murder, he'd contacted the one person he could trust with this particular
situation, IT Specialist Brandon Cole, and asked him to
find out everything he could on the victim. The always-
energetic young man had not wasted a second, working
from home in the predawn hours. And he'd called him
back forty minutes later, following up with an e-mail de-
tailing what he'd found.

Brandon knew the stakes here. He knew what Wyatt

was thinking about this case, about who could be killing these men and why. He didn't believe it. But he knew.

Actually, Wyatt didn't truly believe it, either. And yet here he was.

*You know you have to consider the possibility.*

Was it possible? Of course. Anything was.

But *probable* that someone he knew, someone he liked, someone he'd protected, could be responsible for this?

It seemed beyond belief. The evidence, however, could not be ignored.

"Sounded like you weren't too surprised by what we found here," said Schaefer.

Again surveying the room, the massacred victim, the dried blood, the lingering aura of violence, he shook his head. "No. Not surprised."

Then his gaze focused on one spot. On the item that had most drawn his attention when he'd learned of this particular murder. "A tiger lily," he murmured.

"That what it is?" Schaefer followed his stare. "I don't know shit about flowers."

"I'm fairly certain." Wyatt's even tone betrayed none of the intensity coursing through him all because of that one vivid tropical flower.

"Well, like I said on the phone, I saw the bulletin last week about brutal murders of men in small, out-of-the-way hotels. The flower thing sounded nutty. But once I saw this one, I figured this was exactly the kind of case you were watching for."

"It is. And I appreciate getting the call so quickly."

Drawn to that single blossom, Wyatt stepped to the bedside table, still cautious to avoid the remains and evidence markers littering the floor. Fortunately, the particular type of flower had no scent, unlike the one at the Virginia crime scene. Last time, it had been an Easter lily, the scent of which always made him think of funeral homes, caskets, and grief. The room had already reeked of death, just as this one did. The flower had just made it worse.

This one, though, did not. It was beautiful, its pale orange petals, though brownish and wilted around the edges, still curled closely together. It had obviously been cut just as it began to open and blossom, before it reached its full potential.

The roar of the tiger cut off with a sharp snick of the blade. A symbol for what had gone on in this room? For *why* it had gone on?

There was much to learn about Todd Fuller. Wyatt wanted to know whether there were any hush-hush rumors about him swirling in his community. Rumors that persisted despite his upstanding reputation as a good dentist, a family man, a generous contributor to children's charities. He wanted to understand the man's relationship with his little-girlish wife. And he most wanted to know exactly what he had been doing here, so far from home, in this dingy hotel.

If this case proved to be like the last two, he suspected the answer to all those questions would be found in the man's computer hard drive. His browsing history would show visits to secret, twisted Web sites that appealed to a certain type of sadistic individual. His e-mail file would contain communications between murder victim and killer. And they would invariably involve a child.

Yes, if Fuller was like the others, he had come to this

hotel thinking he was meeting a father with a young son or daughter he was willing to exploit.

"So, what's the deal? Some florist get mad about the prices of roses around Valentine's Day and tumble off his rocker?"

Wyatt forced a faint smile. "Not exactly," he said, barely paying the detective any attention. He had questions for the man, but for now, his focus was on that lily. And on the single drop of blood that lay beside it, congealed and dark on the cheap Formica tabletop. Had it accidentally fallen from the killer's gloved fingertip as he lovingly left the calling card?

More imagery. The soft flower resting beside the ultimate symbol of violence—spilled blood—in a blatantly symbolic display of innocence shattered.

*Not an accidental drop. Intentional.*

A crime scene investigator glanced over. "Place like this, we'll find tons of prints."

"Of course you will."

On the headboard, on the table. On the door, on the walls, on the television remote, on the cracked ice bucket. None of which would matter.

Because none of the fingerprints would match any of the hundreds found in the hotel room just outside Trenton, New Jersey, or the room in Dumfries, Virginia. Any prints, smears, or partials would be from the nameless travelers who had stopped here days, weeks, months ago.

A faint dusting of powder at the previous scenes and a tiny speck of rubber told them this unsub wore medical gloves. And if he took them off, he wiped clean anything he touched. The faucets in the other two cases had been immaculate—the only place without a single smear. Wyatt believed the unsub had touched them bare-handed, while washing the blood off his tools and himself.

He didn't doubt these crimes were the work of one killer. The signature was the same, the means, the locations, everything right down to the type of flower left at each scene. Lilies.

"There is a strange-looking bloodstain on the carpet, over there by the closet door. It's curved, like maybe from someone's heel."

Wyatt's brow shot up in interest.

"But I dunno; it could have been the handle of a weapon or something," the CSI said, sounding resigned. "It was pretty small to be from the man who must have done this."

Too small for a man. The investigator didn't even speculate on something that immediately entered Wyatt's head.

*A woman. God.*

The small-town CSI had never even considered it, obviously not thinking a woman would be capable of such ferocity, such viciousness.

Wyatt knew better. He knew full well what a woman was capable of. Had known since his very early childhood, the memories of which sometimes taunted him with all he'd lost and all the darkness that was possible in this world.

*But this case? This woman?*

No. He couldn't believe it. Not until there was not one bit of doubt.

"We might find some of the killer's own hair or skin.

This victim had to have put up a fight—he wouldn't just lie still for something like this."

Wyatt schooled his expression to reveal nothing of the wild thoughts running rampantly through his head. He forced away the mental speculations about the killer's gender, knowing he would have to deal with them later. Giving his full attention to the CSI, he replied, "He might have been unable to move." If the pattern held, anyway.

"Tied up, you mean?"

"Not exactly." He did not elaborate. The autopsy would have to reveal whether Dr. Fuller's spinal cord had been severed with a sharp blow to the back. In the other cases, the men had apparently walked into the rooms and been struck from behind, left instantly crippled and helpless.

There wouldn't be much other evidence. There almost certainly would be no witnesses. The person doing this was careful and thorough. No one would have heard a thing. These out-of-the-way hotels were cheap and anonymous, barely eking out a living for their owners, with most rooms empty on any given night of the week. The bill would have been paid by the victim, who would have reserved the room by phone. He would also have instructed that it be left unlocked, the old-fashioned key on the dresser. Just as he had been instructed by the person he had come to meet.

And because this place looked to be surviving guest by guest, the staff would have done it.

As if he had read Wyatt's mind, the detective said, "The manager pulled the room records for me."

"The victim paid for the room himself," Wyatt murmured.

"Yeah. With one of those disposable gift-card credit cards."

Harder to trace.

"His wife didn't even know he had it. And he booked the place for four nights."

*Acting to pattern.* Dr. Fuller had paid for a few days on either end of the night in question, thinking to cover his tracks. Arrive anonymously, depart the same way, nobody to mark the time of either one. Which would explain why the body had lain here to decompose thirty-six hours, rather than being discovered by the staff or the next guest.

This type of hotel didn't have regular maid service, changing the beds only between guests—if then—and giving out towels at the front desk. There were no magnetic key cards, never any security cameras, no curious neighbors. Not in establishments like this, which dotted back roads and rented rooms by the hour to cheating couples having clandestine affairs, or by the month to newly released felons with nowhere else to go. The unsub would have parked off-site and walked in through the woods dotting the perimeter, waiting for the prey. Leaving something in sight to draw his victim deeper into the room—a toy, a doll?—he'd have waited behind the door for Fuller to walk all the way inside, presenting his vulnerable back for the ax.

It all played out in his mind, a scenario that had become familiar in the past several weeks, since he'd first read about the New Jersey case and gone up to talk to the investigating officers. The FBI Cyber Action Team he ran was tasked to solve Internet-related murders, so the case had been a natural one to cross his desk. The first victim had, after all, been lured over the Internet by an unsub he had met in an anonymous child-porn chat room.

Yet something about it had stood out since the first moment he'd read the file. Had made him keep that file close to his chest, go up, and poke around on his own.

It had been the name of the child the victim had been going to meet: Zach. Cute little seven-year-old Zach, according to the e-mails the victim had exchanged with his killer. That popular name shouldn't have aroused his suspicion, but it did, some sixth sense telling him this needed his personal attention.

Then came the second case, in Virginia. With it, a second name that was all too familiar.

Laura.

Normal names. Nothing unusual about them and they should have had no significance to the murders. Because there never had been a child, male or female, waiting in one of those hotel rooms. They were phantoms used to draw predators in for their own executions.

But those names had meant something to him.

*Zach and Laura.*

The coincidence had struck him. Just as striking had been the flowers, the lilies. The first a calla lily, the second the Easter one. But this, the tiger lily, was even more important. More telling.

*Tiger Lily. The name she used on that last case before everything went so horribly wrong.*

Damn. This was really happening. And he really was going to have to do something about it. Starting with talking to Brandon Cole about what had gone on here. Brandon, more than anyone, would be stunned by the significance of the type of lily their unsub had left behind this time. *You're the one who started calling her Tiger Lily, aren't you?*

"I should have left you out of it," he muttered, ignoring the curious glance from the CSI. Wyatt regretted bringing Brandon any further into this. It could be explosive—could be the end of both of their careers—and he hoped like hell that if he went down, he didn't bring the younger man with him.

He'd just needed a second opinion, needed to know if he was crazy for reading something into the types of flower, into the children's names. Brandon had acknowledged the possible significance. But there was no possible about it anymore. Not in Wyatt's mind. The names, the flower, the victims, the motivation, the fury—all were too specific.

Other than the two of them, no one else knew about his investigation. None of the special agents or IT specialists who reported to him. So much for the unity of the team, the loyalty, the camaraderie. Their ability to work in sync, to trust one another completely, had been of enormous benefit in solving the cases they'd worked so far. And now he was the one who'd veered off course, taking his youngest and most inexperienced agent with him.

*You had no choice. He's the only one who knows the truth.*

The truth about Lily Fletcher, one of his former team members.

"Lily," he whispered.

Lily, whose seven-year-old nephew, Zach, had been murdered by a sick monster.

Lily, whose twin sister, Laura, had been crushed by the grief of it.

Lily, who'd been taken by a vengeful deviant whose online name had been Lovesprettyboys—a monster who had liked to brutalize youngsters in cyber playgrounds.

Lily. Sweet and bright and lost forever.

Could this murder—all three flower murders—have something to do with what had happened to her?

He didn't know. But he knew where to go to start looking for answers.

Maine.

# Chapter 2

How strange it sometimes seemed that she had ended up living at the beach.

After what had happened, what she'd experienced, she should never have wanted to go near the ocean again. Memories of that night—feeling her life slip away on a cold, windswept shore, the crashing waves hiding her pathetic calls for help—should have made her want to be anyplace else. The salty air should have smelled like pain and tasted like death.

Yet she loved it here. The churning of the Atlantic's waves in an endless rhythm soothed her soul in a way nothing else could. Therapy, meditation, medication, physical training, solitude—they'd all helped. But the tide was what lulled her to sleep each night. And every morning it was what called her forth into the sad world she still sometimes longed to escape.

It could be because it was so steady, impervious to time or humanity. Nothing interfered with the crashing violence of the water against the rocks or the strong lapping of it slipping back out again. It was unstoppable, imperturbable. Strong and aloof. Much like she wanted to be.

When offered this refuge on the rocky coast of Maine, she hadn't been thinking about the sound of the waves or the possibility of being strong and unstoppable. She'd thought only of escaping the darkness. Healing. Being away from the world. Not forever, just for as long as it took to reclaim herself.

Now, though, the months had stretched on and she honestly didn't know how she would ever leave this place. The house hovering on a cliff high above the water didn't belong to her, yet it had become her home. Her sanctuary in the middle of an insane world where the raging currents could sweep those you loved in and out of your life with cold indifference.

A parent. A sweet little boy. A much-loved sibling.

Perhaps that was why she so enjoyed the sound of the surf from far below. Because it was a constant reminder that she was here, high above it and removed from it all. No one left to care about. No one whose loss could be the final blow that shattered her battered psyche.

No one.

Sitting on the terrace, spying on the rest of the world through her laptop, she wondered why she never felt lonely. She went down into town only once a week for supplies, nodding at the postal workers as she checked the always empty PO box. Or exchanging a quiet hello with the woman who ran the local general store that sold everything from apricot jam to weed whackers.

She sensed they all wanted more—conversation, a chance to share juicy gossip. Perhaps even a moment to warn her about living in a house many locals seemed to fear. But she didn't give anyone the opportunity. She remained distant, always paying for her few purchases with cash, never trying to use a phony credit card, or, worse, a real one that could leave a paper trail. That was the extent of her involvement out there in the world.

That world, however, did occasionally come here.

She'd had a few regular visitors at first. Now, though, only two people ever climbed up the steep, winding steps that led from the driveway and detached garage to the house itself, which was practically an extension of the cliff. One was her self-defense trainer, a former army sergeant who came a couple of times a week and worked her until she was so exhausted, she sometimes actually slept without dreaming. *A blessing.* With his help, she had molded her body to match her spirit, making it hard, lean, and dangerous. She would never be anybody's victim again.

As for the other occasional visitor—he came the second weekend of every month.

"So what the hell are you doing here now, a week early?" she whispered as a familiar dark sedan parked behind her Jeep at the bottom of the hill, far below the patio.

Completely in tune to her surroundings, accustomed to the reassuring lull of the surf that was the constant sound track to her new life, she had immediately noticed a new, unexpected sound a few minutes ago. An engine. A car. Coming up the long driveway.

Her heart had begun to thud at the intrusion, but she hadn't panicked. Clicking a few keys on her keyboard, she had switched her laptop over to the surveillance system that monitored every square inch of this property. From the cameras mounted on either corner of the garage roof, she'd identified her visitor and breathed a sigh of relief.

Now, though, she was no longer relieved. Instead, in the few seconds it had taken her to process Wyatt Blackstone's presence here on a sunny, breezy Thursday afternoon, nervous tension had begun to flood her.

This change in routine wasn't like him. Not only utterly brilliant, Wyatt was also reliable and calm, as even and steady as those waves crashing on the shore. Whatever had driven him up here must be important, but she didn't immediately fear the worst. If she was in danger, if there had been any threat at all, he would have called her and told her to get out.

Last winter, or even spring, she would have done exactly that. Now she wasn't so sure. In fact, part of her welcomed the idea of confronting her deepest, darkest fear here, on her turf, with her newfound confidence and highly honed skills.

But Wyatt hadn't called and she sensed no danger. Something else had prompted the visit. He knew she didn't want him here, though, of course, she couldn't force him to stay away. It was his house, after all, even if he did seem to loathe it.

She had made it very clear a few months ago that he didn't need to keep coming up here and checking on her. The trip up from D.C. wasn't an easy or a direct one, and he'd made it every weekend for months. Finally confronting him, she'd asked him to limit the visits.

As usual with the enigmatic man, his reaction had revealed absolutely nothing about what he'd thought of the request. He'd simply honored it.

Until now.

The car door opened. She watched as he stepped out,

clad, as usual, in a dark, impeccably tailored suit. She had only rarely seen him wearing anything else. Designer sunglasses hid the startlingly blue eyes, but didn't disguise the handsomeness of his masculine features—the sculpted cheekbones, strong jaw, chiseled chin, perfectly formed mouth.

How a man who looked like a movie star from Hollywood's golden age had ended up in the FBI, she honestly had no idea.

A soft ocean breeze swept through his thick, black hair, but didn't dare to tousle it. She'd bet Neptune himself wouldn't have the balls to toss ocean spray onto this man's shiny, immaculate shoes. He was that intimidating.

At least, she'd once thought so. He'd intimidated her to near incoherence once upon a time. Left her tongue-tied and awkward, not knowing what to say or how to act. But she consoled herself with the knowledge that every other woman he met had the same reaction. And that she no longer felt that way.

Instead, as she watched him slam the door, then glance up toward the house perched so high above, she realized she felt nothing. At least nothing that could be construed as romantic emotions.

Physical ones? Well, they were another story. No matter how cold a person's heart, the white-hot flame of sexual attraction could be hard to resist. Still, any physical attraction she might feel for Wyatt Blackstone was so deeply buried beneath her own layers of self-defense and wariness, she would never give them free rein.

He reached the bottom step, carved into the rocky hill. Pausing, he glanced down to the right of it, at a clump of sea grass. Then he turned his head up toward the garage.

Toward her. Through the camera, he pierced her with that direct gaze even his dark glasses couldn't disguise, demanding entry.

"Okay, okay," she mumbled, flicking a few keys, disabling the nearly hidden motion detectors that would screech in alarm if he passed them.

He didn't even glance down again to ascertain that the light on the tiny sensor beside the step had changed from red to green. He merely began to ascend, knowing full well she had heard him arrive. Knowing she had been watching every move he made, knowing she wouldn't, couldn't, keep him out. Even if she wanted to.

She shivered, acknowledging the truth: Part of her wanted to.

But worse, another part of her, that tiny, hopeful little spark of her old self that she hadn't been able to entirely extinguish, didn't. *You're just tired of hearing nobody's voice but Sarge's telling you to give him twenty more reps.*

Maybe. Or maybe not.

Either way, she couldn't deny that white-hot flame burned the tiniest bit hotter at the sight of him on the monitor.

Wyatt rose up the hill, step by step, moving as smoothly and gracefully as a cat. She'd never known a man who appeared so fluid, so comfortable in his own skin. He'd always made her feel like an awkward, fumbling klutz.

A faint, humorless smile widened her lips. She was so not that girl anymore. Hard to remember what her former self had even been like. Or what she'd really felt about the man drawing closer and closer to her front door. Had her life once really been so innocent that a steady glance from a handsome man could put a blush in her cheeks? Had she truly sometimes fancied herself in love with him, even as out of reach as he had seemed?

Those reactions were gone, that sweet, innocent part of herself dead and buried. The only reminder of that person was a carved piece of granite marking her grave alongside the graves of her family.

She returned her attention to the monitor. Blackstone was broad-chested and hard. Lean, but not wiry. So in shape that the steep climb probably hadn't even winded him. And keenly perceptive. Which was why, when he reached the top of the steps and the high iron gate, he didn't even try to punch in the security code that would open it. He merely waited, certain she would have changed it since his last visit a few weeks ago.

"Fine," she muttered, again clicking a few keys, releasing the lock.

Then, knowing she'd run out of time, she took her reading glasses off and put them down. Rising from the small café table, she clicked her laptop closed, and headed inside. Her feet bare against the golden oak floor, she noted its warmth and realized she'd been getting cold. It might be only early September, but already the weather was changing. Inside, though, the air was comfortable. A few last remnants of sunlight streamed in from the banks of windows flanking both the east and west sides of the cavernous living room that stretched the width of the house.

This room was her favorite. Light and airy, with just a few pieces of furniture. No shadowy corners. No odd shapes. No place to hide in the dark.

Not that it was ever truly dark. The sun might set; a chill might quickly descend. But with the security lights covering the entire property, her world was never entirely black.

She would not allow herself to be lost in the blackness again.

*Thanks to him.*

Her misgivings about Wyatt's arrival faded. She owed the man everything. If an occasional unexpected visit was the price she had to pay, she'd pay it.

And maybe she'd even manage to prevent him from ever realizing the truth—that she sometimes wondered if it would have been better if he'd never saved her at all.

"Stop," she told herself. "The new you doesn't think that way."

Forcing the frown from her face, she strode to the front door, reaching it just as Blackstone's shadow darkened the grated window set in its center.

Taking a deep breath, she unlocked the dead bolt, the slider lock, and the knob, then pulled the door open. "Hello, Wyatt."

He stared down at her, the glasses still covering his eyes, the handsome face expressionless. Then, finally, he replied.

"Hello, Lily."


"Lily doesn't exist anymore. Remember?"

Wyatt nodded once, acknowledging the point. "I know. I just can't remember what false name you're using these days."

It should have been easy to remember to call this young woman by a false name. After all, she no longer looked anything like the Lily Fletcher he had known.

The one everyone else in the world believed dead. Well, everyone except Brandon Cole.

And the man who had tried to kill her.

Gone was the long, straight hair that had fallen halfway down her back. Now cut short, it hugged her delicate face, emphasizing the haunted twist of her mouth and the gaunt hollowness of her cheeks. It was no longer a soft, sunny blond, instead dyed nearly black, a startling shade when contrasted with her pale blue eyes. He finally understood the comments he'd gotten throughout his own life, about the color combination. It was striking, did draw attention. Which was why she wore brown contacts whenever she left the house.

The hair had been shaved off by the doctors dealing with her injuries. The rest she'd done herself, choosing the contacts, the hair dye, the boxy clothes, all for the same reason she'd donned this alternate identity: for her own safety. She wanted to be anonymous, invisible, someone no one would notice, much less remember.

Funny, though, none of it—the hair, the clothes, the scars, the occasional dark smudges beneath her eyes— could change the fact that she was incredibly beautiful. If anything, the changes in Lily had made her even more so. Because instead of being a delicate, fragile woman, she was now a fully realized one, broken but rebuilt and aware of her own power.

She was almost intoxicating. And frankly, it was no wonder Brandon had gone from flirting with an office mate to falling for the woman they had both rescued. Who wouldn't fall for her?

Wyatt mentally shook off the line of thought, not wanting to go there, even in his head, when it came to Lily. She was his friend, his protégée.

"Can I come in?"

She stepped back, ushering him forward. "It's your house."

Perhaps on paper. Any emotional connection he'd had for this place had been sliced out of him decades ago. If not for it being a safe and secret place where Lily could hide and recover, he would never have willingly set foot here again. And even now, knowing it provided a haven for a young woman he was very concerned about, he still felt his heart skip a beat as he crossed the threshold, determined to see the house as it was now, not the way it had been in his childhood. Not the way it had been the night his childhood had ended all too violently.

Inside, he pulled off his sunglasses while she closed the door, securing every lock, testing them with a pull of the knob. He didn't smile at the overly cautious ritual. There was nothing funny about how seriously Lily took her privacy and self-protection.

Considering she had been shot, kidnapped, and tortured for a week by a madman, the surprise would be if she were not extremely careful. And this house didn't have a history of gentle security.

Perhaps that was one reason he'd brought her here. Because, really, lightning couldn't strike twice, could it?

"Can't be too careful," she said lightly as she triple-checked the dead bolt, wary and serious.

He just didn't know if wariness had slowly transitioned into blind rage. And he needed to know. Badly.

Did he really think the gentle, soft-spoken Lily Fletcher he knew could have killed the three men who'd been cut to pieces in those hotel rooms? That she'd lured them using their own sick desires against them, employing the names of her lost loved ones to do it? That she'd left a tiger lily to autograph her latest crime scene?

No. Deep down, he truly didn't believe she had it in her.

But the human mind could snap if pushed too far. He knew that, more than most.

"So what are you doing here?"

He had anticipated the question. "Monday is Labor Day. I thought I'd take a couple of days off and come up for the long weekend."

"You could have called."

"It's my house," he reminded her, his tone smooth and perhaps even a little bit mocking. This cold aloofness she'd shrouded herself in was almost too much of a challenge. He wanted her to be strong, knew she needed to in order to survive, but he sometimes found himself missing the Lily he'd once known.

He had to be honest, though. This woman fascinated him in ways he hadn't yet begun to evaluate. She was the living example of how a person could drastically change after one horrific ordeal.

Then again, she'd gone through more than one. He suspected the Lily he'd known had been different from the one who had waved her young nephew off to school or shared confidences with her twin sister.

He'd never know who she had once been.

"Suit yourself." She didn't even glance up at him as she spun on her bare feet and walked away from him, annoyance obvious in her tight shoulders. Her hips swayed, her long legs eating up the floor as she moved with determination toward the kitchen.

No, she couldn't be more unlike the young woman he had met a short fourteen months ago. That woman had been gentle and vulnerable, spiritually wounded after the terrible, tragic death of her nephew and her sister's resulting suicide. Lily had been soft-spoken and soft-tempered, with a quick smile, delicate, fluttering movements, and an eagerness to please that sometimes made her appear clumsy. But there had never been anything clumsy about the way her mind had worked. She'd been a brilliant programmer, a genius IT specialist, and he'd been damn lucky to get her.

That genius served her well in her new life. Not a thing could happen within a quarter mile of this house without her computer surveillance system warning her.

"I was just about to make dinner."

He followed, feeling a slow smile tug at his mouth. "Getting any better at it?"

Casting a quick glance over her shoulder, she smirked. "You won't choke."

Considering he'd tasted her dubious kitchen creations before, he'd reserve judgment. On the weekends when he came up, he usually brought fish or steaks to grill. This trip had just been too impromptu for him to do it.

After all, forty-eight hours ago, he would not have imagined he'd be traveling to Maine to try to find out if the young woman whose life he had saved really had slaughtered three men.

*It's crazy.* But he needed to be sure.

"Salad and grilled chicken okay? I went to the market yesterday."

"Fine. And you were careful in town?"

She gave him a *Duh* look. "In case you haven't been there lately, Keating is a tourist town. Tons of people in and out. I make sure not to draw any attention."

Huh. She drew attention no matter where she went,

though she didn't see it. "Well, now that it's Labor Day weekend, be prepared for all that to change. The town is small enough that it will start to pay attention to anybody who sticks around."

"They've paid attention," she admitted, sounding grudging. Rolling her eyes, she gestured around the bright, airy kitchen with the floor-to-ceiling windows overlooking the ocean. Her tone dripping sarcasm, she added, "Enough to drop hints about this *creepy* house of yours."

The muscles in his body stiffened reflexively, but he forced himself to remain where he was, leaning against the doorjamb, his arms crossed. Nonchalant. Normal. Nothing to reveal just how much he hated being here and how right the townies were to think of this place as tainted.

"Just be warned, they're likely to be more nosy when they don't have other tourists to focus on."

"Duly noted."

Lily finally dropped it, thank God, and began to prepare dinner, pulling fresh produce from the refrigerator. As she worked, she would occasionally move a certain way, or her bottom lip would push out in frustration as she tried to decide which spice to use, and he'd catch a glimpse of the old Lily. She even unconsciously lifted a hand to sweep her short hair away from her face, as if forgetting she no longer had the long, silky strands.

"Your hair's really grown out," he murmured, acknowledging that for the first time.

She lifted a brow. "You just saw me three weeks ago."

"I know. But I can't see the scars at all anymore." At least, not the external ones.

This time when she lifted her hand, it was to self-consciously pat and smooth the hair over the top of her mangled ear. She would eventually need to get plastic surgery to repair it, but seemed to have had enough of doctors and hospitals for this year.

Lovesprettyboys, the bastard she and members of another Cyber Action Team had been trying to catch last January in a sting in Virginia, had shot her point-blank, aiming for her face. The bullet had instead skimmed the side of her head, taking off a chunk of her ear.

She'd been lucky. Damned lucky. Especially because the killer's second shot, straight to the chest, had been stopped by her bulletproof vest. He regularly thanked God that she'd been wearing it. She'd ended up with some broken ribs and bruises, but nothing major.

No, the major wound had been the third shot. It hit her in her upper thigh, so close to her femoral artery that another millimeter to the right would have been the end of her.

It almost had been, anyway. He still sometimes found it hard to believe she'd lived, especially given the amount of her blood they'd found inside the surveillance van where she'd been attacked. So much blood, it had been impossible to believe she could have survived, and despite the lack of a body, the world had decided she hadn't. Him included.

The grief of those standing beside a grave that held no coffin, who watched as a small marker with her name and the dates of her brief thirty years on this earth had been erected, had been genuine and heartbreaking. Something none of them had expected to get over. So when he picked up his phone that very night after her memorial service, hers was the last voice he had expected to hear. Weak and agonized, but Lily's voice.

It had been one of the most shocking moments of his life.

They had all believed her corpse had been swept away after the van had crashed from a high bridge. Now, of course, he knew that was what her attacker had wanted them to think. But then, answering that call, he had wondered whether someone was playing a sick joke.

"So how are things in the Hoover Building?" she asked as she reached for an onion and began peeling away the skin, taking a few usable layers of white with it. Talented in the kitchen, she was not.

"Fine."

"Everybody at the office okay? Jackie?"

"The same. She and Lambert still go at each other, especially when they start arguing about who's going to drive."

Her smile was faint, but it did appear. "She's dangerous behind the wheel."

"He's managed to survive."

The smile widened the tiniest bit as her guard began to come down at the talk of normal things. Familiar things. "Lambert turned out okay, though?"

"Yes, he's worked out very well." Jackie's partner, Alec Lambert, had been a new member of the team, on board for only a week when Lily's attack had occurred. "His profiling background has been a remarkable asset. Meanwhile, Kyle still manages to get off one-liners that leave Dean ready to laugh or growl—I can't quite tell which."

That put a sparkle in her eyes. "Mulrooney's a big,

crass teddy bear, but Dean wouldn't trade him for another partner for anything."

Wyatt lifted a surprised brow. Because, though Lily was right, he wondered how she could know that. It had been only a year since the team had come together, and Lily had been absent for seven months of that year. When she left, everyone was still just a bit unsure, cautious, not quite melding into the solid unit they had become.

Funny, in a completely unfunny way. Lily's death had been the unifying moment.

"What about Jackie's family? Her husband? Her kids?"

"Everybody seems fine. The kids are growing up too fast, she says." He couldn't help adding, "She talks about you often."

Jackie Stokes had been the only other woman on the team at the time of Lily's attack and had taken the loss very hard. They had formed a solid friendship, and Jackie, though only twelve or so years older than Lily, had a mother instinct that ran deep. Despite her caustic exterior, the striking, brilliant African-American woman had grown protective of all the younger members of the team.

Many times, Wyatt had wondered just how big a mistake he had made in bringing only Brandon in on the rescue, and in letting Lily swear them both to secrecy about her survival. Jackie could have been a big help. All of them could.

But he'd had his reasons. Valid ones. And he didn't know that he'd make a different decision now, even knowing Lily's recovery was going to take so many months.

Still, he couldn't help wondering whether any of them would understand that, how they would react when Lily decided to rejoin the land of the living. They would be furious, would feel betrayed. And he couldn't blame them. He only hoped they eventually understood the choices he, Lily, and Brandon had all made that bitter January night.

"What about the new ones?"

"Anna Delaney's good, very thorough, although she doesn't have quite the instincts that you do. And Christian Mendez, who came in from the Miami field office, is very direct and single-minded, but I think he'll work out all right."

"Another Taggert, huh?"

"Not exactly. Dean was street-cop gruff. Christian's more quietly intense."

"And Brandon?" Her voice remained deceptively low, her attention on her task, as if she didn't want him to know she really cared about the answer to her question.

"Fine, though he still doesn't understand why you don't want him to come and visit anymore."

Her tremulous sigh reminded him that they had this discussion nearly every time he came up. "Maybe in the fall."

"That's what you said about summer."

She shook her head. "Look, it's bad enough you feeling like you have to come here and check up on me. There's no need for Brandon to go out of his way, too."

Shaking his head, Wyatt wondered if she really felt that way, if she didn't know that Brandon, probably a couple of years her junior, had feelings for her.

Perhaps she did. And perhaps that was why she'd asked

the other man to stop visiting altogether at around the same time she'd asked Wyatt to come up no more than once a month. Lily, it seemed, didn't want anyone to have feelings for her.

Not that she had ever been ungrateful. In the first few weeks after Wyatt and Brandon had rescued her from the bastard who'd held her captive, she'd been able to do almost nothing but thank them. Since then, though, as her body had healed, her heart had developed thick scar tissue, too. She no longer thanked him. He only hoped it was not because she was no longer glad they had found her and saved her life.

"So are you guys still called the Black CATs because nobody has the nerve to call you black sheep to your face?"

It was his turn to smile slightly. "Some things never change. Besides, we've decided we like the name."

"I assume you're still stuck in those crappy offices on the fourth floor that should be used as supply closets?"

He nodded in acknowledgment but lifted an ironic brow. "Which you, especially, should concede is not an entirely bad thing. It's much easier to fly under the radar when we're so far out of view of everyone else."

Her jaw tightened and her cheeks flushed. "I'm sorry."

He waved a hand in disregard.

"I mean it." She dropped the onion onto a cutting board, reached for a large, wicked-looking knife, and started to chop. Quick, hard, efficient. She *had* been practicing.

He shifted uncomfortably, not liking the flash of images shooting through his mind. Ugly ones. Bloody ones.

*Could you? Could you really?*

No. Impossible.

"On top of everything you did for me, saving my life, getting me medical care, letting me live here, faking my death . . ."

Shaking his head, he replied, "That, I did not do. Nobody faked your death, Lily. Not you, not I."

"You know what I mean."

"Yes, but remember, you committed no crime in not coming forward to correct the mistaken impression that you died. Filed no false life insurance claims, made no illegal moves at all. It was not your fault you were declared dead while you were . . ." He cleared his throat, unable to go there, even in his thoughts, not wanting to think about what she'd been going through while he and the rest of the team had been fruitlessly waiting for her body to wash up somewhere. "I repeat: You've done nothing illegal."

"I know. But I'm still sorry." Defiance and anger dimmed the warmth of the apology. "You caught the blame for it, didn't you? For what they all think happened to me?"

Wyatt merely stared, wondering how she could know that.

"Damn, it's unfair. It was nobody's fault but my own. You warned me to let the Lovesprettyboys case go."

Yes, he had, not liking what her obsession with an Internet phantom was doing to her. They had discovered the pedophile while researching a sick online site called Satan's Playground, where sadists and monsters gathered and enacted their ugliest fantasies. From the moment Lily had seen Lovesprettyboys' avatar, and the kind of revolting online games he liked to play, she had been determined to find the man before he could play those games in real life. Even after Satan's Playground had been shut down, after the rest of the team had moved on to other cases, having caught the serial killer who had been using the site to air videos of his brutal murders, Lily hadn't been able to let go of the need to do something.

"I should never have ridden along."

"You were supposed to be protected," he said, the words hard to push from his tight jaw. The whole thing still infuriated him. "Anspaugh should have kept you safe."

She rolled her eyes. "Anspaugh. The jerk. What did he get, a promotion?"

Special Agent Tom Anspaugh, who'd allowed Lily to help in his investigation without Wyatt's knowledge, had definitely not gotten a promotion. In fact, he'd been busted down so low, it was surprising he had remained with the bureau. "Quite the opposite. And you're lucky he doesn't know you're alive, because he holds you responsible for his disgrace."

"Oh, nice, blame the dead chick."

His lips quirked a little.

"Something tells me, though, that he's not the only one who got blamed."

No, he wasn't. Though Wyatt hadn't gotten slapped quite as hard as Anspaugh, he'd definitely taken a hit. But again, he had to wonder how Lily could know that. It wasn't as if Wyatt had raised his voice in Crandall's office when he'd gotten called on the carpet. Their heated conversation couldn't have been heard from beyond the walls of the DD's office, to be then whispered about, for, perhaps, Brandon to repeat to Lily.

"It doesn't matter."

Lily's fingers tightened around the handle, whitening under the nails. Then she tossed the knife down, turned to the cabinet, and retrieved two wineglasses. "After everything you've done, all the cases you've cleared, I can't believe they still treat you the way they do."

Watching her uncork a bottle of Merlot, Wyatt remained silent, not really wanting to talk about it. He'd long since come to accept that his career with the FBI would halt right where he was. His title would never be higher than supervisory special agent and some would never trust him. All because he'd seen some ugly, illegal activities going on and he'd done something about it.

Whistle-blowers, it seemed, were never promoted. Only shoved into the Cyber Division, where he'd never worked, and handed a new CAT that had been so narrowly defined, everyone had expected it to fail.

"Is Deputy Director Crandall still trying to drive you out by any means, fair or foul?"

Wyatt reached for the full wineglass she extended, and glanced at the ruby red liquid. Swirling it around, he didn't answer at first, not wanting her to see his reaction. "What do you mean?"

He was stalling. There had been nothing subtle about that query; she'd come at the matter head-on. The question remained: How did she know Deputy Director Crandall was trying to drive him out? Oh, certainly everyone in the bureau knew the DD hadn't been happy about the embarrassing scandal that had ensued after Wyatt had reported the evidence manipulation going on at the FBI crime lab. Especially because one of the agents implicated had recently been promoted to a position directly under Crandall. What made it worse was that high-level agent—Jack Eddington, now cooling his heels in federal prison—had once been Wyatt's good friend and mentor.

The way Lily had worded the question, it was almost as if she *knew* the deputy director truly hated his guts. That the vengeful man's actions had been personal, more than professional. Having his own office implicated in the crime-lab investigation had made Crandall his enemy for life, and he would have loved to fire Wyatt if he could.

He couldn't. Wyatt had too many friends in high places. Very high. He had a number of powerful supporters, the admiration of media figures who knew him and saw him as one of the few honest men in the FBI. No, Crandall couldn't force Wyatt out.

He could, however, try to get Wyatt to go on his own. And he'd done everything from criticizing him to reprimanding him to accomplish that goal.

That the reprimand had been over Lily Fletcher's death was something he would never let her know.

But how did she know the rest? He had shared details of the tense meetings, the argumentative phone calls, and the sniping e-mails from the DD's office with no one.

Wyatt alone was responsible for the decisions he made. He had known going into it that exposing internal corruption would be career suicide. Not to mention the end of friendships. So he would never bemoan the fully expected results of his actions to anyone now.

Others might whisper about it, speculate that while he'd gotten public commendations and made those high-level friends, in private, in the cutthroat world of the upper echelons of the FBI, he'd been vilified. Yet

Lily seemed to be talking about more than the rumor and innuendo that had been surrounding him in the two and a half years since he'd crossed the blue line and done something about what he'd discovered.

And then he got it.

Wyatt lowered the glass to the counter, no longer trusting himself to hold it upright. The moment it left his grip, his fingers curled together, every muscle in his body growing tense as the truth washed over him. "Lily?"

She opened her mouth to remind him of the name he was supposed to be using, but must have seen the steely flash of anger in his eyes and said nothing.

"You'd better not ever let me find out you've been hacking into our system."

She held his gaze, saying nothing, fearless and emotionless. Not denying it. Not justifying it. As if silently telling him she was good enough that he never *would* find out.

"Damn it," he snapped.

Anger rose. The kind of anger that one year ago he hadn't believed he was capable of feeling, so effective had his emotional control been for most of his life. The frustration caused an unfamiliar pounding in his head and every muscle in his body was hard and tense. What in hell was it with this woman that she continued to take these chances, with no regard for her safety or well-being?

He wasn't used to feeling this way. To ever being thrown off his normal, pace. Yet for the past seven months of dealing with Lily Fletcher, his life had been anything but normal, and sometimes he didn't even recognize himself.

Though Lily remained where she was, her chin up in

silent defiance, he saw a flash of wariness enter her eyes. Wariness of him, which made him incredibly uncomfortable.

"I need some fresh air," he said. "Don't hold dinner."

Then, not trusting himself to discuss the issue with her calmly, he turned and stalked out of the room.

# Chapter 3

"Get over here, Boyd. You got a visitor."

In the middle of a set, Jesse Boyd didn't immediately put down the sixty-pound barbell he was holding against his chest. First, because he needed to stick to the routine, he finished his curls. In here, he had no choice but to keep himself in prime shape, ready to fight off the next con who jumped him in the showers or tried to beat the hell out of him in the yard.

And second, because the guard, Kildare, was a mean prick with a nasty sense of humor. It wasn't a visiting day, nor the right hour. Jesse wouldn't put it past the screw to lie about a visitor, just to get him to leave the weight room without permission and get his ass banned from the gym for violating rules. He'd like nothing better than for Jesse to stop working out, get weak, be unable to defend himself. That was the kind of hateful crap Kildare was infamous for.

Besides, nobody ever came to visit him. His ma had

come to the county jail for a while, after his arrest, and she'd been there during his trial.

But she'd also been sitting in the courtroom when the worst of it had come out, when the testimony got pretty bad. She hadn't come back since. Not one visit. Not one letter. Not one word. It was as if she'd never given birth to him.

"You got shit stuck in your ears?"

Lowering the barbell, Jesse offered the man an insolent sneer. "I heard ya."

The guard glowered, his beefy frame straining against the blue fabric of his uniform. "Then get your ass over here."

It was a risk. Ignore the guard and take a whack from his nightstick, or believe him and land in crap when it proved to be a lie.

Life on the inside was made of such decisions. Choices usually ranged from bad to rotten, and whichever way he went, Jesse was the one who invariably got fucked. But lately he'd been working out hard, building his strength. Now he was strong enough to fight back.

Unlike in the beginning.

Right after he'd come here to the Cumberland maximum-security facility to serve his sentence, he'd learned just how true all those stories were about prison life. About what it was like to go inside on any kind of crime involving kids.

Most people, inside and out, seemed to think his was the worst kind of crime. Paying a debt to society by getting locked in a cell for the rest of his life didn't seem to be enough, apparently. He needed to regularly get beaten and jumped by his fellow inmates, and sometimes guards, too.

Probably the only person who'd had it worse than him in this place was the crazy guy they called the Professor. Because, when you got sent up, the only thing worse than being a convicted child molester was being a former prison warden.

"You got till the count of three. Then I bust your head, toss you in your cell, and tell your fancy new lawyer you're not interested."

That got his attention. "What lawyer?"

The guard peered at him, visibly suspicious. "You weren't expecting her?"

Her? Every one of his previous public defenders had been guys. The last of them, a kid who looked as if he should be going to homeroom and banging cheerleaders, had made it clear he wouldn't be back unless the pope himself showed up to give Jesse an alibi. Just one more in a long line of motherfuckers who'd screwed him over.

Best defense available under the law? Shee-it. His own lawyers hadn't done jack to get him out of this jam. Oh, sure, they'd gone through the most basic of motions to file an appeal, but had given up almost immediately with a "*Sayonara*, sucker." Nobody cared if he rotted in here for the rest of his miserable life.

"Boyd!" the guard snapped.

Putting on his best poker face, Jesse replied, "I didn't think she was comin' today, thassall. Good news."

Yeah, fat chance of that. He couldn't help wondering how the guard would react when he found out this was a mistake. Because it had to be. Jesse didn't have no new attorney.

*It's possible. You never know.*

Maybe it was good news. Everybody's luck had to

turn around sooner or later, didn't it? Maybe it was his time. Maybe somebody had finally realized he'd gotten no goddamn justice and they were here to fix this mess.

"Move it, then."

He crossed the gym, ignoring the glares he got from his fellow inmates. Screw them. Self-righteous bastards. They could slit the throats of old grannies or pop shop-keepers for three bucks, and still thought they were so much better than him? That he was sick and degenerate? Hell, he wasn't no cold-blooded killer.

As Kildare escorted him to one of the meeting rooms, which was used only by inmates and their attorneys, he prepared for the guard's wrath. It wasn't Jesse's fault somebody screwed up and thought he had a new lawyer. But Kildare would blame him for inconveniencing his lard ass anyway.

Reaching the room, he couldn't help peering through the barred glass window to make sure there was a woman inside, and he wasn't about to walk into a guard's birthday party, with him playing the part of the piñata.

She really was there. All prim and snotty looking, dressed in a fancy suit, her hair up off her face and tight. As soon as he walked in, she looked at him over the top of her small silver glasses, shaped like two pointy upside-down triangles, sizing him up. "You're Jesse Boyd?"

Still not quite believing she really was here to see him, he could only nod.

"Sit down."

When he hesitated, Kildare gave him a shove in the back. The hoity-toity lawyer pointed one finger at the guard and snapped, "Watch it or I'll see to it you never put your hands on another inmate."

Okay. He liked this broad, whoever she was.

Kildare fumed for a second, then spun around and walked away, stepping to a corner to give them a little privacy.

Jesse sat. "What's this all about?"

The woman ignored him, pulling a file out of her briefcase and opening it on the table between them. Pen in hand, she jotted something on a yellow legal pad, crossed it out, jotted something else. Without looking up, she snapped, "You're bruised."

Jesse absently rubbed at his forearm.

"Guards?

"Nuh-uh." Not this time, anyway.

"Try to stay out of fights. You'll want to be a choirboy until we get this done."

"Get what done?"

She finally looked up at him. "Your appeal, of course."

"Whoa, slow down, lady. Who the hell are you?"

"My name is Claire Vincent. I'm a partner at the Bradley, Miles & Cavanaugh firm out of Virginia, but our firm has offices in the D.C. metro area and I'm licensed to practice here in Maryland. I've been hired to get you out of here."

Glancing at Kildare and seeing the guard was occupied playing a game of pocket pool while he looked at the pretty lawyer from behind, Jesse leaned over the table a little. "I didn't hire no new lawyer. Did my ma hire you?"

"No. The person who hired me isn't pertinent to our conversation."

"Huh?"

"I mean," she explained, finally putting the pen down, "I was hired by someone who has a strong distaste for injustice. Your benefactor believes you were wronged, and hired me to look into the case, which I've been doing for some time now."

Not quite believing it, Jesse could only stare.

"I have come to agree that you weren't treated fairly. You had the worst of representation and were convicted by the world before you ever set foot in the court-room."

"No shit. I tell ya, I didn't kill nobody—"

She put up a hand, stopping him. "We don't need to discuss what you did or did not do."

He'd heard that line before. His other lawyers didn't seem to care, either. Made 'em uncomfortable, probably, defending all those scumbags who really were guilty of murder.

Unlike him, who'd just had a run of bad luck.

"The simple fact that the victim's aunt was an FBI agent, and that some of the evidence was processed in the FBI crime lab, should have been enough to at least argue for the evidence to be excluded."

Smacking his hand flat on the table, he chortled. "That's exactly what I said! But that pussy public defender wouldn't listen to me. Made one shot at an appeal on some technical garbage, and then gave up."

Her lips thinned. Man, this bitch was cast-iron hard.

"Sorry. Not used to being in polite company any-more," he mumbled.

"It's quite all right." She offered him a small, tight smile. "You won't be for much longer. Perhaps no more than a week."

Stunned and almost not wanting to hope, he asked, "You mean that?"

"I do. I've already gotten us a hearing. It's coming up

in a few days, so I needed to come here to prepare you for it. I apologize for not giving you more time, but I never expected the judge's docket to clear so unexpectedly and give us a date that soon. I was caught off guard, too. I was supposed to go away for the holiday weekend but will now spend every minute of it preparing for our day in court."

Jesse sagged back in his chair, unable to believe his life could be changing so much, so fast. An hour ago, he was wondering how to keep himself alive in here for the next forty years, and now someone was telling him he might be out in seven days?

"Is this really happening?" he whispered.

"Yes. It is. A number of things have happened with regard to your case. No jury on earth would convict you if it came to trial today."

"Like?"

"Like the fact that, aside from the victim's aunt being with the bureau, the evidence was processed within a few weeks of an internal-corruption investigation at the crime lab. A number of other cases were overturned. It falls close enough to the time frame to raise flags."

He could only gawk in disbelief. "Are you shittin' me?"

"Furthermore, the agent responsible for uncovering the tampering was, until recently, the direct supervisor of the victim's aunt. It could be argued that his relationship with her led him to delay reporting it."

"I can't fuckin' believe this."

He smacked his palm sharply on the table, drawing a quick glance from Kildare. Giving him an apologetic look, Jesse drew back.

"The physical evidence—DNA and so forth—should be easily excluded based on those two elements." The lawyer glanced at her pad, flipped a couple of pages, and read something in her notes. "There's also apparently a new witness who can corroborate your alibi. I'm still working on that to make sure his testimony will stand up."

His alibi? That story that he'd been sitting in a crowded bar, drinking, until long after that kid had been snatched?

Who, he wondered, would support that story, considering it was bullshit?

"Things are looking very good for you, Mr. Boyd."

Jesse couldn't help it. He started to cry. Hot, wet tears filled his eyes. "You mean, I'll finally be found innocent? Be able to get back to my real life?"

Get his mother to look him in the eye once more?

The cold, steely expression left the lawyer's face and her voice went a little softer. "No. You won't be found innocent. What we're after is a ruling that there was a flaw in your original prosecution, that the evidence was tainted. The conviction should be overturned, but that's not the same as getting a not-guilty verdict."

Not ideal, but if it got him out of this hellhole, he could live with it. And if he showed up on her doorstep and told Ma they let him out 'cause he didn't do it, she'd believe him, right? He'd make her believe him.

"And that'll be the end of it? No double jeopardy?"

Another shake of her head. Damn, he wanted to smack the woman to get her to talk faster rather than reeling out the information in dribs and drabs. "If the appeals court rules that your first trial was flawed and overturns the conviction, the prosecution will still have the opportunity to refile the case and try you again on the same charges."

He closed his eyes, not wanting to believe it. "Another trial."

A cool hand brushed his. The woman had reached across the table to comfort him. "Jesse, it's inconceivable that the prosecutor would refile. He'll know he'd have no chance of winning. If you have a new alibi, and they have no DNA evidence . . ."

"What about the eyewitness?" he asked, almost starting to believe but not quite letting himself go there yet.

"The child's aunt?"

He nodded once, still picturing that blond-haired bitch who'd put nail after nail in his coffin with every word she'd uttered on the stand.

"Her original testimony can, of course, be admitted, but with the questions regarding her supervisor's involvement in the crime-lab issue, I could argue against it, since she's not available for cross-examination."

"Why isn't she?"

The cool-as-a-cucumber attorney offered him a look of surprise. "Didn't you hear?"

"Hear what?"

"Well, Mr. Boyd, Lily Fletcher, the prosecution's star witness against you, died seven months ago."

She dreamed.

No sweet, pleasant images. No amusing adventures to enjoy while she slumbered. Wyatt's presence down the hall didn't change what happened every time she allowed her weary body to fall into bed, hoping she was exhausted enough to escape the nightmares. The horror.

But no. In the long, empty hours, when sleep should have been a welcome escape, she instead found herself at the mercy of relentless memory. Just like in her conscious times, the images haunted her.

"No, please," she mumbled, twisting in the bed. Lost in that place between asleep and awake, she knew she was falling into the familiar nightmare and tried to swim out of it, to the light of consciousness. But she couldn't pull herself from it.

She could never pull herself from it. Not this night. Not any night.

*The dream that was not a dream.*

Not a dream at all. Pure, dark reality filled the places in her brain that had once been reserved for dreamlike fantasy. Each moment, each tense, terrifying second, of that cold January night played like a movie on an endless loop in the dark theater of her mind.

*Help me, Wyatt. I'm here. Please find me.*

She was there again, on that deserted Virginia beach. Alone. Dying.

Reliving every second . . .

*Help me. Find me.* The words repeated in Lily's brain, lapping over and over like the hard, rolling waves hitting the shore just across the windswept dunes from where she lay dying. Strong at first, each syllable underscored her certainty that he would come for her, would find her before it was too late. That possibility of rescue was a glimmer of weak light in the black void into which she had been thrust.

But as time went on, as the cold night grew more deep and bitter, and numbness spread from her limbs throughout her entire body, those hopes faded. The pleas quieted. She could barely hear her own mental voice anymore. Her heartbeat weakened, too, her breaths growing shallow, her pulse slow and sluggish.

Her body was fading along with her hope of rescue.

*Help me.*

She did not have the strength to send the words across her lips in even the faintest of whispers. Not again. Once had to be enough.

Even if she could find some inner reserve of strength, her only means of communication was gone. She had found her cellular phone tangled in a pile of bloody clothes on the floor of the decrepit, abandoned beach shack where she'd been imprisoned. Miracle enough that she'd located the thing at all. An even greater miracle that the battery had lasted long enough for one call. Just one Hail Mary cry for help to the only person in the world she knew would be there for her. The one who had cautioned her against going down the path of personal vengeance that had eventually left her here, broken and dying, and alone.

*Should have listened to you, Wyatt. Shouldn't have gotten involved. In over my head. Sorry. So sorry.*

At least she had heard him one more time, strong and reassuring. There was some justice in the world that the voice of the vicious monster who'd attacked her would not be the last one she would ever hear. Wyatt Blackstone's would.

*I'm coming. Hold on.*

Did he say that? Had the call really gone through? Or had it merely been a fantasy, a final desperate wish disguised as a lifeline? Was she fooling herself before giving in to the pain and the blood loss? Maybe the physical torment and emotional torture she had endured since that awful night when the FBI sting had gone so horribly wrong, and she'd been taken by a monster wearing a human face, had finally broken her, cracked her mind into a thousand splintered pieces.

*You heard him. He heard you.*

She had to believe that. Yet the hours that must have passed since her desperate attempt to save her own life made her doubt.

Breathing deeply, she struggled to remain conscious, trying not to give in to the dazed, confused helplessness that had clouded her head for the past week.

A week? More? Less? How long since she'd been shot, captured by a sociopathic monster who killed another agent right before her eyes? Time had meant nothing from the moment she'd awakened to the ruthless ministrations of a man who wanted to keep her alive only so he could hurt her some more.

The murderous pedophile blamed her for his losses and he wanted retribution. Badly.

The night lengthened. *Cold. So damn cold.* She had weakly pulled clothes on over her naked body before making her escape, risking the few precious extra seconds to do it. She'd had no way of knowing how long he would be gone. He had believed her unconscious, incapable of movement, but that didn't mean he would take his time on whatever fiendish errand he was running. Still, escaping naked from the hellhole would have given her probably thirty minutes tops before she lost consciousness to hypothermia. So while her clothes were tattered and bloodstained, she was thankful for them.

They wouldn't keep her alive for much longer, though. Even if she had not reopened one of her roughly stitched wounds with her desperate, lurching crawl, foot by foot up the beach, she'd eventually freeze to death.

*Laura. Zach.*

The faces of her sister and nephew filled her mind. Her death wouldn't be as anguished as theirs had been. She'd just go to sleep. Close her eyes on this frigid, wind-swept dune. Never wake up. It wasn't so bad, really. Just sleep, perhaps even with no nightmares to torment her the way they had since everyone she cared about had been so brutally taken from her.

"Lily!"

*Coming, Laura.*

"Can you hear me?

Yes. She heard. It wasn't the first time she'd heard Laura. Somehow the echoes of her voice had rung in Lily's ears back at the shack earlier this evening before she'd escaped.

"Missed you," she whispered. She forced her eyes to open, certain she'd see the faces of her beloved twin sister and the little boy they had both loved more than life. But they weren't there. Above her she saw nothing but dark sky, filled with a glowing white moon shimmering against a backdrop of black, endless nothingness. Eternity.

"Lily, we're here!"

*Laura? No. A male voice.*

Wyatt.

Then he was there, lifting her, holding her close, offering warmth and protection. He whispered soft, comforting things against her hair and her cheek, telling her she was safe. His handsome face was bathed in emotion, tenderness evident in every gentle stroke of his hand on her skin.

Impossible. Wyatt Blackstone was never emotional. Never tender. Her boss never showed weakness.

"I've got you. It's okay. Brandon's right up the beach, too. We're getting you out of here."

She swallowed, trying to process everything. His warmth, his smell, the throaty voice.

"Wyatt?" she whispered, starting to believe. "You heard me?"

His footsteps crunched on the sand and he kept his grip tight around her. "I heard you. I can't believe it—you were like a voice from a grave. Jesus, Lily, we held a memorial service for you one day ago!"

*True. Here.* That voice at the other end of the telephone call had been real, not a figment of her imagination. Tears filled her eyes and erupted from them, freezing onto her cheeks before they could travel down her face. "You found me."

"We found you. You're safe. We'll catch him and he will never hurt you again."

Her blood, already cold, turned to ice. They hadn't caught him. Hadn't captured the man who'd done this to her. She began to shake, and to whimper, thinking of the fists and the wicked needles used to stitch her wounds, with no anesthetic, nothing to prevent her from feeling every rough, agonizing thrust.

"Not safe." Not as long as the psychopath who'd held her was out there. She couldn't even help them find him—she'd been blindfolded until the minute she escaped. She'd never laid eyes on the man; she knew only his voice. And his hateful, brutal touch that had taught her lessons about pain no person should ever have to learn.

Pure terror sent shudders throughout her entire form.

"Shh, yes, you are. I'm taking you out of here. We'll get you to a hospital and you'll be home before you know it."

Home? To her small, sad apartment and her small, sad life? To the four walls that echoed with the voices of those she had lost, and would cage her as she tried to remain out of sight of the madman who would never rest until he had killed her?

No. Home was not safe. No place would ever be safe. There couldn't be enough security or enough guards. She could never return to a normal life, never let herself be visible or live in the light. Not while that monster lived.

She needed to remain in the darkness. Lily, but not Lily.

*Off the grid.*

"Wyatt," she whispered, "please . . ."

"What is it?"

"Please let me stay dead."

*Please let me stay dead.*

The nightmare began again.

Though once a drunk, Will Miller had always considered himself an honest man. He'd never stolen, never injured anybody. He'd only ever lied to avoid hurting his ex-wife and kids about his little problem with the bottle. He'd managed to keep working in a good job, been respected and liked, right up until the day he'd hit rock bottom.

It was the one thing he'd had any pride in—that he was a good man. A weak one, but a good one. He wanted to be that way again. He might have lived in a fog for several years, but now he'd been totally clean for seven months. Clean, sober, and on the path to a new life.

That new life could be made even better with some money to start it.

He stared at the computer screen, having sneaked into his daughter's family room, where she kept her ancient computer, long after she and her baby had gone to bed. She might be a waitress, living in a tiny two-bedroom apartment, barely making it on her own. Yet his youngest child had given him a place to stay. She was the only family he had left, and he owed her a lot. More than he could ever repay.

"Or maybe not," he whispered, keeping his voice low so as not to wake the woman and child sleeping in the next room. "Maybe I could do more for you both than you ever dreamed," he added.

The computer screen wasn't big, but the number in the Balance column was enormous.

All he had to do to get the access code to all that money was tell one teeny, tiny little white lie. Just one. Then all his troubles—and his daughter's—would be over. He'd be able to take care of her, of the kid. Maybe he'd even be able to get his ex and his two sons to start talking to him again. Really get back to his life.

Hell, maybe it wasn't a lie at all. He'd been drunk for a solid four years before getting himself a spot in a rehab center. He could very well have sat next to this Boyd guy in his favorite Annapolis bar one cold February night, two and a half years back. He'd been there practically every night. So maybe they really had shared a bottle and some stories. Just because he couldn't remember didn't mean it hadn't happened. Boyd remembered, right? If the guy had been railroaded by some lying cops, he deserved a helping hand. Just as Will deserved one. And his daughter deserved one.

The number was hypnotic, shining in the darkened room like a beacon toward a new world. A second chance for all of them.

With just one little lie—which maybe wouldn't be a lie—it would be his.

From the next room, he heard his baby grandson coughing. The kid had been hacking and snotting all week, poor little champ. No insurance, no free clinic within bus range. His daughter was trying to make do with that over-the-counter crap that killed little kids if you gave 'em too much.

*You can make this all go away.*

Decision made. His stomach didn't even churn as he reached for the phone, ignoring the late hour since he'd been told to call at any time of the day or night.

Will dialed the number he'd been given. When a muffled voice answered, he said, "Okay. I'm in. Tell me what I gotta do."

# Chapter 4

When he'd brought Lily here last March, after more than a month in the hospital and a private rehab center, Wyatt had stayed with her for a couple of weeks, ignoring his own discomfort and loathing of the house. The renovations he'd ordered had been completed at top speed, with crews working 24-7, so the place at least looked different enough to allow him to pretend it was another building entirely. And the construction, the gutting of the central part of the house so it was now a huge, airy space full of light and brightness, had been worth it, for Lily's sake. He'd wanted to make sure she felt safe and comfortable and had the strength to remain on her own. He'd also overseen the installation of the security system she'd asked for, even while he tried again to convince her that he could protect her and she did not need to stay in hiding.

To no avail.

She had asked him to let the world think her dead. And on that bitter cold night, when she had seemed so close to death anyway, he had given his word. So had Brandon, the one person Wyatt had contacted after getting Lily's pained call for help.

To this day, he honestly didn't know why he had called only Brandon and none of the rest of the team. Maybe it was because he'd been so desperate, panicking when he *never* panicked. Brandon's number had been the one he'd dialed, certain if anyone could trace the cell phone's signal and help him figure out Lily's location from the few clues she'd been able to provide, it was the young computer expert. It might have been because he hadn't entirely trusted his own senses, had wondered if he'd been mistaken, hearing Lily's voice when his rational mind told him he couldn't have.

Hell, maybe even because somehow, with the sixth sense he'd always relied upon, he had already known he was racing into a tangled situation that could very well end up hanging him. *Them.* And while he didn't figure he had much else to lose with the FBI, the others on his team all did. Kyle Mulrooney was too close to retirement. Jackie Stokes had a husband and kids to worry about—and she'd been the most distraught over Lily's death. Why raise her hopes on something that might have been a prank? Alec Lambert was new and already on probation, Dean Taggert just starting to seem to have some kind of personal life again with a new live-in girlfriend. A girlfriend who was also a cop who might ask uncomfortable questions.

Brandon, though, was young and single. Utterly brilliant. And a rule breaker. He'd also been the closest to Lily, sharing an office with her, not to mention a warm friendship.

Looking back, would he have done it any other way? Brought in the cavalry so there would never have been any question of whether Lily Fletcher would return to her life or cease to exist altogether?

He didn't know. And it was too late to worry about it now.

There were other things to worry about.

"Help me, Wyatt."

Her voice was faint, though he heard it clearly. Just as he had the very first night they'd spent here and he'd realized she was tormented by nightmares. The beach house wasn't overly large, just two bedrooms and a loft upstairs. Even over the churning of the surf and the gusty March winds, he had easily heard her tormented cries. Like now.

He didn't go to check on her, to see if she truly needed help. Lily was physically fine, not battling any real demons, just the ones in her head.

In the beginning, he often tried to console her, going to her, letting her know she was safe. He would whisper soft reassurances from the doorway of her room, not wanting to enter and startle her with the presence of a man reaching for her in the darkness. He knew better. She'd told him enough about her ordeal for him to realize that much.

His voice often quieted her and she'd stop thrashing and moaning. He would remain there, watching her slowly drift back into a deeper sleep, the vulnerability of her features stark against the scarred head covered in a layer of pale blond fuzz.

But it hadn't helped every time. On a few occasions, his whispers that he had found her and she was going to be all right hadn't done the trick. And at those times, he had known she was dreaming about something other than the night he'd rescued her.

Those nightmares were more heartbreaking. She wouldn't talk about them, but he had his suspicions about the horrors she saw in her sleeping hours.

Perhaps the face of her nephew, peering in terror through the window of a dark van driven by the sick bastard who had kidnapped him. Lily had, after all, been the last one to see him alive. She had even had to testify in the murder trial against Jesse Boyd, the sexual predator convicted of killing the child.

Or perhaps her dreams were of a few weeks later, when she'd walked into her sister's home and found her twin in the bathtub, her wrists open and weeping blood.

Such sights could haunt a person for life, drive them right into madness. Or into a need for complete, emotionless self-control.

But her dreams might not have been merely about the torture of losing her loved ones. They could have been of the week she'd spent blindfolded in that old shack. Learning the real meaning of torture.

*Which dream are you having right now?*

She cried out again. He got out of the bed, crossing the room in silence, resisting the urge to continue into the hallway, to her door.

He didn't do that anymore. Not ever.

When Lily had been so injured, frail, and helpless, he had felt like nothing more than a friend or caretaker looking after a child. But she was no longer injured, frail, or helpless. And not at all childlike. He'd acknowledged that one night in July when he'd gone to her, only to have her wake up and stare at him from the bed. The full moon and the glimmer of the outside floodlights had brightened her room. Enough for him to see the strong jut of her jaw, the hint of angry determination in her expression as she brought herself under control.

Not to mention the flush of color in her lovely face, the fullness of her lips as she heaved in deep, gasping breaths. Or the clinginess of the thin nightgown that skimmed over her body.

Their stares had met and locked. Her breaths had slowed. His had deepened. Neither spoke, but their thoughts were communicated nonetheless.

In that one long, heavy moment, he'd stopped seeing Lily, the girl he had liked and taken care of. And had begun to see the woman she was now. Strong. Fierce. Beautiful.

It was as if he were seeing her for the first time.

He'd wanted her. Suddenly. Unexpectedly. Completely. God help him, he had wanted to touch her and pleasure her and give her one night of heated sexuality to replace the coldness of her dreams.

Which was utterly impossible. Wanting Lily was almost as unacceptable as actually having her. He was her protector; he'd been her boss. She was a decade his junior and trusted him to keep his distance.

He'd told himself all those things. But still, Lily's image had intruded any time he had even thought about another woman since that night.

So, no. He no longer went to her room when she cried out in her sleep. After fiercely insisting she was strong and capable of looking after herself, and didn't need to be coddled, Lily probably suspected that was why he had backed off.

It wasn't her strength he had doubted. It was his own.

Frankly, he was also beginning to question his own sanity. Was it possible he was really considering her a suspect in the lily murders?

"It's insane," he whispered, all the suspicions that had driven him here to see her this weekend having faded into ridiculous conjecture once he was back in her company.

Ridiculous conjecture or not, he had a job to do. And ruling Lily Fletcher out as a suspect was chief on his to-do list.

Ruling her in, he didn't even want to contemplate.

He heard movement and leaned closer to the door, silent, quieting even his breaths. Lily's bedroom door opened. She stepped into the hall, her footsteps firm, as if she had leapt out of bed, angry at her own subconscious. But they faltered when she reached his room.

Wyatt closed his eyes, his hand flat on the middle panel of the door, his fingers splayed.

Would she knock? Would he answer?

A moment more. She moved on.

Not sure whether he was relieved or disappointed, he remained there, waiting for her to return. She had likely gone downstairs to get a drink of water, take a sleeping pill, perhaps. But the minutes stretched on. And on. Until finally, he needed to make sure she was okay.

He moved silently through the house and down the stairs, expecting to find her in the kitchen. It was empty, as was the living room.

"I'm out here," a voice said from the darkness without.

The coldness inside finally registered, as did the open

patio door. He stepped out to find her at the railing, staring down at the beach. She wore simple cotton shorts and a T-shirt and should have been shivering from the night air, but seemed oblivious to it. Oblivious to everything, really, except the sound of the waves and the newly lit cigarette in her hand.

"Haven't quit yet, hmm?"

She gestured toward the table but didn't look around. "That's the same pack I bought in May."

The small package was still half-full. It rested beside her laptop, which was open and turned on, an Internet news page displayed on the monitor.

"You know, before the nightmares, I never smoked a single time in my life."

"I know."

She'd told him once that on the worst of those nights, it was either light a cigarette or down a few glasses of vodka. Still on pain meds and antidepressants at the time, she'd figured smoking was the lesser of two evils and apparently hadn't kicked the habit.

"I've never done it in the house."

"I know that as well." Not that he'd give a damn if a stray match burned the entire place to the ground, once Lily was well and had no need for it anymore.

He'd certainly considered it over the years. Just demolishing the place. But something had stopped him. Perhaps just knowing his grandparents had held on to it for him, never even letting him know until their declining years that it was his, still there on the cliff, silent and dead.

He'd never come to see it before last winter. Nor, however, had he let it go.

She glanced down, then wordlessly crushed the unsmoked cigarette into the railing. Finally turning to look at him, she admitted, "I guess conversation beats inhalation."

He smiled faintly. "You ready to talk?"

"Well, you sure had nothing to say at dinner."

No, he hadn't. At dinner he had been too busy wondering how to break the news to Brandon that Lily had been able to get around whatever firewalls and constraints he had placed around the group's files. Not to mention how to get Lily to open up and tell him why she was doing it.

While he was lying in bed trying to fall asleep a little while ago, the answer had, of course, come to him. "You know I'd tell you if we had anything on him."

Her brow lifted, though her tone sounded unsurprised. "What?

"The Lovesprettyboys investigation is stalled. That doesn't mean it will never be solved. You've got to trust me."

He couldn't imagine how frustrating it must be for her, knowing the man who had attacked her had gotten away and had never been identified. Lily had never stopped believing he was out there, looking for her, wanting to finish what he started. Not only because he held her responsible for his downfall, but also because she might somehow be able to identify him.

"Damn it, Wyatt. It's been seven months," she said, her anguish clear. Her voice, her face, her twisting hands, her shaking arms, all confirmed how far on the edge she truly was—and confirmed that she might do something crazy, like a little hacking, to get some answers. "How the hell can you still not know who he is?"

They had leads and theories, but hadn't been able to prove a thing. "You know how these things go. You said yourself it would be almost impossible for you to ID his face."

"Yes, but someone else could! The vagrant he picked up to help him that night. He was an eyewitness, for God's sake."

"Not a reliable one," he replied evenly. "Just a drugged-out guy from the street who could remember only that the man who picked him up was Caucasian and middle-aged."

Lily shivered a little, as if finally noticing just how cold and damp it was outside.

"Let's go in," he said.

She shook her head, grabbed a beach towel from the railing, and draped it over her shoulders, tucking her arms into the folds. "Why isn't this going any faster?"

"Do you really have to ask?" He said the words carefully. The woman already bore a lot of weight on her shoulders. He didn't want to add to it. But he did need for her to understand. "The world thinks you *and* your assailant were killed in that van crash. So not only is the case not a high priority right now, since they're assuming he's dead, but the official investigators are looking for anyone who went missing or died the same night you did. Only you, Brandon, and I know he did no such thing and might very well have gone back to his real life once he realized you weren't coming after him."

"But you can't tell anyone that," she whispered.

"No. I can't."

Moving slowly to the table, she dropped onto one of the chairs. "Of course."

Joining her, Wyatt noted the way she'd visibly deflated. "Look, it doesn't mean we won't find him. It just makes it a little harder."

"Maybe I should just come forward, let the media make a big deal out of the FBI agent who faked her death, and let the bastard come and find me."

Wyatt stiffened, not even wanting to consider that option. "You're not using yourself as bait."

"Don't coddle me, Wyatt."

He intentionally sneered, knowing the very last thing Lily wanted was to be treated like a fragile object. Besides, she wasn't fragile. Wounded, yeah. Weak? No way in hell.

He didn't like having to remind her that she owed him, but damned if he would let her take unnecessary risks and lose everything she had gained. "We didn't save your ass, put our careers on the line, just so you could go out and get yourself killed."

It was a cheap shot and he knew it. Lily flinched, but she also lifted her chin, glad he'd treated her as an equal, a strong woman capable of taking as much as she dished out. It wasn't difficult, because despite how much he wanted to keep her safe, he knew she was strong, his equal in every way.

"Understood." She tapped her fingers on the surface of the table and dropped the idea, as he'd known she would. "The owner of the vehicle he ditched before he grabbed me, did you talk to him? Make sure it truly was stolen?" she asked, going back to the case.

"She was a well-known, respected plastic surgeon. Very convincing, very reliable."

The unsub had stolen a car parked at a ritzy Richmond hotel, intending to break into a house where two young children were supposedly alone, unsupervised. He'd found the children, stalked them, by lurking on a kids' community Web site.

Those two unattended children had never existed. Lily had played the role of young girl irritated at having to babysit her little brother for the first time. She'd lured him in like a slimy fish on a baited hook. She'd called herself Tiger Lily, in answer to the handle he'd been using on the site: Peter Pan. The boy who never grew up.

Sick fucking bastard. At least the one he'd used at Satan's Playground, Lovesprettyboys—the identity he had admitted to using when he had Lily in his clutches—had been unambiguous. It had revealed him for the twisted degenerate he was.

On that January night, fearing a trap, the unsub had waited down the block from the undercover house, slipping a vagrant a twenty to scope out the place first. When he'd realized the whole thing was a setup, he'd tried to run, but he couldn't start the car. The closest vehicle was an FBI van doing exterior surveillance. Inside it, Lily had been watching, listening, waiting for the end of the investigation that had consumed her.

The rest of what had happened that night had been thought about, talked about, wondered about, by everyone on the team and others in the bureau. Considering Lily's memories were fuzzy, he doubted they'd ever know the whole story. How, for instance, the killer had stashed Lily in the dilapidated beach shack and then gotten back to the bridge to stage the crash. How he'd gotten away from the crash site without being spotted. If, perhaps, he *hadn't* gotten away and had just blended in as onlookers and rescue workers filled the scene.

One of the biggest questions: Had someone helped him?

He needed to know all those things. But the only one who could answer the questions was the unsub.

At first, as he'd told her, Wyatt and everyone else in the bureau had looked for any Richmond-area middle-aged man who had disappeared unexpectedly the same night Lily had. They'd thought, of course, that he had died. When Wyatt realized one week later that the unsub was still alive, he'd still looked at anyone who was missing, likely in hiding.

Then he'd realized the truth. The unsub might have hidden out at the shack with Lily for a day or two, waiting for any hint that his identity had been uncovered, despite all his precautions. When that day hadn't come, though, had the slime simply returned to his real world? Gone back to a normal life, believing no one would come after him? At least as long as nobody ever found out Lily was still alive.

How he must have panicked when he got back to the shack and found she had disappeared. Had he been somewhere on the long, deserted beach himself that night, searching for his victim even as Wyatt and Brandon were rescuing her? It was possible. Because he certainly hadn't returned later, when they had been staking the place out. Wyatt imagined that, like a character out of a Poe story, the unsub was tormented by the possibility of discovery, the chance that his victim might have her vengeance on him yet. That waiting and uncertainty would be enough to drive a sane person mad.

No one had ever called Lovesprettyboys—Peter Pan—sane.

"Tell me what you have." Apparently seeing the instinctive refusal about to come out of his mouth, she urged, "Please. I'm healed; I'm healthy. If you talk about it, maybe it'll spark something and give you a new lead."

He stared at her intently, unable to see the depths of blue in those eyes out here in the moonlight. The floodlights over their heads might brighten the cliffs and the stairs. But here they were almost caught in a small pool of night that existed between the house and her security perimeter. Caught between light and darkness, being in the open and remaining hidden in the shadows. Just as Lily was caught. And would be, until he captured the person who had tried to kill her.

"Please," she repeated.

Sighing heavily, he tried to give her what she wanted, knowing he could not reveal too much. Especially since he was currently investigating two cases that somehow involved Lily Fletcher: her own "murder"... and the murders of three men who had a lot in common with her attacker.

"As I just said, the owner of the car was a plastic surgeon from Williamsburg, Virginia, attending a medical convention at that hotel."

"Are you *certain* she—"

"She isn't a suspect. Just the owner of the stolen car. A number of people remember seeing her at the banquet at which her father received a humanitarian award that night, and her sister-in-law shared an elevator ride with her right around the time you were being attacked. We have the surveillance video to prove it."

"Where was the car?"

"It had been parked by a hotel valet."

She immediately leaned forward. "Meaning the valets had access to the keys."

He nodded. "But the keys to that particular car were still at the valet stand the next morning."

"Hot-wired? That would indicate a certain kind of criminal."

"No. Dr. Kean admitted she kept a spare key to the car in a magnetic box inside the fender."

"Leaving a key hidden right on the vehicle in this day and age?" she asked, sounding astonished. "Good grief, some people are so naive."

She used to be one of them. Not that he intended to mention that. "Apparently, the doctor has a teenage son, a new driver, who has already locked himself out of the car several times."

"What, and she never heard of OnStar?"

Wyatt ignored her sarcasm. "When the vehicle was searched after your attack, that magnetic box was open, the key gone. It's very possible the unsub just went hunting for a car with a spare key hidden on it and struck pay dirt."

Lily's frown remained.

"Dr. Kean was very upset and concerned about being implicated in any way," he said, seeing she still had doubts. "She was entirely cooperative."

"Well, she can rest easy, anyway. I know Lovesprettyboys was not a female." A bitter laugh escaped her mouth. "Though I did hear a woman's voice during those final hours I spent in that shack."

Stunned, he leaned closer. *"What?"*

Lily immediately shook her head, negating his assumptions. "No, no, it wasn't a real voice. Just one in my head."

Probably her own voice encouraging her to not give

up, to get away while she still had the chance. He blessed that voice; he really did. "Your own?"

"No. A ghost's, I think. My sister's."

Wyatt couldn't stop himself from reaching out and clasping her hand, noting the coldness of her fingers. He quickly pulled away, knowing physical contact wasn't what Lily wanted right now. She might never want it again. Besides which, it shouldn't come from him.

"Don't be so sure," he said. "It's possible the unsub spoke with a woman, maybe someone walking on the beach, who had no idea he was holding you captive inside. It's one more avenue to explore."

"Maybe."

He got back to the things they knew for sure. "Dr. Kean claims she had no idea someone had taken the car from valet parking until the next morning, when she reported it stolen and found out it had been used in a crime. Since she was staying at the Richmond hotel, the police hadn't been able to use the vehicle registration to reach her at home the previous night."

"Okay, back to the valet parking. What about surveillance video?"

"The valet lot was full because of the conference. The attendants started parking overflow in the back alley of the hotel. No cameras."

She reached for the cigarettes, drew one out, twisting it between her fingers but making no effort to light. "And the witness? Were you able to get anything from him at all?"

"The vagrant told us the unsub had been wearing thick gloves, a heavy coat, a furred cap that disguised his features. Considering he was having withdrawal shakes after just a few hours of interrogation, I'd say that description was pretty good. He also admitted he'd grabbed the key from the ignition while the unsub was retrieving something from the backseat, worrying he would be left behind if things went wrong."

"Good move for him. Not so good for me and poor Vince Kowalski."

Special Agent Kowalski had been shot dead in the street right in front of Lily's eyes.

"Brandon's been working on the cyber angle, of course, and tracked the computer used by the unsub to an IP in central Virginia. The ISP led to a Wi-Fi hot spot in a mall."

"Sure. Why not sit in a food court and stalk little kids in an online chat room?"

He hadn't been in the food court. Wyatt had gone over every inch of the mall's surveillance tapes. Wherever the unsub had been when he'd picked up the signal, it hadn't been within camera range.

Sighing, she mumbled, "That's about all you know, then."

She didn't ask about the forensics from inside the stolen van, or the beach shack. Some issues were apparently too much, even for her. Nor did she ask him about the other online leads, what other information they'd gotten from the chat rooms and message boards where she, posting as a little girl, had attracted the attention of their unsub.

He suspected he knew why. If Lily hadn't been up here doing her own online investigating, then he was no judge of character at all.

*Maybe you're not. Look what you're doing right now, wondering if she could possibly be a killer.*

Every instinct he owned screamed no. But he had to

make certain. He didn't want to spy on her, but he'd gone ahead and checked the mileage on the Jeep. He'd bought it slightly used and had a good idea of what the original mileage had been. If there'd been another several thousand miles on it, his suspicions would have increased. There wasn't, however.

That didn't mean she couldn't have driven to the closest bus station, train station, or airport. He always left plenty of cash for her personal use.

She remained silent, still, moving only the tips of her fingers on the surface of the table. Her nails tapped out a nervous beat, and she averted her gaze as she mumbled, "I've been doing some thinking."

"Undoubtedly." Wyatt stiffened, red flags going up in his head. He already knew that when Lily announced she'd been doing some thinking, he would probably end up trying to talk her out of something. Like, for instance, this whole obsession with tae kwon do and additional weapons training.

"We've known all along he was someone with money."

"Yes." The unsub had once offered a small fortune to a serial killer to have his ugly fantasies enacted online.

"And though he hurt me, he knew enough to keep me alive. To stitch me up."

He already knew where she was going. "Of course we've considered all the medical personnel who were at that convention. We've looked into their backgrounds, investigated their location the night in question and the week following. We showed the witness photos of every registered male attendee we could get a picture of. Nothing."

She waved a hand. "I know that."

"Damn it," he muttered, wondering if she knew her

ass might not be on the line for staying dead, but certainly could be if she'd been hacking into an FBI computer system.

She came up with a quick explanation, as if realizing he was holding himself on a very short tether regarding his suspicions about her hacking. "I mean, I know you would do that, not that I *know* know."

Of course.

"I was just thinking about it the other day, though, and wondered if I might be able to help."

"How? Do you want to see the pictures?"

"I've seen most of them."

He closed his eyes and shook his head.

"Oh, come on, would you relax? I'm not spending my days nosing around in your precious system, okay? It didn't take me more than sixty seconds to find out which hotel and which medical convention was going on that weekend. Nor to find a list of the speakers, honorees, and attendees. Most doctors have Web sites now, you know, and most of those sites have photos of their staff members."

He didn't take the news as good or bad, knowing from the beginning that she would probably be unable to visually identify the man.

"What I was thinking is, if we could possibly get any tapes or recordings from that conference, and I listened to the voices . . ."

He immediately followed. "I'm sorry. I just don't see that working. It was months ago. You were wounded. And you know he was drugging you."

She nodded once, undeterred. "Wyatt, I hear that man's voice in my dreams every single night. It is imprinted on my brain."

Maybe. But dreams were tricky things.

"I'd know him," she insisted. "Maybe six months ago, I wouldn't have. My head was too clouded. I was too scared. Now, though, I'm thinking rationally, seeing things with utter clarity. And I honestly believe I'd know that voice." She shivered slightly. "That cold, mocking voice."

He believed her. No, he wasn't certain it would work, but he genuinely believed she thought it would.

That didn't mean it was a good idea. "It could be risky for you, emotionally. Are you sure you're capable of doing that?"

She leaned over the table, dropping her forearms onto it. "You might be surprised by what I'm capable of doing these days."

Seeing the narrowness of her eyes, suspecting the soft blue irises looked more like hard, gray flint right now, he very much doubted that.

The soft-spoken Lily he had known might not have been capable of swatting a fly.

The woman she had become, on the other hand, appeared capable of just about anything.

"Very well."

Her expression softened. "Thank you. I can't tell you how much I appreciate it that you don't treat me like some fragile flower in need of protection."

"You are in need of protection," he said, blunt and to the point. "There's a man out there who wants you dead. And you can't afford to forget it."

"Don't worry," she whispered, haunted, weary. "Not one single minute of one single day goes by without me remembering that."

\* \* \*

Jesse wasn't supposed to take any unapproved documents back to his cell, and knew he'd have to hide this one before morning. That was fine—he had a few cubbyholes that hadn't yet been discovered during the weekly surprise cell tosses.

If it was found, it would be confiscated and he'd find himself punished in all the little ways the guards liked to punish the inmates in this place. Yet Jesse had been unable to give it back to the lawyer after she'd let him read it. He'd carefully slipped it into his jumpsuit before the guard had returned him to the block. He'd just needed to keep it close. Keep it all real. For as long as he possibly could. He needed to keep convincing himself that it had really happened. That next week could really happen.

That he could be set free.

He read the letter again, alone in his cell, very late that night. The security lights spilling in from the rest of the cellblock provided ample illumination. His fat, stinking cell mate, who had watched while Jesse was held down and assaulted his first week here, snored on, but Jesse was still careful not to rustle the paper, to make no sound at all. Not even a happy sigh as he studied the words he had almost memorized.

*Dear Mr. Boyd:*

*I suppose you have many questions regarding my intercession on your behalf, which is why I am writing this letter, which Ms. Vincent was instructed to deliver to you. My altruism may seem unusual, but I am, in fact, merely a person with a loathing for injustice in any form. Call me someone who has seen it firsthand, who wants only to see that the guilty are punished and the innocent protected. Therefore, please accept my assistance with your legal dilemma in the spirit in which it was offered: with nothing but positive thoughts, well wishes, and hopes for your speedy release.*

*I am convinced an injustice was done to you and look forward to the day when the rest of the world sees that as well. I am sure that with Ms. Vincent on the case, that day is fast approaching. After it comes, I do hope we can meet, face-to-face, to discuss everything that led you to this difficult point. The choices you made, the people you met. The people who wronged you so terribly.*

*How unfortunate, in a way, that your main accuser is not alive to see her lies exposed and your good name restored. I do hope that, wherever she is, she learns of your change in fortunes . . . and weeps.*

*I will be anxiously awaiting the results of your hearing next week and wish you all the best.*

*Sincerely yours,*

*A friend*

# Chapter 5

The next morning, shortly before dawn, Lily left the house and made her way down to the beach. She'd taken care to creep past Wyatt's bedroom door, not wanting to awaken him, as she'd obviously done during the night. She had put the man out enough to last her lifetime.

By asking him to let her help in the investigation, she had done so again. He had already gone so far out on a limb for her, he was on the verge of falling into a very deep pit of trouble. Yet he had agreed, knowing, as Lily did, that with so few people aware of the truth, she could be a genuine asset.

Just as the need to do the job—to keep other families from being hurt—had been enough to help her survive what had happened to her family, now, needing to know who had done this to *her* gave Lily the same motivation. She'd been recovering for months. Rebuilding her strength. Preparing. Now she needed to act.

The sun was just on the verge of rising when her feet finally hit the sand at the end of her long descent. By all rights, she should have slept much later herself. She and Wyatt had remained outside on the patio talking until at least two a.m., and though she had fallen into bed shortly thereafter, sleep had been a long time coming.

At least her dreams had not been dark ones.

"No, they were almost worse," she muttered, shaking her head at her own foolishness. Because instead of dreaming about the terrifying night Wyatt had saved her, she had instead been troubled by intense, surprising visions of some other nights she had spent with him. Other moments, when she had been less vulnerable and he less noble. When he'd let down his guard and looked at her with eyes that weren't pitying and protective, but instead piercing, hot, and perhaps even interested.

*You're imagining things.*

He was as interested in her as any good person would be in a wounded animal. That was all. Dreams inspired by solitude and a long drought of physical intimacy didn't mean a damn thing other than that she needed to be extra vigilant to keep her feelings hidden.

Not romantic feelings, she had to believe that. She felt only friendship and genuine appreciation for Wyatt.

But she couldn't deny that when she let herself really think about the idea of him desiring her, something deep inside the untouched, cold part of herself flashed with unexpected warmth.

"Forget it," she reminded herself. "It's never going to happen." She had never been the kind of person who could separate sex from emotion, so the idea of just taking a bit of physical relief from the most attractive man she'd ever known was out of the question.

At least, Lily had never been that kind of person. The Lily she'd once been.

"You're not that Lily anymore."

Maybe the woman she was now could take what she needed, get it out of her system. Maybe that woman even had the nerve to try to take it from Wyatt Blackstone.

It bore consideration. But not now, not while he was here, filling the house with his magnetic presence. She'd think about it long and hard after Wyatt left and she was again alone, lost in her own thoughts and free from any outside distractions.

Remaining at the base of the steps, she sat down on the weathered wooden plank, cut into the side of the rocky hill, and rested her forearms loosely on her knees. The bottom cuff of her sweats pulled up a little, enough to reveal the ankle holster and small-caliber handgun she carried at all times. Self-conscious, though she was entirely alone, she pulled the fabric down. Wyatt knew she had weapons— he just didn't need to know she carried them every time she set foot outside the perimeter of the house.

Streams of orange and pink had begun to appear far away where the black ocean met the dark blue sky. As always, Lily held her breath, waiting for it, enjoying this one moment of the day more than any other.

She was soon rewarded, paid off for her patience. Between one blink of the eye and the next, the golden globe of the sun popped up to send streams of light racing across the water. Within seconds, day had broken, bathing the beach, and her face, with the very first hints of warmth that cut through the morning chill.

"Okay, another day," she told herself. "Make something of it."

Though she seldom ventured far from the house, she did enjoy her occasional workout on the beach. The stretch of shoreline, called Dead Man's Beach by the lo-

cals, probably because of some ancient shipping trage-
dies off the rocky coast, was far from any of the crowded
tourist areas. Not private and exclusive to Wyatt's house,
it was still far enough from civilization to discourage visitors. A lighthouse, long abandoned, remained perched
on a jutting bit of land a half mile to the north, but almost no one ever came by to explore it.

Today was no exception. No human was visible, as far
as her eye could see. So she took full advantage, first
with a quick jog along the shoreline, up to the lighthouse,
then back, followed by stretches and position practice
for this afternoon's lesson with the sarge.

Something else Wyatt seemed to disapprove of, though
he had never said a word. He had been all for her taking a few martial arts lessons after she'd gotten through
physical therapy to strengthen her badly damaged leg.
He had, however, somehow sensed that she was no longer doing it just as a way to get back into shape, or even
entirely for her own peace of mind.

They had not discussed it, but he was no fool. He knew
what demons drove her, knew she felt with an undeniable certainty that the man who'd kidnapped her would
come after her if he ever found out she was still alive.

And she was getting ready. Not just to defend herself.
But perhaps to avenge herself.

"The way you balance, no one would ever guess how
badly damaged that leg was," a voice said.

She didn't turn around. She'd been aware of Wyatt's
approach down the steps for a minute or two. She just
hadn't allowed herself to think about it, not wanting the
old self-consciousness to interfere with her workout. Especially because she knew if she glanced at him, she'd
end up staring.

Wyatt almost always wore suits. Expensive, well-tailored suits. But he did, on occasion, dress down, which was almost worse for her peace of mind. His faded, worn jeans hugged his strong legs, and the casual polo shirt, with the collar turned up, highlighted the broad shoulders and thick arms. He looked a little less the boss she'd known and a little more the sexy man she'd had wicked dreams about.

"Just don't look too closely at the scars," she replied, smoothly moving from Intermediate to Position Four.

"Something else for the plastic surgeon to take care of."

Another soundless turn. "Maybe I'll go down to Williamsburg to see one."

He crossed his arms, his strong jaw jutting out. "Don't even think about it."

She'd gotten the reaction she expected. "You said yourself that hearing the voices of some of the doctors from that symposium might be of use."

"I meant recordings of their voices," he insisted, "which I'll have from Brandon sometime this morning. You are absolutely not going to stroll into the offices of the doctor whose car was stolen and try to listen for the voice of the monster who attacked you."

*Position Five. Breathe deeply. Slow and steady.*

"Maybe he'd see me and drop over dead from a heart attack, sure he was seeing a ghost," she said, not really serious. She wasn't crazy, and she certainly wouldn't waltz into a place that could put her face-to-face with someone who wanted to kill her.

Well, at least not until she'd tried it Wyatt's way, listening to the recordings or searching for any other audible resources she could find.

If all else failed, however? Well, she didn't think anyone else she had worked with on a daily basis would immediately recognize her now. So while she wouldn't necessarily make an appointment and walk right into the lion's den, perhaps there was another way. Shadowing a group going to lunch and sitting nearby? Delivering a package, or flowers? Something that would get her close—but not too close.

"Stop thinking about it," he ordered.

She paused to stare at him. "You can't control what goes on in my head."

"No, but I can control whether I leave the keys to my Jeep here or not. And if I get the idea you're thinking of making any long-distance trips, I guarantee you I'll be taking them with me."

A humorless laugh escaped her lips. "Gee, thanks for the reminder that I'm completely at your mercy."

He thrust out a frustrated breath and stalked closer. "Damn it, Lily, you're not a charity case. I don't begrudge you anything. I just don't want you to get hurt again."

"You're being kind. You have to admit, I *am* a charity case." The reality of that rankled. Lily had never relied on anyone, not since her parents had died and she and her sister had played a game of here-we-go-round-the-foster-care-system. She didn't like being completely supported by anyone. "I'll probably never be able to repay you for all my medical expenses, even if I can get back my unclaimed financial accounts."

He waved a hand, as if money meant absolutely nothing. Though she didn't know a lot about Wyatt's background, other than the fact that his family owned this house—and that he never used it, for some deep, dark reason that the locals hinted at but she had never pried into—she had no doubt the man had money. So much money, he hadn't batted an eye when paying her bills, whisking her up here, renovating the house, buying the Jeep.

That didn't mean she wasn't going to try to pay him back, somehow, someway. Sometime. Even if it took the rest of her life.

"I don't care about the money. I only care about your need to do something leading you into a dark, dangerous situation."

Hearing the genuine intensity, she had to try to mollify him. "Look, you and I both know I'm a hermit and the chances of me going more than ten miles from here are very slim, meaning a trip to Virginia is almost inconceivable."

"You really have no desire to leave? Haven't had any impulse to just go?"

Though his expression remained neutral, he seemed very interested in hearing her answer. She couldn't help wondering why he seemed so concerned. "What is it you're really trying to get at?"

He shook his head slowly. "Just curious."

Yeah, right. The man never asked idle questions; he was also after something. Now he seemed to be asking if she had the nerve to leave here, or if she just intended to give up and hide from the world forever.

*Well, haven't you considered it?*

She ignored the inner voice. "What is it you're accusing me of, Wyatt?"

He countered with a question. "Should I be accusing you of something?"

"Don't pull that interrogator garbage on me, okay? If you have something to say, just say it, would you?"

"Will you do the same?"

She managed to smother a groan that he'd done it again, and think about what he'd asked. Would she do the same? Be honest and open? About most things, probably. About the case, her physical well-being, the house, what was going on in the outside world. Yes. Absolutely.

But what went on in her head? What she was really thinking, feeling?

Not bloody likely.

"Forget I asked," she snapped.

Deliberately turning away, she tried to get back into her exercise, closing her eyes and breathing deeply. She heard the sarge's voice in her head as she moved, remembering how hard such simple movements had been a few months ago, when her muscles had only recently healed after the slash job the bullet and her attacker's instruments had done on them. After a few moments, she found her center, rediscovered her calm, and was able to focus.

"So," she asked, ready to resume their conversation, "Brandon agreed that my voice idea was solid?"

Wyatt backed off, too, as if knowing she had already put their harsh words out of her head. "He did. The owner of the car, Dr. Kean, was interviewed on tape, along with her sister-in-law, who provided an alibi and backed up her claim that she knew nothing of the stolen vehicle until the morning after your attack. Brandon is sending me a snippet of that interview."

"Anyone else from the convention?"

"All of the workshops were recorded, the audio copies offered for sale online. We're gathering every one of them. We'll have a lot of material for you to listen to." He glanced at his watch. "Probably starting by this afternoon."

*Position Eight. Flow. Calm.*

"Brandon must have gotten an early start."

Wyatt leaned against the handrail at the base of the stairs, his feet crossed at the ankles, arms at the chest. "He responded to my e-mail at six forty-five this morning and said he'd work on this from home so there'd be no delay due to his commute to the office."

"He's a good kid."

He laughed softly.

"What?"

"That kid is only a couple of years your junior."

Maybe in physical years. Not in experience. Not in the journey of the soul.

"He's also in love with you."

She closed her eyes briefly, then opened them to glare at him. "Damn it, Wyatt, I'd just gotten my calm back."

He shrugged, unrepentant. "You need to deal with it."

"I did deal with it," she snapped. "Why do you think I asked him to stop coming up?"

Despite asking him to stop coming to visit her, as he'd done every single week last spring, she did miss him. Brandon was the closest thing to a brother she'd ever had. Putting a stop to his visits had been for his sake, more than hers.

Lily wasn't blind. She had known before she was kidnapped that Brandon was a flirt and a player, and that he liked trying out his cocky charm on her. But after he'd been part of the rescue, he'd turned into a hovering, cautious caretaker who treated her as if she needed to be wrapped in cotton. And he wanted to be the one wrapping that cotton around her and carrying her in his pocket.

Nothing brought the protective romantic gene out in

a man like thinking he had a fragile, wounded woman to take care of. With Brandon, it had gone a step further. It hadn't escaped her notice that he had feelings for her. That—the thought of him wasting his time and emotion on her when she would never return it—had been the primary reason she'd asked him not to come back.

"Well, now that we've gone to a subject you really want to avoid, shall we go back to the previous one?"

She gritted her teeth.

"Tell me something.

Despite the mental warnings to remain focused and steady, she couldn't help stiffening. There were any number of questions Wyatt could be about to ask her. Many of which she didn't want to answer. Starting with what she was thinking, and ending with what she intended to do tomorrow. Next week. Next month. "What?"

"Would you really go down to Williamsburg? Leave here?"

Lily stopped the workout. "Why wouldn't I?"

"You haven't left in months." His stare intent, he prodded, "Have you?"

"I'm not a surf fisherman—I've had to eat," she said, finally giving up altogether on her workout. She couldn't concentrate with anyone watching, much less when Wyatt's unfiltered, undiluted attention was zoned in squarely on her. She shook her arms out and walked across the sand, toward the stairs. "I go to the market."

"Maine," he insisted. "You haven't left Maine?"

"Why do you ask?"

He shrugged. "I'm just wondering how you're doing. If you're starting to think beyond this place. Going back to your real life."

"What's there to go back to?" she asked. "I have no

family. My apartment's gone. I won't get my job back once the bureau finds out I've been hiding all this time."

He stepped in front of her, blocking her access to the steps. "So are you saying you haven't left, and don't intend to?"

Lily didn't want to answer any questions, especially right now. Wyatt was too big, too close, too intent. Too damned curious.

"I can leave anytime," she insisted. "Maybe even later today, after we listen to the recordings. Might just necessitate that trip down to Virginia."

"What would cause you to make that trip, Lily? *Not* hearing a voice you recognize?" His dark blue eyes glinted in the early-morning sun. "Or hearing one you know all too well?"

She knew what he was really asking. Which did she want more? Justice? Or revenge?

If she heard the voice of the man who'd held her, would it make her long to see him brought to justice so she could begin living her life again? Or merely prompt her to take things into her own hands, pay her own debts, and give the son of a bitch exactly the same tender care he'd given her?

She thought about it. Right at this moment, she honestly didn't know the answer to that question. Vengeance, she had often heard, was a dish best served cold. But the need for it was like an incendiary wire, jolting her with heat and flame. With anger. It sometimes seemed it could drive her to madness.

Drive her to almost anything.

"What does it matter?" she finally replied, going

around him onto the bottom step. "I'm not going to do anything until after we listen to the recordings."

He didn't let it go, reaching for her, dropping one strong, solid hand on her shoulder. "And afterward?"

Lily dipped out from under that hand. Seeing his immediate remorse, and knowing he probably assumed he'd frightened her, she felt a moment's regret. She hadn't shrugged off his touch because he had frightened her, but because the idea of Wyatt touching her didn't frighten her one little bit.

It excited her.

Reason enough to get away from the man. But she couldn't see how she could do that, considering he owned the house in which she slept.

There was, however, one place where she knew he wouldn't follow. "I need to cool down after these exercises," she said, completely ignoring his last question. Though she was weary and wanted nothing more than a shower, she added, "I think I'll jog for a while."

Without another word, she spun around and jogged up the beach, heading toward the lighthouse. Wyatt wouldn't follow; he hated the damn place. He'd warned her it was a falling-down ruin and had asked her to never go there. But she knew by the frank disgust in his face whenever he caught sight of it that there was more to it.

Maybe it wasn't nice to go where she knew he wouldn't. But Lily Fletcher was no longer ruled by her need to be nice.

When Brandon Cole had learned that Lily might be able to recognize the voice of her attacker, he'd scrambled to get samples of every voice Wyatt had suggested. Especially the attendees of the medical convention at the hotel from which the car had been stolen.

He hadn't gotten it at first, why they thought it could be a doctor from the hotel, rather than some random thug who'd stolen the first available car.

Then he'd remembered what had been done to Lily. The way her kidnapper had worked on her, stitching her up, however brutally, then shoving narcotics and even antibiotics into her system. All, he believed, to keep her alive for more torture.

He'd had to force that image out of his head by sheer force of will and by throwing himself two hundred percent into the job. Staying home, he'd spent all morning working on the audio clips, sending them to Wyatt around noon. Which was why he didn't hit the office until one p.m.

He'd called early this morning, telling Jackie, who was running the office today while Wyatt was out on leave, that he had forgotten about a dental appointment. She hadn't asked questions. But there had been that heavy, questioning silence she was so good at that made him wonder if she suspected him of something. Jackie sniffed out prevarication the way a dog sniffed out liver treats.

Though only in her forties, Stokes seemed to have adopted the role of mother in the group. Perhaps because she was the only one with kids. Once a forensics expert, she had transferred to the Cyber Division when her son and daughter were babies. She never talked about it, but he'd heard she had come a bit too close to a bullet for comfort, and had decided that a nine-to-five job suited her better while the kids were young. Now that they were a little older, she was back in the field, getting her hands dirty, combining her IT expertise with her field-agent background.

He got in while the others were at lunch, and nodded to the new receptionist. They seemed to get a new one every other month. The members of the team might like the privacy of their ancient suite of offices on the fourth floor, but the support staff was never quite as content.

Reaching the office he had once shared with Lily, he couldn't help thinking about how much he missed her. His new office mate was Anna Delaney. She was good, but so coolly confident he sometimes felt as though she looked at him as an overanxious kid. Lily had been like him. A bit of an outsider. A little untried.

He sat at his desk, flipped on his CPU, then went right back to work on the files. He'd sent them to Wyatt, as well as forwarding copies to himself, but Brandon wanted to keep working on them, cleaning them up as much as possible, to see if he could enhance them in any way. Lily deserved to have every advantage when it came to identifying the man who had kidnapped her.

It wouldn't be easy for her. And would probably be incredibly painful.

*I could have been the one to stay with her, help her this weekend.*

He *should* have been the one to stay in Maine with her. He ought to be up there with Lily right now, holding her hand, helping her through this. Taking care of her. After all, they'd been so close once, while she and Wyatt had always had nothing more than an employer-employee relationship.

Brandon had thought it over, wondered, stressed about it, but for the life of him, he just didn't know why Lily didn't want him to come see her anymore. All he had ever wanted to do was protect her, keep her safe. Never again let ugliness or violence intrude on her life if he could possibly help it. And she didn't even want him in the same state.

If she hadn't insisted that Wyatt come only once a month as well, he might have wondered if she had some kind of feelings for the other man. That had sounded crazy when he'd first thought about it—Lily was years younger than their boss and she'd always been nervous and jittery around Wyatt. But he'd noticed a few occasions when she'd looked at Wyatt, or Wyatt had looked at her, that had left him curious.

Still, Brandon knew there was no way Blackstone would take advantage of someone as wounded and fragile as Lily.

"Hey, you made it in, huh?"

He looked up from his computer screen. Seeing Special Agent Jackie Stokes, he offered her a smile, wondering if she could read the tension that had made him sit close to the monitor, his ear almost pressed against the state-of-the-art speaker. "Yeah, sorry about this morning."

"It's okay. We managed one morning without you." Her friendly smile slowly faded and he knew one instant before she opened her mouth again that something had happened. "I want to know what's going on."

He somehow managed to remain completely still. "I don't know what you mean."

Stepping into the office, she pushed the door closed behind her. Her sensible, low-heeled pumps clicked ominously above the whir and hiss of all the computer equipment as she crossed the room. Dropping onto Anna's empty seat, Jackie leaned over, dropping her elbows onto her knees.

It was all Brandon could do not to minimize the screen now that she had a direct line of sight. But there was nothing to see—just a paused audio screen. Nothing out of the ordinary. He was simply being paranoid.

Damn, this was hard. Keeping Lily's secret from the world had been difficult enough, but keeping it from those who had loved her? People like Jackie? He honestly didn't know if she was ever going to forgive any of them.

"I know you, Brand," she said with a frank stare. "I know when you're up to something and you have been up to something for quite a while." She glanced at the closed door. "I also know some things are going on in this office that the rest of us aren't aware of."

Brandon put on his best poker face. "Like?"

"Like, some cop called this morning, got put through to me when he heard Wyatt was out. He was asking about something he called the tiger lily murder?"

*Oh, shit.*

"I had to tell him I didn't know anything about it. It appears Wyatt went out there to walk a crime scene the other day." Jackie sat up in the chair, crossing her arms in front of her chest. "And something tells me you already knew that. It seems as though every time I turn around, the two of you are having quiet conversations, one-on-one meetings. Care to share what's going on?"

"I'm sorry, but I can't help ya," he said, shrugging. It wasn't a lie—he hadn't said he didn't know anything, just that he couldn't help.

She obviously saw right through the hedge in his words. "You *can't*, huh?"

Brandon shook his head once, not relenting.

Jackie waited a long moment, then nodded. "Okay.

Guess I'll just talk to SSA Blackstone when he arrives back in the office Tuesday morning."

"You do that," Brandon said, turning his chair around to face his monitor once more. "I really need to get back to work."

He didn't, of course, get right back to work. Not until he heard the office door close quietly behind her as Jackie left.

Maybe it was just as well that Jackie's suspicions were up, that she'd be confronting Wyatt. Perhaps she wouldn't then be so blindsided by the truth. Because if this lead panned out, and Lily was able to recognize a voice on one of those audio files, they might very well have a viable suspect.

Which meant Lily Fletcher might be returning from the dead in the very near future.

# Chapter 6

Brandon was as good as his word. By one, Wyatt had received the audio files. The IT specialist had taken the workshop recordings from the conference, narrowing most of them down to a one-minute clip of the speaker in an effort to save time. The two multispeaker panels were full-length, but hopefully they wouldn't have to listen to the entire things.

He'd also sent the audio interview with the car owner and her sister-in-law, which Lily wanted to hear for herself, just in case.

The two of them sat at the kitchen table, the doors and windows closed to cut down on any audible interference from outside, and listened, starting with the interview. It was cursory, since the doctor had never been a real suspect, but the voices came through clearly. Clearly enough for Lily to proclaim she hadn't heard them before.

Dr. Kean came across as crisp and professional. Competence laced her tone, though she sounded genuinely dismayed by the idea that her vehicle had been used in a crime. "I'm sorry I can't tell you more," said the voice on the digital recording as the interview came to a close. "Will you please let me know as soon as you've finished with the car?"

"We'll do that," a male voice replied. "We so appreciate you, and you, Dr. Underwood, talking to us."

"Anspaugh," Lily muttered. The disdain in that single word told him all he needed to know about Lily's feelings for the other agent. The one who was supposed to protect her.

"I'm sure you're anxious to get your vehicle back. We're terribly sorry to inconvenience you."

"Has he ever not sounded like such a sleazy suck-up?" Lily said. "If I didn't already know from the pictures on their Web site that Dr. Kean is very attractive, and her sister-in-law utterly gorgeous, I'd have been able to figure it out just by the sound of Anspaugh's drool hitting the microphone."

"He shed a tear or two at your funeral, before realizing he was going to catch hell for what happened to you."

"Only because he never succeeded in getting in my pants before he got me killed."

Wyatt couldn't contain a small half smile. The old Lily had never been so blunt. And she'd been a whole lot nicer. Frankly, he liked this one better.

Not that there was anything wrong with nice, but he'd worried about whether she was tough enough to meet the demands of the job. He had also found her hard to read; he'd never quite been able to see what the young agent was thinking.

What she was feeling? Well, that hadn't been difficult.

Lily had always worn her emotions on her sleeve. Which hadn't been the best asset in a field that required dispassion and analytic thinking.

Funny, the woman the world considered dead would probably be better at her job now than she had been before.

"I don't want the car back. Ever. I simply want to get rid of it," said the voice on the recording.

Lily sighed, reached out, and closed the audio file with a click. "Moving on."

Yet, she didn't immediately start the first of the workshop snippets. He suspected he knew why. Part of her was anxious to hear every voice, screen every possibility. Even knowing this whole enterprise was a long shot and she probably wouldn't recognize a single person.

But another part of her had to be very afraid she would. Hearing words spoken by the man who'd held her, hurt her, would be shocking. Possibly even terrifying. His voice rising like a ghost from the computer speakers could push her over the edge into that panicked state she'd been in all those months ago when she'd been rescued.

Wyatt honestly didn't know how she would react. Which was why he slid his chair a little closer, ready to offer a steadying hand on her shoulder.

Positioned so close to her, he suddenly realized he should have thought twice. The soft, delicate fragrance of honeysuckle rose off her skin. Her favorite lotion. He'd seen it in her apartment, which he'd gone to clean out after her "death," and made sure she was stocked in it. So she smelled like the same sweet, soft young woman he'd known.

*She's not that woman.*

No. She wasn't. Though his immediate sensory reaction to the scent was a familiar jolt of tenderness and protectiveness, it didn't counteract his other senses. The scrape of her bare leg against his jeans ratcheted up the tension, as did the sound of each of her slow in-and-out breaths. Her hand, resting beside his on the table, was so damned slim, fragile, yet the arms revealed by the sleeveless tank top were toned and sculpted with muscle.

She was strong and soft, sweet and tough. The biggest distraction of his entire adult life.

*And you think she could be a killer?*

No. He didn't. From far away, in the middle of a crime scene, the evidence had seemed damning. But being back here in her company for one single day had reminded him of all the reasons why Lily could not be the vicious, cold-blooded murderer he sought.

Could he see her picking up a gun and shooting the man who'd attacked her if he came at her again, intending to do her harm? Oh, absolutely. As easily as he could see himself doing the same thing in her position.

But murdering random strangers so violently, with all the foresight, planning, and brutality those cases had involved? He just didn't believe it and felt almost foolish for coming up here with the intention of spying on her.

Something else was going on, the ties to Lily either completely coincidental—

Or not.

It was the *not* that worried him. The not that would keep him up nights until he discovered who the lily killer was, and how he was connected to Lily Fletcher.

There was, of course, one very obvious possibility. Lovesprettyboys, having been thwarted in his efforts to find out what happened to Lily after she'd escaped his clutches, might be trying to get law enforcement to do the job for him. He had to be going out of his mind, believing himself to be one of only two people who knew Lily hadn't been in that van when it crashed off the Route 17 bridge into the York River. Yet having absolutely no idea what had happened to her, he had to be wondering if she might reemerge and point her accusing finger in his direction.

Setting her up to look like a serial killer was one way to get the authorities interested in making absolutely certain of Lily's fate, since they'd never found a body. If the vicious crimes raised doubt about her "death," the ensuing investigation could lead everyone—the police, and the unsub—to the truth about Lily Fletcher. What had happened to her. And where she was today.

The unsub wouldn't want her to be arrested and tell what she knew. He just needed her to be found, possibly drawn back to Washington for an investigation. So he could get one clear shot at her.

*Jesus.*

So far it seemed that Wyatt was alone in associating Lily with the murdered men in those hotel rooms. God help them all if someone like Anspaugh, who had such an ax to grind against both Lily and Wyatt, stumbled across it.

Wyatt had to move faster. He needed to find Lovesprettyboys, because doing so might very well solve both cases. And only once the man was caught would Lily Fletcher be both physically safe and out from under the cloud of suspicion.

"Okay, let's proceed. I'm ready to hear the clips from the various workshops," Lily said, as oblivious to their closeness as he was affected by it. "I don't need to listen to the content, obviously, so this should go much more quickly."

The quicker they finished, the better, in Wyatt's opinion. He honestly didn't believe this idea was going to lead to something useful. There were just too many variables. Not only might Lily's memory of her attacker's voice be unclear, but it was a long shot that the unsub had in fact attended the convention at the hotel. The odds were even slimmer that he was a speaker whose session had been recorded.

But Lily wanted to try. So they'd try. The sooner they finished, and the sooner he could back away and reconstruct that professional, polite barrier between them, the better.

Lily started the first clip, listened to a few words from the speaker, then moved on. Again. Again. With each click of the touch pad, her shoulders seemed to droop further, her full lips tighten even more.

There had been two dozen workshops and it took less than an hour to listen to the clips from all but the two panels.

Though disappointment rolled off her, Lily didn't give up. She pulled up the first panel, listened long enough to hear a few words from every speaker. Then came the second group workshop, the final possibility.

The panel featured five speakers, including the sisters-in-law Drs. Kean and Underwood, both of whom they'd already heard. Relaxed at first, Lily began to physically tense as they finished their presentations, giving way to the other speakers on the panel. Because the other speakers were all men—ones they hadn't heard before. Theirs would be the final voices, the last chance to hear the echoes from her nightmares. Lily appeared to hold her breath, waiting for them to get their turns at the microphone.

Then they did. And her last hope died.

"Nothing," she said, shaking her head in utter disappointment, shock tugging her mouth down and lowering her lashes over her eyes.

"Look, it was a good idea. But we both knew it was a long shot."

"I guess." She leaned back in her chair, lifting her face to stare at the ceiling. When she spoke, her voice was so soft, he almost didn't hear her, especially over the voice of the workshop presenter, still droning from the computer's speakers. "Maybe it's better."

Though he thought he understood, he still asked, "Why?

She continued staring straight up, not meeting his gaze. "Because now the only time I hear his voice is in my nightmares, when I'm asleep. If I hear it when I'm awake, I might never be able to get the sound out of my head."

Wyatt couldn't stand the defeatist tone, or the awful weariness in her body. Jesus, the woman had survived so much, she deserved some peace. And knowing the man who wanted her dead would never be able to touch her again would give her that peace.

"We'll find him," he insisted. He put a hand on her shoulder, squeezing it in reassurance. This time, she didn't pull away. "I promise you we're going to find him."

She turned her head, watching him with pale blue eyes that swam with emotion. "I'm treading water, Wyatt. Just treading. Barely keeping myself from drowning, but getting no closer to shore."

He should have murmured something comforting, maybe squeezed her shoulder again. Instead, he reached for her, pulled her out of her chair and into his arms, until she sat on his thigh. Lily offered no resistance, coming to him freely, as if needing the warmth, the physical connection, the reassurance that she really wasn't alone.

"It's all right," he murmured. "You don't always have to be so damned strong, Lily."

Holding her close, he tangled his fingers in her short hair, rubbing its fineness, picturing its blond shade. The movement brought his fingertips to her scars and he touched them lightly. The feel of them made him instinctively grip her tighter, wanting nothing more than to keep anyone from hurting her again.

Lily's head rested on his shoulder, her mouth so close to his neck he experienced her every warm exhalation flowing across his skin. Against his chest, he could feel her heart thudding.

As was his.

Hunger rose within him, surprising, insistent, and compelling. Sweat broke out on his brow and every muscle in his body tensed. He closed his eyes, willing away any personal thoughts, any emotions. He'd become adept at doing so at such a young age, it was second nature now. Yet while he could bring his physical reactions under control, getting a grip on the tenderness he felt for the beautiful woman in his arms proved more difficult.

He could feel her heart pick up its rhythm in her chest. Beating faster in confusion. In surprise. And those warm breaths against his neck grew more rapid, more shallow. Closer. Until he wasn't sure whether he was feeling her exhalations or her soft lips.

Then she lifted her head, stared into his eyes with intense emotion—curiosity? Surprise?

Want.

Groaning, he muttered, "Lily ..."

He didn't know what he was about to say, if his impulse would be to apologize or to let her know exactly what she made him feel, but he ended up saying nothing. Because Lily suddenly shot straight up, leaping to her feet with a shocked cry. Her eyes shifted wildly, her mouth open as she gasped for air. Her hands fisted by her sides, she remained very still, rigid with tension.

"What—"

She cut him off with a slash of her hand through the air. "Shh."

Then she leaned closer to the computer. Listening. Concentrating.

She'd heard something, or someone. A familiar voice.

He froze. The speaker was a woman—Dr. Kean, maybe?—talking about the psychology of plastic surgery, how it changed lives.

"Does that answer your question?" the woman said as she concluded her remarks. "Or do you need me to spell it out a little further?" There was a mocking tone there, as if she felt some sort of antipathy toward the person she addressed.

"Nothing further," a man's voice said faintly, almost in the background.

"That's him," Lily whispered. She lifted one trembling hand to her mouth, pressing the other tightly to her stomach as if she had suddenly become nauseous. "That's him, Wyatt."

He didn't know if she was right. He knew only that

Lily believed she was. That she was convinced she'd just heard the voice of her would-be killer.

The audio continued for a few seconds, both of them still and silent, thinking of the ramifications. Then Lily suddenly snapped out of her daze. Mumbling something, she bent over the laptop, skimming her fingers across the touch pad. Pausing the digital file, she backed it up by about two minutes, then resumed.

"He asked a question. That's what I heard."

"What did—"

"Shh!" She leaned close to the monitor. A speaker droned on, then asked, "Are there any further questions?"

A moment of silence. Then a voice said something, indistinct and distant. Wyatt shook his head, not sure he could recognize his own voice if he'd been the one on the tape.

"Could you approach the microphone, please?"

Ah.

Another hesitation, then a man's voice spoke, loud and clear. "Yes, Dr. Kean? I was wondering if you'd tell us just how long a person should try to combat nature by buying a new face or body. When is it time to give up and age gracefully?"

Lily closed her eyes, nodding once, then slowly lowering to crouch down until she was eye level with the screen. "That's the man who kidnapped me, who held me prisoner."

"You're certain?"

She nodded once. "More certain than I've ever been about anything in my entire life. That cruel tone, that edge of sarcasm, did you hear it?"

Of course he'd heard it. The question had been an intentional insult, a taunting gauntlet thrown at Dr. Angela Kean. As if the unsub was mocking her.

Was the doctor, perhaps, an advertisement for her own practice? Someone who lived life that way—putting off aging with expensive surgery?

If so, the question would imply that the questioner knew her. Or at least knew of her.

They might just have broken this case. After all these months, one simple recorded question might have handed them the identity of Lovesprettyboys.

Lily listened to the answer, then the mumbled acknowledgment of the questioner, who once again had spoken off mike, having apparently returned to his seat. When it was over, she paused, scrolled back, and started the exchange again.

"He sounds cold, doesn't he? Jovial on the surface, as if he's intending just a harmless poke at someone he knows. But beneath it . . ."

"Cold. Yes." More than that, they knew now. He was vicious.

After the third playing, Lily stopped the recording, but this time, she didn't rewind. Instead, her fingers still resting lightly on the keyboard, she slid up onto her chair, staring vacantly at the paused screen. He sensed she was hearing that voice saying any number of other things. Words he whispered in her subconscious.

But she didn't give in to it. She didn't shrink, draw into herself in fear. Did not pull back whatsoever. If anything, the set of her jaw screamed determination and her entire body leaned forward, tense, as if ready to fight to defend herself.

She wouldn't have to. Damn it, he never wanted her to have to do that again.

"Dr. Kean might be able to identify the person speaking, since it sounded like there was some personal tension there," he said, believing every word.

"Exactly. Then we'll have a suspect."

"That's all we'll have, though," he said, warning her not to get her hopes up. "Remember, I can't do a thing to this guy, can't prosecute him, or even get a warrant to bring him in, without evidence. Namely you."

She nodded once.

"Meaning Lily Fletcher would have to come back from the dead and testify."

Her cheeks, so flushed with color this morning when she'd worked out down on the beach, were powder white. "Will it matter? My testimony, I mean?"

"Of course it will."

"I'll have no credibility. The frightened agent who pretended she was dead."

Wyatt could handle Lily fearing for her own life; she had good reason for that. But he was not about to allow her to question the choices she made to stay alive. He reached for her, taking her chin in his hand and forcing her head up so she'd meet his eye.

"The world decided you were dead without your help. Just because you had the fight-or-flight instinct and hid out so you could stay alive, hoping the monster who tried to kill you would be caught, does not reflect badly on you."

She licked her lip, nodding her thanks for the pep talk. Wyatt dropped his hand.

"I need to go call Brandon," he said, immediately turning toward the door. "I want him to segregate that snippet out, enhance it as much as possible."

"And then?"

"And then," he replied, "I'm going to make an appointment to see a doctor."

Something was going to happen. Soon.

After all these months, all the manipulation, all the effort, this whole ordeal was going to come to an end. The uncertainty, the fear, the worry that one day Lily Fletcher would crawl out of whatever hole she'd hidden in and ruin everything, would stop. No more worrying. No more waiting for a knock on the door from the police or the FBI. No more speculating about what the agent knew, what she remembered, how much she'd heard, or whom she could identify.

Fletcher had been badly injured during that entire week. Incoherent most of the time. Feverish and in pain, she'd held conversations with her dead sister and her sister's kid, and she should, by all rights, have died all on her own.

"*Did* you die?"

At first, in those early months, it had seemed the most likely scenario. That the media didn't report what would have been a pretty major story didn't mean anything. Maybe the FBI agent had staggered out onto the beach, died of her injuries, and been swept away by the tide. Or buried in the blowing sands of the dunes swept wildly on a cold winter's night.

A month had gone by. Two. Three. But instead of growing more at ease, more confident that no one would ever find out, the tension had built. Because, wouldn't something have been found? If she'd been buried in a dune, wouldn't she have been discovered come spring when people started filling Virginia's beaches? Or if she'd been swept away, wouldn't her remains have washed up somewhere? Why had there never been a single piece of evidence, as if the woman had simply never existed?

*Because you're hiding, aren't you, Lily?*

Yes. Lily Fletcher was in hiding. Even though she had had no family and no close friends, she'd still found someone to help her get away. Then she'd stayed away, managing to remain dead in the eyes of the world for seven long months. The more time that passed, the more certain that seemed. The passing days of silence didn't comfort; they merely increased the insane uncertainty until it had become nearly all-consuming.

Until Lily was found, and dealt with, life could never go back to normal. Not really. Because, despite her injuries, the woman might have seen something, could remember something damning. If not an outright physical description, then the clothes, the eye color, the height, the build, the voice, a chance incriminating word. Something.

Damn it. Why hadn't *he* just killed the blonde when he'd had her at his mercy?

Weakness. Panic. Fear. Vindictiveness. Who knew?

And it was far too late to dwell on now. Fletcher would be found, one way or another. All that had been set in motion this past summer would come together to force her out of her hiding place and put her in position for elimination.

Scenario one: Jesse Tyrone Boyd, with his excellent legal representation, no eyewitness, and an alibi provided by Will Miller, would be released. That release would serve to draw out the woman who would want to see him put back behind bars.

If not that, the other option would put a whole lot more people on Lily's trail and make finding her ever so much easier. Somebody at the FBI would finally bother paying attention, do his job, and connect the murders of those three men with their own supposedly dead agent.

God, they must be complete fools not to have done it so far. How much more obvious did the crime scenes need to be? Would leaving the former agent's picture, writing her damned name on the wall in blood, do it? How about dropping off her tattered bulletproof vest, kept hidden all these months? What in heaven's name would it take?

It had all been so carefully planned. Easy enough that a child could put it together. But apparently not a police officer.

There'd been the specific victim type. The Internet connection. The obviously vengeful crime scenes—passionate, planned, full of rage. The names of the supposed children. The flowers, eventually even a damned tiger lily, which had been the fake online name the agent had used when trying to capture the man Lily Fletcher had known as Lovesprettyboys or Peter Pan.

All of that and they didn't even suspect yet. There'd been not one news story, not one speculative article, about the FBI's involvement in a tristate murder investigation. Local outlets were covering the cases, but hadn't put them together. It truly seemed that nobody had noticed the perfectly chosen clues.

So perhaps it was time to be just a little more obvious. If the FBI couldn't figure out subtle hints, it was time to drop some not-so-subtle ones.

*You could wait for Boyd.*

Yes. If Boyd got out next week, Lily would come slinking back into town on her own. There could be no doubt about that. She would never let the guilty man walk free as long as she had breath in her body.

But if the appeal failed, and the man didn't get out to serve as a lure for the woman, even more time would have been wasted. And this had gone on long enough. Hiding the secret, keeping Lovesprettyboys' true identity locked away forever, returning to the real world and a real life, had been a tremendous strain. The pressure had become nearly unendurable and just couldn't continue.

This had to end. Maybe it would, with Boyd's release. Yet it never hurt to cover all bases. Meaning the lily murderer needed to act once more. And this time, there would be no ambiguity whatsoever. Only raw, bloody violence and blatant clues nobody could miss.

Perhaps a strand of hair from Agent Fletcher's own blond head—kept ever since that last night before she'd disappeared? Or something even more blatant?

It was, perhaps, time to look through a few mementos of Lily Fletcher's stay in Virginia last January. They were locked away in a storage locker, had been all along. Just in case of emergency.

"Smart. So smart. Always thinking ahead." Everyone said so.

There was only one thing left to do: reel in the prey. It was soon, mere days after the last killing. But the irons were already in the fire, the contacts established. The Internet connection was live, secure, and untraceable. Which meant it was time to ramp up the e-mail communications with one Frank Addison, a truck driver out of North Carolina, who loved to hang out at a site with a triple-X-rated name any search engine would warn against visiting. They'd already exchanged many pleasant e-mails. Even an IM session, during which they'd compared stories. Shared fantasies society frowned upon.

Now it was time to bring the matter to a close. Set the date, the time, the location. The trucker thought he was arranging to meet a drug-addicted mother and her son.

A mother named Lily Fletcher.

"And if that doesn't wake you the fuck up, not a single one of you deserves to carry a badge."

# Chapter 7

Once she'd recognized the voice on the conference audio recording Friday, both Lily and Wyatt had expected he'd go immediately to Williamsburg to find out whom it belonged to. Unfortunately, that hadn't happened as quickly as they'd wanted. Because when he'd tried calling to arrange a meeting, they'd learned Drs. Kean and Underwood, who needed to listen to the recording, had gone away for the holiday weekend. Several other members of their family, many of whom also worked at the same private practice, had gone as well. Meaning there was no one around to tell them how to reach either woman. Since an outside physician was covering any emergency medical calls, the answering service hadn't been helpful, either.

They'd looked up the other speakers in the panel workshop—all of them were from faraway states, one even from another country. None was likely to remember one question from a long-ago convention. Kean, who had seemed to know the person questioning her, was the best bet.

Without a warrant, and with the need for extreme discretion, there hadn't been much they could do. Which was why, instead of leaving on Friday, as she'd expected, as she'd wanted, Wyatt had remained here with her throughout the holiday weekend.

It had been an awkward couple of days. Lily didn't really understand why, but this trip, this time she'd spent with Wyatt, had been more difficult than the times before it. Something had disappeared. Their ease with each other, perhaps. Or the quiet comfort she'd felt from him, the sense of security from knowing he was in the next room.

There had been no more intimate, late-night talks on the patio, no visits to her room to drag her from her night terrors—of which there had been a few. She'd stayed in her bed, telling him she was fine when he'd asked through the door if she was okay the previous night. They had, in fact, almost been tiptoeing around each other since Friday, talking only about the case. Keeping a physical distance, and an emotional one.

*You know why.*

She tried to ignore that little voice as she showered late Sunday afternoon. Just as she'd been ignoring it all weekend. But she couldn't fool herself forever.

She knew.

In recent months, Wyatt had consoled her and lent her a strong arm. He'd carried her; he'd shielded her. Recently, he'd even begun to verbally spar with her, acknowledging—as Brandon would not—that Lily was strong enough to take it. And, in fact, wanted it.

But then he had pulled her onto his lap Friday when she'd nearly broken down. He had held her close, letting her feel his hard, muscular form, smell the warm aroma of his skin, even share every breath because their mouths were so close. During that unexpected encounter, everything had changed. *Everything.*

It was probably a good thing she had recognized the voice on the tape at just that moment, for any number of reasons. One of which was that her leaping to her feet in shock had prevented her from doing something crazy. Like, oh, wrapping her arms around his neck, sinking her hands into his thick, dark hair, and tugging his mouth to hers for a crazy-hot kiss that she had fantasized about since she'd first set eyes on his strong mouth.

She'd been fooling herself the other morning, thinking she could ignore the sexual attraction she felt toward the man, or think about it rationally, coolly, and decide if she wanted to act on it. Because there had been nothing rational or cool in that long, intimate moment. And while it had started as an embrace of comfort, she'd known, somehow, that his awareness had been as strong as her own.

Never in her former life had Lily believed she had a chance with Wyatt Blackstone. Never had she imagined him looking at her with dark blue eyes made darker with want. Yet in that one single moment, when she'd lifted her head and met his stare head-on, she'd seen that want. Maybe even had that chance.

It had scared the hell out of her. Though she didn't believe there was much that could surprise Wyatt Blackstone, she suspected it had even taken him off guard.

He wasn't supposed to lust after wounded, innocent little Lily. He'd been so careful around her since Friday afternoon. Watching her closely, yet not coming close. Offering his support, yet never touching her. Providing a comforting presence without really being wholly present, at least not mentally. Because his thoughts were guarded, somewhere far away, and he wouldn't reveal, by word or expression, what he was really thinking.

Part of her was glad he was holding back, acting as if it hadn't happened. Another part wanted to grab him and demand that he look at her like that at least one more time before he left.

"Maybe you'll get your shot," she whispered as she got out of the shower and dried off. Because, almost against her own better judgment, she had agreed to go out to dinner with him tonight. Not on any kind of a date, of course. He just wanted to drag her out into the world, away from the beach house for a little while, and knew she'd be more likely to go sit down at a restaurant if a familiar face was across from her.

It was her first step into some semblance of a social life since before last January. The first meal she'd eat in a restaurant since she and Jackie had gone out to lunch a few days before the attack.

She was nervous. Her hand actually shook as she tried to apply a little of the makeup she'd picked up at the local general store but had never even opened. She'd bought it thinking she might try to disguise the scars around her ear. Not out of vanity, but to make herself less recognizable as someone who'd been shot in the head. Now that her hair had grown in, though, she didn't need to. Yet she still put a little foundation on her face to even out her tan lines and a swipe of mascara across her lashes to make them look a little prettier despite the drab brown contact lenses.

When she was finished, and looked in the mirror, she saw the woman the world would see. Relief flowed through her. Compact and slender, with her short, dark hair, dark eyes, and serious set to her mouth, she looked nothing like her old self. While it should have been a little disconcerting to see a stranger staring back at her, she liked the feeling.

Lily felt . . . anonymous. Free. Confident enough that no one would know her, she was almost looking forward to going out in the world for one evening to try to forget about everything else.

Maybe she'd be this way forever. Maybe she'd never go back to her old life. She could stay dark-haired and dark-eyed and tough. Could leave here and go prowl the world, seeing what it had to offer, no longer marked by the sadness or the violence of her past.

Then she thought of Wyatt and Brandon, and everything they'd done for her. She thought of Jackie, of Dean, Kyle, and Alec. They had been more than her co-workers; they had been her friends. They had mourned her. Grieved for her.

When she did decide to return to the real world, every one of them deserved the chance to tell her to go to hell for what she'd put them through.

She frowned at her reflection, then turned away. The guilt over keeping her survival hidden from people who cared about her was another heavy weight, one she knew she had to get off her back someday. After that, though, all bets were off. Unless somebody gave her a better alternative, she would be free to go out and live whatever life she chose for herself. It was almost something to look forward to, though as recently as a few days ago, she hadn't been able to fathom it.

What, she wondered, had prompted it? Their breakthrough in the case, knowing they might soon find the man who'd taken her? Or Wyatt's presence? Maybe it had been the realization that whether he wanted to admit it or not, there was something between them, something far more than friendship or gratitude.

Heading downstairs promptly at six, as promised, she managed not to trip over her own feet on the bottom step as she saw Wyatt waiting for her. Damn, did the man really have to go and put on one of those perfectly tailored suits? In her long, flowing skirt, formfitting tank top, and cropped sweater, she was in no way a match for his elegance.

"Good," he said, nodding approvingly.

Not "You look good," she noted. He wasn't complimenting her looks. Just her disguise.

Typical man.

"Gee, thanks so much."

One of his brows quirked at her sarcastic tone. He didn't even realize what she might have wanted to hear from him. And she wasn't about to explain it.

"We really don't have to do this," she insisted as he retrieved her jacket and came over to help her put it on, the movement so graceful, so Wyatt, she wondered why more men didn't realize the appeal of such basic gentlemanly actions.

"Yes, we do," he murmured. "Don't tell me you're not exploding with frustration about this wait, because I know you are. And so am I. So let's just go out and try to be normal for the night. All the rest will still be here in the morning."

She nodded slowly, appreciating the thought, even if his words made it eminently clear this was in no way any kind of date.

*You knew that already, dimwit.* She just had to keep reminding herself of that fact. Wyatt wasn't ready to even consider letting their relationship turn into any-thing other than friendship.

Even if she knew, deep down, that a part of him wanted to.

It didn't prove an easy task. As she sat by his side in the car, breathing in the fragrance that was uniquely Wyatt, listening to the soft strains of jazz coming from the car speakers, it was hard to remember this was just a way to kill some time. Arriving at a small oceanfront restaurant a couple of towns away and being seated at an intimate corner table, with chairs placed side by side, rather than across from each other, made it even harder.

Obviously the seating was designed with the beach view in mind. And it was glorious, watching the purple shades and shadows of twilight begin to descend over the sand and the surf. Under other circumstances, she might be grateful for it. It was hard to be grateful, however, when with every move he made, his trousers brushed her bare calf, or his arm the tips of her fingers.

By the time their appetizer was delivered, she was ac-tually shaking a little in her seat.

"What's wrong?" he asked, waiting until the flirty waitress, who'd been much more interested in taking Wyatt's order than hers, had moved out of earshot.

"Nothing. I'm just a little edgy. This isn't easy for me."

"You're going to have to get used to it sooner or later, aren't you?"

"To going out to dinner with you?" she asked, the words popping out of her mouth in old-Lily fashion be-fore she could stop them.

He didn't acknowledge how that must have sounded—

like a hint that she wanted this to be more than a simple dinner between friends. Thank God.

"I meant, you have to get used to being out in the world. Doing such normal things as going out to a restaurant."

Before, her words had been impulsive, nervous. Now she put a little thought into them. And still she had to ask, "Going on dates, you mean?"

She wondered if he'd be able to maintain that cool, impassive front. She shouldn't have. As always, he kept his emotions, his reactions, entirely in check, as if he was so accustomed to guarding them, he couldn't be surprised by anything or anyone.

"Going anywhere," he told her. His faint smile emphasized the strong curve of his lips and the sparkle in his beautiful eyes. "Not that I think you ever lacked for dates."

"You might be surprised," she admitted wryly as she reached for a breadstick and snapped it in half. She twirled one half in her fingers, as if it were a big, fat cigarette, and suddenly realized she hadn't even had the urge to look for her lone pack since the night he had arrived.

"I know things had been pretty bad for a while. But before that, you must have had some sort of personal life. Friends, relationships. Something resembling normal."

"Do you have anything resembling normal?" she shot back, almost in challenge.

He hesitated; then the smile widened. "Touché."

"I don't think it's entirely possible in our line of work," she said, half-glad Wyatt had just admitted he didn't date and hadn't had any recent relationships. Half-sad for the very same reasons, because it confirmed what she'd known about him from the very start: that he was a loner, an enigma wrapped in secrets, surrounded by mystery, and almost untouchable by anyone he didn't invite to get close.

She had once wanted to get close. Very close. Emotionally, anyway.

Now she wanted to get even closer. Not emotionally— Lily wasn't about to get her feelings tangled up in anything anytime soon. But physically? Yes. She'd been thinking about it for months and Friday had confirmed it. She wanted Wyatt Blackstone. And if she thought he'd say yes, she'd ask him to take her back to the house right now and spend the rest of the weekend in her bed.

But he wouldn't say yes. Of that she had no doubt.

Despite the self-realization, for the next hour, she somehow managed to act normal. Nibble on the breadstick, sip her glass of wine. Chat lightly, actually laughing a few times when he made one of his dry observations about the not exactly four-star food and service.

In fact, once she allowed herself to acknowledge the truth about what she wanted—even knowing she'd never get it—she actually managed to let her guard down and start to enjoy herself. Almost enough to imagine this was just a normal dinner date, and they were a normal man and woman.

"You can't tell me there was no one."

The sudden change in subject confused her. They'd just been talking about the way the chef must have stock in Old Bay seasoning, since he used it with all the subtlety and lightness of a road crew spreading salt after an ice storm. So at first she didn't follow. "Huh?"

"Before."

*Before.*

"You haven't been alone your entire life."

Oh, hell, they were back to personal talk about romance and relationships. Food, bad cooks, spices, and road salt she could deal with; they could cover those subjects all night long. Sex? No way, nohow.

"You have been in love, haven't you? Isn't that something you want for yourself again?"

The quiet tone didn't disguise the piercing curiosity in his eyes. It was as if all this time, all this light conversation, had merely been the camouflage he'd used to creep in under her defenses, so they could get right back where they'd been an hour ago.

"You're good," she said, shaking her head ruefully.

"So they say." Wyatt was never cocky, only confident. So the words that could have sounded wrong coming from another type of man sounded sexy and absolutely right from him.

He lifted his drink, sipping the martini, watching her over the rim of the glass.

"I've been in love," she admitted with a shrug. "Or in very strong like."

"What happened?"

"He didn't appreciate being with a woman who carried a gun."

He laughed softly. "Terrified him, did you?"

It was rather funny. Before this year, she'd fired that weapon only during her bureau training and never removed it from its holster once in the line of duty. "I guess so. I'm terribly intimidating, you know." With an impish grin, she added, "Or so they say."

His amusement didn't quite reach his eyes. "Didn't he know you were an office nerd, and couldn't hurt a fly?"

"You wound me."

"Just stating the obvious."

"You think you know me so well?"

His voice intense, thick, he replied, "I hope I do."

Maybe he did. A year ago, she would have agreed with his assessment. Now, though? Well, she couldn't be entirely sure of who she was anymore. "I guess you never know what you're capable of until you're in the heat of the moment."

"Heat, yes." He leaned closer over the table. "In the white heat of danger or passion, I believe, anyone is capable of anything."

She swallowed hard, ignoring the word *passion*, focusing on the other. "Exactly. In danger, would I pull out that weapon and use it on someone?"

He waited for her to continue.

"You're damn right I would."

"And were you not in danger?"

She knew what he was asking, where he was going. Wyatt was still carefully dancing around the whole idea of vengeance. Her going after the man who'd attacked her and getting even in the most violent way possible.

Part of her wanted to lie, to be the kick-ass woman she'd told herself she'd become. But she couldn't. Not to him. Not convincingly, anyway. "No," she admitted. "I couldn't kill someone in cold blood."

"Even someone vile? Someone you hated?"

Like she hated Lovesprettyboys? "I wouldn't cry if someone else did it. But no. Not even then. Taking a life is something I simply couldn't do unless I were forced into it. Not even a villain's. Certainly not someone innocent."

"Taking a life is a very difficult, ugly thing to do. Even if it's your own," he murmured, so softly, so calmly, she at first thought she had misheard him.

Lily's heart splintered with the pain that suddenly stabbed into it. That was one hell of a low blow.

She drew in a deep, even breath, not trusting herself to reply. Which was good. Because she almost immediately thought about his words and realized why he'd said them.

Wyatt would never cause her pain intentionally—she knew that with every cell in her body. He wasn't throwing her sister's suicide in her face. He was simply forcing her to baldly acknowledge what she had only admitted in the utmost silence of the night, in her own head.

He knew. Somehow, he knew the secret feelings she'd tried so hard to repress. The bitterness. The anger. The *fury*.

"Suicide is a contemptible act," she finally replied.

"Yes, it is."

"Hateful and cruel. Almost unforgivable."

Not that she hadn't forgiven her sister. She had. That didn't mean she hadn't cursed her twin almost as much as she'd cried over her in those first few months, when she'd wondered why Laura had left her alone in this world. Entirely alone to grieve *all* of them.

"I know," he admitted, something in his voice clueing her in that he meant it. He knew.

As if he also knew they'd both gone far afield from their original conversation, he managed to move them back on the normal path with a noncommittal shrug and a sip of his drink. "Okay, tough girl. We have the gun-hating wimp. Who else?"

Though glad he'd changed the subject, she couldn't help frowning at the description. It was a little too accurate. "I didn't date only wimps."

"You don't seem like the football-jock type."

"Hardly," she said with a forced shudder.

No, she'd been the brainiac type. The kind who'd always had a thing for men who were smart enough to know they didn't need to rely on brawn.

Maybe that was why she'd always been a little infatuated by this one. The thought made her think twice before continuing. The conversation was a little too getting-to-know-each-other-on-a-first-date-ish for comfort.

"You know, if I'm going to answer these kinds of questions, you're going to have to as well."

"I'm not the one who's scared to return to her real life."

Her jaw dropped. "Scared? Excuse me?"

"Not that you don't have reason to be scared, obviously; you went through a lot and you could still be in danger." He shook his head slowly. "But it's more than that, isn't it? This whole situation, as ugly as it's been, has been a perfect excuse for you to hide away, protecting yourself physically, but also protecting your emotions." His voice almost hypnotic, he went on. "Safe from grief, from heartache. From risks and expectations."

She swallowed hard, responses spinning in her mind, so many she couldn't settle on just one. He was wrong. He was right. He was rude. He was sympathetic. He was intrusive. He was intuitive. He was keeping her off balance, unsure what he'd say next, what he'd ask next, relentlessly battering at her defenses to get her to admit everything he wanted her to acknowledge.

She should feel manipulated. She didn't. Instead, she could feel only a strange sense of relief at finally having someone to admit it to. The truth about how she felt.

He was that someone. He had been that someone for a very long time. "Yes."

"Yes to?"

"Yes to all of it." She thrust a hand into her hair, taken briefly by surprise, as always, that most of it was gone. "Trying to get back to any kind of normal life after what happened to my family hadn't been working out so well. I was floundering, even way back then, long before the attack on me, long before Friday, when I admitted it to you that I was treading water, staying alive, though not really living."

"And then you no longer had to even try to keep treading. You could just sink, hide away, stop trying to be part of the world that had moved past you."

"Exactly," she whispered.

Until he *made* her by doing things like staring at her with heat in his eyes from the doorway to her bedroom one hot summer night. Showing up and treating her like a woman rather than a fragile doll. Challenging her, arguing with her. Holding her in his arms and wanting her. Dragging her out here and forcing her to admit the truth.

Over the past few days, she'd begun to acknowledge the changes within herself. She actually thought about leaving here. Being free. Being alive again.

Because of him.

He was making her come to life whether she liked it

or not. And now that it had started to happen, she sensed he was not going to give up until she became the woman he expected her to be.

Wyatt had taken Lily out to dinner specifically so she could escape her worries for a little while. So why he'd felt the need to segue into the role of amateur shrink and try to analyze her, he didn't know. Having started, though, he couldn't deny he wanted to know more. He wanted her to admit more. Perhaps exposing more of herself, letting the dark, unhappy thoughts out into the open, would keep her from dwelling on them so incessantly in her daytime hours and her nighttime ones.

But it wasn't to be. He had no sooner opened his mouth to ask her to continue talking about her feelings about her sister, her past, than a large man appeared by their table, and intruded in a loud voice. "Hey, you're him, right? You're the kid from that house up Dead Man's Beach? The murder house?"

Wyatt froze, his spine snapping hard against the back of his chair. Across from him, Lily's eyes had widened in shock, her mouth falling open on a tiny gasp.

Damn it. The span of years might have been long, but memories in small New England towns ran longer. He'd avoided going to Keating, driving out of the way to come up here to an even smaller town farther from the old beach house. Putting distance between himself and anyone who might recognize him had been an instinctive move.

He hadn't gone far enough.

"I don't know what you're talking about," he finally replied.

"I remember that story," the stranger said, as if Wyatt hadn't even spoken. "I was a teenager and read every one of the newspaper articles. Damn, you look just like your dad. That black hair and those blue eyes—you don't forget a combination like that. Good-looking fella, ayuh. And your mother, what a beauty."

Wyatt didn't even look up to acknowledge the man, whose slur outed him as drunk. The alcohol had obviously stripped the stranger of his inhibitions. Not to mention his common sense, considering he continued to shoot off his mouth, despite the deepening scowl Wyatt couldn't keep off his face.

"The whole town talked about nothing else that whole summer. Tragic."

"You're mistaken," he managed to say, forcing the words through clenched teeth.

"No, no, I remember like it was yesterday!"

Wyatt's entire body remained rigid, tense, and ready to spring into action, even though his mind cautioned against doing anything impulsive, anything he might regret. Laying out a stupid drunk who shot off his mouth regarding things he had no business asking about was definitely something he would regret.

"Let's go," he said to Lily, immediately rising, pushing his chair back hard against the wall. He tossed several bills on the table, then turned to fully face the stranger, a red-nosed guy with weathered, lobsterman's skin and milky eyes. "Excuse me, I think you've mistaken me for someone else. We were just leaving."

The stranger didn't budge. Still oblivious, blind to Wyatt's mood, he also missed the tension that had fallen over the entire restaurant. "Come on, at least admit it's you.

They found you in the lighthouse, right? Or was it in the house? Either way you were covered with blood. I mean, you *are* the kid who survived after that insane—"

Wyatt didn't think; he merely reacted, losing himself to some primal drive that his own intellect hadn't been able to completely subdue. He grabbed the man's beefy upper arm, clenched his fingers tightly around it, and spun him toward the wall, twisting the arm around until the shoulder had to be screaming. Leaning close, their backs to every other person in the place, who probably watched wide-eyed, he snarled, "Don't say another word. Not one word. Do you understand?"

The drunk grunted. Wyatt tugged farther.

"I repeat. Do you understand?"

With a wince, the man nodded quickly, at last recognizing the explosive situation he'd been about to kindle. "Sorry," he whispered. "Hey, I'm sorry. Obviously I mistook you for someone else."

As instantly as it had arisen, Wyatt's anger dissipated. His fingers jerked open and he let the man go, already regretting that lapse, that loss of control.

If Lily hadn't been here, an audience to the truth about the dark past Wyatt had tried so hard to put behind him, would he have been so quick to try to shut up a loud drunk? Maybe. But maybe not.

Of course, if Lily hadn't been here, nothing on heaven or earth would have induced him to come to within a hundred miles of this place. Ever.

"Wyatt?" she said, her voice subdued. She watched from a few feet away, no fear on her face, no flashback of a man's voice raised in anger, thank God. Just concern. "Are you ready to go?"

He nodded once. As the waitress hurried over, finally

noticing the situation, he waved toward the cash on the table. "Thank you very much; we'll be leaving now," he said. "I trust that will take care of everything."

The young waitress stared goggle-eyed at the pile of bills. "Sure. You bet. Come back any old time."

Not very likely. Especially not now, when he knew that within hours, all the tiny towns up and down a sixty-mile stretch of coast would be whispering about his presence. The return of the boy who'd survived such an infamous crime.

Not glancing left or right, he put his fingers on the small of Lily's back and led her to the exit, impervious to the stares, almost hearing the whispers.

*Was it really him? How old was he, five or six? Did they ever find out how much he saw? Whether he went to the lighthouse on his own, or was brought there? All that blood! I remember the pictures in the paper—they looked like such a nice couple.*

It was almost as if he had a sixth sense and could hear the buzz of conversation, the words swirling around and around in his mind, present and past mixing up. The questions were all the same now as they had been then, exploding in the silence, crowding out the quiet hum of the engine and the deep, even sound of Lily's breaths in the seat beside him.

Tension filled the car throughout the drive back to the house. Whatever conversation he and Lily might have had before, now they shared only the uncomfortable memory of Wyatt losing his famed cool.

She asked no questions. Didn't pry, didn't try to tease him out of his dark mood or tell him that fair was fair— she'd done some talking, and now he should.

For all of that, he was most grateful.

But that still didn't stop him from dropping her off, escorting her to the door, then turning around, getting back in his car, and driving all the way back to Washington that very night.


The murder house. Wyatt's handsome father and beautiful mother. The boy who'd survived.

Had his family really been killed in this house? God, had he really witnessed the murders of his own parents when he was just a small child?

Lily couldn't get those thoughts out of her head during the ride back to the house or in the moments after Wyatt had unceremoniously dropped her off and left. Her mind had, of course, filled in the gaping blanks left by the drunk man's story. She suspected finally filling in those blanks would provide a complete explanation for the varying facets of the supervisory special agent's life: his brilliance, his secretiveness, his intensity, his solitary lifestyle. His enigmatic personality.

All those answers, just waiting to be discovered.

The information was out there. She knew it. A trip to the local newspaper office or the library would provide archives. That failing, a talkative resident familiar with the history of this town would almost certainly answer any questions she cared to ask about this house.

"So many questions," she whispered, looking out her bedroom window, as she had been for several minutes, since his taillights had disappeared down the steep driveway and up the lonely beach road.

Lily didn't know that she could do it, or even that she needed to. She already knew the basics. Something awful had happened here. Something that had scarred

Wyatt for life, making him the man he was today. It had shaped him the way a piece of raw metal was hammered and formed in the punishing fires of the furnace.

"But could I do that? Intrude on his past like that, ask those intimate questions?" she added, her own breaths making misty circles against the glass, proof that autumn was indeed coming fast in this part of the world. She turned to the other window, on the eastern wall, which overlooked the ocean. Staring down at the shore, at the blackness of the water, the faint outline of the faded lighthouse up the beach—the place he seemed to hate even more than this house—she knew she could not.

No research, no digging, no questions. She couldn't do that to him. It was Wyatt's story. His secret. His history. When he wanted her to know about it, he would tell her. Until then, she could only treat him with the same kindness and respect he'd always shown her and mind her own goddamn business. That was the very least she could do, given all she owed him.

She wandered back to the bed, eyeing the room, studying the curve of the antique four-poster, the soft, honeyed oak of the dresser, and the gently billowing sheers on the window.

*The murder house.*

Strange that it still felt so safe to her. So comforting, even if it had a horrible history she might someday learn about.

Stranger that he'd brought her here. She'd nearly been killed and her savior had brought her to the site of his darkest, most vicious nightmares to hide her from the world. He'd set aside the seething emotions he must have for the place and installed Lily within it, coming back here, month after month, despite the memories that had to ooze from every wall, seep from each crevice in the floor.

The sacrifice was staggering.

So at the very least, to repay the man, she could be patient and wait for him to tell her the truth. Even though she knew full well that day might never come.

# Chapter 8

Frank Addison wasn't as gullible as the Pennsylvania dentist had been. Or the first two victims, who had been so caught up in their own excitement that they'd walked right into their own massacres.

Not this man. He was cautious, wary. He hadn't moved forward two steps without taking one back since the minute he'd exited his pickup, which was parked by the side of the motel. In fact, for a moment, it appeared he was going to slip away without ever entering the dark, dingy room where the scene had been so carefully laid out. The man's sixth sense had alerted him that something was off, and he'd hesitated before coming in, not driven by his insane need and anticipation of the clandestine evening awaiting him. Maybe because he was another predator, he'd smelled a trap.

Thankfully, though, the man's defenses had dropped when he heard little "Zach's" voice coming from inside the room right after he'd pushed open the unlocked door. Pitiable and soft. Vulnerable and alone. "Do you know where my mom is?"

Those small digital recorders were remarkable. They could not only distort voices in any number of ways, but they could also throw sound to make it appear that it was coming from another area of the room altogether.

"No, I don't," the man said as he stepped inside. "Did she leave you here . . . ?"

In silence, the ax began to swing through the stale, cigarette- and skanky-sex-smelling air that lived in all rooms like this one. But the trucker was quick on his feet, alert and ready. He spun around, as if sensing someone was behind him, lurking behind the door. For one second, it appeared the blow would glance off a beefy shoulder, and then there would be serious trouble.

But fate decided otherwise. The newly sharpened blade, originally meant for the broad, flannel-covered back, instead kissed Frank Addison's throat, slicing across it as delicately and precisely as a scalpel. It really was surprising, a complete accident, certainly not the result of a carefully aimed blow. The blade could easily have swung across nothing but air, and then they'd be fighting to the death.

Instead, though, the sharp metal cut through layers of skin and clumps of sinew and cartilage as though they were blobs of congealed gravy. When the ax blade emerged from the other side, it took a good inch of the man's windpipe and most of his Adam's apple with it.

Blood immediately gushed out, spewing wildly. That hadn't happened before. The more typical blow, to the lower back, was neater, less messy, with a shirt or pants often sopping up the initial spurts of blood.

This was raw, violent, and explosive. Warm, viscous

blood flew everywhere, hitting both their bodies, both sets of hands and feet and everywhere in between. Having taken the precaution of stripping down to bare skin, as always, and wearing only thin gloves and equally thin surgeon's booties, that wouldn't be a problem. Just a bit more to wash up in the mildew-stained bathroom when this was all over.

And it would be over soon. Addison gurgled, lifted his bloody hands to catch the larynx hanging out of his open throat. Finally, after what seemed an age but was probably less than thirty seconds, he fell to his knees, landing hard, his eyes widened in shock and pain. His mouth twisted, moved to try to form words, undoubtedly to ask the same question all of them asked.

*Why? Why me?*

"It's nothing personal."

Frank didn't reply. Couldn't reply, of course.

"You really should be glad it turned out this way."

"Gaaahh . . ."

"You see, chances are that you're going to bleed to death long before I cut your cock off and shove it into that hole in your throat."

Funny, for a nearly dead man without a voice box, Frank Addison still managed a sort of scream.

Not so funny, at least not for Frank Addison, was the fact that it took him a few minutes longer to bleed to death than he'd probably have liked.

Wyatt reached Williamsburg by two thirty on Tuesday afternoon, well in time for his three p.m. appointment with Dr. Angela Kean. He'd called the office first thing this morning, telling her it was urgent, and she'd offered to fit him in between other appointments.

The timing couldn't have worked out better. Throwing himself back into the case would help keep his mind off what had happened Sunday night, off the image of Lily, sitting up in that damned house with her computer, clicking away and reading about his past.

*She wouldn't.*

The thought calmed him. Because he knew it was true. She wouldn't pry. She would wait for him to tell her the truth.

"You're going to be waiting a very long time," he muttered before thrusting thoughts of that whole situation out of his head. As he always did when the memories threatened to arise.

Armed with the digital file he wanted Dr. Kean to hear, he parked outside the expansive, new-looking offices of Eastern Virginia Plastic Surgery, a few spaces down from the row of Mercedes-Benzes, BMWs, and Lexuses that filled all the Doctor Parking Only spaces. Most of them had cutesy personalized tags containing messages like DRS-TOY, and none appeared to be more than a year old.

Nearly every space in the lot was filled. It appeared that, despite the economy, the plastic surgery business was booming. Possibly because, from the research he'd done, this particular practice, staffed by Dr. Alfred Underwood and several members of his family, was among the most renowned in the state. The rich women of Virginia trusted no one else with their lifts, rhinoplasties, implants, and ever-so-discreet liposuction procedures.

Before he even exited his own government-issued sedan, he saw a man, probably around thirty, bound out of the office doors. Dressed in khaki pants and a golf shirt, he also wore an expression of lazy self-indulgence. His clothes, though casual, screamed old money. Though he might have been one of the practice's own clients, the man headed instead for the reserved lot. He hopped over the driver's-side door of a hot red convertible, parked in a space reserved for Dr. Philip Wright.

Gunning the engine, the young doctor backed out of his space as though he were launching a rocket. As he threw the car into drive, grinding the transmission, he hesitated, staring at Wyatt from across the parking lot. He grinned slyly, then pointed one index finger in Wyatt's direction. The tires squealed as he hit the gas, but above the sound, Wyatt heard him call, "Don't let them touch the face. It's perfect."

A doctor warning away the patients. Amusing.

The car sped away. "Doctor's hours," he murmured, glancing at his watch. He couldn't help wondering if Dr. Wright would have gone zero to one hundred if he'd known an officer of the law was in the vicinity.

Probably. The wealthy didn't always acknowledge that such mundane things as laws applied to them. Having come from such old money himself, he knew that to be true, even if he disagreed with the philosophy.

Heading inside the building, he noted the obvious elegance and atmosphere of the lobby and the waiting area. The place seemed more high-end spa than doctors' office, with plush carpeting, tasteful artwork on the walls, and massive bouquets of fresh flowers. A large silver punch bowl filled with ice and stocked with bottles of Evian water stood just inside the door, and the seating areas in the waiting room were separated into distinct alcoves, offering privacy in a nonprivate setting. Even the underlying music, emerging from some hidden speakers, was soft and classical, no canned Muzak or local radio station blaring tire ads or traffic updates.

Several of those semiprivate alcoves were occupied, and he drew the attention of every waiting client as he approached the receptionist's desk. Most of the women were well dressed, their faces smooth, with a faint sheen that said this was not their first visit to the center. But there were also a few male clients, a couple of businessmen types, probably looking to tighten up the paunch of middle age.

"Good afternoon," he murmured as he reached the front desk, where a young, attractive brunette greeted him with a smile. "I'm here to see Dr. Kean."

The woman leaned forward slightly. Keeping her voice low, she asked, "You're, uh, Mr. Blackstone?"

Obviously the "Supervisory Special Agent" part was to be their little secret. "Yes."

The woman rose. "This way, please. Dr. Kean asked me to bring you right back."

Following, he made a point of moving slowly, taking stock of his surroundings. He surreptitiously counted the number of exam rooms, and peered into offices with large, executive desks visible through open doorways.

On the walls between the offices were a number of framed photographs and articles. These pictured Alfred Underwood and various members of his family/staff with the rich and famous. Politicians. Actors. Many of whom had probably received their perfect noses and chins in this very building.

He did, however, also note the number of plaques and civic awards. Most of them honored Dr. Underwood for his good works, his donations to charities, especially those involving children. Wyatt paused before one particular photo, a large framed shot of a crowd of at least twenty people standing and sitting outside a lofty, beachfront house. Underwood stood in the center, several beaming adults surrounding him. One or two sullen, bored teenagers appeared on the fringes, and a few young children were rolling on the lawn. A big family photo shoot, apparently.

He took a few more steps, then paused again in front of the largest framed portrait yet. It depicted a handsome, smiling man, probably in his late forties. Hanging alone, it stood out, singular and dignified, at the very end of the corridor where two others branched off in a T. At least three feet tall and two feet wide, it was illuminated by a spotlight from below. Beside it, an engraved plaque read, *In loving memory of Dr. Roger Underwood. Beloved son, brother, and husband.*

They apparently grew physicians on the Underwood family tree.

"Handsome, wasn't he?"

Wyatt slowly turned as another voice intruded. A few feet away, watching from the open door of an examination room, was a stunningly beautiful woman. Eyes a warm shade of blue, with champagne-colored hair falling in a long, loose curtain over her shoulders, she was the kind of female who turned men stupid.

Men like Tom Anspaugh, he thought, remembering the other agent's stammering when he'd interviewed the women of this family. Because he immediately recognized the blonde as Dr. Judith Underwood, the plastic surgeon who'd provided her sister-in-law with an alibi the night the car was stolen.

If she was an advertisement for the skills of this practice, she was a damned good one. There wasn't an imperfect spot on her, yet she managed to look entirely natural and untouched.

"My late husband," she said, stepping over to stand beside him and eye the portrait. "Father . . . I mean, my father-in-law set up this pseudo-shrine. I think it's a little morbid, but I'm only an in-law, so I didn't have much say." Sadness visible in her eyes, she stared at the enormous portrait for a moment longer. "It's like he's still here."

Curiosity got the better of him. "He appeared young."

"Doctors make the worst patients, I suppose. Especially vibrant, otherwise healthy ones. He apparently didn't even recognize the chest pains for what they were. Heart attack at forty-nine, can you imagine?" She shook her head, adding in her soft voice, "One evening we're having a lovely dinner with his sister and her husband, who live right down the street. The next morning I find him dead on the living room floor, still holding the broken neck of the wine bottle he'd been opening when he collapsed. It's still hard to believe, even after all this time."

"I'm so sorry for your loss."

"Thank you." She looked up at him, flashing those blue eyes ringed with ultrablack lashes. "I'm Judith Underwood, by the way."

He nodded once. "I know."

"You're the FBI agent coming to visit Angela."

"Yes, I am." Ignoring the curiosity glittering in the young widow's eyes, he added, "And I'm afraid I'm keeping her waiting. Nice to meet you."

The receptionist, who'd been tapping her foot on the

marble-tiled floor, flashed him an appreciative smile and led him up the hall. "Here we are." She knocked twice, then began to push the door in. "Your visitor is here, Dr.—"

The door was suddenly yanked open from within. A tall, distinguished-looking man with dark hair graying at the temples appeared, his expression glacial. Without a word to the receptionist, much less to Wyatt, he stalked down the hallway and stormed into one of the empty offices. The slam of the door punctuated his displeasure about whatever had just happened with Dr. Kean.

"The other Dr. Kean," the receptionist whispered, looking a little terrified. Something told him the angry scene was nothing new.

"Does this happen often?" he asked, sensing the woman was a talker.

"I'm just a temp and have only worked here a few days, but I hear they fight like cats and dogs."

"Come in, please," said a voice from within.

Doing as she'd asked, Wyatt assessed the woman rising to greet him from behind the desk. She was probably in her mid-forties, quietly confident. The same gray-green eyes he'd seen in her late brother's portrait watched him enter. Her attractive face was not pulled taut and immaculate like those women he'd seen in her waiting room. In fact, the doctor had a few wrinkles beside the eyes, a less-than-perfect chin, and a perfectly average nose and mouth.

He remembered the speaker on the tape, the one who had asked about women defying age through plastic surgery. And he began to worry. Perhaps the questioner hadn't been jabbing at the doctor after all. Because, though she was very attractive, he would lay money that this woman was not a physician who healed herself.

"Agent Blackstone," the woman said as she extended her hand to him. "Please forgive my husband's little display of temper. We disagree on treatment for a patient and," she said with a tiny smile, "the boss likes me better, so I'm sure to get my way."

The boss. Her father. Though the comment could have been snide, instead Angela Kean appeared quietly amused, as if she was only joking about going over her husband's head.

Wyatt had to wonder if her husband was in on the joke.

"Please sit down."

"Thank you for seeing me on such short notice."

"It sounded very important," she said. She watched Wyatt take the chair opposite the desk, then returned to her own. "I received several messages from last Friday. I'm terribly sorry you were unable to reach me. As you can imagine, with a family business, we rarely get to take time off all together. It's become a sort of tradition that we close for the Labor Day holiday and go to our beach house. Extended family comes, too, from all over the place."

"I understand. Quite a few of you work here, don't you?"

Dr. Kean laughed, which emphasized those tiny lines beside her eyes. She was prettier when she smiled. "You've no idea. Father drilled family loyalty into our ears from a very young age. My husband's office is right up the hall, my father's down from his." Her smile faded a little. "My late brother was right across from Father, his wife one down from that."

"I just met her."

Dr. Kean's smile didn't fade, but the warmth in her eyes certainly did. "How nice."

He filed away that tidbit, knowing at once that the sisters-in-law were not close.

"There's also Philip Wright." Displaying more of that coolness, and an even tighter smile, she explained, "Father's stepson. He joined us last year, right out of medical school."

"Father's stepson." Not "my stepbrother." He made another mental note, remembering the young doctor who'd blasted out of the parking lot in his Ferrari.

"Everyone in the same field. I imagine you have pretty limited dinner-table conversations during family gatherings," Wyatt murmured.

"Oh, there are a few nonmedical types in the extended family, at least. Politicians, lawyers, even a novelist."

He noticed she didn't say sanitation workers, schoolteachers, or deliverymen.

"But as for the rest of us?" She shrugged helplessly. "What can I say? The family who does face-lifts together . . ."

*Gets rich together.* Very rich, he suspected.

"That's not to say shop talk doesn't get exceedingly tiring. That's why I insist on living close to Richmond rather than in one of the local neighborhoods like the rest of the family. My husband and I commute here every day." Laughing a little, she added, "It's a hike, but still a small price to pay to get away from everyone else at night."

"I understand."

He didn't, not really. Not ever having siblings, or much family, he honestly couldn't relate. But agreeing with witnesses, building a rapport with them, was an important part of the job.

"Now, your message said you wanted to ask me about my stolen car?" She shuddered visibly. "I still have nightmares thinking it was used by a murderer who wanted to harm little children. Imagine if he hadn't abandoned it, and had used it to kidnap a child?"

Wyatt schooled his features to remain utterly impassive. This woman—this witness—should not know so much. But since she'd been interviewed by Anspaugh, he wasn't entirely surprised. Dr. Kean was attractive enough to incite the other agent to puff up his own importance. And shoot off his mouth.

That was the one good thing that had come of this entire mess. Anspaugh, at least, had been put on a leash even tighter than Wyatt's. He only hoped that, like a chained dog, the brute didn't get meaner and hungry to bite anyone who came within range.

"I was hoping you might listen to a recording for me." He lifted the small digital recorder and placed it on the desk. Brandon had loaded the pertinent clip onto it. "I'm interested in identifying a man who asked you a question at the panel workshop you gave that weekend at the medical convention."

One of her brows shot up in surprise. "A voice identification? From over seven months ago?"

"I know it's a long shot, Dr. Kean. But it sounded to me as though this person knew you, and perhaps you, him. It could be someone who moves in your circle, someone whose voice you already know."

The doctor did not nod in agreement. Instead, she eyed him steadily. Warily. "Are you implying that someone I know, a physician at that workshop, was the one who"—she thought about her words carefully, then concluded—"stole my car?"

He knew what she was really asking. Did he think someone she knew was a cold-blooded murderer and potential child molester? "I'm not implying anything. Just following up on a lead. Now, would you please just listen?" he replied evenly.

A long pause, then she nodded once. "All right. But I'm not making any promises."

"I don't expect any."

He pulled his chair closer to the desk, sliding the digital device toward Dr. Kean. When she murmured her readiness, he pushed play, hearing the now-familiar voice asking his snide question.

Wyatt never took his eyes off the woman. She kept her head tilted down, staring at her hands, which were tented on her desk, as if she was in deep concentration. The pose also, however, gave her a chance to evade his stare, to keep him from seeing her immediate reaction. He was denied the opportunity to witness any flare of the eyes, a loss of color in her cheeks, a startled inhalation, or a frown that said she did recognize the voice.

When the clip ended, she remained very still. Then, her voice low, she said, "Would you play it again please, just so I can be sure?"

Wyatt's pulse picked up its tempo. The doctor was a calm, intelligent woman who would be deliberate and certain in her responses. Of course she would want to hear it again before confirming she knew the speaker.

He played the file, still watching her. Again, she remained still, so very still. Until finally, a full thirty seconds after the recording ended, she lifted her head and met his stare with an impassive one of her own.

Dread filled him. He knew what she was going to say before the words left her mouth.

"I'm sorry, Agent Blackstone. Truly. But I cannot identify that voice for you."

"You're certain."

"Yes. I'm certain."

Damn it. She didn't shift her gaze, made no obvious signs that she was lying. Her voice didn't quiver.

Of course, she had no reason to lie, so he shouldn't have been looking for such signs. But something about her hesitation before listening had made him wonder whether the doctor would be entirely honest. He didn't imagine anyone would relish the possibility of hearing a familiar voice, knowing the person might have done some horrible things.

By her demeanor now, however, the coolness of her tone and completely unflinching gaze, it appeared she was telling the truth. She couldn't help him.

He wasn't about to give up, though. Not when he finally had a solid lead for the first time in months. "Someone else might recognize him. Another of the speakers, conference attendees. Perhaps your father?"

Her mouth tightened an infinitesimal amount, and so did her jaw. "Can't help you there. My father is away. He and his wife decided not to return from the beach house for a few days. And my husband didn't even attend the convention. He was ill."

Ill? Or taking advantage of a night away from his strong-willed wife and her family?

"Philip, my stepbrother, just moved back to Virginia last year and knows very few professionals outside our office. He attended only the banquet, to show support to Father. None of the other weekend events. Besides all that, he just left to return to the beach. . . . He and Father have a standing golf date every Tuesday."

How chummy.

The doctor's tone said she didn't like that one single bit. A jealous daughter, perhaps, envious of her father's closeness to a young stepson who'd waltzed in to take the place of the son he'd lost? If he remembered correctly from the brief family background Brandon had put together for him, the senior Dr. Underwood had married his second wife, who had been raising two children of her own, at least twenty years ago. He hadn't adopted the children, but it sounded as though there was a father-son bond.

Not a sister-brother one, however.

"And your sister-in-law? Judith?" he asked, undeterred, wondering why she was trying to keep her family out of the situation. "She was one of the speakers on that panel with you, wasn't she?"

Again that hint of coolness appeared. "Yes, she was. But I doubt she'll remember any more than I do. There were hundreds of people there, our panel was hugely popular, and we could barely see a soul in the audience from up on the stage."

"Just the same . . ."

She waved a hand. "If you insist, though I hate for you to waste your time during what I sense is a very important investigation." She glanced at her watch, then rose to her feet. "I believe Judith is with a patient, and I have one to see myself. Why don't you wait here and I'll return with her when we're both free?"

Wyatt shook his head. "No, please don't trouble yourself. I can ask the receptionist to track her down. I've taken up enough of your time."

"It's really no trouble," the woman said. "Just stay here."

But before the doctor could leave, a knock sounded on her door.

"What is it?"

Dr. Judith Underwood herself opened the door and stuck her head in. "Sorry to disturb you, Ang. I need to consult with you when you have the chance."

Dr. Kean frowned, though whether because she just didn't like her sister-in-law, or because she no longer had an excuse to avoid letting the woman hear the audio file, he didn't know. But Wyatt wasn't about to waste the opportunity he'd been given.

"We were just talking about you, Dr. Underwood. I wonder if you might be able to help me." Ignoring Angela Kean's deepening frown, he explained the situation, concluding, "If you don't mind listening, perhaps you'll have more luck than Dr. Kean did?"

"Of course," the other woman said, "I'd be happy to."

Like replaying the same song on an old record, Wyatt found himself again placing the digital recorder on the desk. This time, though, Dr. Kean remained standing, facing the windows, staring outside with her arms crossed over her chest. Judith, the blonde, sat on another visitor's chair, leaning down and listening intently.

He pushed play. He waited, listening to the familiar voice that had imprinted itself on his brain.

The tape ended. A long silence ensued. Then he was entirely disappointed once more.

"I'm sorry, Agent Blackstone," Judith said, as wide-eyed and impassive as her sister-in-law had been. "I just don't know anyone who sounds like that."

It had been a long shot. A stab in the dark. He should

have known he wouldn't be fortunate enough to find someone who recognized that voice on the very first go-round.

This would crush Lily. She'd pinned a lot on this lead, hoping, as he did, that her nightmare of uncertainty would soon end.

The two women watched him impassively, never glancing toward each other. The tension between them could fill a lake. But whether it was simply because they disliked each other, or it had something to do with his presence—and the audio recording—he simply didn't know.

He wasn't about to give up, either. There were other ways to proceed. He had a few ideas and had already mentioned them to Brandon. Including gathering files from previous conventions, seeing if they could find the same man, identified for the recording this time.

That, however, would take a while. It would be easier if he could question anyone who had actually been in the room during the workshop in Richmond, when they knew the unsub had been present. Had, he wondered, Dr. Underwood's father been there? Her stepbrother?

Her angry husband, who might not have been as ill as she claimed?

A simple thing to ask, yet Dr. Kean didn't seem to want any other members of her family questioned. She didn't even seem to want Wyatt to meet them face-to-face.

Could it be because she didn't want him learning the identity of the man on the tape?

The idea might immediately have left the mind of someone like Anspaugh, who was easily cowed by the trappings of wealth and couldn't picture the dark, seedy side of the lifestyle. Wyatt, however, didn't discount any possibility, however violent, however bloody. He knew rage and bloodthirstiness were in no way limited to the average person.

He suddenly wanted to dig around. More so than before he'd come here. Because if these women weren't hiding something, then he had no business calling himself an FBI agent.

"Thank you both, very much, for your time," he murmured, rising to say good-bye to the two doctors. He wanted out of here, away from the ornate office and the aura of privilege and wealth. He would happily leave them to their tension and their family drama, to their rich patients and their soap opera lifestyle.

He didn't envy them one bit. And the idea that he might have been raised much the same way, if not for a twist of fate and a single night of bloody rage, served as a reminder that he was on the right path. He'd gone in the right direction with his life, and wouldn't trade places with the golf-playing surgeon or the angry husband controlled by his wife's family for anything in the world.

He headed through the building, hesitating near the front desk. The receptionist wasn't there. For a moment, he considered tracking her down to ask her to listen to the recording, but since she'd admitted she was new here, he didn't think it was worth it. Doing so would be an obvious sign that he didn't trust Drs. Kean and Underwood. And while that was true, he didn't see the need to put their guards up so quickly on a long shot with a temporary employee.

Wyatt proceeded to the front door. Opening it, he

stepped back, out of the way, to allow yet another patient to enter, this one already attractive, though her severe hairstyle hardened her features. Her eyes widened
behind her trendy glasses and she gave him a quick
once-over, then quickly averted her gaze. She didn't
even thank him for the courtesy, probably wanting to
keep a low profile for this, a visit to a plastic surgeon
who would remove a chin or fill a wrinkle or smooth
some age spots. Holding on to youth and physical beauty
had never been more important, or so it seemed in this
little microcosm of society.

Funny. Even with her shaved head, her scars, her
bandages, stitches, and bruises, Lily Fletcher was more
beautiful than any woman in the building.

Outside, he walked toward the car, already planning
his next move. He had come here looking for a witness.
He wondered, though, with all the little details he'd
heard from Judith Underwood and Angela Kean, if he
might have stumbled upon a clue that could lead him to
a suspect.

The family certainly bore more investigation.

Getting in his car, Wyatt couldn't deny his disappointment that he still didn't know whose voice was on that
tape. He dreaded calling Lily and telling her. But he'd
also make it clear that he wasn't about to give up. There
had been hundreds of people at that convention, dozens
in that workshop. Someone, somewhere, would recognize that voice. He had to believe that.

For Lily's sake. For all their sakes.

Standing shoulder to shoulder, she and her sister-in-
law watched the handsome FBI agent exit the building.

They had been completely silent, just staring at each other for a long moment after he'd departed, before they moved, almost in unison, to the large tinted window overlooking the parking lot. And it wasn't until he was in his car, driving away—hopefully never to return—that she finally broke the silence. "You lied."

A shrug. "So did you."

Well, of course. There'd been no other choice. Not lying would have brought a damned murder investigation down on them. Reputations could be destroyed, all they'd worked for torn apart, the family crucified in the press.

And what happened to the family happened to the practice.

"Do you think he believed either one of us?"

"Probably not. But let's not panic just yet."

"Why now?" she murmured, torn between fear and resentment. "Why, after all this time, and why that one recording? What can it possibly prove?"

With a frown, the other woman replied, "I have no idea. But one thing is sure: We can't let this go any further. Do we have anyone in the family with FBI contacts? Somebody who can nip this thing in the bud, get rid of that tape?"

Good point; she should have thought of it herself. "I'll work on that." Lowering her voice to a thick whisper, she added, "Do you believe it? That *he* was involved, somehow, with stealing the car? Stalking those children?"

A bitter laugh was her only response.

Yes. Her sister-in-law believed. God help them, they both did. Because there had been other signs, other children. And they were all damned for having known about it and yet doing nothing.

"We have got to get this under control. To make sure that agent never gets near Father."

She shuddered at the very thought, rubbing a shaking hand over her eyes. "This could destroy us all. Child molestation. Murder." Then, not sure she even wanted the answer, she asked flat out. "I thought it was under control. That he'd been scared off after whatever happened last summer with that Web site he was so obsessed with."

The other surgeon, so brilliant, so charmed, sneered in response. "Only a fool would think he could resist those baser urges for long."

She shuddered, hating to even imagine it. Had he always been that way? Had the rest of them just been too blind to see? Was she herself one of the fools?

"If he did it, he certainly timed it well, knowing how busy the rest of us would be with the conference, while he would be assumed to be there, as well. Though we both know he made himself scarce that weekend and was hardly around."

"Almost as if he had planned it that way," her hated sister-in-law replied.

Perhaps he had. It hurt to think about someone she had once so loved. But perhaps he had.

They each turned from the window, walking toward the office door, saying nothing else. They were allies now, though neither of them liked it—or each other. But they had no choice. The family had to be protected; Dr. Alfred Underwood's legacy and the practice's reputation could not be tarnished by any hint of a scandal.

And a pedophilia/murder investigation would make for quite a scandal. It could bring down every single one of them. So for now, the two of them were trapped, helpless, and forced to shield each other. She and her sister-in-law would remain silent conspirators.

Together, they would have to make sure that the entire family wasn't headed for total destruction because of the actions of one sick, unbalanced member of it.

# Chapter 9

"Come on, you can do better than that. Hurt me. Take me out the very moment I come at you."

Lily blew out the side of her mouth at an errant strand of sweaty hair that clung to the side of her face. Her head down, she backed up and forced her body to relax, bouncing a little on her bare toes on the exercise mat beneath her feet. Sarge, aka Sergeant Wally Devlin, U.S. Army, Ret., stood a few feet away, his big body clad in desert camo, his head down as he studied her from under bushy brows. Any second now, he would come at her, giving her no warning as to which move he intended to use, where he might grab her, if he'd lunge or kick or dive.

And she would fight back.

"Don't think," he snapped. "Don't plan. And for God's sake, don't dwell on what you might have done to change what happened in the past. Just do it *now*."

What she might have done to change the past? Considering she'd been shot a few times within milliseconds of seeing her attacker's hand—and his weapon—come around the side of the surveillance van door, she didn't chide herself for not doing more.

Getting involved in the Lovesprettyboys investigation to begin with? Well, that was another story. High kicks and fast punches might not have stopped her from getting shot. But minding her own business, doing her own job, and not lying to her boss about what was going on probably would have.

"Come on, Lily, get—"

He lunged without warning, midsentence. Went left. Her body reacted instinctively. She swung right, curled her left leg for a Crescent Kick, then immediately spun farther and hit him with a Double Side Piercing Kick.

"Good girl!" he chortled as he fell to the mat.

She stepped back into a waiting position, not even winded. "You okay?"

He rolled onto his knees and looked up at her. "That's the kind of response I was looking for. Instinct kicks in. You don't overanalyze—your body tells you what to do."

The sarge was powerfully built, stubborn, and tough, but he was also a sixty-year-old man. She'd put him on the mat pretty hard, and it hadn't been the first time today. They'd been at it for an hour, enjoying the afternoon session outdoors on the patio to savor the warmth of the September day. She extended a hand to help him up.

He stared at it, rolled his eyes, then ignored her help and rose with a grunt. "Don't go getting cocky, girlie."

She grinned. At first, the man had seemed like a grizzly bear. He'd pushed her hard when she hadn't believed she was ready to be pushed. He'd made her strong and made her want to be even stronger. But she'd come to recognize him as more teddy than grizzly. She didn't remember her father very well, since she'd been five when her parents had died. But she hoped he would have been at least a little bit like this man.

Reaching for a towel on the nearby table, he wiped his brow, then grabbed a water bottle and downed half its contents. Lily wasn't fooled by his weary demeanor or his heavy breathing. The man had set her up on more than one occasion. She looked for a tiny twitch of his mouth, or the shift of his eyes as he studied her position, something that would indicate a surprise assault.

"Want some?" he asked, lifting a second water bottle.

Still prepared, she nodded once, and extended her hand.

He grabbed it, tugged her forward, tried to twist her around. She responded with two quick jabs and a kick that dropped him to his knees on the mat.

"Excellent!"

"Wow, remind me to never offer you a bottle of water," a voice said.

Lily tensed, the way she hadn't when preparing for Sarge's next move. Because she recognized the voice.

A small part of her, the part that was still Lily Fletcher, who couldn't seem to get through a day without doing something klutzy, reacted with pleasure. Pure happiness at the thought of seeing a friend poured through her before she could stop it.

But the rest of her responded only with wariness, wondering what Brandon Cole was doing here, and what the visit meant.

"Brandon," she said, nodding at the spiky-haired blond who stood in the open doorway leading from the kitchen. He'd once been her friend, someone who'd somehow been able to make her smile, even on days when she thought she'd never smile again.

She'd missed him. But not enough to invite him to start coming back around again, building up his expectations that their relationship could be something it had never been, and would never be.

"Hey, gorgeous." He stepped out, arms wide, smiling so gently, genuinely happy to see her, she couldn't be annoyed that he'd surprised her. Or that he'd ignored her instructions not to come up.

She allowed him to tug her close for a hug, but quickly pulled away. "I'm a sweaty mess," she said with a forced laugh. Gesturing toward his trendy-as-always clothes, which looked as though they'd come off the pages of a men's fashion magazine, she added, "I couldn't afford to have that outfit dry-cleaned, much less replace it if I ruin it."

Knowing Brandon wouldn't have come alone, especially not on a Thursday afternoon, and that he couldn't have gotten in without Wyatt to bring him through the security checkpoints, she glanced past him into the darker depths of the house. A shadow stood there, tall, solid. Then he stepped closer and she saw his eyes.

Those wary, worried eyes.

Lily tensed. "What's wrong?"

She hadn't spoken to him since the previous evening. After his unproductive visit to the Virginia doctor's office on Tuesday, he'd dived deep into other possible witnesses. He and Brandon had contacted convention attendees, and when he'd called her last night with an update, he'd said they were striking out with every one. Some of the doctors genuinely didn't recognize the voice of the monster on the tape. Others, however, wouldn't listen at all; they just weren't willing to cooperate. Which made her wonder if someone had asked them not to.

Of course, that could just be the pessimist in her.

"Hello, Wyatt," she murmured. "Two Thursdays in a row. I'm honored." She wondered if he heard her insincerity, or her sarcasm. Frankly, she didn't know why she enjoyed jabbing at him, letting him know she wasn't exactly chomping at the bit to have him around. Maybe it was because she had once liked being around him a bit too much, and the feeling had never been reciprocated. Or because on that one night when she wondered whether it might be reciprocated, he had backed off so fast he might have sprouted wings and flown off the side of the cliff from the beach house.

Then she remembered the way he had left Sunday. The way he'd stormed out into the night, desperate to get away from her curious eyes, from her questions. From any responsibility to explain anything about himself to another human being.

And she realized why she was a little annoyed. Yes, she'd been sympathetic and she knew he had been horrified by the drunk at the restaurant. But part of her had really expected him to at least mention the incident, apologize for practically dumping her without a word. Yet he hadn't. He'd acted as though it had never happened. Which meant he had absolutely no intention of ever discussing the matter again.

"Hello, Lily," he replied evenly before glancing at Sarge. "Wally."

The army sergeant extended a hand, shaking Wyatt's firmly. Lily didn't know how the men knew each other, but she did know Wyatt trusted Devlin completely. The older man had made a comment or two that made it sound as though he'd known Wyatt from childhood, but he'd quickly clammed up whenever the subject skirted too close to Blackstone's sheltered past. She would bet Sarge was one of those people with some answers to the questions she wouldn't allow herself to ask.

"Good to see you again, son. We were just finishing up, but we can work out a little longer if you'd like to join in."

Wyatt managed a small smile and shook his head. "I'm afraid not."

The two men eyed each other steadily and, like Lily, the sarge realized Wyatt was not here to pay a social call. "Guess I'll run, then," he said. Turning to Lily, he added, "You're getting too good. Be ready for me to try out one or two new tricks on you next time."

"Anytime, anywhere," she said with a genuine smile. The man was a true friend. He'd helped her regain not only her physical strength but her mental strength as well. Because the more confident Lily became in her ability to defend herself, the more sure she was that she would, eventually, leave this place. Go and have that real life for herself.

"Let me walk you out. I want to get a cold drink, anyway," Lily said. She headed for the door, brushing past Wyatt, touching him ever so lightly, arm against arm.

Whatever that drink was, she didn't imagine it would be cold enough to wash away the small flash of heat still singeing her arm where it had brushed her former boss's. Nor to douse the confused warmth that arose when his eyes flared the tiniest bit and his handsome mouth opened on a surprised inhalation.

He'd felt the spark, too.

She led Devlin to the door, smiled her thanks, then closed and locked it behind him and headed for the kitchen. Wyatt had remained outside on the patio, but Brandon had come in. The refrigerator door was open, and he was half-visible behind it as he rooted around inside.

"Sorry, you won't find any Mountain Dew." As if he needed it. The young man was a cyclone of energy. She had often felt exhausted just watching him work in the office they'd shared.

"Don't need it. This'll do fine," he said, pulling out two bottles of water.

He tossed one to her. Lily caught it in midair, the condensation slick and cooling against her hot skin.

"Wyatt?" he asked, glancing past her at the doorway. "Want one?"

She hadn't needed Brandon to confirm Wyatt's presence behind her. Her whole body had grown tense and aware the moment he'd stepped inside off the patio. The very air had felt different as it parted and shifted around him. The subtle scent of his masculine cologne teased her nose and she felt warmth fill her cheeks.

Not embarrassed warmth, as she'd often experienced with the man in the old days. Rather, her body's warm, womanly acknowledgment of how he affected her.

"No, thank you," said that deep voice. "Lily, we need to talk to you."

Opening her bottle, she drank deeply of the cold water, then pulled out one of the kitchen chairs and plopped down onto it. "Phone broken?"

"It's serious."

She knew that. She'd known that from the minute she realized Wyatt had brought reinforcements on this visit. She'd known by the way her heart kept thudding at the look of undeniable concern in Wyatt's deep blue eyes.

This was bad. So bad, she'd needed to sit down to listen to it. She just hadn't wanted him to know she'd already realized that much.

"Okay. Shoot."

Wyatt and Brandon exchanged a look, then took seats with her at the table.

"After I left here Sunday night, what did you do between then and Tuesday night when I called you about my trip to Virginia?"

She tapped a finger on her temple, as if thinking about it. "Hmm, I had the girls over for a game of Bunco, and I performed in the local community theater's production of *Annie*, and I bought a round for the guys down at the bar." She managed to avoid rolling her eyes. "What do you *think* I did?"

He didn't rise to the bait, remaining on subject. "You stayed here, alone, no trips to the store, nothing?"

"Nothing. I did some shopping last week and had plenty of supplies."

"Any visitors? Was the sarge here on Monday?"

"No. Because of the holiday, we changed our schedule to Tuesday afternoon and today."

"But he called you Monday to do that?"

She shook her head slowly. "No, we arranged it last

Friday when he came. You must have been inside at the time."

His taut jaw grew even tighter and she wondered if he was going to crack his own teeth by clenching them so hard.

"Did you go for a walk on the beach? Any chance anybody drove by, saw you jogging, maybe waved?"

A low throbbing began in the base of Lily's skull as she shook her head. "No. And that's enough questions. I want to know why you're asking them."

He hesitated, exchanging another of those glances with Brandon. Then, with a low sigh, he admitted, "Because a long-distance truck driver from North Carolina was murdered and dismembered in a Pennsylvania hotel sometime between midnight Sunday and Tuesday morning. The coroner hasn't given us the time of death yet."

Not understanding what that could possibly have to do with her, she mumbled, "That's very sad, but what does it have to do with me?"

He thrust a hand through his thick hair, more visibly anxious than she'd seen him since those first days after he'd rescued her.

"Lily," he finally informed her, never looking away as he hit her with the rest of it, "your badge was found clutched in his bloody hand."

Jackie Stokes had known for weeks that something was up with her boss and her coworker Brandon Cole. But she hadn't even begun to imagine it might have anything to do with Lily Fletcher, her late friend. Now, though, she was beginning to wonder. Because today,

Brandon and Wyatt were both gone, and Lily was all anyone was talking about.

"Can you friggin' believe this?" Kyle Mulrooney snapped as he—as all of them—watched Tom Anspaugh and one of his goons dig through the box of personal effects from Lily's desk. They'd kept her things, since there was no one to give them to. And Anspaugh apparently knew it. He'd also demanded access to case files from any investigation she'd worked on.

"It's like watching a gorilla sort through a china tea set," Alec Lambert murmured. "The destruction doesn't matter, just finding whatever it is he's looking for."

Wasn't that the truth?

Anspaugh had shown up here a couple of hours ago, claiming the team—the Black CATs, as they thought of themselves these days—needed to hand over every bit of information they had on Lily Fletcher. When Jackie, who was again acting as supervisor in Wyatt's absence, demanded to know why, Anspaugh had snarled something obscene. He'd then handed her the phone, asking her if she wanted to call Deputy Director Crandall and question him directly, or if she just wanted to get out of his way.

She'd called, of course. Screw Anspaugh. Lousy little scumbag. None of them had ever gotten over how badly he'd messed things up with his Lovesprettyboys investigation, letting one of his own agents, as well as poor, sweet Lily, pay the ultimate price.

But Crandall had confirmed the other agent's story. Jackie had been told to give the man full cooperation. Considering Anspaugh had gotten slapped pretty hard over the balls-up in Virginia, she had to wonder just what it was he had that Crandall wanted so badly.

Maybe Wyatt knew something. Crandall seemed to think so, because he'd ordered her to get her boss in from wherever he'd gone off to and have him report to the DD's office by the end of the day.

Good luck with that. Wyatt was in Maine—he'd told her that much when she'd called him to tell him what was happening. And he didn't seem to give a damn that Crandall wanted him back.

"What's going on?"

Christian Mendez, who'd been with them for about a month now, walked into the office, having just returned from interviewing a witness in a murder-for-hire case they were investigating. The agent, with his sultry Latin looks, was good at talking to witnesses. As good as Alec had been before he'd gone so gaga over his new fiancée and seemed to lose any interest in flirting with other women.

Not that Christian flirted. Oh, no. He just steamed up a room enough with all that dark intensity to get any woman talking, if only to get him to stick around a little longer. If she were ten years younger and, of course, single, he would definitely have been someone she would want to keep around.

Good God, it wasn't always easy being one of only two women to work among several of the hottest men she'd ever seen. Even a happily married, settled wife and mom could occasionally be overcome by all the sexy testosterone heating up these offices.

"What are they looking for?" Christian prompted when no one answered his original question.

"We dunno. Dickhead's going through all of Lily's things," said Kyle, not looking away from the atrocity taking place in the next room. "Lily Fletcher's."

Christian probably hadn't needed the clarification. Jackie imagined that in the month he'd been here, the murdered agent's name had been mentioned a hundred times.

"Why?"

"That's what we'd all like to know." That came from Dean Taggert, whose brow was pulled down over a fierce glare cast directly at Anspaugh's back.

All of them were huddled in the hallway outside the conference room, which also served as the team's only storage closet. Boxes and files were stacked in all four corners, and Anspaugh was busily sticking his nose into every one of them. It was all Jackie could do to remain calm when the thickheaded bastard took the framed photograph of Lily's sister and her boy, which used to sit on Lily's desk, and slid it into a plastic evidence bag.

"Did you say they're investigating the Lily Fletcher case?" a woman's voice said. Anna Delaney joined them, having just returned from going over the ACES report on the computer used in the hit-man case.

"Not sure what the hell they're investigating," Jackie mumbled, not wanting to go into yet another explanation as every member of the team came through the door. She was too busy watching Anspaugh, making sure he didn't try to abscond with evidence or confidential files. Or any personal item of Lily's that he could never justify touching, much less taking.

"Maybe it's because of the hearing."

Jackie turned her head toward Anna. So did all the others.

"What hearing?"

The other IT specialist, as efficient and self-confident

as Lily had been unsure and quiet, who occupied Lily's chair and did her former job, lifted a brow. "You hadn't heard about the hearing? It's been on the news. I recognized the name immediately, of course, knowing the connection to Agent Fletcher and her family." She shook her head sadly. "Maybe it's just as well she didn't live to see the day."

Thoroughly distracted now, as was everyone else, Jackie stepped closer to the other woman and put a fist on her hip. "You know, I think you better start at the beginning and tell us exactly what it is you're talking about."

The color fell out of Lily's face in a rush, as if someone had pulled the plug on her every vein. Her mouth open in astonishment, she remained silent, having immediately grasped exactly what Wyatt was telling her.

Someone was trying to implicate her in a murder. Someone who had access to the FBI badge that had been lost when she'd been attacked all those months ago. Someone known as Lovesprettyboys. Wyatt had been tipped off to the situation by an old friend in Crandall's office and had immediately gotten Brandon to come up to Maine with him to see Lily.

"Tiger Lily, baby, are you okay?" Brandon scooted his chair closer, putting his arm around Lily's shoulders, his other hand on her clenched ones. He appeared ready to draw her into a comforting hug.

Wyatt suddenly had the urge to pick Brandon up by the front of his shirt and toss him through the patio door.

He resisted.

He had no business getting bent out of shape because another man's hands were on her, another man's arms about to draw her into an embrace. No reason for his body to tense and his breathing to grow labored just because Brandon was whispering soft, consoling words to her, treating her as delicately as a paper-thin seashell that sometimes washed up on the beach below. One that would break apart simply if touched the wrong way.

No business at all.

Yet knowing that didn't stop his temples from pounding and his teeth from slamming together in his mouth.

Then something surprising happened. Lily ducked out from under Brandon's arm, pulled back from him physically, almost imperceptibly shifting her chair an inch or two away. Though still pale, she didn't look distraught, or soft. In fact, her flinty-hard eyes were glued on Wyatt, any signs of dismay having vanished.

"What else?" she asked. "I know there's more."

Wyatt couldn't prevent a slight smile. Maybe it wasn't so surprising. Not from the Lily he now knew.

He didn't try to spare her. He didn't need to. "It's not the first murder."

"I only had one badge."

"Three other men have been brutally murdered in the past six weeks," he explained baldly. "All were lured to motel rooms by someone promising an encounter with a child."

Her eyes drifted closed for a moment, her lashes sooty black against her cheeks. That would, of course, hit her where it hurt, far more than the news that someone might be setting her up for murder.

"We don't have to go into all the details right now, do we?" asked Brandon, shooting Wyatt an annoyed look.

"Yes, you do," she said, opening her eyes again, calm and in control again, brave and forthright. Not to mention utterly magnificent.

Wyatt threw off the thought. "Each case had small clues, minor things, that pointed to you. The names of the nonexistent children were your loved ones' names. Their supposed backgrounds reflected your own. The e-mails worded like some of the communication you'd engaged in with 'Peter Pan' on that last case—the unsub used the term 'loves pretty boys.' It was all there."

"Making it appear I was still alive, out there, having turned into a vigilante, a rogue agent getting my revenge on anyone like the man who attacked me?"

"Exactly. And a flower was left at each scene. Last week's was a tiger lily."

She didn't flinch, didn't even suck in a breath of surprise. "Last week."

He nodded once, knowing how quickly her mind worked.

"Last week, right before you showed up here to check up on me?"

Brandon interrupted. "You have to believe us, Lily—we never actually suspected you. Not for one second. Neither of us thought you were capable of hurting anyone, of even considering doing something so violent."

She didn't even glance at the younger man; her attention remained strictly on Wyatt. Her brow lifted, her chin tilting up in challenge. "Is that true, Wyatt? You never suspected it of me, not even for one second?"

They had come way too far for him to lie. Besides, he didn't lie. Not if he could help it. Certainly not to people he cared about.

"Well?" she prodded.

Brandon shot him a warning glance, obviously still worried about Lily's fragile state.

Fragile? Maybe once. Not anymore.

Though the situation was incredibly grave, Wyatt couldn't help lifting one side of his mouth in a half smile. "Maybe for a second. Or two."

Lily didn't react for a moment, and then she actually grinned in return. "Thanks."

"You're welcome."

At that moment, Brandon got it. He saw. Wyatt almost felt sorry for the younger man, who suddenly sagged back in his chair, his jaw unhinged, surprise filling his face. He supposed it would be pretty shocking to realize you knew absolutely *nothing* about the woman you fancied yourself in love with.

Wyatt knew her, though. He knew her very well. And liked her all the more for it.

"So your little visit last weekend, you were investigating me, right?"

"Right."

"Seeing if I, poor little lost Lily, was a ruthless, cold-blooded killer." She didn't seem the least bit distressed by the idea. "All those conversations, those questions about whether I'd ever left here, about whether I could seek revenge. They were part of your investigation."

"Exactly."

"And?" she asked, almost beaming with approval that he had taken off the kid gloves. "What did you decide?"

He dropped all hints of amusement. Wyatt leaned forward, until his hands slid across the table to within a few inches of her own clenched ones, and his reply held absolutely no doubt. "That you're innocent. Not because you're not strong enough to do such a thing, but because you're so strong, you can rise above the base, human urge to."

Their stares locked. Held. In her blue eyes he saw the full breadth of her feelings—fear, worry, gratitude. And something more. A certain warmth, an intimacy that had been building between them for months, that they'd both fought so hard to ignore.

There would be no more ignoring it. Lily's seeking, searching stare promised that.

Unable to do anything else, Wyatt returned the stare, silently affirming it as well.

"Thanks again," she finally said.

"You're welcome again."

After another long stare, Wyatt glanced at the third person in the room, whom they'd almost forgotten. Brandon was watching them both intently. Though his mouth was slightly pulled down at the corners in a frown, he didn't appear angry. Merely a little disappointed. Because he'd seen the truth—that something was happening between Wyatt and Lily. Maybe it hadn't happened yet, but it was only a matter of time. Even Wyatt had begun to acknowledge that, if only in the deepest recesses of his brain.

"Thank you, too, Brandon," she said, finally turning her face toward the other man. "I really appreciate everything you've done."

The young man, sometimes a hothead, sometimes a computer geek, merely nodded. "I just want you to be happy."

"I will be. As soon as I get past this." She addressed Wyatt. "Give me the rest."

"Up until yesterday, nobody else had put these cases together. They were in three different states—the feds hadn't been called in, strictly local police. This was something only Brandon and I were investigating."

"I imagine the badge put an end to that."

"Oh, hell, yeah," Brandon said, having regained his usual cheery energy. "I don't know who you wronged in another life, babe, but the call ended up getting put through to Anspaugh."

She groaned audibly.

"And he is on the warpath, with the full support of the deputy director's office. He's going to use every resource he's got to find out if you survived."

Wyatt watched as Lily put a hand over her eyes and rubbed wearily. He honestly had to wonder whether she knew what she was in for. How ugly this was likely to get before it was over.

"If he finds out I'm alive, Anspaugh will try to crucify me for these murders."

Okay. She knew.

"It's not Anspaugh I'm worried about," Wyatt told her. "He might try to build a case, and he might even take you into custody. The bigger problem is the person behind all of this."

"Ahh." She wrapped her arms around herself, rubbing her hands up and down on her bare arms, as if suddenly chilled. "That's what he wants, right? To draw me out? He's got himself convinced I'm still alive, and was using these murders as a way to get the authorities to lead him right to me." Her voice lowered a bit. "To finish the job."

Wyatt shook his head, silently telling her she could trust him to make sure that didn't happen. He was about to open his mouth to say so. Before he could, a ringing interrupted.

"Sorry," Brandon said, tugging his cell phone out of his pocket. He glanced at the caller ID screen and frowned. "It's Jackie again. I asked her to update me on what was going on with Anspaugh and his goon squad searching our offices. I wonder if she and the rest of the team have found out about Lily's badge being at the crime scene yet."

"Don't say anything if she hasn't," Wyatt instructed.

Nodding, Brandon answered the call.

As Wyatt watched, Lily sucked her bottom lip into her mouth, as if truly surprised. At first, he figured it was because of the thought of Anspaugh actually investigating her. Then he wondered if it was simply hearing Jackie's name, knowing she was on the other end of that phone call. Of course she knew Jackie Stokes and the others were out there, living their lives, doing their jobs. But there was always that distance. Now her old life was intruding, a voice from the past speaking to a person who sat right beside her.

Brandon appeared to notice her discomfort. He rose, covered the mouthpiece with his hand, and murmured, "I'll take it in the other room."

"Be careful what you say," Wyatt replied, his voice just as low. Jackie might suspect the two of them were together, working on the mystery case she'd confronted him about a couple of days ago. Still, the less she knew, the better. For her sake, for the sake of all the rest of the team, plausible deniability was the way to go.

Lily reached for her half-empty water bottle and brought it to her full lips. Tilting her head back, she drank deeply. Every swallow emphasized the slender lines of her vulnerable neck, the smoothness of her supple skin. Jesus, was she really going to be hit with yet another nightmare by way of a murder investigation? How much did one woman have to endure in a lifetime?

She apparently noticed his sudden worry, because as she lowered the bottle, she said, "I'm fine. I'll get through this, just like I've gotten through everything else." Her voice lowered. "As long as I know I have people I can count on."

"You know you do."

"Okay. So maybe it's best that I just go in, give myself up. Now that I know the unsub's looking for me, that he's killed other people and left evidence that can be used to track him down, there's really not much point in me hiding anymore, is there?"

The very idea stunned him. "There's more reason than ever for you to stay here. You think I'm going to let you go back, watch Anspaugh make a big production out of bringing you in, then leave you exposed and unprotected for a psychopath to target?"

"What do you suggest, that I just stay here? Continue to let other people fight my battles?"

He opened his mouth to reply, but before he could, Brandon did.

"No, Lily. I don't think you're going to be able to stay here. I don't think you'll even consider it."

Wyatt and Lily jerked their attention toward the doorway, in which Brandon stood. He was tucking his phone into his pocket, staring at Lily's pretty face, his frown deep, his expression troubled.

"What is it?" Wyatt asked, slowly rising.

Lily rose as well.

"It's Jesse Tyrone Boyd," Brandon said, drawing out each syllable of the hated name, which Wyatt immediately recognized. His sympathy rang in his tone and shone in the sadness of his eyes. "His conviction has been overturned and he's been released from prison."

# Chapter 10

The last time Lily had been in Washington, D.C., had been on a brutally cold day in January when everything was dead and lifeless, and every resident burrowed inside except when forced out by necessity. Late summer in the nation's capital was an entirely different experience. People were out and about, jogging, pushing baby strollers, playing softball on the lawn at the National Mall. Tourists laden with cameras and shopping bags lined up to board their buses, SUVs jockeyed for the limited parking spaces, pigeons hovered over every park bench, and everything felt entirely, totally alive.

Including her.

She wasn't afraid. Even knowing someone was after her, she felt no fear at being back here on her old turf. D.C. had been home for most of her adult life, and wasn't far from Annapolis, where she had been born and had spent her entire childhood. Despite all the challenges that lay ahead, she felt good here. Connected. Her heart racing, she experienced no sense of foreboding, merely determination. Lily was ready to meet all challenges.

Starting with getting that son of a bitch who had killed her nephew back behind bars where he belonged.

They didn't know a lot of details yet, just what they'd read on a news Web site out of D.C. *Convicted Child Killer Released—New Evidence and Death of Star Witness Key to Case.*

Lily shook her head, still stunned at the whole crazy sequence of events. Some high-priced lawyer had gotten Boyd an appeals hearing. The article said there was some problem with the original prosecution, and some complete stranger had appeared out of the woodwork with an alibi. Those things, combined with Lily's supposed death, had prompted the court to let the man go and the DA had not commented on whether he intended to refile charges in the case.

As Wyatt had explained, he probably wouldn't without a witness.

She had come close to getting sick when Brandon had told them. The very thought of that degenerate being back on the street was enough to make her ill. It also made her wonder if she really could commit some of the violent acts Wyatt had described.

"You're sure we shouldn't just go straight to the DA's office?" she asked him as he drove across the Key Bridge. They had landed at Reagan and driven into the city to drop Brandon off at his place. Now they were headed to Wyatt's town house in Alexandria. With no home of her own to go back to, they'd all just assumed she'd be with Wyatt.

Brandon, she noticed, hadn't even suggested otherwise. In the hours since they'd sat in the kitchen of the beach house this afternoon, he seemed to have begun to drop the overprotective, lovesick act and started acting like the high-energy friend he'd always been to her. Because he'd noticed how she looked at Wyatt? Had he seen the depth of feelings in her eyes, heard the shuddery sighs she couldn't contain whenever their arms brushed or he touched her, however slightly?

She honestly didn't know how he could have missed those things. Nor did she think Wyatt had.

"No. We need to plan this, Lily. Figure out the right time for you to come forward. And it's not going to be until after I find a way to make sure Anspaugh, Crandall, and the others take your safety seriously. If they think you're a serial killer, that's not going to be the primary interest."

Being thought of as a serial killer. Who ever considered that happening in their lifetime? "You'll keep me safe," she murmured.

He didn't even sound worried as he replied, "I'll be on suspension and they won't let me anywhere near you."

Lily turned to glance out the window, not wanting him to see the sudden misery she felt. She'd cost this man so much. How on earth could he still want to keep taking care of her? Knowing he would not want to have that conversation now any more than he'd wanted to have it any other time she brought it up, she let it go. For now.

"They'll figure out that I'm innocent, Wyatt." *And I'll fight with everything I've got to make sure you don't get the blame.*

"Of course they will. But in the meantime, if you come forward, you're a sitting duck. If they don't arrest you, you'll be exposed and vulnerable. And if they do, well, you can't tell me you think Lovesprettyboys is just going to wait for you to talk about whatever you remember. The man is murderous and desperate. We know he has money and reach. It's not such a stretch to think of his finding a way to get to you, no matter where the bureau decides to lock you up. We have to think this through."

"Okay, you're seriously depressing me," she said. "I get it. No DA tonight. No anything tonight."

"Good. Let's just go back to my place, get settled, and work on our game plan. Boyd's not going to disappear in one night, not when he thinks he's totally in the clear."

Brandon had promised to come down in the morning so they could decide, as a group, how to handle telling the others on the team that she was alive. The last thing Lily wanted was to cause any of them more pain, and she had no idea how they would react.

There were other decisions to make as well, including *how* she should report to FBI headquarters. Should she go in with a lawyer? Go straight to Crandall's office? God knew there was no way she was putting herself in Anspaugh's hands.

Unwilling to sit back and do absolutely nothing while they figured out their next move, she also wanted to know what she could do to help in the investigation while she was stashed away in Wyatt's house. Brandon, he'd told her, had come up with other audio clips for her to listen to. That would occupy her for at least a little while tomorrow.

As for the rest? It all remained to be seen.

About the only thing they had decided for sure since Jackie's shocking phone call about Jesse Boyd was that Lily could no longer remain dead. Justice demanded that she do the right thing. No matter what it cost her.

"I was thinking I might try calling Boyd's defense attorney. I'd really like to know how she ended up with this case."

She rolled her eyes. "Like she'd talk to you?"

"She might," he said. Then he lowered his voice as if speaking to himself. "I suspect she could be very interested in talking to me."

"What do you mean? Why would she?"

He didn't reply, merely mumbling under his breath about how impossible it was that this could all be a coincidence.

The same thought had flashed through her head more than once. "It does seem pretty odd that Boyd lands some new high-powered attorney and gets out right around the same time somebody's trying to set me up for murder. Sounds a lot like a desperate person covering all his bases, finding me by fair means or foul."

No matter who got hurt. No matter what little child Boyd might target next.

Not that Lovesprettyboys would care. The unsub was a sociopath, not a classic pedophile at all. When they'd first discovered him, he'd been part of a violent virtual world, Satan's Playground, and offered to pay a fortune to see such violence performed against a child in real life. So the idea of a convicted child killer going free probably delighted him.

How such people could exist was beyond her. It seemed as though every time they caught one, another two took his place. That didn't mean she'd ever give up on catching them and putting them away. Especially Jesse Tyrone Boyd.

While the courts might think he didn't get a fair trial, she didn't for one minute think anybody really believed he was innocent. Especially not her. She'd seen Zach's little face through the window of the man's panel van. She'd seen his tags. And when she saw him in a lineup, she'd easily picked him out as the man who'd been lurking around the neighborhood in the days preceding Zach's kidnapping. The man Zach said had talked to one of his friends about a lost puppy.

*Why did you let him go back to that park, Laura? Why?*

She thrust the anguished thought away, focusing on the case. The things she could do something about. Not the past that was gone, out of reach, inalterable, and resolute.

"You know, Boyd's mother came up to me in the courthouse during the trial."

He took his eyes off the road long enough to give her a quick, worried glance.

"She was teary-eyed, and she came to tell me how sorry she was for what her son had done. The way he had destroyed my family, cost me everyone I loved." To this day, she couldn't forget the look on the woman's face when she'd admitted what her son had done. What he was.

How did a mother survive that?

She hadn't brought it up to be maudlin, or dwell on it, only to illustrate a point. "She is his only family, and she made it clear that when she listened to his testimony, she knew right away that he was lying. And had no doubt he was guilty. She cut him off then and there, said she would never be back."

"Meaning," Wyatt said, understanding immediately, "it is very doubtful he has family members on the outside paying for a new lawyer."

"Exactly."

"So who did?

"That's a very good question. And I suppose it's the reason you want to talk to this lawyer, Claire Vincent?"

"Yes."

"She won't tell you who she's really working for. She can't, can she?"

"No, I'm certain she won't. But I want to talk to her anyway. Call it my sixth sense. I have the feeling there's something to be learned there."

She didn't doubt Wyatt's sixth sense, having seen evidence of it more than once. Primarily on the night he'd found her on that cold, dark beach. Because the odds had been astronomical. By all rights, he should never have even ended up on the right beach, much less actually tracking her to the dune on which she'd fallen.

Oh, no, she didn't doubt Wyatt's inner voice.

"No harm in trying," she said.

They pulled up to his place, and Lily blinked. Once again, Wyatt's wealth was made clear. The graceful, mellowed-brick old town houses in this neighborhood, some four or five stories tall and a hundred years old, were a far cry from the one bedroom/one bath cubbyhole she'd called home last winter.

He definitely didn't afford it on an FBI agent's salary.

He glanced over, obviously saw her wide-eyed stare. "I grew up here and inherited the house from my grandparents."

Grew up here in his grandparents' house. Well, they were making progress, weren't they? That was about as much personal information as he'd revealed in the past six months. At this rate, she might actually learn his middle name sometime before she died of old age.

This enigmatic thing was sexy, but it was also frustrating as hell. As someone who'd been living a secret life for months, she suddenly found herself damn well sick of mysteries and enigmas.

She reached for the door handle and yanked it open, stepping out into his driveway before he'd come around to open the door, as he always did.

"You okay?" he asked.

"Fine. Just anxious to get this over with."

He said nothing, merely reaching into the backseat and grabbing the small suitcase she'd brought with her. Clothes bought and paid for by this man. Just like everything else she owned.

Maybe it was being back here, in the city where she'd been so independent, overcome all the hardships of her youth to get her degree, then her master's, and land a job with the FBI. She'd never let anyone hold her back; she'd paid her own way.

Until now.

Following Wyatt, she quickly glanced around the inside of the house as they walked through the back door into the kitchen. As she could have predicted, it was immaculate—dark cherry cabinets with glass-front doors, a swirling brown and black marble countertop, state-of-the-art appliances. Perfect. Just like the man who owned it.

Her apartment's Formica cabinets had been chipped, the handle broken off the one under the kitchen sink so she'd had to pry it with her fingertips whenever she'd needed to get trash bags or dish detergent.

His floors were a deep, rich hardwood, highly shined. Hers had been linoleum, with a burned spot in one corner where she'd made the mistake of putting the hot oven rack.

She so didn't belong here. At the beach house, it had been easier to pretend, because she'd been hiding. But she no longer wanted to hide. She also most definitely no longer wanted to be kept. "This needs to be over soon," she muttered.

Wyatt put her bag on the table, then turned to stare at her, his arms crossed over his chest as he leaned against the back of a chair. The immaculate suit didn't even shift out of place with the pose; it just moved with him as if it had been perfectly tailored. Well, it probably had. That was what perfectly tailored meant, right?

She shook her head.

"What is it?"

"Nothing," she said. "I'm just tired and ready to get on with things. Two weeks ago, I thought I'd be happy to never leave Maine. Your beach house. Now all I can think about is how desperately I want to get out of here, put all of this behind me, and go out there and actually live somewhere, in my own place, on my own dime, without being a drag on someone else all the time."

He straightened and stepped over, lifting a hand to her chin. Tilting her head up so she was forced to meet his eyes, he silently urged her to listen to him. He appeared understanding, not irritated that she was throwing his generosity right back in his face like some selfish teenager bitching because she got the wrong color iPhone for Christmas.

"Let's get one thing clear. I have more money than I could spend in my lifetime," he admitted. "My father was disgustingly rich, my mother's family pretty well-off also. And the day I turned twenty-five, I got the keys to a large trust fund."

Lily sucked in a breath, not because of the fact that he was a rich man, but because he was telling her so much, revealing more and more of himself.

"I hate the beach house," he added, almost gritting out the words. "And I don't particularly care about this one, beyond the good memories of my mother's parents and the fact that it provides a place to sleep at the end of every long, fourteen-hour workday. But I feel no attachment to anything, Lily. I put no value on things or on dollars."

Spoken like someone who had never lived without them.

"If you can't handle having someone else cover your bills for a few months, then when this is over, you can go back to work and start giving me twenty dollars a week to pay me back. Now, could we please get past the money issue? Because you're going to be sleeping in my . . ." He looked away, frowning as his words tangled in his mouth. "Under my roof, and I don't want to have this discussion again."

All the rest of his words fell away as she focused in on just one part of that speech.

Sleeping in my . . . what? *House* would have been the easy word, the natural one. But he hadn't said it. He'd stumbled on his own sentence and come up with a clumsy alternative. Which meant whatever that first instinctive thought had been, he hadn't been happy about it.

She knew. Of course she knew.

"*Am* I going to be sleeping in your bed, Wyatt?" she asked, needing to stop dancing around this thing that was between them. Needing to know if he felt it, too, and what they were going to do about it.

He hesitated for a split second. Then, with a groan that said he just couldn't help it, tilted her head back farther and bent to cover her mouth with his in a deep, hard kiss.

Lily parted her lips for him, hungry and excited. She licked at his tongue, tasted him, begged him silently for more, then demanded more. He met every thrust, sliding his hands up into her hair to cup her head. She tilted one way, he another, so their mouths could meld more perfectly.

He tasted as she'd thought he would—spicy and hot. Intoxicating. And he felt better than absolutely anything she'd ever experienced.

Then he ended it, slowly, disengaging a little at a time until their lips were barely brushing, then weren't touching at all. He stepped back, stared down at her, studying her face with something like shock in his eyes. She saw worry there, too.

"Don't you dare," she warned him, her voice shaking with intensity. "Don't you tell me you're sorry. Don't ask me if I'm all right. Don't you even think about it. And if you apologize to me, I'm going to show you firsthand how much I've learned from Sarge."

He closed his eyes, dropped his hand, and sighed heavily. "I'm not going to apologize for doing something I've wanted to do for a very long time," he finally admitted. "But that doesn't mean I'm exactly happy with myself for having done it."

He didn't even give her a chance to argue about it. Instead, he simply turned and walked out the door through which they'd entered, leaving her standing alone in the middle of his completely unfamiliar house.

Smiling.

\* \* \*

Jesse Boyd was a free man, out of jail, with his whole life to live. His wildest dreams had come true—he'd beaten the odds. When the lawyer had shown up at the prison to tell him he'd won his appeal hearing, he'd almost fallen over. He'd walked like a zombie through the prison discharge procedures, barely hearing the words or seeing the faces, scrawling his name over and over to a dozen different forms.

Then, donning the old clothes he'd been wearing at his original trial and clutching his few possessions, he'd walked out of that place for good. He hadn't spared a glance at anyone, not a single good-bye, silently wishing them all nothing but misery for what they'd done to him.

He was free to do anything, to go anywhere.

Only, he had nowhere to go. They had given him some money, barely enough to survive for a week or two. He'd used some of it to pay for a cheap hotel room the previous night, needing a little time to adjust to the strange sensation of freedom. But he couldn't stay longer, not when he didn't know how long he had to make his money last.

He'd asked his lawyer why he couldn't sue for wrongful imprisonment, win a million bucks like some other cons he'd heard about. She'd said he'd have had to actually be exonerated, not just had his conviction overturned. Greedy bastards. They got to fuck him over and he got 580 bucks and a pair of sneakers.

Jesse had been sure he could go back to his ma's house, which was where he'd headed Friday, after taking a bus down to Baltimore. Throughout the trip, he pictured their reunion. When she saw him at the door to her duplex in the old Dundalk neighborhood and learned he'd been freed, she'd know he was innocent for sure. She would welcome Jesse home by drawing him into her big arms and pulling him into the kitchen for a bowl of her famous crab soup. Her pudgy face would grow wet with tears of happiness. Then she'd lead him to his old room, kept just the way it had been while he was growing up.

But it hadn't worked out that way. She'd opened the door all right. Then she'd shrieked a little, made the sign of the cross, and slammed it closed in his face.

He'd knocked for five minutes, pleaded through the door that he was free, he hadn't broken out of jail, and she ought to turn on the news if she didn't believe him. She'd apparently called a neighbor instead. Because that fat fuck Mr. Watson from the other side of the duplex stepped outside onto the porch, butting his nose in where it didn't belong, like always.

"She don't want to see you, son," he said.

"I'm out," Jesse insisted. "They let me go. It's not like I escaped or anything. But she won't listen to me."

The front door finally opened. His mother peeked around the edge of it, smiling in relieved appreciation when she saw Mr. Watson. The man stepped back into his own doorway, but didn't close it, remaining right there in plain sight. Then Ma glanced somewhere behind the still mostly closed door and said something to another person who had to be in the tiny living room. "Just hush, now, it's okay. I'll step outside and be right back."

"Who you got in there?" Jesse asked, knowing his seventy-year-old mother would never be with a man. Then a curtain shifted in the front window, and he saw a kid's face peer out.

He tensed, a familiar sensation crawling up his body, from his toes all the way up his legs and throughout the rest of him. His mouth went dry, his throat tight. A buzzing started in his ears, as if a fly had gotten inside his skull and was whooshing around, trying to find a way out.

"Who's the boy?" he whispered.

"I'm babysittin' him." She planted herself in front of the door, crossed her arms over her big chest. "And you ain't comin' in."

How crazy was that? She didn't trust him around some neighborhood kid.

Such a cute little neighborhood kid.

He swallowed, wondering why he felt dizzy. Why he always felt this way when he saw some bright-faced boy, all grins and big teeth.

Seeing how closely she watched him, he forced himself to stand up straight and not let his eyes shift to peek at the window again. "Ma, they let me go. You gotta let me in," he said. He turned his back to Watson, who stood so close, probably able to hear every word. He acted as if he needed to be a bodyguard, protecting Jesse's mother from her only son.

"I know what you are. I know what you have always been. And you've set foot in my house for the very last time."

Shock made his jaw fall open. That was ugly, what he saw in her eyes. It looked like disgust. Maybe even close to hatred.

"But they let me go," he said weakly.

"Not 'cause you didn't do it, though." She stepped closer, until he could see the way the wrinkles had deepened in her face and the dark circles had imprinted themselves under her sunken eyes. She'd aged a lot more than two years. Lowering her voice, to keep Mr. Watson from hearing, she snarled, "Because you *did* do it. I don't care what they say on the TV, what the lawyers say—I know you and I know you're guilty."

Jesse started to cry, sniffling as though he were some damn little kid who'd been caught out doing something dirty. "No, Ma. No, I got a bum rush. It wasn't fair."

She lifted her hand and shook one quivering index finger in his face. "Don't say nothing more. I don't want to hear it. I don't want to see your face. Whoever let you out of that jail was crazy, because I know you ain't gonna be able to last long without hurting somebody again."

"I didn't hurt him!" he insisted, hearing the whine in his own voice. But it was true. He hadn't hurt him enough to kill him, at least, not on purpose.

That had been an accident. Just an accident. He wasn't a killer—he'd never murder anybody. Who could be blamed for an accident?

She stepped back inside for a moment, and when she came back out, she was holding a small plastic bag, thick with folded bills. She shoved it toward him. "Your money, all you had in your room and your account before you got picked up. I held on to it for you. Plus I put in every dollar I had in my purse. Now, get gone, boy. Just get gone. I'll keep praying for you—just like I pray for that little boy you killed. But prayers are all you're getting from me."

She slipped back into the house without another word, shutting the door again, slamming the bolts home, leaving him standing there on the porch. Alone. Rejected. Homeless. And completely loathed by the woman who'd given birth to him.

Anger flooded through him. Not at her; he couldn't be angry at her, not ever. But at the authorities who'd hunted him, who'd thrown him in that courtroom and dragged out that ugly trial that his ma had had to sit through. She'd been in the courtroom when that blond cunt had testified. She'd seen the pictures of that kid.

It was their fault he was in this mess. It should never have happened—that FBI lab was corrupt; his own lawyer had said it. He should never have had to go on trial. Should never have had to see that look of hatred in his own mother's eyes.

He staggered off the porch, wandering aimlessly down the street. Nowhere to go. Nobody who even wanted to know him. Jeez, he might just as well go back to the prison and give himself over to rape and beatings for the rest of his life. Or just die now.

Suddenly, a ringing sound intruded on his misery. He'd forgotten all about the cell phone Ms. Vincent had given him. It was in his pocket, untouched, since he hadn't had a single person to call.

He gingerly removed it, not even sure how it worked, then pulled it open. "Hello?" he said, cautious and tentative.

"Hello, Jesse."

The voice sounded strange, tinny and fake. Like one of those automated ones you got whenever you tried to call just about any customer-service number. "Who is this?"

"I am your benefactor, Jesse. The person who hired Ms. Vincent to represent you."

Reaching a covered bus stop, which was deserted, he ducked inside for privacy. "You heard, then? That she got me out?"

"I heard. Congratulations. How are you enjoying freedom?"

He kicked his toe against some gravel on the cement floor. "S'okay."

A pause, then the voice said, "I almost hate to tell you this, but there might be a problem. I have heard through some very reliable sources that the FBI agent who testified against you, the one whose body was never found, might not actually be dead."

Five minutes ago, Jesse had been ready to give up, to die or go back to prison. Now, though, when he thought of that woman, realized she might still be out there, sheer fear, combined with a healthy dose of panic, roared through him. He lurched back in the shelter, collapsing onto the bench, sucking in deep breaths. "This is some kind of joke, right?"

"I'm afraid not. I believe the authorities are seeking her out now, and expect if anyone will find her, it's her former colleagues. One Supervisory Special Agent Blackstone might even know where she is already."

Jesse pounded his head back on the wall of the stand. "This can't happen. Can't. Happen."

"Cheer up. I don't think it matters. Obviously she was wrong about your guilt, and now that you have an alibi, it really isn't an issue. At least, as long as that alibi holds up."

Fuck. The alibi from some guy he'd never even heard of, this Will Miller he'd supposedly been drinking with at the bar he'd never been to in his entire life? How well would that hold up if they tried to put the screws to him again, with that Fletcher bitch leading the way?

"Lucky for you, Mr. Miller remembered talking to you at the bar that night. It certainly wouldn't be good for you if anything happened to him. If it did, and Ms. Fletcher were to return, you could be in some very serious trouble." The person on the other end of the call suddenly *tsk*ed. "Or, well, I hate to even bring it up, but if this Agent Fletcher is a vengeful woman, things could be even worse."

Vengeful? Despite being slim and pale, the woman had looked ready to rip him apart with her bare hands from up there on the stand.

"I mean, she was an FBI agent, after all. Good with weapons, I suppose. And if she thinks you got off on a technicality, well . . ."

"Oh, God." He leaned over, clutching his stomach, sure he was gonna puke. "She might come after me. What am I gonna do?"

There was a long hesitation. Then his anonymous benefactor quietly murmured, "If this does come to pass, Mr. Boyd, I think there is only one thing you can do."

"What?"

Something clicked, like some kind of metal against the mouthpiece of the phone. And when the voice came back, it sounded different. Thicker. Almost seething.

"You have to get her before she can get you."

# Chapter 11

Wyatt spent most of Thursday night calling himself an idiot. All the promises he'd made himself, all the resolute certainty that what he felt for Lily was sympathy and protectiveness, and he'd let himself kiss her as if he needed her kiss to survive.

He wished he could regret it. He really did. But when he evaluated his most base response, his innermost reaction, it wasn't regret he found.

It was hunger.

Hell, maybe he did need her kiss to survive. Maybe he needed that warmth, that vibrancy, that keen mind, and the will that seemed to grow stronger by the day.

Maybe he did. That didn't, however, mean he should take it. Because he wasn't what she needed. Whatever she said about not regretting it, not wanting him to, and not needing to be protected, he was still her former boss, still the man taking care of her, still ten years older and a good deal more jaded.

Well, perhaps not that. Lily had seen things in the

past few years that could harden even the most tender-hearted person.

"She's not hard," he reminded himself as he sat outside on the back patio Friday morning, sipping the steaming cup of black coffee he'd just made. The enclosed courtyard behind the town house offered privacy and was lush with vines and vegetation that made it seem more like a secret garden than a backyard. He'd had the stone wall heightened and the plantings increased soon after he'd inherited the house, so now neither next-door neighbor could look down from a higher floor and see anything other than the top canopy of shady trees and flowering shrubs.

No, Lily was not hard. The strength she'd fought for, that stamina and will, hadn't come at the cost of her kindness and her good heart. Lily hadn't buried her former self to become the powerful woman she was today. She'd simply blended two parts, the old and the new, until an altogether different woman had been formed. Not the innocent girl she'd been long ago. Not the angry, scarred woman he'd known this past spring.

She was neither. She was both. She was so much more.

And she was walking out the back door toward him right now, wearing a short, silky bathrobe and carrying her own cup of coffee. Wyatt looked away, not liking the sudden flash of interest that had shot through him at the sight of her long bare legs, revealed nearly to the tops of her thighs. High enough for him to see the puckered flesh, the scars. Yet she wasn't self-conscious about it anymore, as if she knew there was nothing about her he could look at and find unattractive.

"Morning," she said, sitting opposite him. She smiled,

as if their tense evening hadn't happened. And it had been tense. After he'd come back into the house, they'd barely exchanged ten words beyond his telling her how to find her room.

He wondered if her sleep had been as restless as his.

"Good morning." About to ask her how she'd slept, he was interrupted by the ringing of his cellular phone, which sat on the table. He'd already spoken with Brandon this morning, and with Jackie, who had asked him if he was going to come in to deal with the increasingly furious Deputy Director Crandall.

Yes, he would, but not until he was ready to. Not until he knew what he was going to do with the woman watching him with sleep-heavy eyes from across the table.

He glanced at the caller ID and saw the name *C. Vincent* with a Virginia area code. "Boyd's attorney," he said, nodding in approval. He'd suspected the woman wouldn't be able to resist returning the call Wyatt had placed to her less than a half hour ago. Lawyers were nothing if not predictable, and she was probably strutting her stuff over her big win in appeals court. The chance to throw that win in the face of an FBI agent—so often the enemy in a criminal trial—would probably be irresistible.

Placing his finger over his lips to instruct Lily to remain silent, he flipped the phone open. "Blackstone."

"Hello, Agent Blackstone, this is Claire Vincent. I just arrived in my office and was given a message that you called."

"Yes, I did. Thanks for returning the call." He winked at Lily. "I wasn't sure you would."

The woman on the other end of the line laughed softly.

"Oh, don't be silly. I'm always happy to talk to law enforcement." Her laugh ended abruptly. "Especially when they do me such enormous favors."

He sat straighter in his chair. "Favors?"

"Of course. If not for you, my client Jesse Boyd might still be sitting in his prison cell."

Wyatt slowly rose to his feet, tucking the phone into the crook of his neck. He lifted his coffee mug and walked to the edge of the patio, sipping slowly, waiting for the lawyer to explain.

"You are calling about Jesse, aren't you?"

"I am."

"I'm not surprised. It must be difficult for you. I mean, you must know that your exposure of the shenanigans in the FBI crime lab couldn't have helped my client any more than if you'd gotten a signed confession from another suspect."

He lowered his mug to his side, closing his eyes. This was what he hadn't wanted to hear, but what he'd feared he would discover from Boyd's attorney. The details hadn't been laid out in the article. It had said only that there had been some problems with the original case against the man. Problems involving evidence and, of course, the loss of the witness.

"The fact that the victim's aunt was your employee didn't hurt, either. But the real icing on the cake was you reporting that evidence tampering when you did. I mean, if you'd blown the lid off that a few months later, I might not have had as much legal maneuvering room. As it was, the timing was just close enough for the judge to buy it as a reason to throw out the evidence."

An almost tangible wave of red washed over his vision and a vicious headache began to pound in his brain. Each thud of his pulse ratcheted it higher until the pressure felt likely to blow through his temples.

"Can't imagine how tough it must be for you, since Fletcher worked for you. Thank God she's not alive to know your whistle-blowing helped get the guy accused of killing her nephew off the hook."

The woman's chipper voice assaulted him with every syllable. No, he hadn't been taken completely by surprise. A tiny part of him had worried that his actions might have had something to do with this case.

He had long ago accepted the fact that, by doing what he had done, reporting what he knew, he could be costing the convictions of some pretty horrific criminals. That knowledge had kept him up night after night, racking his brain, trying to find some other way. In the end, there had been no other way. He was an officer of the law surrounded by lawlessness. He'd done what he had to do, fully prepared to accept all consequences.

*But not this one.*

Jesus, not this one. He did not want to put the phone down, turn around, and admit the truth to Lily.

"Now, is there something I can actually help you with, Agent Blackstone? Or did you simply call out of morbid curiosity?"

Wyatt pulled his thoughts together, focusing only on getting information. Not on past cases, not on old mistakes. Only on now.

"I'm curious," he said, wondering whether she could hear the tightness, the barely controlled anger in his voice, "about how you got involved with the case."

The woman didn't answer.

"I mean, you weren't the original attorney of record. Who brought you into the case at this late date?"

Ms. Vincent sounded a little less amused and a lot more cool when she answered. "I am not at liberty to discuss my clients. You know that."

"I'm not asking you to. I'm simply curious. From what I remember, Boyd doesn't exactly come from a wealthy background. He couldn't afford more than a public defender at the original trial."

"I repeat, I'm not at liberty to discuss my clients, nor who's paying their bills. Now, if you'll excuse me, I am due in court this morning. Good—"

"One more thing," he interjected smoothly. "I was wondering, since I haven't seen your name in any local cases, where your practice is located."

A brief hesitation said she was considering whether to respond. The question was a perfectly innocuous one, though Wyatt very much wanted to know the answer. Finally, as if realizing he could get the information if he dug for it, anyway, she admitted, "My firm is located in Williamsburg, Virginia, Agent Blackstone. Now, I really must go. Good-bye."

Brandon lived close to headquarters, so rather than taking the Metro down to Alexandria first thing in the morning, he went to the office first. He had something he needed to retrieve.

As soon as he got there, though, Jackie waylaid him, pulling him into her office before he could even get close to his. "Anspaugh's here again," she explained as she softly closed the door behind him. "And he's been barking your name since yesterday. The minute he sees you, he's going to want to question you."

"Does he have a warrant?" he snapped.

"Get real. You know you can't refuse."

Right. Which meant he better make sure he remained scarce so Anspaugh never got the chance to ask.

"Where's Wyatt?"

"At home, as far as I know," he replied.

"Crandall has called twice and he sounds like he is going to shout his office walls down if Wyatt doesn't show up this morning. He calmed down about yesterday when I forwarded him Wyatt's actual airline itinerary, proving he'd gone up to his place in Maine, and couldn't come in. But that also means he saw the trip was for one day only and he was coming back last night."

Brandon smiled. Forwarding the itinerary as a way to get Crandall off their backs for a day had been his idea. It had, however, as Jackie had just reminded him, bought them only one day. Which wasn't enough.

He and Wyatt had already been on the phone this morning, and they'd both agreed they needed more evidence before they allowed Lily to turn herself in. Evidence in both cases—to show that not only was she not the lily killer, but somebody else was setting her up to take the fall. And that she was in very real danger.

They needed time. They also needed help. Which was why he was about to take one of the biggest gambles of his life.

"Jackie, do you have some sense about what's going on around here?" He stared at her directly, letting her know he was done covering up, skirting around the real story.

"It involves Lily."

"Yes, it does."

Jackie lifted a shaking hand to her throat. "You know what happened to her."

He nodded once. But before he could say another word, the door to her office burst open. Kyle Mulrooney stuck his head in and said in a loud whisper, "Anspaugh heard somebody say you were here, Cole, and he's looking for you. He's in Alec's office right now, but Alec won't be able to stall him for long. Get outta here unless you want to be questioned all day."

No, he couldn't afford that. Lily couldn't afford that, either.

"My office is next in line. I'll try to hold him up, too," the gruff, older agent said, shooting him a conspiratorial look. It was as if all the other team members knew Brandon was up to something, and they trusted him enough to cover his ass without asking a lot of questions.

He had never been more thankful to work with this team, these people, than right now. He only hoped every one of them didn't hate his guts when they found out he'd helped Wyatt cover up the truth about Lily for so very long.

After Kyle ducked back out, Brandon strode toward the door, peering out into the hall. Anspaugh's blustery voice was easily heard from down the hall, two doors past his own office.

It was incredibly risky, but he wasn't leaving here without what Wyatt had asked him to get. Namely, the audio files from the other medical conventions that he'd been working on until yesterday's impromptu trip to Maine.

Before he left, he grabbed Jackie's arm. She was watching him, wide-eyed, tense, and silent. "Come to

Wyatt's when you can," he insisted. "Just come and you'll understand."

Then he checked the hallway again, dashed down it as quickly as he could, and ducked into his own office. The audio files were backed up on a flash drive. Considering a lot of his stuff had been gone through, he only hoped Anspaugh had been as inept in his search as he was at everything else.

The voices moved closer, out in the hall. Then he heard Kyle Mulrooney ask Anspaugh to step into his office on some pretext. He was almost out of time.

Spying the drive still sticking out of his CPU, Brandon yanked it free, breaking every one of his own rules about how to handle his backups. He shoved it into his pocket, then, still certain the voices were coming from inside the next office, dashed out of his own. He didn't turn around, didn't even hesitate; he simply hurried to the main doors of the suite and burst through them into the outer corridor.

"Secret Agent Man," he told himself with a laugh as he hurried toward the elevators. "Running away from your own damn desk. Pathetic."

He'd wanted to do fieldwork, wanted to get away from the lab and the computers and see some action. Well, now he was seeing it. Hiding from an idiot like Anspaugh—it was fricking embarrassing.

But a little embarrassment he could handle. He only hoped it didn't end up costing him his job altogether.

Or landing him in jail.

Brandon looked like a kid playing a dangerous game when he showed up at Wyatt's later that morning. Lily almost found herself laughing as he described his game of hide-and-seek with Tom Anspaugh. She knew the game could have had very serious consequences if he'd been caught out, but couldn't deny she would have liked to see Anspaugh's face when he realized he'd been misled.

"You rule breaker," she said, shaking her head and eyeing him with affection.

He dramatically threw himself down on the lounge chair, which stood beside the patio table. "God, I need a drink. All this clandestine stuff is giving me the jitters."

"I think it's your hyper personality that gives you the jitters."

"Hey, I'm not hyper." He shot her a wide grin. "I'm just exciting."

This time, she didn't control her laughter. She let it spill from her lips, so happy to have Brandon flirting with her, acting completely at ease, like a playful little brother, that she just couldn't help it.

His happy smile widened when he saw he'd made her laugh. And when it faded, he reached for her hand, squeezed it, and said, "It's good to have you back, Tiger Lily."

Thoroughly relieved he'd gotten over whatever kind of feelings he'd thought he had for her, and gone back to being the adorable, roguish player she knew him to be, she squeezed back. "It's good to have you back, too."

"If you two are finished, we have work to do."

She hadn't even heard Wyatt return from the house, and he nearly growled the words. He'd been in an awful mood since that lawyer had called, barely meeting her eye, not wanting to even have a conversation until after Brandon arrived. Now he looked even more irritated.

It didn't take a genius to figure out why. He'd been

kicking himself for kissing her, and tried putting up that wall between them afterward. Now, though, he was afraid someone else might be going around it.

It almost made her laugh again, the idea that Wyatt might think she would prefer Brandon. Men were such strange creatures. He wanted her but wouldn't take her. Yet he didn't want her with anyone else, either.

When, she wondered, would Wyatt realize he was falling in love with her?

"Are you ready to listen to the new clips?" he asked, not meeting her eye.

"I suppose."

For some reason, since the moment Wyatt had finished his call with that scumbag Boyd's attorney—who, judging by whom she took on as a client, had to be pretty scummy herself—he'd been anxious for her to listen to the audio clips Brandon had brought down. The speakers had been recorded at the same annual medical convention she'd listened to before, only one year previously. He hadn't said why it was so important, just that something the lawyer had said made it even more imperative that she listen again for the voice of the man who had attacked her. With any luck, he'd attended the previous year as a speaker. That was the hope, anyway. Then they'd have his identity.

She was due for some luck. Right?

"I've uploaded the files off the flash drive onto your laptop," Brandon said, sitting up in the chair. "Whenever you're ready, Lily."

"Are you sure you don't want to go inside to make sure there are no outside noises distracting you?" Wyatt asked.

"Now that I know exactly who I'm listening for, I

don't think I'll miss him even if your next-door neighbor decides to jackhammer his driveway."

She'd never forget that voice. Never.

Lily scooted close to the table, sipping from the glass of iced tea she'd poured for herself when she'd gone in to change her clothes. Coming outside in a short bathrobe might not have been a big deal with Wyatt, but she wasn't nearly as comfortable with Brandon or anybody else.

When, she wondered, was he going to realize *she* was falling in love with *him*?

Oh, yes, falling so hard. This was nothing like the silly crush she'd once had on the man. It was no longer about being dazzled by someone smart and handsome and mysterious. She wasn't awed by him anymore; she'd become his equal. And the way he'd acknowledged that more with each passing day—how she'd changed, how she'd strengthened—had made her fall for him even more.

She no longer doubted she was woman enough for him. She doubted only whether he'd let her be.

"Okay, let's do this," she said, forcing all the crazy personal thoughts out of her head. There was still a long road to travel before she could think about any kind of future, a life with Wyatt, or one without him. For now, she just needed to focus on staying alive.

Wyatt handed Brandon a sheet of paper he'd carried out from inside. He'd gone to check something on the Internet, and he'd returned with a list of the medical workshops presented two years ago. "Go right to number nine," he said, putting the paper on the table. He tapped his finger on the line in question. "This group workshop."

Lily glanced over, catching sight of the first speaker's name. "Alfred Underwood . . . Why does that sound familiar?"

Wyatt remained standing behind her, blocking out the sun with his broad frame. "The woman whose car was stolen—Dr. Kean? Her maiden name was Underwood. Alfred is her father."

Lily gasped in surprise. "You said you didn't suspect her!"

"I don't suspect her of being involved in your kidnapping. But I think she and her sister-in-law might be hiding something. Why would two women who strongly dislike each other stick together to cover up for someone unless it was a member of their own family?"

With all that had gone on in the past forty-eight hours, Wyatt hadn't had time to tell her everything about his interview with the surgeons, but she didn't think he'd have kept such a tidbit from her if he'd suspected before now. The only thing she could think of that could have led him in this direction was this morning's phone call.

"What did the attorney tell you?" she asked.

He didn't seem surprised that she'd put it together. "She told me her office is located in Williamsburg."

Interesting. But certainly not a stop-the-presses revelation. "We knew Lovesprettyboys was in that area back during the initial investigation. That's why the stakeout was conducted there. So why do you think the attorney might be specifically linked to Dr. Kean or her family?"

"Call it a hunch. I had some misgivings when I left the office Tuesday."

"I trust your hunches more than I trust most people's studied findings."

"Ditto," said Brandon.

"Hearing the attorney's location just made me a bit more suspicious and I wanted to check a few things out." He reached into the inside pocket of his suit jacket and pulled out a small stack of folded pieces of paper, handing her the top sheet. On it was a printed screen shot from a Web page, one of those doctor report-card sites, and it was focused on Dr. Alfred Underwood. He had been sued for malpractice twice, which, in his line of work, probably wasn't a bad record.

"Look who represented him," Wyatt said.

She did, and felt absolutely no surprise when she saw Claire Vincent's name. "You really ought to patent your hunch method."

"It gets better." He handed her the next sheet. This time, the page was a printout from an online newspaper article. Wyatt had cropped out most of the text to focus only on the photograph, a woman identified as the attorney Claire Vincent herself.

"She might be attractive if she got the stick out of her ass," Lily muttered, predisposed to disliking the woman intensely.

"And got rid of the awful hairstyle and glasses," Wyatt agreed. "She's rather distinctive, isn't she? I recognized her immediately when I saw the photo."

Lily tilted her head in sheer surprise. "You've met her in person?"

Shaking his head, he explained cryptically, "No. Just held a door for her."

"Must have been a pretty impressive door."

His eyes glittered as he dropped the next bombshell. "It was the door to the Eastern Virginia Plastic Surgery

Center. Ms. Vincent was coming in just as I was leaving the other day."

"Bingo," Lily whispered, realizing why he was so confident that this whole case was somehow connected to Dr. Kean and her family. It all made sense now.

Someone in that practice had gotten the family's trusted attorney to work on Jesse Boyd's appeal and there could be only one reason why.

They were getting close—she could feel it right down to her very core.

"Ready?" Wyatt asked. When she murmured her assent, he nodded at Brandon. "Go ahead."

Brandon clicked the touch pad to start the clip, skimming through the introductions to the meaty part of the workshop, when the actual speakers all got their turn at the microphone. Lily listened intently as the first one began educating his audience about the most recent procedures in sucking the fat out of people's posteriors. *Charming.* And his pompous, older-sounding voice was utterly unfamiliar.

"Not him?" Wyatt asked, frowning.

Almost feeling as though she'd disappointed him, she slowly shook her head.

"Continue." He bent over the back of her chair, his hand on her shoulder, listening along with her to the next speaker. This one sounded younger, forthright, and brusque. And, again, was no one she'd ever heard before.

Wyatt's hand tightened on her shoulder, not a lot, just enough to indicate his rising tension. "Keep going. We're not finished yet."

Lily nibbled on her bottom lip, leaning so close to

the laptop's speakers, her hair brushed the screen. Her heart pounded furiously. Wyatt seemed so sure. She almost held her breath as the next speaker began. Then disappointment made her release it in a gush.

"No," she said after the third man spoke only a few words. He sounded young and even a little flirtatious. Not the cold, arrogant voice she remembered. "It's not him. None of them are him."

Brandon sank back in his lounge chair, muttering a curse. Wyatt straightened and turned away, crossing his arms and tilting his head down, as if studying his feet. Though he appeared disappointed, he certainly didn't look thrown. Nothing ever really threw the man for long.

"A miscalculation, then," he said, sounding thoughtful. "I don't believe in coincidence, of course. I still strongly believe Dr. Kean and her family have something to do with this and that they brought that attorney into Boyd's case. But who . . ." He shook his head, visibly frustrated. "I'm sorry I got your hopes up."

"Don't apologize to me," she said. "Not for anything, not ever. I intended to listen to clips from every workshop, anyway. This just knocks one out of the way. We'll figure it out."

He nodded absently, rubbing his clean-shaven jaw.

"Hey, there a party going on back here?" a woman's voice suddenly called, shocking all three of them into near immobility. "Nobody answered out front, so I decided to come around."

Lily didn't have to turn completely around to recognize Jackie Stokes, who had opened the gate at the side of the house and stepped into the courtyard. Her heart started to pound, and on the table, her hands clenched into tight fists.

*Please don't let her hate me.*

Jackie, who still stood just inside the gate, suddenly froze. Her keys, which she'd been holding in one hand, slipped unnoticed from her grasp, landing on the flagstone walkway.

She hadn't even gotten a good look at Lily yet; from where she stood, she couldn't have seen more than her profile. But it had apparently been enough.

"Oh my God," the other woman whispered. She appeared in shock, her mouth open in confusion, her eyes wide and quickly filling with tears. "Is it you? Is it really you?"

Lily pushed the chair back and rose, turning to face the woman who'd become so close to her in the months they'd worked together. "It's me, Jackie."

They stared at each other from about a dozen steps away, not moving for a second, as if Jackie needed to give her brain a chance to catch up with what her eyes and ears were telling her. Then, with a shriek, she cried, "Lily!"

Flying across the courtyard, Jackie threw her arms around Lily, hugging her tightly enough to cut off her circulation. "It's you, it's you, it's you," she kept whispering, stroking Lily's short hair, wetting her cheek with her tears. "Oh, thank you, Jesus."

Lily was crying, too, by the time Jackie released her and stepped back to stare her in the face. Jackie might be angry when she found out Lily had been hiding all these months, but at least for a few minutes, her friend had made it clear that she was very happy Lily was alive.

Offering Jackie a tremulous smile and reaching for

the other woman's hand, she drew her over to where Wyatt and Brandon stood, watching silently, shoulder to shoulder.

"If you're going to thank somebody, these two would be a good place to start. Because they saved my life."

# Chapter 12

The private investigator called at eleven a.m. Friday. It seemed far too early for news, but there was always hope. "Do you have something?

"You could say that," said the PI, who called himself Jonesy, an ex-cop who'd been fired for roughing up suspects. Though obviously an alcoholic, with the spider veins on his nose, the sloppy clothes, and the bright red cheeks to prove it, Jonesy was good at what he did. And, most important, discreet. "Easiest job I ever took."

He sounded as if the case was solved. Was it really possible? After such a short time, just twenty-four hours since he'd been put on the job, had he really come up with a lead on Lily Fletcher? There had been no doubt the woman would come crawling back to D.C. when she heard the news about Boyd, but *this* soon? It seemed almost too good to be true.

"You discovered something about Agent Fletcher?"

"You could say that."

"Tell me everything."

The man made a smacking noise as he cracked his gum, which seemed to be the second-most frequent item in his foul mouth, after the lip of a beer mug. "I been sittin' outside that Blackstone guy's house since last night. Told ya I saw him pull up with a black-haired woman, who spent the night."

"And I told you, I'm not interested in Blackstone's girlfriends. I hired you to follow him in case he goes to meet up with Fletcher." Or even to arrest her, a strong possibility. If Lily was ready to come back to life, whom else would she trust to bring her to the FBI building than her former boss? And wasn't she in for a surprise when her former supervisor picked her up and informed her she was a suspect in four murders?

Blackstone was good, his team's reputation strong. Even if Lily didn't turn herself in, they would be on her tail by now, considering she'd been well and truly exposed as a murderous vigilante. With Wyatt Blackstone's reputation as a scrupulously honest, by-the-book straight arrow, he'd bring Lily in the minute he located her.

It would be easier to take the woman out before she was in FBI custody, but if it had to be done afterward, there were ways.

"I'm getting there," Jonesy said, his voice puffed up with self-importance, as if he knew he had something good.

Maybe he did. Maybe this really was all going to be over with very soon. With Lily taken care of, it would just be a matter of cleaning up a few loose ends, like Jesse Boyd and Will Miller. And, perhaps, Jonesy. Then life could go back to normal and the infuriating worrying could stop.

"So I stay up the block in my car all night long. This morning, this young guy shows up—one of the agents in the file you sent me. Cole."

Interesting that the younger agent would show up at his boss's house on a workday. Why hadn't Blackstone gone into the office?

"I try to inch a little closer. See his neighbors leave for work, both of 'em, and slip into the backyard on the right. Blackstone, the blond dude, and the woman are outside on the patio talking. The wall's real high, so I can't see 'em, but I hear their voices. All three of 'em."

"Could you hear what they were saying?"

"Nah, nothing specific. But a few minutes later, this other one shows up. Good-looking black woman wearing a dark pantsuit. Obviously another fed."

Special Agent Jackie Stokes. Her picture lay on the desk, part of the complete dossier on Blackstone's team.

"She tries the front, gets no answer, then comes around to the back. I edge as close as I can get, hoping to see or hear something when she goes in the gate."

He hesitated, probably for dramatic effect. *Fool.* There was no time for these games. Impatience sparked an angry prompt. "Well? Tell me the rest, now!"

"Okay, okay. The woman, she goes in, but she stops right there with the gate open. Then she kinda squeals. She calls out a name. A woman's name. I risked taking a peek, and I see her running toward the black-haired woman, giving her a big hug, the two of 'em sobbing their faces off."

"You can't mean . . ."

"Yep. That's exactly what I'm telling you. The name she calls out? I heard it clear as a bell. It's Lily."

"Good God."

It was true. Lily was back.

This validated everything, especially the sixth sense that had been whispering for months that she was out there somewhere. Everything that had been done had been worthwhile and the right thing to do. The confirmation should have felt good, but there would be no time to feel good until Lily Fletcher was dead and gone, for real this time.

The biggest surprise of all of this? Lily was with Wyatt Blackstone. No-nonsense, scrupulously honest Wyatt Blackstone, who, according to rumor, had let a number of other agents, and friends, go down when he'd seen some illicit behavior in the FBI crime lab.

Mr. Squeaky Clean was hiding a suspected serial killer. A woman who'd faked her own death.

*Her lover?* There had been no indication of that in any of the background checks.

Merely her protector, then? Her white knight?

This made things a little more difficult. Because while there were always people to be bought, bribes to be offered for a guard to look the other way while a suspect was being transported, there was no weak link in Blackstone's group. Not a one. Especially not the man himself.

If she was under his protection, Lily would be very difficult to get to.

There were two obvious options. Call in an anonymous tip to another FBI agent. Perhaps one who had an ax to grind against Blackstone—there were, reportedly, quite a few. That might kill two birds with one stone, resulting in Lily's arrest and Blackstone being tossed on his ear, stripped of his credentials, his title, his weapon.

A good choice. But also a risky one. Killing Lily while she was in federal custody had always been the last resort. A better one was getting at her now.

"You still there?" Jonesy asked.

"Sorry. Yes. Listen, you've done an excellent job. I just have one more for you to do."

"What's that?"

"I want you to stay there and try to get a photograph of Lily Fletcher. Do you think you can do that?"

"Might not be easy. That wall is high as shit."

"It's worth twice what I'm paying you now."

He whistled. "Double, huh?"

"That is generally what *twice* means."

Jonesy obviously didn't understand sarcasm. "Oh, sure. Okay, you got a deal. Gotta go."

The man hung up without another word, which was fine. Hopefully it meant he was returning immediately to do what he'd been asked to. Which meant a picture of Lily should soon be forthcoming. Even without a firm plan in mind, the photograph was a good idea. If Lily's looks had changed too drastically, she might not be recognizable even to someone who knew her well. Someone like, say, Jesse Boyd.

Because he was, of course, option two. Jesse was desperate to avoid going back to prison. The man seethed with hatred and rage toward the woman he felt had helped send him there.

By now, he should also be in something of a panic about his personal safety. The seed had been planted. Boyd had to be wondering if his victim's aunt would come gunning for him now that she knew he was free.

Hmm. There might be a way to make that more plausible, more frightening. A way to convince Boyd his nemesis was coming after him, going through whomever she had to in order to gain her revenge. Starting, perhaps, with the man who'd given Boyd the false alibi?

"Will Miller." His address and phone number were a few key clicks away.

How frightening would it be for Boyd to hear his anonymous alibi had been murdered? For a man like Boyd? A coward? Probably utterly terrifying. And a frightened man was a desperate man. In that state, he would practically be a lethal weapon.

It merely remained to point that weapon in the right direction, and see if he could get past the protective circle Wyatt Blackstone had placed around his vulnerable young lady friend.

Jackie Stokes was one of the most coolheaded, intelligent people Wyatt knew. So for her to have to sit in a chair and put her head between her knees to keep herself from passing out said a lot about how she was taking Lily's miraculous reappearance. So far, she'd been focused on her happiness. But he knew her well enough to know the questions would begin firing out of her mouth any second now.

"I can't effing believe this; I just can't. This only happens in movies, doesn't it? Is this for real?"

"I'm so sorry, Jackie," Lily said. Her voice was tremulous, as if she, too, knew Jackie would transition from shock to raging curiosity any second now. She sat close to the other woman, one slim hand on Jackie's shoulder, repeating the apologies he knew came straight from her heart. "I can't tell you how sorry I am to have put you through such pain. I know you mourned for me, grieved for me."

The words gave Jackie something else to focus on, and she shot straight up in her chair. On came the curiosity, and some of the anger he'd anticipated.

"You know. You *know* that. How do you know that?" She glanced up at Wyatt and Brandon, her dark eyes accusing. "Because they told you?" Rising to her feet, she stalked toward Wyatt, sticking her index finger out. "How long have you known? How long have you kept this from the rest of us?"

He didn't even try to downplay it. "Since the night of the funeral."

"The funeral," she whispered. "Lily's funeral." She closed her eyes briefly, obviously remembering that day, that whole vivid time. When she reopened them, he noticed some of the fire had left them, but not that obvious need to know the truth.

"And you?" she asked Brandon.

"The same," he said.

"Seven and a half months. You've known all this time." She slowly turned and looked at Lily, walking over and brushing her fingers in the soft black hair. Apparently noticing the scars on her head, she bent over and, like she probably did with her own kids, gently brushed her lips over the top of Lily's damaged ear, as if wanting to kiss away the pain. "My God, what did he do to you, child? What did that madman do?"

Jackie had reached the right conclusion, her quick mind filling in the pieces without needing them all laid out for her.

"Did *he* have you that whole time? Between the night you disappeared and the night of your, uh, funeral?"

Lily nodded once, and tears rose to Jackie's eyes, spilling from them onto her pretty cheeks. The woman was about as strong as they came; the one place she was vulnerable was when someone she loved got hurt.

She slowly returned to her chair. "Okay. Tell me everything."

Wyatt began, going over every detail he could recall, from the minute he'd picked up the phone and heard Lily's voice, until this very morning. Brandon added bits here and there, reiterating, as often as he could, that they hadn't involved anyone else on the team strictly for the agents' own good, because the others all had more to lose.

Lily spoke only once, to set the record straight. "I asked them not to tell a single soul, Jackie. I wasn't . . ." She swallowed hard, twisting her hands in her lap. "I wasn't well for a time. Physically or emotionally. Please, don't blame Wyatt and Brandon—they were only doing what I asked them to."

Jackie dropped an arm over Lily's slim shoulders and tugged her to sit even closer. "Honey, with what you went through, I'm still shocked, and very grateful, that you had the ability to call Wyatt."

"Me, too," said Wyatt.

"Don't you ever apologize, to me or to anyone else, for doing what you had to in order to stay alive and get well. Just in case you're worried about it, everybody else on the team is going to feel exactly the same way." Jackie hugged Lily again, as if she wanted to keep her close. "I'm so glad you're alive."

After that, Lily remained silent, as if it was better to just hear her story succinctly told by someone else than to have to repeat all the ugly details herself. Wyatt tried to gloss over some of them, like the extent of her injuries, and some of the more brutal methods her kidnapper had used, but Jackie's glassy eyes said she wasn't fooled.

Finally, when he was through, Jackie blinked those tears away and thought for a long, silent moment. Then, instead of getting sentimental or dwelling on her disappointment that they hadn't called her, that sharp mind went right where he most needed it to go. "How much have you got on this Lovesprettyboys? Where does the investigation stand now and what are we going to do?"

Relieved, and glad Brandon had talked him into bringing Jackie into this, he answered, "I thought we had a good shot at finding him." He waved toward the laptop, where the audio file from the convention workshop still droned on at a low volume, completely forgotten in the reunion. Explaining what they'd been doing, he added, "It's still possible he was there, and that she'll hear him. We'll get back to that shortly."

She frowned. "Meantime, while she's listening to tapes from a bunch of plastic surgeons, recorded two years ago, this psychopath is out there setting her up to take the fall for another murder?"

"Hey, it'd almost be better if he was. Now that she's with us, at least she's got an alibi," Brandon said. As soon as the words left his mouth, he winced, realizing how they'd sounded. "Not that I, uh, wish anyone murdered. Especially not as viciously as this guy's killing them. The sick bastards deserve to be locked up, not chopped up."

"As always, Brandon, your eloquence astounds," Wyatt murmured.

Lily's lips quirked and she glanced at him sideways, through half-lowered lashes. Their eyes locked and they shared a brief moment of amusement that was completely out of place, but still felt right. Like everything about them felt right lately. Everything except the very idea that someone out there wanted to hurt her. Again.

He tore his gaze away, needing to keep his focus, not get distracted by thoughts of what was happening between them. Lily was in danger, with enemies closing in on all sides. The last thing she needed was him losing his impartiality, letting his personal feelings make him careless.

"I have another idea," Jackie said. "Let's say this scumbag really is a doctor, and he was at that convention. We know the unsub stayed at the shack, hiding out for the first couple of days, until he knew they weren't on to his real identity, right, Lily?"

"Time seemed a little fuzzy to me," Lily admitted, "but I'm pretty sure he did, yes. He was muttering, over and over, about how he couldn't go home, he could never go home, that they'd be looking for him. Then one day, he disappeared. He came back in a good mood, telling me he'd gotten away with it completely." Her voice shook as she added, "And that meant he had lots of time to pay me back for inconveniencing him."

"Sick motherfucker," Jackie muttered. But she quickly returned to her point. "Okay, back to this convention. How about if we get a list of the male attendees? We exclude everyone whose alibi is unshakable—anyone on surveillance video during the time of the attack, or checking out of the hotel Sunday morning."

"We've already done that," Wyatt said. "And done background investigations on the rest."

"Okay, good. From the rest, we narrow down the ones who are local, say within a hundred miles of Richmond. There can't be that many, maybe a few dozen? We call their offices, say we're calling from an insurance company, doing an audit or something. Ask whether the doctor treated patients on the Monday after the convention."

"If he did, then it's a pretty good bet he's not our guy," Brandon said, sounding impressed with the idea. "So we look a little closer at any of them who weren't in that day."

The idea certainly wasn't perfect, and had a number of holes, like the fact that Lily's memory could be faulty. But it was something, another angle, at least. At this point, Wyatt was willing to try anything. "Brandon, do you have that list with you?"

"Nope, but I can get into it remotely," he said, turning in his chair to swivel his laptop around. "As long as numb-nuts hasn't changed my passwords or anything to get even with me for not bowing down after his summons."

"Anspaugh. Man, oh man, he's gonna run this all the way into the end zone to try to get his career back on track." Jackie sounded completely disgusted.

"He really hates me."

"Yes and no. I think part of the problem is he felt anything but hatred for you once. Now his feelings are all screwed up." She wrinkled her nose in distaste. "I swear, watching him search through your stuff yesterday, I wasn't sure whether he was gonna smash your old coffee mug, or put his mouth on it, just so his lips could touch something yours had."

"Excuse me while I vomit," Brandon mumbled, though he remained focused on the laptop screen.

On the laptop, the audio file continued to play, the volume turned down, mere background noise. Wyatt was about to tell the younger man to turn it off when Jackie announced, "I think it's pretty obvious that Lily needs to just hide out here, lay low, not let anybody know she's alive yet."

"That's impossible," Lily said, shaking her head.

"Why? It's gone on this long. What's another week or two, so we can find the real killer and keep you from getting hauled in for questioning? Or worse?"

"You know why." Lily wrapped her arms around herself, looking at all three of them, as if wondering how they could have forgotten what had brought her out of hiding in the first place.

Wyatt hadn't forgotten. Of course he hadn't.

"Jesse Boyd is out there walking the streets. The DA is not going to refile that case and have him rearrested unless he knows he has a shot at winning. And because of whatever happened with the other evidence, I am the only shot he has left."

Her testimony was the only shot because the other physical evidence had been tossed out. The DNA, the fibers on her nephew's clothes that had come from the rug in Boyd's van, the boy's hair found on one of Boyd's shirts, a spot of his blood on Boyd's shoe. All excluded. All because of him.

He abruptly rose, not even able to look at her any longer. He'd have to tell her someday. When the time was right, he would admit it was his fault and apologize from the very depths of his heart. Right now, though, he just couldn't stand to do it. Seeing that look of devastation, of betrayal, on Lily's face was something he simply couldn't bear right now.

About to walk into the house, knowing he couldn't put off going into work and dealing with Crandall for much longer, he paused when Jackie said, "Okay, then.

If the world's going to find out Lily's alive, we have to act as fast as we can to clear up the lily murders and remove her from suspicion. We've got to find something that clears her in those cases while we're also trying to find the unsub."

"I know," he said. "Brandon's been working on the victims' computer hard drives when he can, tracing IPs in the communications between killer and victim."

"And I bet those IPs aren't in Maine. It should be easy to prove Lily didn't send the e-mails to lure them in."

Having thought of that, he shook his head. "Anspaugh won't go for it. Once he finds out where Lily's been, that she has almost no witnesses to confirm her location for most of the summer, he'll decide she left the area to e-mail her victims. Just like the Professor did last winter."

"It only takes one," Jackie insisted. "One message sent from another geographical area when we can *prove* Lily was in Maine."

"Then he'll claim she used her computer expertise to fake the IP."

Jackie blew out an irritated breath. "Come on, you know we can prove she's innocent."

She was right; he was just being pessimistic, still too focused on the damned evidence in the Boyd case. "I know; of course we can. We *will*. I would just prefer to do it before she gets arrested." And before Lily was put in a cell where somebody with a long reach and a lot of money might be able to get to her. Wyatt had too much experience with the criminal-justice system, with courts and prison security, to trust them entirely. Especially not with the safety of someone he cared about.

A lot.

"We have to bring the others in, you know, get them working on this—"

"Quiet!" Lily, who had been listening in silence, launched herself from her chair. She yanked the laptop right out from Brandon's typing fingers and spun it toward herself. And just like last week, she leaned close to the speakers, her frightened face a mask of concentration.

That audio file had been droning on in the background. Lily hadn't been intently listening to his conversation with Jackie; she'd been listening to the medical workshop they'd started on nearly two hours ago.

"You heard him again?" Wyatt asked.

She nodded once. "Yes, and it's the same situation as before. He's on there not as a speaker but someone in the audience." She found the volume button on the front of the laptop and jabbed it a half-dozen times.

They heard voices, laughter; then one of the original speakers came on. "As you might have guessed, that *cheeky* man in the audience knows a little bit about my methods. He has had his hands on the posteriors of half the women in the state of Virginia."

"I learned from the best," another voice called from the background, though not too far from a microphone to be heard.

It was that voice. That same voice Lily had singled out before. Not as cold and condescending this time as it had been toward Angela Kean, but there was still a note of arrogance that rang clearly, even through the humor.

"What can I say, like father, like son!"

*Father. Son.*

Impossible.

"That's him, Wyatt!" Lily's blue eyes gleamed with tension. "It's him, and now we've got him! Who was he talking to? Which speaker was that, the one he said was his father?"

"It was Alfred Underwood," Wyatt murmured.

Alfred Underwood, whose stepson, Philip Wright, had been another speaker on that panel. One of the men Lily had already excluded this very morning.

There was only one explanation.

Without another word, he reached for the laptop and pulled it from her, just as Lily had taken it from Brandon. Around him, their voices swelled. Lily launched into a number of questions, plans, with Brandon and Jackie adding their own. The louder their voices, the less Wyatt could hear their words. They simply became a hum of background noise as he focused all his attention on his own thoughts. Because though the answer was now clear to him, and so many things made sense, several others did not.

They most definitely did not.

Opening a search engine, he typed in a name. Hundreds of hits came back almost immediately and he pulled up the first one, scanning the article, checking the dates.

*Pay dirt.*

It fit. The timing all fit. Everything that had happened right up until the night he had rescued Lily, it all made sense.

Beyond that? Not so much.

Scrolling down, he came to a black-and-white photograph of a man, which dominated the center of the article. Clearing his throat, he turned the laptop around so the others could see the screen. "Here he is. This is the man you just heard."

As Lily stared at the picture, emotions washed over her face, anger, fear, and sorrow. He saw no recognition, though. Her attacker had done a good job at concealing his face from her. But not his voice.

"That's him?" she whispered. "That's Lovesprettyboys?"

The man of her nightmares. The man they'd all hunted so desperately one year ago when working on the Reaper case. "Yes."

She shook her head slowly. "He looks so normal. It's hard to believe he's completely insane, killing Kowalski, kidnapping me."

"'What evil lurks in the hearts of men?'" he quoted softly.

"Evil. Yes. He has to be utterly evil. Not just for what he did in the heat of a desperate moment, but to be so calculating to have lured and brutally murdered three or four other men to try to find me."

"That," Wyatt said, his voice low and intense, "he did not do."

The others all eyed him with confusion. Then Lily exclaimed, "You just said—"

"I said this is the man we knew as Lovesprettyboys, and yes, he's the man who attacked you. But he's not the one who has been killing those other pedophiles, trying to set you up for murder. He's not the lily killer."

Wyatt scrolled the screen back up to the top, so they could see the headline from the Williamsburg paper. It had been published months ago. Seven and a half to be precise.

And it raised more questions than it answered.

"Oh, my God!" Lily said, shock pulling every bit of color from her face.

"What the hell?" Jackie asked.

Brandon remained silent, shaking his head in confusion.

They all grasped what it meant, but Wyatt laid it out, anyway. "Roger Underwood, the man who kidnapped you, died last January, Lily. On the very night of your escape. Lovesprettyboys is *dead*."

No relief washed over her beautiful face, no moment of obvious satisfaction that the man who'd tortured her was no longer out there, waiting for his chance to do it again. How could she be relieved or satisfied?

"Then who . . . ?"

She didn't need to finish the question. They were all wondering the same thing.

If Roger Underwood, the original unsub, was dead, who was out there now, still trying to destroy Lily Fletcher completely?

# Chapter 13

Though she knew he didn't want to leave her, especially not after their amazing discovery, Wyatt left at noon to head to the office. He couldn't put Deputy Director Crandall off any longer. Brandon, who couldn't keep ducking Anspaugh, either, accompanied him.

They had, of course, refused to leave her alone and Jackie remained behind. It probably wasn't necessary. Lily felt as safe here, in his Washington home, as she had in his Maine one. Well, almost. This place didn't have the security setup, nor was it easy to stand on the upper floors and be able to see movement in any direction from a quarter mile away like she could at the beach house. But if she had lost her ability to survey the entire world spread below her, at least the town house was private, hidden from prying eyes. She might not be able to see out, but nobody could see in, either.

In the hours since Wyatt had gone, she had spent most of her time trying to readjust her thinking about what was happening in her life. Though the danger hadn't ended, and though she was still in legal hot water, mostly all Lily could focus on was the death of Roger Underwood. Her tormentor.

It was strange to realize he was gone, and had been gone for so many months. All this time, she'd pictured him out there in the world, an immense black shadow waiting for the chance to envelop her in all his darkness again, pull her back in that place where life had seemed far away and death infinitely preferable.

"Roger Underwood," she murmured, her eyes again drawn to his face, printed out in full color from the newspaper article about his "tragic" death.

## FAMED LOCAL SURGEON SUCCUMBS TO EARLY DEMISE

Not early enough, as far as Lily was concerned. Too bad the son of a bitch hadn't dropped dead of a heart attack one week earlier.

She had no doubt he had, indeed, been the monster of her nightmares, the instrument of her near destruction. Once she and the others were armed with his name, the first thing they'd done was look for more samples of his voice, finding them almost immediately. He'd appeared in no less than three other recordings Brandon had tracked down, and each time she heard a syllable come out of his mouth, her stomach heaved and her skin crawled. Once, when he described some new stitching technique, she shuddered, despite the warmth of the day.

That was before Wyatt had left; he'd been there right beside her. When she'd begun to tremble, his hand had appeared on her shoulder, as if he knew exactly what she was thinking, what awful, brutal moments she couldn't help remembering. He knew just how to comfort her, to reassure her she was no longer alone and would never be hurt again. Whether it was with the touch of that hand, or just a glance from the other side of the table, with concern warring with promise in his eyes, he knew exactly how to calm her.

Every additional piece of information they'd gathered about Underwood confirmed his identity in Lily's mind, even if she'd had any doubts about his voice, which she did not. Though his name was listed on a roster of registered attendees, he hadn't been a speaker at the Richmond event. And judging by the photographs of the banquet on the organization's Web site, he also hadn't been sitting at the head table when his father had received his humanitarian award. The lure of two unattended children must have been irresistible for him to risk missing the event, when he would almost certainly have been expected to be there.

The car. Had he taken it because his own was parked in the traditional valet lot, where there were cameras to mark every entrance and exit? It certainly made sense. He obviously knew his sister kept a spare key hidden inside the bumper. Wyatt had said the woman used it because of her teenage son.

God, it made her sick to think of that man being some child's uncle.

No, he wouldn't risk exposing his true nature so close to home. He liked his secret life. The one at Satan's Playground, and as Peter Pan on those message boards.

He would prey on other people's children.

Lily knew the rest of what had happened that night, right up until the moment his arm had appeared in the back of the van and he'd shot her. Then, nothing until she'd awakened in the beach shack the next day, to his furious whispers about all she had cost him and how he wanted to make her pay.

*So why did you bring me here? Why haven't you killed me already?*

Though she hadn't remembered before, she now knew she'd asked him those very questions.

She also remembered his reply. *Killing's too good for you.*

He'd left her to think about that answer, dazed, bloodied, and in such pain, for at least a day.

"You hangin' in there, chickie?" Jackie asked.

"I'm fine, really."

Depositing a tray of sandwiches on the table, Jackie ran her hand over Lily's hair before sitting down, as if she couldn't stop touching her simply to make sure Lily was real and alive. "For a bachelor, that man has one heck of a kitchen."

"It's mostly used by his housekeeper," Lily said. "Though he's not a bad cook." Better than her, anyway.

Jackie grabbed a sandwich. She'd made them a late lunch since they'd been working so hard they'd forgotten to eat. "I guess you two got pretty close all that time you were living with him."

Hearing the extremely innocent tone, Lily couldn't help casting a quick glance at her friend. Jackie's expression was equally as innocent. Too innocent. "He wasn't there most of the time," Lily reminded her.

"Really? I seem to remember that man taking a whole lot of vacation time this year. Kind of out of character, I thought at the time. I suspect he built up some major frequent-flier miles taking trips to Maine, and I doubt it was because of the weather. Especially not in March, when he seemed to be gone almost the entire month."

March, when she'd first arrived at the beach house, had been violently windy, with raging storms including one the locals called a nor'easter. Newly released from the hospital, weak, and entirely dependent upon Wyatt, Lily had actually found herself liking the weather. Tucked safely inside, listening to the wind whipping the surf into a frenzy, and watching tornadoes of sand fly off the beach, she'd felt completely protected by the storm that surrounded her. No, they couldn't get out. But neither could anyone else get in.

"So, not to be nosy or anything," Jackie said, the way someone who was about to be incredibly nosy always did, "but is something going on there?"

Lily intentionally misunderstood. "Going on where? In Maine?"

"Ha. I mean, what's with you and Wyatt? I noticed some serious vibes."

Knowing Jackie well enough to know she wouldn't be palmed off by some flip, trite answer, Lily admitted as much as she could. "There are vibes. I just don't know where they're going to lead."

The other woman bit off a corner of her sandwich and chewed, appearing thoughtful. Finally, she said, "I guess it's pretty natural to be really appreciative of someone who's done so much for you."

"This has nothing to do with appreciation, Jackie." Lily wanted to be sure that was understood. "I think it's more about finally knowing who I am, who I'm going to be for the rest of my life, and knowing he likes that person."

"No more hero worship?"

With a soft laugh, Lily asked, "Was I that obvious?"

"Maybe just to me."

"No. No more hero worship, even though he really is my hero now. But I'm not the timid little ingenue anymore."

The other woman snorted. "I already noticed you don't drop anything you're holding just because he says something to you."

God, that seemed like such a long time ago.

She opened her mouth to reply, but before she could, she heard a muffled sound coming from near the stone wall surrounding the courtyard. Jackie heard it, too. They both fell silent, glancing in that direction, and Lily couldn't deny her heart skipped a beat or two. She found herself wishing she hadn't left her gun up at the beach house, even though, legally, she no longer had the right to carry one.

A bird suddenly appeared. Flying up from the yard next door, it cawed loudly as it arced over their heads and was silhouetted against the bright afternoon sun. Just a bird.

"Damn, you've got me jittery now," Jackie said.

"It's fine," she insisted. "I'm fine."

"I know you are. And I promise you, Lily, you're going to stay that way. You've got a whole team of people behind you who are going to make absolutely certain of it."

Deputy Director Fred Crandall had worked his way into his position by way of intelligence, determination, drive, and luck. But his complete lack of a conscience certainly hadn't hurt. Nor had the generally slimy factor of his personality.

Wyatt couldn't stand the man and the feeling was entirely mutual. From the moment his boss had landed the job, thanks to the ass-kissing at high levels that it always took to reach this office, he'd done what he could to fuck with Wyatt. The man had just disliked him from the get-go, despite Wyatt's record, the cases he'd closed and the commendations he'd received.

Crandall's former right-hand man, Ray Letterman, who had recruited Wyatt right out of college and had once been a close friend, used to say it was pure jealousy. That while Crandall might own several thousand-dollar suits, he still wore them as if they'd come off the rack from Kmart, while Wyatt could be in a bulletproof vest and jeans and look more stylishly dressed.

Wyatt didn't believe it. It was inconceivable that a man at Crandall's level would let class envy dictate how he did his job. But something had definitely crawled up the man's ass about Wyatt even before the scandal that had cost so many—including Letterman—their careers. Since then? Well, Crandall hadn't declared outright war, but it had come pretty close. This next skirmish could end up becoming a major battle.

"Just when were you gonna let the rest of us in on your little private investigation, Blackstone?" Crandall's jowly face quivered with fury. "Do you know how fucking embarrassing it is to find out one of my own people is conducting a private investigation nobody else in the bureau knows about? If the local police hadn't contacted Anspaugh about the badge, and asked if the case was connected to the other flower murders *you* put out a bulletin on, we might never have known. Just how many more murders would it have taken for you to do your job?"

"I was under the impression I was doing my job," Wyatt murmured, impassive, as he'd been from the minute he'd stepped into the office. Keeping a slight smile on his mouth, with his legs crossed, and his fingers laced together on his lap, he knew the mere sight of him was sending Crandall into a frenzy. The man was all rage and bluster and Wyatt's very demeanor offended him. Yet the louder the deputy director got, the more quiet and pleasant Wyatt's response.

"Oh, right. When did it become your job to investigate serial killers? Isn't that why we have the BAU?"

"I believe, sir, that's exactly what you tasked me to do when you ordered me to form the team. Isn't catching serial killers what we've been doing since day one, starting with the Reaper?"

Crandall smirked. "Right, the one you let get away?"

The killer, Seth Covey, hadn't exactly gotten away. He'd hanged himself to avoid being taken into custody. Something Crandall and his ilk liked to call the team's failure.

"The point remains, you asked me to lead a team that would solve Internet-related murders, and that's what I've been doing."

"This case isn't about Internet murder and you know it!"

Wyatt shrugged. "I disagree. The victims were chosen specifically because of the Web sites, chat rooms, and message boards they frequented. They were stalked on those sites. Their meetings were arranged in cyberspace. How much more wired does a case need to be?"

Crandall smacked his hand on his desk. "I meant this case is about a whole lot more than the Internet."

"Perhaps, but are you denying the basic elements are

all there?" Wyatt wasn't about to let it go, needing Crandall to admit he had no reason to take the investigation away from him. "My interest was captured purely by virtue of the Internet lure, the e-mail communications and the child-pornography sites visited by the victims. Unless the definition of Internet connection has changed, I was doing absolutely nothing other than my job."

The other man frowned, but couldn't deny it. He leaned back in his chair, his pig eyes narrowing to twin slits. "Why didn't the rest of your team know about it?"

"We're a very busy group. That murder-for-hire case was at its peak, and we hadn't officially been asked to help on the first few murders. I was, essentially, gathering information, laying the groundwork for bringing the team in."

"You sure about that? You sure you didn't keep it to yourself when you figured out it had something to do with Lily Fletcher?"

This was the first time Lily's name had come up, but of course Wyatt had been expecting it, so he managed to remain completely impassive. "Fletcher?"

"Don't be coy."

"Why would I connect the case to her? I didn't receive the call about the latest victim, found holding her badge. What other reason was there to think she might have some connection?"

Crandall yanked a file folder off a pile on the corner of his desk and flipped it open. "How about because the killer left lilies at every scene?"

"You would have preferred daisies?"

Crandall sputtered.

"My point is there are probably hundreds of varieties of flowers. Why would one variety make me think of a woman lost in the line of duty so many months ago?" he added, emphasizing the *line of duty* part. Because Crandall might be thinking of Lily as a suspect already, but that didn't mean he should be. "The next time we find a body lying near a rosebush, should we put out an APB on anyone named Rose?"

Crandall's face reddened more as he grew more irritated, more distracted from the main point. That was good. Wyatt wanted him distracted, kept off guard, and going in the wrong directions, if only to prevent the man from asking the right questions.

Trying to keep the exchange normal, not give Crandall any reason to think he could get away with treating him like anything other than an equal, Wyatt said, "I apologize for not being here yesterday when the new case came in. I was, as you know, out of state. I'll look forward to seeing the details on it."

Crandall didn't respond, just watched him in silence, staring right into Wyatt's eyes. Wyatt had absolutely no problem holding that stare, maintaining his calm, aloof demeanor. He had faced men far more intimidating than Deputy Director Fred Crandall, and if the man thought he could browbeat him, he was sorely mistaken.

Crandall had exactly one weapon he could use against Wyatt. One card he could play that would bring him to heel and have him doing whatever the man wanted. Fortunately, though, he did not yet know that one weapon was still alive.

If asked directly, would Wyatt have lied about it? Said he didn't know if Lily had survived, or where she might be? Considering his aversion to lies of any sort, he wasn't sure. Thankfully, he'd been spared from having to decide because the question had not come up.

A knock on the closed office door was quickly followed by someone opening it and stepping in uninvited. "I heard you were meeting. I think I should be a part of this."

Tom Anspaugh. The agent, with his ill-fitting suit, his crooked tie, and his red-rimmed eyes didn't look well. In fact, he looked like someone who had filled a lot of long, sleepless nights with a lot of cheap liquor. But he had apparently begun to work his way back into Crandall's good graces by bringing news of Wyatt's secret investigation to the deputy director's office.

"Oh, excellent," Wyatt said, forcing himself to nod politely at the other agent, whom he had disliked for a long time, but truly loathed after he'd left Lily unprotected and vulnerable. "Deputy Director Crandall was updating me on the new information you've received about my case."

He didn't know who looked more shocked at his gall, Crandall or Anspaugh.

"*Your* case?" Anspaugh finally snapped. "I'm working this case now."

Ignoring him, Wyatt addressed the deputy director. "Is there some problem here? Didn't we just agree about the Internet aspects of these murders?"

"Yes, but—"

"Then why is this even being discussed?" He tossed a disdainful look Anspaugh's way. "I mean, Special Agent Anspaugh has most recently been working on bankruptcy-fraud cases, hasn't he?"

The other agent's eyes nearly bulged from their sockets. He didn't like being reminded about his loss in status.

Crandall, however, needed the reminder. In his zeal to

screw with Wyatt, he'd somehow managed to forget he'd made Anspaugh a fall guy as well.

"Look, Blackstone," Anspaugh said, "you're out of this thing now. I got the call about Lil. You can't very well investigate one of your own employees for murder."

Wyatt managed to convey a look of complete surprise. "Excuse me?"

Crandall cleared his throat and frowned at Anspaugh. "To be clear, we're not assuming Agent Fletcher is a suspect. We're not even assuming she is actually alive, despite the evidence to the contrary."

"You have evidence that she is alive?"

"The badge—"

"Was obviously taken from her by the man who shot her and drove off with her in the back of that van last January. Who knows where it ended up after that night? Besides, even if she were alive, do you really think she'd be stupid enough to leave her own badge behind at a crime scene?"

Anspaugh, beginning to appear nervous, shot off his mouth again. "Look, maybe she's not actually alive, but this case involves her somehow. And her last boss can't be the one investigating it."

His tone silky smooth, Wyatt replied, "As I recall, Tom, on Lily's very last assignment, she was under your supervision." Pure, unadulterated anger must have shown through his eyes, because Anspaugh almost imperceptibly drew back under his stare. "Your *protection*. You did promise me she'd be protected, remember?"

The other man's neck worked as he swallowed, hard. "We couldn't have known."

"Anybody knows you don't leave two inexperienced agents used to doing only electronic surveillance alone in a van with no backup." Wyatt crossed his arms over his chest, needing to hide his hands, which were clenching into fists. "Kowalski was a computer specialist, just like Lily, not a field agent. They should have been covered at all times."

Crandall tilted his head back, his disdainful mood now focused on Anspaugh as much as on Wyatt. Anspaugh had been crucified in the investigation, and Crandall hadn't forgotten the black eye it had given him, as well.

Apparently seeing he was losing ground, Anspaugh jumped right back in the fight, stubborn and belligerent. "Look, Blackstone, we all know her body was never found and she could be alive. If she is, then she's gone rogue, turned into some kind of vigilante. And you know as well as I do that rogue agents aren't investigated by the Cyber Division."

A slight smile touching his lips, Wyatt addressed Crandall. "Excuse me; I was under the impression that Agent Fletcher's employment with the bureau expired when she did."

He didn't have to go on. Crandall's frown and the sneer on his lips said he understood. An FBI agent suspected of a crime would require an internal-affairs investigation. A former agent? Now it got sticky.

Anspaugh gave it one more shot. "Come on, I've done a lot of work on this. . . ."

"Since yesterday?" Wyatt asked, lifting one brow. "I can't imagine how you could possibly have more information on this case than I have accumulated in the past several weeks. Especially considering I was on the scene of all of the first three murders, two of them before the bodies were even removed."

Another argument Crandall could not deny. This time,

he didn't even try to stall, or wait for Anspaugh to throw up another false objection. He merely waved a weary hand in the air, gesturing them both out. "Fine. Get back to work. Blackstone, I want to be kept apprised of this situation every step of the way."

Tom Anspaugh shot to his feet. "But I need to be part of this! I lost everything because of Fletcher, the stupid little—"

Before he could even form the final word of his vicious comment, Wyatt leapt up as well, leaning in until his face was two inches from Anspaugh's. The fury he'd felt toward the man for so many months made his voice shake and every muscle in his body contract. "Don't you blame somebody else because you couldn't manage to keep your own people alive during your fucked-up undercover operation." He stepped closer, lowering his voice to a near growl. "Don't you even dare."

Then, knowing Crandall had to be as shocked as Anspaugh appeared to be, Wyatt spun around and strode toward the door, not casting a single look back at either of them.

In the old days, by four o'clock on a Friday afternoon, Will Miller would be parked on a stool at his favorite bar, having had an appetizer of Bud while he worked his way toward the main course of Wild Turkey, with a few shots of schnapps in between strictly to cleanse the palate.

Not anymore.

"We've come a long way, baby," he told his young grandson as he unbuckled the car seat he'd just bought for the kid from the car he'd just bought for himself. This weekend, he would take his daughter out and buy her one, too. Nothing ritzy or glamorous, something reliable and used like this one. He had money to spend, but not millions. He wanted it to last, to give them all a chance at a better life.

Whatever she drove would be an improvement on the bus. Even better, if he had his way, she would soon be driving it to the community college, to work on the degree she'd given up on when she got pregnant. Getting her to quit that lousy job at the diner was his number-one priority.

"She's gonna ask us questions about the money, isn't she?" he asked little Toby. "Can you say lottery? Lot-ter-y."

The kid babbled something, his stuffed-up nose making the gibberish even more impossible to translate. The medicine he'd just picked up for him would fix that.

"Mommy's gonna be happy, isn't she? She thought I was just babysitting you today, but we surprised her with a trip to the clinic, didn't we?"

A clinic with a real doctor, who'd taken one look at Toby's nose and prescribed him a good antibiotic to clear up the infection. He'd be better within a day or two.

His grandson would be healthy and his daughter would get to go back to school. He'd move them both to a decent place, out of this ratty, run-down neighborhood. Will was finally going to be able to pay back the people who'd stuck by him.

For once, his life was really looking up.

Toby wrapped his chubby arms around Will's neck, twining his slobber-wet hands in the short gray hairs behind his ears. And Will's heart welled up, the same way it had many years ago, when he'd first started to see the real person his *own* firstborn son was becoming, after months of looking in a crib and seeing nothing but a crying lump.

This little guy had personality. He was also just about the cutest baby anybody had ever seen—even the nurse at the clinic said so.

"I'll keep you safe, buddy," he whispered.

Safe from sickness. Safe from poverty. Safe from bad people . . .

Jesus. His thoughts had taken him there again. Right to the place he'd tried so hard to avoid going in the past few days, ever since he'd gone into a lawyer's office and sworn in an affidavit that some guy named Jesse Boyd had been drinking with him in a bar on one specific night a few years back.

If he'd done some research, if Will had gone on the computer to look up the guy's crimes, would he have still gone through with it? What did it say about him as a person that he'd lied, for money, to help set a god-damned child molester and murderer free?

"Pop-pop-pop-pop," Toby said with a sleepy smile, mumbling the words Will had been teaching him every day for a week.

*God forgive me.*

A little kid. A little boy not much older than Toby. Boyd had taken him. Hurt him. Killed him.

If there was a hell, Will would someday be there with the man he'd helped set free, both of them sitting front row, center.

"Pop-pop."

"That's right, I'm your pop-pop," he said, kissing the tousled blond curls on the top of the baby's soft head. "And I'll always be there for ya, kid. I'm gonna watch over you, take care of—"

A loud noise cut off his sentence. *Pop! Pop!* Something hit him, then something else, *bang-bang*, two in a row.

The bullets struck hard, pain erupting in his lower back, and in his left shoulder. He stumbled forward from the impact, staggering onto the sidewalk, dropping to his knees. Even as he fell, he was careful to hold the baby up so his tiny frame didn't smash onto the cement.

The sharp pain from each gunshot rapidly expanded, spreading throughout his body before merging to create one enormous torrent of anguish. He'd never known a person could hurt so much.

"Toby." The word lingered on his lips. As he started to fall forward, knowing he was going to land on his face, he gently pushed the boy to the side, out of harm's way.

"Help," he whispered, not even sure he understood what had happened. "Help."

Toby began to whimper. Then to cry. But his cries were drowned out by the sound of a car's engine, revving up and roaring away, the tires spinning and screaming on the blacktop as the vehicle tore up the block.

"Pop-pop?"

Will reached for the boy, his own flesh and blood, the kid who was supposed to be his chance to make everything right, to do it all over again. He wanted to touch him, to stroke that hair, brush his fingers against that little cheek, and promise it would all be okay.

But his fingers were bloody and his arm was weak and he was dying, and Will could only stare at the child as the world went dark and he headed for his front row, center seat.

## Chapter 14

Though Lily knew her former coworkers had been informed of her miraculous resurrection and wouldn't be caught by surprise as Jackie had been, she couldn't contain her nervousness as it drew closer to seven thirty. That was when the other three men she had worked with, all good, fine agents, would be coming over to Wyatt's to help work on Lily's case. Late this afternoon, Wyatt had called Dean Taggert, Kyle Mulrooney, and Alec Lambert into his office and had told them the whole story. He'd given them a choice: Walk out and pretend they had never heard a thing, staying out of the mess that was almost surely headed their way. Or help.

All three of them were on their way over here to help.

Though Wyatt, Jackie, and Brandon swore the new members of the team, Christian and Anna, could be trusted, Lily had made the decision not to bring them in. She didn't know them; they didn't know her. Why should they have any loyalty to her, especially if it could hurt their own careers? It was better that they remain in the dark. More of that plausible deniability. And as Brandon said, at least there would be two members of the Black CATs still employed if this went down badly.

*Oh, God, please don't let it come to that.* What an awful repayment that would be for the sacrifices and the loyalty, the friendship, and the never-ending support these people had offered her.

That support could make all the difference. Because with those brilliant minds working on both cases, something would happen. It had to. They would all take on different assignments, providing backup, doing legwork, chasing down clues, leaving Wyatt free to pursue their one hot lead: Roger Underwood. He intended to go back down to Williamsburg the next day, to try to surprise the bastard's widow at her home, see if he could shake her story and get any more information out of her. At the very least, confronting her about her lies regarding her husband's voice on the tape should get a reaction out of the woman.

She'd obviously lied about the voice in order to protect her husband. But did she know what she had been protecting him from? How far would someone go to cover up for a loved one? How much would a person do out of love for someone else, a husband, a brother, a son?

Wyatt wanted to know. So did Lily.

"Would you stop pacing?" Wyatt asked, interrupting her.

"You're sure they aren't angry with me?" she asked him again as she prowled the huge living room, which encompassed the front half of the downstairs. Every time she passed one of the windows, she peered out, looking for a dark-colored sedan, and a familiar hand-some face emerging from it.

"If they're angry, it's at me for not bringing them in and letting them help long ago," Wyatt insisted. "Not you. Never you."

"Unlike Anspaugh."

"Unlike Anspaugh," he admitted.

Wyatt had told her all the details about his meeting in the deputy director's office today, leaving out nothing. Afterward, she had come around to his way of thinking—coming forward now, today, would land her in jail, not in a witness stand testifying against Jesse Boyd. Besides, as he reminded her, if she wanted to maintain any credibility as a witness whatsoever, she couldn't get up there and be introduced as a suspected serial killer herself.

She'd clear her name, then go after Boyd. Even though the delay nearly killed her.

Tense, Lily perched on the corner of a chair, sat for a moment, then stood and resumed her pacing. Wyatt finally stepped closer, put both hands on her shoulders, and ran them up and down, warming the skin she hadn't realized had grown cold. "It's okay."

His hands, so strong, solid, and tender, brought not only warmth but calm. It was as if with each inch his palms slid against her skin, another bit of tension was pulled free from her, replacing worry and fear with comfort and calm.

Lily's eyes drifted closed and she remained very still, letting him touch her, stroke away her cares. She swayed a little on her feet, until her hip brushed against his, and the tips of her breasts scraped the front of his jacket. She tried to hide the intense pleasure she got out of not just his touch, but that Wyatt was the one touching her. Wyatt, the dream man she'd once thought so out of reach, Wyatt the hero, the savior, the friend.

She wanted him to become Wyatt the lover.

It was crazy—Jackie was in the kitchen throwing together some dinner, and the others would be arriving at any minute—but Lily couldn't stop herself. Her eyes slowly opening, she lifted her hands, sliding them onto his shoulders, the tips of her thumbs caressing his neck. Held back by nothing, not pride or fear or intimidation, she looked up at him, silently asking him for the world, or just the little part of it he inhabited.

He smiled faintly, shaking his head. But he wasn't saying no. That expression told her that as crazy as it might be, the answer was yes.

"When this is over," he whispered.

"Tonight's meeting?" she asked, intentionally misunderstanding.

He barked a quick laugh. "You know what I mean."

Now it was Lily's turn to shake her head. "No."

"Yes, you do."

"I meant no, that's not acceptable."

"It's not, huh?"

She leaned closer, rising up onto her tiptoes so their mouths shared the same inch of air space. Then she eliminated it, pressing her lips onto his in a kiss so fleeting, so soft, that if not for the way her mouth tingled, she wouldn't have been certain she'd kissed him at all.

"If there's one thing the past few years have taught me, Wyatt, it's to take nothing for granted. Don't put off something you want for a future date, because for all you know, your future might not extend beyond today."

He opened his mouth to reply, and she didn't know

whether he was going to start with another warning about why this was a bad idea, inform her he couldn't take advantage of her, caution that he was older, had been her boss, blah, blah, blah. She'd heard it before.

"I don't give a damn," she whispered before he got a word out.

"You should," he told her. "There are some things you don't know."

"Sweet man, all the things I don't know about you could probably fill the hard drive on my laptop. But there's one thing I do know, and it's all I need to know." She smiled. "I'm alive not only because of you, but merely because I am *with* you."

"Lily." He thrust a hand through his thick, dark hair, shaking his head. "You don't understand. There are issues we need to clear up before you decide to do anything." He appeared almost mournful as he added, "I've done things for the right reasons that have ended up hurting people. Even you."

She put her hand up, touching the tips of her fingers to his warm mouth. "I don't want to hear it."

He stepped away. "You're going to have to. Because we're not going to do anything about"—he waved a hand between them—"this until I tell you the truth."

"Your past is yours to keep, Wyatt. I didn't go snooping after that awful drunk shot off his mouth at the restaurant and I am not waiting for you to tell me all your secrets before we go to bed together."

Wyatt couldn't quite believe Lily had put that bald comment out there so readily. And while part of him was incredibly turned on by her certainty about where they were going, another part reacted with utter guilt. He sucked in a raw, shocked breath. His own past, his dark, awful, ancient history, hadn't been what he was referring to. He'd been thinking only of the role he'd played in Jesse Boyd's release from prison.

Now that she mentioned it, of course, all the other reasons he shouldn't be with her flooded into his head. The darkness that surrounded him and his family, the awful things he'd seen, and the way they had affected him merely added to the stockpile of ammunition against them as a couple. Lily was someone who deserved to be loved, who needed to find whatever happiness she could in her life, to get over the darkness and rediscover things like laughter and joy. How on earth could Wyatt be the man to help her do those things when he hadn't done them for himself and didn't really care to?

"That doesn't mean I don't expect you to tell me all that stuff eventually," she said. "I know you will."

He was already shaking his head before she finished.

"You think I can't handle it? Good Lord, Wyatt, with everything I've seen in my life, do you really think I can't deal with hearing you've had a tragedy or two in your own?"

"Not like this," he admitted, forcing the words from a throat tight with tension. "Not just what happened, but the reasons why it happened."

The betrayal. The rage. The madness. How was he supposed to explain away all the ugliness in his own family tree, and expect her to trust that none of it had been visited on his own psyche? Or, hell, stamped onto his own genes?

"Reasons or reactions, they're not much different, are they? Are you holding it against me because my twin sister slit her wrists in a bathtub? Some could say I'm tainted with the same kind of blood, that I'm as weak and selfish, predisposed to doing something like that, too, no matter how much it hurts those who are left behind."

Wyatt drew her into his arms, needing to hold her. She nearly shook with emotion, as she'd done the other night at the restaurant. She might mourn her sister, but that didn't mean she didn't carry the same impotent rage felt by every person who'd lost a loved one to suicide.

She melted against him for a moment, though he knew she wasn't trying to seduce him, or to initiate another kiss. She was merely taking what he offered, letting him support her. Then Lily nodded once and pulled away, looking up at him with clear eyes that held no tears.

Maybe she really was getting over everything.

"Tell me something," she said, proving how adept she had become at putting the past behind them. "Do you *really* want to have a big expository meeting before we finally give in to this and find out whether what we've been thinking about, dreaming about, fantasizing about, for months is as good as we both suspect it will be?"

Wyatt didn't answer. He couldn't answer. Because saying yes would be a lie, and saying no a catastrophe.

"Because I don't, and I'd really like to avoid wasting one more night on sleeping in the wrong bedroom of your house."

Before he could come up with some kind of response, they both heard a door slam outside. Lily turned away, visibly disappointed that their conversation had been interrupted. "They're here," she whispered, bending over to look out the front window again. "Guess you were saved by the car door."

"Lily . . ."

"Don't. We'll talk later, all right?" She kept her attention glued to the window, as if she didn't trust herself to look at him yet. "Though I'm really hoping this is settled and we don't have to talk about it anymore at all."

Damn, the woman could be stubborn. She didn't even look over her shoulder to see how he reacted, as if she'd reached the limit of her own brazenness. As if she knew he needed time to mull it over and eventually come around to her way of thinking.

It wasn't that he didn't think she was right. There was no doubt they wanted each other. They needed to be with each other. But that wasn't the end of the story.

"It's Dean and Kyle," she said, still focused on what was going on outside the front window.

Dean Taggert, dark-haired, intense-looking Dean, had just gotten out of the driver's seat of a car, his partner, barrel-chested, always smiling Kyle Mulrooney, leaving the passenger side. Kyle said something and laughed. Dean shot him a glare.

"I see nothing much has changed with those two."

"No, it hasn't."

Pulling up behind them was another familiar car. Parking, Alec Lambert got out of it. Lily hadn't known Alec very well at the time she'd been taken from them, since the former profiler had joined the team only a week before. Wyatt hadn't been sure she would want him included tonight. But Lily hadn't hesitated. As she'd reminded him, Alec had been the one who'd convinced her to talk to Wyatt about the side investigation she was conducting on Lovesprettyboys.

If only she'd come to him sooner. If only he'd forbidden her from riding along on the stakeout. *If only.*

"There's Brandon," Lily added, watching the young man step out of Alec's car. "I wonder what he was able to find out today."

"We'll know soon enough."

Brandon had remained in his office all day, looking for information on Dr. Roger Underwood. He'd intended to start from the man's birth and work his way forward, using public records and private mentions that turned up on the Internet. Anything that would help build a picture of the man, something they could use to figure out who his accomplice had been. They had to know who had gone on a murderous spree to try to incriminate Lily. Had there been someone else at the shack where he'd imprisoned her? The homeless man who'd ridden with Underwood to the house where the sting had been set up back in January hadn't mentioned another person being involved. But there must have been someone else. Otherwise, why would someone be trying so desperately to find out whether Lily had survived, unless he believed he himself could be identified?

It was possible the plastic surgeon had hooked up with another pedophile along the way. Perhaps someone he'd met in Satan's Playground, or on some anonymous Web site where deviant minds shared their twisted fantasies. Someone he trusted, whom he could call for help after everything had gone south. Having backup would certainly explain how Underwood had been able to fake his death, crashing the van off the bridge, and yet get all the way back to the beach where he'd left Lily.

Wyatt just wished Lily remembered more, but she swore she couldn't. It wasn't too surprising, really, given her injures, the blood loss, and the drugs Underwood had shot her up with. When she did focus all her energy on filling in the blank places in her mind from that week, she usually descended into shivers, mumbling about the pain, the fear, and the cold. Here and there would be snippets of conversation with Underwood, words he'd used that she would repeat. Not much else. The only other person she ever mentioned was the ghost of her sister, her only companion on that long night when she waited for Wyatt to come for her, not even certain her call for help had actually gone through.

Of all the moments she had endured, those were the ones that most haunted him. The torture, the pain, Underwood's taunting, they hadn't broken her. But he strongly suspected that in those dark, cold, desperate hours, she'd come as close to breaking as a person ever could.

"They're at the door," Lily said, watching him curiously. He'd been so lost in thought, he hadn't even heard a knock. "Ready?"

"Yes," he replied. "Are you?"

Her throat quivered as she swallowed hard, as if working up her nerve. "As I'll ever be."

This would be an ordeal, he had no doubt, but it wouldn't be as bad as she expected.

"Don't worry," Wyatt said. "They're on your side, Lily. We're *all* on your side, watching out for you. We have your back. And not one of us is going to leave you unprotected until this is all over with."

How was he supposed to kill the fucking bitch when she was surrounded by all those people?

Jesse hunkered down lower behind a hedge at the side of a house a few doors up from Agent Wyatt Blackstone's house. Though he wasn't one hundred percent certain Lily was in there, it sure seemed to make sense. His benefactor, and new best friend, said she'd been spotted at the place, and there'd been enough strange activity to make it likely.

Jesse didn't know what he had done right in another life to deserve his secret helper. Helper—hell, more like a guardian angel. Because not only had he gotten the warning phone call, but it had been followed up with a text message, sent right to his fancy new cell phone. Attached had been a grainy picture of a woman with short dark hair. Supposedly Fletcher had changed her look when she'd been hiding. Thank God his anonymous friend had been worried enough to hire somebody to stake out the FBI agent's former coworkers and friends. Without this picture, he might have walked right past Lily on the street and not even recognized her.

Now he couldn't miss her. And just as soon as he had a chance to take her out, he *wouldn't* miss her.

The neighborhood was an older one, with fully mature landscaping and dim old streetlights, so he felt pretty confident that his hiding place would conceal him from any prying eyes. The yard in which he'd hidden was overgrown, out of place in the upscale neighborhood, a For Sale sign out front. A peek in a window confirmed the house was empty. It was a perfect hiding spot, totally private and hidden from view. Unlike Blackstone's house, which had been in Jesse's sight for three hours, since just after sunset.

He'd seen them arrive, two by two, those FBI agents in their dark blue suits with their matching tough-guy expressions. Bastards. Like they were so much better than him? They were criminals, too, weren't they? Covering up for a woman who'd faked her own death, helping her get away with murder, they obviously thought they were above the law.

And Lily Fletcher was a murderer—of that he had no doubt. Jesse shivered, though not because it was getting chilly as the evening wore on. No, his very blood was cold, and it had been since he'd gotten that second call from his mysterious friend today. The unnatural, altered voice had spoken quickly, barking panicked words about how, incredibly, this morning's dire warning had appeared to come true. Somebody had shot down that Will Miller guy, Jesse's own alibi, right in the street. Shot in the back like a dog, left to bleed to death in front of his own grandkid, according to the coverage on the local news. What a sick, sick world. And his anonymous friend believed Lily Fletcher was the person who had done it.

There could be only one reason—because Miller had helped him, Jesse, get out of prison. The coincidence was just too great for it to be anything else. The only person who would go into a murderous rage over Jesse's release was Fletcher.

"Psycho whore," he whispered.

The FBI agent had apparently gone off the deep end. Now, having taken Miller out, she would almost certainly move on to him. Who else was there to target? As his benefactor had said, Jesse had to get her before she got him.

He had a sudden thought. Damn. He'd been in such a panic to get over here and start figuring a way to get at her, he hadn't paused to warn the second person who'd done so much for him lately. Glancing around the quiet yard, to make triply sure nobody could possibly be watching or listening, he risked pulling the phone out of his pocket. He dialed the number Ms. Vincent had given him, but got a machine. Not wanting to leave an incriminating-type message on a voice mail, like, you're-in-danger-but-I'm-gonna-kill-the-bitch-before-she-can-get-to-either-of-us, he merely muttered, "It's Jesse Boyd. Call me back; it's important," and hung up.

Before he even had time to put the phone away, it rang. But the information on the caller ID wasn't Ms. Vincent's name—the caller was unidentified.

He knew what that meant.

Yanking it open, he whispered, "This is Jesse."

"Are you all right?" the machine-voice asked.

"Yeah, yeah. I'm outside Blackstone's house."

"And?"

Frustrated and tired of lying on the cold ground, he mumbled, "It's been pretty quiet. A bunch of FBI agents showed up a while ago and they've been inside ever since. I can't even get close enough to see if a dark-haired woman's in there, much less if she's Fletcher."

"She is," the voice said. "I am sure of it."

So was Jesse. He felt it in his bones, the creepy-crawly sensation that somebody was out to hurt him, or to screw him over. He had no doubt it was because Lily Fletcher and her gang were thirsty for his blood.

"So what are you going to do, simply stay there all night?"

"It's getting cold," he said, a hint of a whine creeping into his voice. "And I gotta figure out where I'm gonna sleep tonight." He shifted uncomfortably on the ground, arching a little. Then an answer popped into his head, like magic. "Wait a sec. This house is empty—there's a foreclosure notice on the door."

"In Blackstone's neighborhood?"

"Yeah." The idea sounded better and better. "I can get in through a back window or something, flop here for a little while so I don't have to waste money on a hotel, and watch every second for a chance to get at Fletcher."

"And once you get that chance? What are you prepared to do?"

"Whatever it takes," he said. "But it's gonna have to be close-up—I don't have no way to get a gun or anything." He hadn't actually reached the point of thinking about how he would do away with Lily, focused entirely on making sure it was her. Now, though, he could think of a few methods. There was an old, broken clothesline in the backyard, cords dangling free. That would be nice and quiet. Or some broken glass from a bottle stolen out of one of the recycling bins. He knew just where to slit a throat to cause the quickest bleed-out. Hell, even a knife from Blackstone's own kitchen drawer.

He'd find the weapon. He just needed to wait for the opportunity to get close to her.

"Blackstone will never leave her alone."

"He has to go to work doesn't he?" Jesse replied.

It wasn't easy, but even the machine-sounding voice managed to sound impatient. "Not until Monday. Are you going to sit there all weekend, waiting for her to track you down and kill you?"

Oh. Right.

"I think there is a way you can get him to leave the house without telling Fletcher about it. You can draw him away, but you're going to need to wait and do it late at night, when there are no others in the house to guard her while he's gone."

He liked this idea. Get the big guy, and all his FBI buddies, out of the picture so it was just him and the skinny bitch? It would be as easy as it had been to subdue her nephew.

"Okay, then. Tell me exactly what I gotta do."

# Chapter 15

Jackie was the last to depart that night, staying until after ten, as if loath to leave Lily now that she'd found out she was alive. The others had gone about a half hour earlier, though none had appeared to want to, for the same reason.

Considering the situation was dire and they were surrounded by murder and betrayal, the evening had taken a strange turn. Dean, Alec, Kyle, Brandon, and Jackie had been so happy to have Lily back, the war-strategy session had become a big after-hours happy hour, sans booze, since they were working. But the mood had been almost celebratory. For a few moments, at least, they all managed to forget that Lily had to remain in hiding and that someone still wanted her dead and merely enjoy the fact that she was alive.

Though his team had become incredibly close at the office, blending together to form a great working relationship, this was the first time they had all socialized outside of work, much less at Wyatt's own house. To his surprise, Wyatt had found himself enjoying it. As for Lily, she hadn't looked so happy in months.

But even her pleasure at having been forgiven for her deception, and welcomed with open arms by her colleagues, hadn't been able to prevent pure exhaustion from washing over her eventually. Her huge yawns and sleep-heavy eyes had prompted all the others, and eventually Jackie, to say their good-nights. Just like everyone else, Jackie swore to return over the weekend to keep working on the case, knowing the sooner Lily was cleared, the sooner she could return to her own life. And her own home.

That should be a good thing. The right thing. Why, then, he wondered, did he feel a strange sort of emptiness at the very thought of it?

Funny, she'd been in his Virginia house for only twenty-four hours, and he already knew it would feel empty when she left. Well, emptier. Because it had always felt a little empty, since the day he'd inherited it from his grandparents. It was only since he'd walked into the kitchen and seen Lily at the stove, making a mess out of the simple task of scrambling an egg, or drinking a cup of coffee and twirling an unlit cigarette on the back porch, that he realized how much more he liked the place when he wasn't alone in it.

He couldn't say the same of the beach house. That place he would never like.

"Wyatt!"

He tensed, cocking his head, as he heard Lily call from upstairs. She'd gone up a few minutes ago to get ready for bed.

She called again. "Wyatt?"

Jesus. Was someone in the house?

Launching up from the couch, he ran to the stairs, taking them two at a time. The guest room door was closed, and he threw himself against it, bursting inside. He half expected to see her defending herself against a dark intruder. The other half wondered if she had fallen asleep and landed in the middle of one of her dark, terrifying nightmares.

The actual situation proved to be much more simple, and a whole lot more complicated. Because instead of looking terrified, or threatened, Lily merely looked shocked at his intrusion. She stood in the middle of the floor, nearly naked, staring at him through the neck opening of the white T-shirt she'd just been about to pull on. Other than that, she wore nothing but a tiny pair of pink underwear, and an expression of surprise. "What are you doing?" she asked, tugging the shirt—one of his—down over her smooth, creamy stomach and curvy hips.

Not soon enough, though. God help him, not soon enough.

"You screamed."

"I didn't scream."

"I heard you call for me."

"Yes," she explained, sounding exasperated, "I called. That's not the same as screaming. I wanted to remind you to turn off the coffeepot."

Relief washed over him, but since his tension had already transitioned into discomfort at that glimpse of her stunning body, the slim waist, the curves of her full breasts, he didn't immediately laugh off the incident. Usually able to maintain his cool despite the circumstances, to his surprise, he let his frustration drive his reply. "Are you kidding? You yell my name at night, when we both know you're being stalked by a psycho-path? What was I supposed to think?" he snapped. Immediately realizing he was reacting emotionally, rather than logically, he closed his eyes briefly, then turned to go. "I apologize."

"Don't even think about it."

He paused and glanced over his shoulder. "What?"

"I said don't even think you're going to turn into Mr. Calm, Cool, and Collected and walk back out of here. Not after you burst in like that. Not after you finally lost a little of that famed self-control."

She sounded happy about that.

"I'm so glad I amuse you."

"You don't amuse me, Wyatt. You thrill me and excite me and you drive me a little crazy, especially when you say dumb things like I'm not allowed to call out your name."

"There's a right time and place and a wrong one."

"The wrong time and place, huh?" she asked, lifting a brow in utter challenge, not at all intimidated by his annoyance. Her lips were quivering, as if she was trying not to laugh; she couldn't have been more different from the timid girl he'd once known if she'd been physically replaced by a kick-ass stunt double.

One word crossed his mind as he stared at her. The same one that so often occurred to him when he beheld the amazing, strong woman she had become. *Magnificent.*

Something in his stare must have revealed his thoughts, the sudden jolt of hunger he always felt for her at his most unguarded moments. She almost sauntered as she came closer.

"Meaning there is a right time and place, correct?"

Each step she took sent the tension up a notch. Her sweet, feminine fragrance filled his head, he could hear the warm, even rasp of her breathing, and every inch of her looked like warm, sultry female, earthy and elemental. Someone who knew what she wanted and planned to take it.

"I suppose," he said, still not heading for the door. He should; God knew he should.

There were a million things he needed to tell her, to make her understand, yet he knew one thing: Right now, at this point in her life, Lily didn't want to know anything except what it was like to feel physical pleasure again. Seeing her like this, sexy and strong and playful, he realized she was ready for that pleasure, almost demanding it.

She lifted one slim yet somehow strong hand and placed it on his chest, near his heart. The tips of her soft fingers brushed the bare skin revealed by the unbuttoned collar of his shirt, the coolness of her skin somehow burning and sparking with every slow, delicate stroke. Still silent, she leaned even closer, her dark hair soft against his cheek, her body pliant and yielding, held not more than a half inch from his own. Then her lips brushed his throat, and her whisper stabbed through his last bit of self-control.

"The right time, the best time, for me to call out your name is going to be when you're inside me."

*God help me.*

They had been building toward this all evening, all day. All week, all month. Their being together had been inevitable since that night when their eyes had met in her darkened bedroom up at the beach house. Though part of him knew he should resist, should wait until all the darkness surrounding them was gone, washed away, and replaced only by light and the possibility of tomorrow, deep in his very soul, he knew he couldn't.

He'd been waiting too long, waiting for her, waiting for them. Not just since that July night, not just since the night he'd saved her. Not since she'd come to work with him. No, Wyatt had been waiting for Lily for his entire adult life.

He hadn't realized it, but he had always been waiting for a woman who made him feel like this. Hungry. Hopeful. Crazy and at peace, all at the same time. She had worked her way inside his heart, mind, and soul, making him believe, for the first time ever, in something other than logic, reason, self-control, and dispassion.

He'd never trusted himself with passion before. In fact, Wyatt had worked for decades to cut it from his life, from his personality. His previous sexual affairs had been physically satisfying, but, always, a part of him had remained detached. Removed from what he was doing.

With Lily, he not only wanted to be with her; he felt almost desperate to be, overwhelmed with the need to taste and touch and have and take.

There were a thousand good reasons for walking away. But he'd sooner cut off his own legs than do it.

"You're sure?" he asked, sliding his hands into her hair, fingering the short, silky strands.

"Never more sure," she admitted. She kissed his throat again, sliding her tongue delicately in the hollow, then kissing her way to the pulse point beneath his ear. "I want you, Wyatt. I want to touch you and be with you, want you to drive every thought out of my head except how good your hand feels on my hip and your mouth feels on my thigh." She pressed closer, the puckered tips of her breasts scraping against his chest, wanting him to know that her heavy, sexy whispers were affecting her as much as they were him. "I want you to bury me with sensuality, not with conversation. Fill my body, not my ears. Take me and give to me and satisfy me until I am so physically pleasured I can't even remember what pain feels like."

She meant it, each and every word. He knew it without doubt.

Her words and her nearness seduced. But the slight catch in her voice as she revealed the very deepest part of her need—the need for sexual connection to drive away the darkness—grabbed at his heart and twisted it hard.

Right now, he would do anything for her, to her, or with her. Whatever she wanted, whatever she would offer, he would give it and take it and gladly. Then he'd do it again, and again, for as long as he had strength in his body. He opened his mouth to tell her so, to give up all resistance and admit she had cut the very foundation out from under him, not with her demands, but with her raw, honest want.

But showing her was so much easier.

Staring up at him, Lily knew the moment Wyatt gave up all objection and acknowledged what she had known for so long. That they were meant to be together. Lovers. Whether they would be long-term ones or would have only this night, she couldn't say. Because of that, she intended to make this night as unforgettable as she could.

He wrapped one strong arm around her shoulders, another around her waist. Pulling her closer, Wyatt hauled her up a little so all her curves melted against the angles of his body, breast to hard chest, thigh to thigh. The feel of his rigid erection against the vulnerable hollow below her belly button sucked at her strength and she sagged harder against him.

"I've had so many nightmares," she admitted in a whisper, "but there have been some good dreams as well, and every one of them was about this."

He lowered his mouth to hers, their lips parting instantly, tongues sliding together in deep, hungry tastes. The ravenous kiss continuing, she sighed in pleasure when he bent to pick her up, cradling her in his arms. She wrapped hers around his neck, knowing that tonight he carried her not with tender, protective care but with driving need.

Instead of carrying her to the guest room bed, he turned and walked out the door, heading down the short hallway to his room. He didn't let the kiss end when they reached the bed. He placed her there, and followed her down onto it. No longer holding her, he was free to run his hands over her cheeks, her neck. He filled one palm with the curve of her shoulder, then traced his fingertips over her collarbone until she drew back from his kiss just so she could beg him for more. "Don't go slow," she ordered. "Don't make me wait anymore."

She reached for the buttons of his dress shirt, slipping them free as fast as she could, finally yanking at them when they resisted. He let her push it off him, and tossed it out of the way, each movement emphasizing the thickness of his arms and the breadth of his shoulders. He was incredibly solid, toned, and perfectly sinewed with rippling muscle.

She wriggled beneath him. "Take the rest off."

Though she had been talking about his clothes, he reached for her shirt. That'd do.

As he tugged the T-shirt up and off, those strong hands worked magic on her body. Every touch aroused all her senses. Each tender caress made the skin just beyond his fingertips throb in anticipation of being the next place he visited. Her limbs shook, her breasts grew taut and heavy, her nipples tight. She arched toward his hands, not wanting soft and tender, needing it a little fast, and a whole lot wild.

He knew. With a groan, he moved his mouth to her throat and his hand to her breast, cupping its weight, sliding his fingertips across her nipple.

"Yes," she hissed, writhing beneath him. When he replaced his hand with his mouth and sucked her nipple, hard, she rose off the bed with a groan. "God, yes."

Even as he kept sucking her to new heights of pleasure, he managed to unfasten his pants and shove them out of the way. Lily wriggled beneath him. Now only her skimpy underwear separated their naked bodies, but he didn't immediately tear them off. She taunted them both, heightening the tension by rubbing against his massive erection, gaining immense pleasure from the press of his thick heat against her sensitized clit.

"It's been so long," she groaned. She didn't just mean sex. It had seemed like a lifetime since she'd felt the intense spiral of pleasure, building, taking her higher toward the orgasm she desperately needed. She rocked against him, greedily taking more of those thrilling sensations, using him, though she knew he didn't mind. Judging by the way he watched her with dark, hungry eyes, she knew he didn't mind one damn bit.

"Wyatt," she cried, feeling the climax rise higher. He returned to her breast, sucking deep even as he ground against her, giving her the pressure where she most needed it. And the waves of pleasure lifted her that last little bit, making her quake. She gave herself over to it, barely even able to remember to breathe as she was racked by deep waves of delight.

As if seeing her reach that point had robbed him of his very last remnants of control, Wyatt reached for her underwear and tore them off her. But before he moved between her thighs, he reached into a bedside-table drawer and grabbed a condom. Watching him put it on, Lily arched up for him, wanting him inside her even before the last throbbing sensation ended. "Now, Wyatt, please."

"Yes, now," he murmured, then drove hard, plunging to the hilt, stretching and filling her completely. Shockingly, another orgasm rocked her instantly, and this time, she didn't just cry out—she gave a little scream.

"Good Lord, Lily," he whispered. He threw his head back, his face set in lines of intense concentration, as if the rhythmic spasms of her body were almost enough to pull him into an explosion of his own. But he seemed to gain control by pressing his mouth against her hair, the top of her damaged ear, then the side of her neck. He kissed her over and over, remaining deep inside her, filling her completely. But it seemed like forever before he trusted himself to move.

Then, finally, he brought his lips to hers and kissed her again. Their tongues mated, their breaths joined, and he began to stroke her, sliding out, easing back in, in a careful, easy rhythm. It had been so long since she'd been with anyone, and she'd certainly never been with him, yet she found herself immediately matching his every move. She took when he thrust; she released when he pulled away. Slow at first, then faster, deeper, wilder.

Wild, yes, but still so infinitely tender and loving, she found tears welling up in her eyes. Feeling so good had never felt so *lovely* as well.

"I've wanted this for a long time, Wyatt," she whispered.

"So have I."

It wasn't an admission of love, but as he slid home again, touching her somewhere deep inside, she felt pretty sure that was more than desire gleaming in his eyes.

Lily wrapped her legs around his lean hips, wanting to hold him closer, to imagine she could keep him right there, joined with her, forever. Their movements grew more frenzied, and before long, he took her to the very highest height for a third time. And this time when the physical bliss bubbled up and burst inside her, Wyatt let himself go, too.

Lily fell asleep almost immediately. It had been a long day, of course, but he had the feeling she'd just been wrung out by the responses of her own body.

Judging by how lethargic and sated he was himself, he completely understood.

He made no move to disentangle their bodies, liking that she slept while he was still inside her. He did, however, roll a little to the side, tugging her with him so he bore her weight instead of the other way around. Studying her beautiful face in the moonlight spilling in from the front window, he found himself wondering why this time, with this woman, seemed so different from any other time he'd had sex before.

Was it the emotional connection he felt to her? Was it true, what the poets said, that adding that single ingredient had taken an act he had always enjoyed but never lost his mind over, and made it the earthshaking interlude they'd just shared? *Is it because you're in love with her?*

Maybe, because he undoubtedly was. Wyatt hadn't planned to be—he didn't particularly want to be—but it had happened.

"I know what you're thinking," she whispered, though he had thought she was still asleep.

"You do?"

"You're thinking you're hungry."

He laughed softly. "No, I suspect that's what *you're* thinking."

"Oh, yeah, right. That's me." She yawned, her eyes still closed, and nuzzled closer to him, her head tucked into the curve of his neck. "So what is on your mind?"

"Just wondering what I'm going to do with you now that I've got you."

Her rumble of laughter said she didn't take his slightly bewildered comment the wrong way. She knew him too well; Lily had to realize this wasn't what he'd planned for, what he'd wanted. "That's easy. You have to keep me."

Keep her? Be with her? Have a normal life with her?

Wyatt's amusement faded a little. Because those things implied a future, commitment, all the things he knew he wasn't cut out to have.

She seemed to sense him pulling back. Lily kissed his shoulder and added, "I'm joking, Wyatt. You know I have no expectations."

"You should," he told her, meaning it entirely. "You should expect more. You deserve the whole works, someone younger and more open. Someone who wants the same thing you do."

"What might that be?"

"A nice, steady, normal life. One that's peaceful and includes a house with a white picket fence."

"I prefer a security gate and motion detectors," she said, pulling back to emphasize that with a stare. "And frankly, I consider a nice, normal life to be sitting with you outside in the middle of the night, wishing I wasn't craving a cigarette while you tell me about the psycho killer you're going after next."

He barked a helpless laugh. "That's pretty demented."

"Maybe. It's also as honest as I can be. If you think I'm holding out for a marriage proposal, babies, and a house in the suburbs, you can think again. I'm not sure I'll ever want any of those things."

"Which is a good thing, since I already *know* I don't."

She stared, and he almost regretted laying that out so baldly. But the last thing he would do was lead her on.

"Why not?" she asked, no longer half teasing. On the surface, her question might seem a simple one, but with those two words, she was asking so much more.

He understood. She wanted to know the truth, not about his future and how it might include her. No, Lily was asking about his past, what had shaped him, made him who he was, and led him to make those kinds of decisions about what the rest of his life would be. She'd respected his privacy, kept out of it, not intruding on what was none of her business. But now he was her lover, she'd moved into his innermost circle, and she deserved to know.

Wyatt never spoke about it. Not ever. Nor did he plan to now. At the very least, though, Lily was entitled to a brief explanation, if only in gratitude for the way she hadn't researched him or pushed for answers before now.

The subject wasn't one for warm, cozy, after-sex talk. He slid out from under her, sitting up on the bed. Lily reached for him, sliding her hand down his back, caressing his bare hip. Glancing over his shoulder at her, he said, "I'll discuss this only once."

She nodded. "Understood."

"And this conversation will not evolve into a discussion about feelings or emotions or psychobabble about poor-little-me. I don't need sympathy over how screwed up my childhood must have been or speculation that it drove me to become the man I am today. I know all that already. Do you understand?"

"Of course I do," she said simply. "I've always known that, even without knowing what exactly happened."

He didn't hedge, didn't soften it. Instead, he simply explained as briefly and succinctly as possible, as if describing a case, something that had occurred to another family, another son.

"You know they call it the murder house."

Her hand stilled on his hip. "Yes."

"My father died in that house," he admitted. "He was killed there, shot down right on the back patio."

Lily closed her eyes and shook her head. "I'm so—"

He cut her off. "My mother was the one who killed him."

This time, she made no soft gestures of comfort, offered him no look of pity. Pure, unadulterated shock twisted her features as she slowly sat up. In the long, silent moment that followed, Lily moved to the edge of the bed to sit beside him, staring at the floor, absorbing it, inexorably changed by the knowledge.

It did change everything, didn't it? Learning your new lover's father had been murdered by his mother?

That was only part of it, though. Finally, Wyatt felt she was ready to hear more, and he was ready to say it, wanting only to get through it, get it over with, so it never had to be discussed again. "My father was a rich, spoiled playboy and my mother was out of her element. Her family was well-off, but nowhere in his league. She didn't know how to handle it, didn't know how to turn a blind eye to his affairs, which came one after another."

She closed her eyes briefly.

"Finally he had one too many. She followed him to the beach house and watched him with his latest mistress. After the woman left, she went to confront him. The next thing I heard was a gunshot—"

She gasped. "My God, you were there?"

"Of course. I was the boy who survived, remember?"

A mumbled curse told him she did remember the words the drunk man had said at the restaurant. A sad little sniff told him she was crying about it. Apparently, she remembered all of the drunk's words . . . *the boy they found covered in blood.*

He forced himself to go on, remaining focused on the here and now, relating this just as if it were one of his cases. "I don't believe she was really insane, despite what that idiot at the restaurant started to say."

"I don't doubt it. People do desperate things when they're hurt."

He nodded, glad she understood. "She was very hurt. She hated what he did, but she had loved him wildly.

And he was gone—she'd killed him. Strangely enough, though, she knew one thing: She did not want to live without him. Not even for my sake. So she took me down to the beach, walking in the surf as she cried and raged and figured out what to do."

"She ended up at the lighthouse," Lily murmured.

"Of course."

"You don't have to say it."

He nodded his appreciation, knowing she meant it. She didn't need to hear the details. She knew without him telling her that his mother had gone into that place and put the gun to her own head, unable to live with what she had done, much less go through the rest of her life without the man she loved.

"Where did they find you?" she whispered.

"Back up at the beach house. I vaguely remember walking back and forth, one place to the other, all night long, hoping one of them would wake up."

She sniffed again and reached for his hand in the semidarkness. "How old were you, Wyatt?"

In a movie, this was where the violins would build to a crescendo and the drama would well up as the dam on his emotions finally broke. Only this wasn't a movie; this was life. His life. He'd dealt with it for years and he was far beyond the point of needing to break.

"I was five."

Lily dropped her face into her hands.

"Don't," he cautioned. "You don't need to do that. I have very few memories. And after that, my very warm and nurturing grandparents took me in and raised me in a loving home. I'm not the poor little lost soul you're imagining."

"Maybe not. But everything you are, every choice

you've ever made, has been a result of that one awful event." Not looking up at him, she added, "And you can't tell me not to cry for you. I can if I want to."

He loved her for wanting to, even if he genuinely didn't need her sympathy. But sweet, tender Lily needed to give it to him.

She shifted, curling against him, burrowing into his arms. Wyatt held her close, feeling her shake as she shed her silent tears. They wet his chest as he stroked her hair, comforting her, telling her over and over that he was all right and had been for a very long time.

Finally, she fell asleep again, still in his arms, half on his lap. He held her for a long while, knowing this time she was out for the night, wrung out physically and emotionally.

He hadn't intended to wring her out, hadn't meant to hurt her at all. He'd simply wanted to tell her the truth because she deserved to hear it. And also, he supposed, to offer her warning. Whatever he might be feeling for Lily, and she him, that didn't mean he envisioned himself truly changing his life for her. He was solitary and self-contained, driven and focused on his job, used to culling emotions that threatened to weaken him. He didn't like distractions, didn't want entanglements.

Just because he'd fallen in love with her didn't mean he envisioned anything actually changing. He'd simply do with that love exactly what he'd done with all the other emotions he'd dealt with in his life: acknowledge it, give it a half second to burn brightly, then get it completely under control. That had always worked for him before.

As he studied her sleeping face, however, he began to wonder if what had always worked in the past would do the trick yet again. And if he really wanted it to.

Mulling it over, he was surprised to hear his cell phone ring interrupt the late-night silence. It had been in his pants pocket and the pants had been tossed somewhere across the room. Disengaging himself from Lily, he quickly got out of bed and followed the sound of the ringing. As soon as he located the trousers, he dug the phone out and answered it on the fifth ring, not even glancing at the caller ID. "Blackstone."

"Agent Blackstone? I need your help," a man's voice said. He sounded shaky, nervous.

"Who is this?"

"You don't know me."

"How did you get this number?"

"That doesn't really matter. What matters is, I think somebody's trying to kill me, and you're the only person who can protect me. I need to see you."

Lily moved in her sleep, mumbling something.

"Hold on a minute." Wyatt headed for the door, stepping out into the hallway, not wanting to wake her. Shutting the door behind him, he lifted the phone to his ear again. "Now, tell me who you are."

"I'm scared."

"I can't help you if you don't tell me your name."

The man hesitated again. "You don't get it. Nobody will help me. Nobody will care that she's coming after me."

Wyatt tensed, not even sure why. This call could be just about anything, from a prank to someone he'd worked with on a previous case. Something, however, put him instantly on alert, making him realize something big was happening. Very big.

"I'm going to give you until the count of five to tell me who you are. Then, if you haven't told me who you are and exactly what you want from me, I will hang up."

The man fell silent for a moment. Then, when Wyatt had mentally reached the count of four, he finally admitted his name, shocking Wyatt so much he almost dropped the phone.

"My name is Jesse Tyrone Boyd. And I think one of your former employees, Agent Lily Fletcher, is going to try to kill me."

# Chapter 16

Wyatt Blackstone might be some famous, tough-guy FBI agent, but as far as Jesse was concerned, he was a fucking pussy.

The fed had refused to meet with him. Even now, shortly before dawn the next morning, Jesse could hardly believe it. The plan had been perfect, all laid out, and it still hadn't worked. When Jesse had called, saying he had proof Lily Fletcher was alive and gunning for him, and needed to see Wyatt in person, right away, the agent was supposed to say, "You betcha." He should have been all curious and worried, wondering how Jesse could know the blond troublemaker had survived, and why he thought she was gunning for him.

The son of a bitch had refused.

Well, he hadn't exactly said no. He'd just said there was no way he would come in person to talk to him last night. Blackstone had offered to have another agent pick Jesse up. He'd demanded to know where Jesse was, said he'd make sure he was protected. But he had absolutely hands down said there was no way he was coming out to meet him before this morning.

"Probably too busy screwing the lying bitch who's hiding in your house," he muttered sourly as he stared out the window of the dark house in which he was hiding.

Blackstone's place remained pretty quiet, though one of those dark blue sedans was parked out front. It hadn't been there last night, showing up sometime while Jesse had slept. For all he knew, the whole gang of them were in there right now, working on tracing Jesse's call to Blackstone, all ready to come at him like a gang of vigilantes.

"You're not such a genius after all, are ya?" he mumbled, staring at his cell phone and thinking of the person who'd called him on it last night. His so-called benefactor had put the whole scheme into Jesse's head, promising Blackstone could be lured out with the right bait. Once the agent was gone, off on a wild-goose chase to meet with Jesse—who had no intention of showing up—Lily Fletcher would have been alone in that house. A sitting duck. Jesse could have taken care of her and been gone again before her boyfriend ever figured out he'd been had.

No Lily to come after him for revenge. No Lily to testify against him now that Jesse's alibi was dead and gone.

Wrong. What a big screwup the entire idea had been.

Now what was he supposed to do? Just stay here in this house, waiting for a real estate agent to show it and figure out someone was flopping here and call the cops? Or leave and hang out in the old neighborhood, begging his ma to take him in, just waiting to feel Fletcher's bullet hit him right between the shoulder blades, like it had poor Will Miller?

"No way," he said aloud, wishing he had a way to call back the mysterious person who'd been helping him out. He was entirely on his own.

Well, fine, then. He'd do this on his own—he was no dummy. Frankly, now that he thought about it, the whole scheme to get Blackstone out of the house so Jesse could get to Lily seemed way over the top. As much as he would have liked the satisfaction of choking the life right out of the woman, the main thing was to keep her from getting to him.

There was one surefire way to do that. If Lily had killed Miller, the police were probably looking for her. And if she'd been hiding out, faking her own death and shit, the FBI would find her. Either one would do. Didn't really matter to him which of them picked her up and tossed her into a cell, as long as she was off the street and off his trail.

He thought about it, wondered which would have more pull to keep her ass in jail, and decided to go for her own former colleagues. Because not only did Lily deserve to get picked up, but so did that Blackstone dude. If he was hiding her, he was guilty and deserved to get in trouble with the FBI, too.

Decision made. He didn't need some anonymous voice on a phone telling him what to do. Jesse had covered his own ass more than once, and he'd do it again now. Which was why, with no hesitation whatsoever, he called information and got the number for the FBI. And after several explanations and transfers, he finally ended up getting a promise that an agent would be calling him back real soon, that he just had to be patient since it was so early on a Saturday.

Okay, he'd be patient. But this agent better call pronto,

because the idea of just getting on a bus and riding until his money ran out was sounding better and better to Jesse.

He glanced at his watch. Six thirty. He'd give it till noon. Then, call or no call, he was outta here. Meaning this agent, this Tom Anspaugh, had better get to work.

Facing a long drive down to Williamsburg, Wyatt prepared to leave very early Saturday morning. He'd been distracted, quiet, and at first Lily had wondered if it was because he had regrets, not just about making love to her, but about telling her his secrets.

"Is everything okay?"

He glanced at her from across the shadowy bedroom, buttoning his shirt, slipping a jacket on over his broad shoulders. Donning the uniform that turned him from passionate lover to aloof FBI agent.

"Fine."

"You're quiet." She walked into the room and sat on the edge of the bed. Jackie was downstairs, so she probably shouldn't, but she couldn't help it. As far as mornings after went, this situation wasn't ideal.

He seemed to know it. Crossing the room, he lifted a hand to her cheek, brushing his thumb across her bottom lip. "It's fine, Lily, I promise. I'm just focused on what I have to do, how I'm going to question Roger Underwood's widow." He leaned over and touched his mouth to hers, softly, sweetly, adding, "All I can think of is catching this guy. Making all of this go away."

As long as he meant all the bad stuff, and none of the good that had come out of it, she found that a fine idea. Unfortunately, she couldn't be sure of that. He was being tender now, but did he see her sharing that big bed with him again tonight? They were together, but that didn't mean they were some kind of "happily ever after" couple.

"Okay," she said, "good luck, and please keep in touch."

He kissed her again, lightly, not taking her in his arms. Mentally, he was already gone, back in that place where reason and intellect completely banished emotion.

She liked that about him, but as she watched him walk down the stairs and exit the house, she couldn't deny she would have liked a single whisper about what he was feeling.

Lily was no fool; she had no illusions that being Wyatt's lover meant she had a permanent place in his life. Honestly, she didn't think he wanted anyone to have a place in his life. On his pillow for a night or two? Maybe even for a week or two? Okay. Beyond that, though, she strongly suspected Wyatt had decided years ago that he was meant to be alone. He'd flat out admitted he wasn't cut out for the marriage-family routine.

"In case you haven't noticed," she muttered, "I'm not exactly dying for that, either."

A couple of years ago? Oh, yes, she'd wanted the whole nine yards. Wanted the family she'd never had growing up, wanted to be a mom like her sister, wanted a beautiful little boy and a nice home and a life partner.

Now she just wanted life. Big and dynamic, to be lived full throttle, with an eye toward savoring, not surviving, because any day could be the *final* day. Love could fit into her vision of that life, even if Wyatt didn't see it in his. She might even see marriage working its way in there.

But children? Oh, no. Not ever. Not after Zach.

It was kind of funny, in an odd way. She'd found out last night that Dean Taggert was engaged to be married to his girlfriend, Stacey Rhodes. It seemed Stacey was pregnant. The news had surprised her, because Lily remembered well how the other woman had felt about raising children. The female sheriff had seen some dark times, including a campus shooting spree, and she'd told Dean, already the father of a young son, that she never saw herself having children. Yet here she was, happily pregnant and engaged.

Some would tell Lily that the story was an example of why one should never say never.

"Never," she repeated, meaning it wholeheartedly, not affected by the other couple's situation at all. With everything she had seen of this world in the past few years, she would never willingly bring another soul into it. So, no, maybe she and Wyatt didn't have the radically different dreams of the future he seemed to think they did.

She and Jackie spent a quiet morning together, catching up a little, chatting about the other woman's kids and her husband. Both of them seemed to want to put off the day, as if holding the investigation at bay for another hour might make it easier to deal with when the time came. Finally, though, they could avoid it no longer. Lily asked for a half hour to shower, then promised to come back down ready to get to work.

She took a hot, steamy shower, using Wyatt's bathroom, his shampoo, his soap. She even dried off with the same towel he'd used. It still smelled of him, and she wanted to hold on to that scent.

Afterward, she dressed quickly, pulling on loose shorts and a T-shirt, knowing Jackie had been waiting patiently. Together, they were going to look through the background check the other agent had conducted on Roger Underwood. Before heading to the guest room to grab her own brush, though, Lily paused to glance at the clock. Wyatt would be in Williamsburg right now, possibly even inside the offices where Underwood had worn the normal, surgeon's face over the secret, twisted devil's maw that reflected his true self. He'd somehow lived nearly fifty years disguising what he was, fooling the community and his patients, even members of his family.

Well, maybe not all the members of his family. They might have known. In fact, Wyatt seemed pretty sure his wife and sister had suspected something about the man, since they'd both lied about not recognizing the voice on the tape.

Maybe because she was in law enforcement, she couldn't understand the concept of lying to protect someone who committed such hideous acts. She'd loved her sister. But would she have covered for Laura if she had been guilty of such brutal crimes?

"No way," she whispered as she walked across the hall to the other bedroom, with the pristine, unmade bed.

But Roger Underwood's loved ones had. So what did that say about them?

"That they're all equally as twisted," she told her reflection as she pulled a brush out of her purse and yanked it through her hair. The dark strands were almost long enough to pull into a short ponytail. For now, though, she just tucked them behind her ears, not even caring about the scars about which she had once been so self-conscious. She barely even noticed them anymore, maybe because she had been healing from the inside out for so long, they'd almost become invisible to her eyes.

Taking the steps two at a time, she jogged downstairs barefoot, seeing Jackie sitting in Wyatt's dining room. The other woman didn't even look up, simply pushing a file folder across the broad, gleaming table. "Check these out. Names of every registered sex offender in the Williamsburg area. Nothing that screams a connection with Underwood, but it's a place to start."

"Maybe one of them went to him to get a face-lift and they bonded over a Cub Scout calendar," Lily said, shaking with disgust. "Gotta look youthful and handsome if you want to try to hide the fact that you're a monster."

The other woman nodded. "Judging by the number of names on that list, they could have kept Underwood's office busy all on their own for a year."

"Maybe that's why the practice is open on Saturday mornings."

That had surprised her, realizing the plastic surgery office was open today, and Wyatt wouldn't be confronting Underwood's widow at her home.

"Just as well," Jackie said. "By showing up unannounced, during business hours, when patients might be around to see and hear, Underwood's family might be more quick to usher Wyatt in for a private talk."

Lily wasn't holding her breath. "Until the very moment they realize he's there to confront them about their lies. Then they'll lawyer up and invite him to come back when he has a warrant."

Though she could be wrong. Wyatt had a way of making women want to talk to him. Maybe it was his calmness, the sense that you could tell him absolutely anything and he would remain understanding, sympathetic, and controlled while coming up with a solution to any problem. It was a rare talent, one she found incredibly appealing. Though Lily had to acknowledge she also liked it when he lost a little of that control. Especially when he lost it with her, in his bed.

Hoping Jackie didn't correctly interpret the satisfied smile she couldn't contain, she turned her head away and said, "I think I'll go get some coffee. Want some?"

"Sure."

Lily started to walk toward the kitchen, but got only a few steps when Jackie stopped her.

"Wait!"

"What is it?"

Jackie was reading over a document on her laptop screen, her eyes narrowed, a frown line between them. "I was just going over this family history and something struck me. A name that looks really familiar."

Lily walked over to stand behind her, staring down at the screen. Jackie moved the cursor to the name in question, highlighting it.

"What does it mean?" she asked, equally surprised.

"I don't know."

"We should probably let Wyatt know," Lily said. She reached into the pocket of her shorts for her cell phone. "I'll try to reach him—"

A squeal of tires from outside interrupted her. A door slammed; someone yelled.

Jackie leapt up and hurried to the front window. "Oh, my God," she whispered, staring out at the street.

"What is it?"

"You've gotta get out of here." The woman spun

around, putting her hands in the middle of Lily's back and physically pushing her so hard the phone flew out of Lily's hands. "Out the back door. Fast."

*"What?"*

"It's Anspaugh," the woman said. "It looks like he brought a whole posse, and I suspect he's gunning for you."

As expected, Judith Underwood hadn't been pleased to hear he was waiting to see her.

Wyatt didn't let that stop him. After informing the receptionist that he'd wait, despite the woman's claims that Dr. Underwood couldn't possibly squeeze in a meeting, he'd taken a seat in the waiting room. It had taken one conversation—just one—and he'd gotten the meeting he wanted. Apparently the grieving widow didn't like hearing that he was talking to the patients about being here to question one of the doctors about a crime.

He was whistling as he followed the receptionist down the familiar back hallway. But he found it hard to maintain the cheery facade when he reached that T in the corridor and came face-to-face with Dr. Roger Underwood's portrait. Wyatt had to pause, stare at the man, search for any glimmer of insanity in his eyes or utter evil in his half smile.

There was nothing. No hint that the man was the kind of depraved monster who would abuse young children. No malice in the smile to show he would gladly slaughter anyone who got in his way.

"It was so sad. A real tragedy," the receptionist said. "Dr. Roger being so young and all."

"Had he had a history of problems with his heart?"

Wyatt asked, wondering so much more about Roger's death now that he knew just what a fiend he had been in life.

"Never," she said. "It really was a mystery. He played tennis all the time, ate right, had regular physicals. Never sick a day."

Very unusual.

The receptionist, who was not the same one he'd seen on his last visit, meaning she might have been around long enough to know something, inched a tiny bit closer. Wyatt knew the move signaled a desire to spill a little more information. With the right prodding she'd do just that.

"Did they do an autopsy?" he asked, trying to sound only mildly interested.

"Uh-uh," said the woman—girl really, who was pretty in a vacant way. "They probably would have if the family hadn't been who they are. But I guess since there wasn't a mark on him, other than the tiny cut where he fell on the wine opener, they didn't suspect anything." She lowered her voice a notch. "There were some whispers, though."

"Oh?"

When she didn't elaborate immediately, Wyatt intentionally pulled his gaze off the portrait and stared down at the young woman, offering her a smile of encouragement. She lifted a hand to her throat, her cheeks turning a soft pink as she stared up at him. She wasn't the first woman to look into his blue eyes and see something she wanted to see there, and she almost certainly wouldn't be the last.

"Well . . ." The girl looked quickly over her shoulder, then peeked past Wyatt down the other short hallway.

Confirming they were not being observed, she continued. "I'm not one to speak ill of the dead."

Everyone spoke ill of the dead. It just took them an hour or two.

"Dr. Roger was a little hard to work for." She swallowed visibly. "And I don't imagine he was much easier to live with. Dr. Alfred loved him to bits, but other than that, he wasn't really well liked around here."

"Not even by his wife and sister, or his stepbrother?"

She frowned, shaking her head. "Sometimes it seemed like all three of them were united in hating him, others like they were fighting over a boyfriend they were crazy about. It was really weird. Dr. Judith and Dr. Angela sometimes act the same way now about Dr. Kean."

Dr. Kean. Angela Kean's angry husband? What must it be like for him, working down the hall from his domineering wife, across from his overbearing father-in-law?

And right beside his stunning, widowed sister-in-law?

Somewhere nearby, a door closed, and the young woman stepped back, guilty and nervous. "I think I've said enough."

Wyatt moved forward, staying close, maintaining that intimate air that silently told her she could trust him. "Dr. Roger's death . . . do you suspect someone did something to him?"

She pulled her lips into her mouth, as if clamping down on them to keep herself from saying something she shouldn't.

He persisted. "You don't think he had a heart attack?"

After a brief hesitation, she shook her head once, keeping those lips sealed. As if as long as she didn't say the words aloud, she wasn't really talking about her employers.

"His sister?" Jealous of their father's attention, perhaps?

No response.

Wyatt zoomed in on his own favorite suspect. "His wife?"

The eyes flared briefly, confirming it. The receptionist believed Roger Underwood's wife had done something to him. Having met the woman, he thought it highly possible. She was beautiful, brilliant. How difficult would it be for a woman with so much to offer to find out her own husband had such vile preferences? A blow like that could drive any woman to a sudden rage. No doubt about that.

Had she found out about her husband on that very night—perhaps figuring out Roger had stolen the car and was involved in the planned attack on two young children? What possible excuse had he given her for disappearing for those couple of nights? Might he actually have admitted what he'd done?

A sound penetrated from just inside the closed office door to their right. Without hesitation, Wyatt put the tips of his fingers on the receptionist's shoulder, turning her and pushing her forward, so she appeared to be leading him. A second later, the door swung inward and Dr. Judith Underwood appeared there.

She stared at the receptionist, her pretty eyes glacial, her face as cold as a mask carved of pure ice. "I was beginning to think you got lost."

"Sorry," the young woman said.

Wyatt interrupted. "It was entirely my fault. I'm so sorry to have kept you waiting."

He offered her an intimate smile, extending his hand. Judith took it, her eyes widening as he kept her fingers clasped in his own for a moment longer than was technically necessary. "Once again, I've interrupted your workday," he murmured.

"You'll have to make it up to me sometime," she replied, her tone intimate, matching his. The icy expression melted as she gently tugged him inside, seeming to forget all about the receptionist, who had already scurried away.

"How should I do that?" he asked, stepping aside as she shut the door behind him.

"Lunch?"

She might not be hungry after their meeting, but he merely offered her a noncommittal shrug. As if he were instead silently saying, *Dinner?*

"Please, have a seat." She didn't go to her own, behind the desk, instead gracefully lowering herself to a small love seat in the corner, grouped with two comfortable chairs. He assumed the coffee-klatch setup was designed to make skittish patients feel more at ease before submitting their laugh lines or extra chins to the knife.

"Thank you," he said, taking his time, as if keenly interested in the office. He glanced around, noting the degrees, the awards, the thank-you letters from grateful patients. There was only one photograph, the same huge portrait of the Underwood family in front of their beach house that hung in the outer hallway. He recalled it also graced one of the walls in Dr. Kean's office—the senior Dr. Underwood's contribution to the building's decor, perhaps?

He also realized one more thing. There was no photo of Roger Underwood. Not a single snapshot to remind the grieving widow of her dearly departed.

That was all right. He had something else that would bring the man to mind.

The understated flirtation had relaxed her. She had correctly interpreted the intimacy in his smile and that second-too-long handshake, felt comfortable and mildly flattered at his attention. Meaning it was time to pull the rug out.

Wyatt unceremoniously pulled the digital recorder out of his pocket and set it down on the coffee table, hitting the play switch even as he sat down across from her. Roger Underwood's voice emerged from it.

The color dropped from Judith's face. "What is that?"

Lifting a brow, as if confused by the query, Wyatt replied, "I believe it's your husband's workshop on a new piece of laser equipment, isn't it? From a speech he gave in 2007?"

The woman moved as if to stand, but Wyatt put a hand on her arm, not restraining, still intimate. And he threw her off balance again. "Judith, I understand," he said softly.

She hesitated.

"Of course you would want to protect your husband."

She didn't settle back in her seat, but she did at least stop trying to get up.

"You loved him."

The muscles beneath his hand tensed.

"Or at least you wanted to protect his reputation. For the sake of the family, of the business."

She finally leaned back in the chair. Which was when he knew he had nailed it.

Wyatt let go of her arm and sat back himself, eyeing her with sympathy. "It can't have been easy."

"What is it you want?"

"I mean, knowing what he had been planning to do.

It must have been so difficult. How long had you known the truth about him?"

Blinking, she simply stared and he could almost see the wheels turning in the intelligent mind. *How much does he know? What is he asking? What do I say?*

Wyatt tipped the balance again, intentionally leaving her to wonder. "Forgive me; we can discuss that later. Let's talk about the night in question. The night he took your sister-in-law's car. Did you notice he was missing?"

Judith hesitated before finally admitting, "Yes. Right before the banquet."

"He hadn't told you he was going anywhere?"

"He mentioned something about having to make some calls."

"Did you find that strange?"

"Of course. Roger usually made an effort to keep his daddy happy, even though Alfred would forgive him absolutely anything." Judith glanced out the window, staring at the blue sky beyond. "I later wondered why he didn't just claim he was sick, but I suppose Ben already had the corner on faking illness to cover what he was really up to that night."

"Ben?

She pulled her attention back to his face. "Benjamin Kean. Angela's husband. He backed out of the entire conference at the last minute, claiming illness."

Wyatt suspected he knew the answer, but he still asked the question. "Do you know why?"

"Of course. He was down here screwing the little receptionist who just escorted you back here and filled your head with lots of rumors and speculations."

Wyatt didn't try to deny it, staying on the offensive. "Was that a frequent occurrence?"

"Ben's a slave to his own penis and his own legend. He nails any woman who will say yes, singing the poor-put-upon-husband song to anyone who will listen."

"Including you?"

The woman shrugged. "Occasionally. If I was bored or was angry at my husband for some reason and wanted to punish him."

Wyatt allowed himself a second to process it—Ben Kean sounded like a slime; the condition obviously spread like a cancer in this family. But he did not sound like a man who shared his late brother-in-law's tastes. That didn't mean the men hadn't been friends, and he hadn't helped Roger in his moment of utmost need, but Wyatt doubted it. He couldn't see Underwood turning to a man who'd had an affair with his wife. Men like Roger tended to dislike it when other people played with their possessions.

"When did you next see your husband after the night of the banquet?"

Judith met his eye directly. "About forty-eight hours later, on Monday night. He showed up at the house looking like he'd been at a Roman orgy."

"You hadn't reported him missing?"

She shrugged, as if to say it had not been the first time. Probably it hadn't.

"Any explanation as to where he'd been?"

"None."

"Did you have any suspicions?" he asked, making no insinuations either way. He wasn't sure how much Judith knew, and didn't want her to clam up now by his bringing up the one subject she wouldn't touch.

To his surprise, she didn't just touch it; she hit it with a sledgehammer. "Sure. He was probably out at some sick party where rich perverts paid lots of money to partner swap, to see someone being tortured, or to have sex with helpless little children."

Wyatt didn't react with as much as a blink. She might have thought she was going to shock him, might have worded her answer to do exactly that. But it hadn't worked. "So you did know."

She nodded once. "He'd gotten tangled up in a role-playing Web site a few months before and I found him acting out the kinds of fantasies that would land most people in a mental ward."

*Satan's Playground.*

"You hadn't known before then?"

She finally rose, her slim body graceful and elegant, innately sensuous. How on earth had she ended up in Roger Underwood's bed? "His cruel streak was a thing of legend, though of course nobody filled me in on it until after we were married." She wrapped her arms around herself. "I don't know if I can explain it. Some people are just . . . magnetic. Sadistic—you can see it in their eyes—but seductive just the same. They become almost an addiction."

Wyatt began to see the answer to his own unasked question. For a while, anyway, Roger had been her obsession.

"He cared about no one and could be utterly vicious, which just made you want him even more."

Underwood had obviously been a charming socio-path. Wyatt had met a few like him. Manson, so they said, had possessed that same quality to inspire utter devotion to the point of insanity, his cruelty never driving away those who were madly in love with him.

"There was no depravity too low. I found out things

about him after we married. . . ." She shook her head, glancing toward the door, then back at Wyatt. This time, she lowered her voice, visibly shaken for the very first time since she'd opened up. "No one was off-limits if he wanted that person. You understand? *No* one."

He understood. It made him sick, but Wyatt understood.

"How long had it gone on, do you think?"

"Oh, years. I know he started in with his stepbrother, Philip, when the boy was eight years old and Roger was in medical school. Philip's teenage sister, too."

And his own sister? The one who'd hated him, loved him?

Vile. But not impossible.

So Roger had been molesting children for decades. He'd found his victims close at hand. Which led Wyatt to believe that his plans on the night he'd attacked Lily had involved far more than a sexual attack. Had those children really existed, Wyatt truly believed Roger would have kidnapped, then slaughtered them, choosing strangers with whom he had absolutely no connection in an effort to cover his crime. The homeless man who'd assisted him would more than likely have been found dead the next day, too.

"His father never suspected?"

"Who knows what that old man thinks?" Bitterness oozed from her. "Precious Roger could do nothing wrong, and if he suddenly decided he wanted to fuck the family dog, Alfred would have found a reason to justify it."

It was only eleven thirty, but Judith seemed to need a bracer. She walked over to a small wet bar, opened a miniaturized wine refrigerator, and pulled out a pricey-looking bottle. "Care to join me?"

Though he couldn't blame her, he declined.

"Suit yourself." Judith was almost ruthless in her movements as she peeled the foil off the bottle. Retrieving a small device, a plastic tube holding a tiny air canister, with a long, slim needle at the end, she plunged the sharp point into the cork, pushed a button to release the compressed air, and watched as the cork erupted out.

Violent, but expedient.

"That's unusual-looking," he murmured.

Judith pushed the cork off the needle with her thumb. "Wine has always been the unhappy wife's best friend, hasn't it? Anything that gets the cork out of the bottle a little faster is okay by me."

He hadn't been thinking of how fast that needle could get a cork out of a bottle, but of all its other potential uses. "Your husband was opening a wine bottle when he died, wasn't he?"

Glass clinked against glass as she poured herself a generous helping of Chardonnay. "He was a connoisseur, had already gone through a few bottles earlier that night with his sister and her husband, who had come over for dinner."

Wyatt narrowed his eyes in concentration. "You mentioned that when I was here the other day. Can you tell me more about that night? What happened?"

Carrying her drink, she returned to her seat. "There's not much to tell. We ate, drank. Roger and his sister were very tense with one another, so she and her husband left early to walk back to their place." She smiled bitterly. "I assumed they were having a lovers' quarrel."

Seeing the flint in her eyes, and remembering how little she and Angela liked each other, he took that for nothing more than spite. "Go on."

"There's nothing else. After they left, I told Roger I was going to bed. I came down the next morning and found him on the floor in the living room, surrounded by broken glass and reeking of wine." She shook her head. "Unfortunately, he'd been opening a bottle of really nice white Burgundy he'd brought back from France last year. What a waste."

Wyatt leaned forward in his chair, dropping his elbows onto his knees. "Can you back up a little, to before the dinner? What had you noticed that week?"

"Roger had been gone a lot and his mood vacillated between foul and violent. He wasn't happy when I reminded him we had dinner plans. Considering he was the one who invited his obnoxious sister and her weak little husband over, I wasn't going to let him bow out."

"They were close?"

Judith merely stared.

*Good God.* "Even at that point?"

"She was absolutely insane for him and had been for years."

Wyatt suddenly had a suspicion, and while it didn't make things much better, it made them a little less degenerate. "Wait a minute, we're not talking about Angela and Ben—she told me they live in Richmond."

Judith's eyes flared in surprise and a soft, humorless laugh emerged from her mouth. "Oh, goodness, you thought I meant ... Well, I wouldn't be surprised to learn some of the things that went on in the house they grew up in after their mother died. But I was referring to his stepsister, Cece. She and her husband live a few doors down from us."

"Philip's sister."

"Yes."

"The one Roger seduced when she was a teenager."

"Exactly."

"No offense, Dr. Underwood, but this is like an episode of some high-melodrama soap opera about the lives of the rich and shameless."

"Think I could sell the movie rights?"

He'd bet she'd like to do just that. Earn as much money as possible and get as far away from her in-laws as she could. Though he didn't know her well, he sensed Judith Underwood was desperate to wash the stench of Roger Underwood and his family off her forever.

Almost conversationally, he asked the question that had been most on his mind. "So did you kill him?"

The query didn't shock her; she merely shook her head and took another sip of her wine. "No, Agent Blackstone, I did not," she eventually replied. "I believed, and I still believe, that his own evil eventually broke him. How long can a corrupt heart keep beating?"

Too long, as far as Wyatt was concerned.

"Evil or not, I did cry a real tear or two at his funeral." A crocodile smile made a mockery of any tears she might have shed. "But that night, I went home, got good and drunk, danced naked around my living room in sheer joy, then had sex with my gardener."

Wyatt reached for the recorder, pocketed it, and stood. "Thank you for your time."

She stood as well. "I suppose I shouldn't have said that last part. Does this mean you're no longer interested in lunch?"

He extended a hand and answered truthfully. "If I weren't already involved with someone else"—*and completely in love with her*—"I suspect I might like to have lunch with you, Dr. Underwood."

She nodded her appreciation, shook his hand, then turned to lead him toward the door. Before he reached it, though, Wyatt stopped, glancing at the huge Underwood family portrait. "I'm curious. Which one is Cece?"

Judith stepped close, leaning toward the framed picture. Then she tapped one long, perfectly manicured nail on the glass frame, pointing toward a woman standing a few feet from Roger Underwood.

Wyatt stared. And stared. He couldn't move, just letting it all sink in, all the puzzle pieces move around, twist, turn, then come back together to form a picture in his mind.

"Even here you can see she's making goo-goo eyes at him, despite the fact that she's standing right beside her own husband, and I'm there on Roger's arm. I think the woman would have cut her own heart out of her body to save Roger's when his went bad."

His stepsister would have died for him. And yes, indeed, she was making goo-goo eyes in the photograph, wearing her emotions on her face so obviously anyone could see them.

She might be brilliant, but the woman with the severe hairstyle was not good at masking her own feelings. Not even behind those trendy silver eyeglasses.

"Good-bye, Doctor, and thank you again," he said as he turned and opened the door, now knowing exactly where he was headed.

Wyatt no longer had any interest in going down the hall to try to talk to Dr. Angela Kean. He wanted to pay a visit to Cece—the woman who had gotten Jesse Boyd out of jail to draw Lily out of hiding. The woman whose job made her the perfect person for Roger Underwood to call for help in a legal emergency. The woman who was madly in love with her stepbrother, would die for him. Might even kill for him.

Claire Vincent.

# Chapter 17

Lily refused to run.

Jackie had pushed and prodded, ordered, and tried to strong-arm her into at least hiding, but in the end, she had been the one to walk over to the front door and answer it after Anspaugh had nearly pounded it down. The look of shock on the man's face when he saw and recognized her would live in Lily's memory for a long time. But probably not as long as the flash of sheer furious hunger she'd seen there before he could disguise it.

Anspaugh had always desired her. Now, though, his desire had been overshadowed by anger. Wyatt hadn't been exaggerating. Anspaugh didn't just resent her for ruining his career. He hated her. Probably because he'd once so wanted her and she'd chosen to fake her own death and let him swing in the wind.

Never mind the fact that his ineptitude was what had caused her to nearly die in the first place.

"You can't just take her," Jackie snapped, not for the first time, as Anspaugh insisted Lily accompany him to headquarters. "If you're going to arrest her, do it, and I'll have a lawyer waiting for you by the time you arrive downtown."

Hearing the anger in Jackie's voice, Lily reached over and touched her friend's arm. "It's all right. We knew this would happen, and it *needs* to. I've got to clear my name. I'm innocent and I want to get that established so I can move on and make sure Jesse gets put back in jail where he belongs."

Anspaugh sneered. "Yeah, right, save it for the judge."

Maintaining her dignity, Lily eyed him without flinching. "I need to go upstairs and change," she said, gesturing toward her shorts and bare feet.

"Fine, let's go," he said, grabbing her arm.

"Whoa, whoa, big boy," said Jackie. "I'll escort her up and keep an eye on her."

"Whadda you take me for? You're her damn accomplice."

"I'm an FBI agent with more than a dozen years on the job," Jackie snarled. "I was in the field while you were still trying to pass high school algebra for the third time, boy, and don't you forget it."

Anspaugh signaled to another agent, one of the three men who had accompanied him. All were loyal Anspaugh flunkies, from what Lily remembered. "Keep Agent Stokes here. As of now, she's a suspect in aiding and abetting a criminal."

"What the hell?" Jackie jerked away as the other agent grabbed her arm. "You touch me again, you're gonna be pulling back a stump."

"Jackie, don't," Lily insisted, sensing the situation was getting ugly. This wasn't professional, wasn't courteous.

Anspaugh was out for blood. Hers. He didn't seem to be thinking clearly and she couldn't be entirely sure he wouldn't do something crazy if he sensed they weren't cooperating. "It's fine. I'll go downtown, clear this up. It'll be fine."

"Yeah, you might want to worry a little less about her and a little more about yourself," Anspaugh told Jackie. "In case you haven't realized it, you're an accessory after the fact, just like your buddy Blackstone." He smiled in utter malice. "Where is he, by the way? I really can't wait to put the cuffs on him and take him in."

"He's not here," Lily said, hanging on to her temper by its very thin edge. "And I can dress myself." She tried to brush past him to head for the stairs.

He wouldn't let her, grabbing her upper arm and squeezing tight, then pushing her forward. "Let's go."

*Keep your cool, keep your cool,* an inner voice reminded her. It sounded a lot like the sarge's. Not that she was thinking along those lines, doing anything physical. She couldn't deny, however, that the idea she might be put in a position of having to defend herself had crossed her mind. Anspaugh's mood was strange, his voice thick with barely suppressed anger. And again, she suspected it had more to do with the fact that she'd once rejected him than anything else.

Or maybe the fact that she'd rejected him, and then turned to Wyatt Blackstone to be her savior. And her lover.

He crowded her as they walked up the steps, breathing his hot, heavy breaths on her neck, squeezing her arm hard enough to leave bruises. At the top of the stairs, she pointed toward the guest room. "My things are in here."

He escorted her in. Lily turned, waiting for him to leave, but he merely crossed his arms and smirked, shutting the door behind him.

She didn't get truly worried until he twisted the lock.

Lily hid her concern. If he thought she was the same timid girl he'd known, the man was sorely mistaken. Lifting her chin, not about to let him shame her, she peeled off her lightweight cotton shirt, and unzipped the shorts, pushing them off her hips. She still wore a plain white bra, and modest cotton underwear, but he reacted as though she'd stripped down to nothing. His bloodshot eyes devoured her and his mouth parted as he licked his thick lips.

*Scumbag.*

"You know, of course, that this is all going to go away. Proving my innocence is going to be incredibly simple once the entire Cyber Division gets involved. They'll take the computer equipment I used, confirm I was nowhere near where the unsub's messages originated from, and finally get to work looking for a real suspect." She reached for her jeans and stepped into them, knowing he was trying to peek down the top of her bra.

"Oh, yeah? Then why haven't you just come in? Why'd you have to fake your death, make everybody think something happened to you?"

Anger sparked. She dropped the jeans again, turning to show him the vicious scar on her upper thigh. "Want to hear how many surgeries it took to repair the muscles in my leg? How long it took me to walk again?" Then she yanked her hair back to display her ear. "How about this? Want to talk about how lucky I am that I didn't lose my hearing? How about the week I spent being tortured by the psychopath you *said* you had under control in that house?"

His face paled. For the first time since he'd arrived, he began to look uncertain.

Lily cursed herself for trying to explain a thing to the Neanderthal. She quickly pulled the jeans on, then grabbed a sweater from the top of the dresser and donned that as well. Shoving her feet into a pair of tennis shoes, she said, "I'm ready. Let's go do this. I'm sure they're going to be really interested to hear that you called an all clear on the site and told me and Kowalski to leave the van without ever even checking to see if the man you'd caught had an accomplice outside."

The man's face reddened again and he lurched toward her. "It wasn't my fault."

"I didn't say it was," she replied, "but you sure didn't help the situation."

"Goddamn it, Lil, I never wanted anything to happen to you!" He grabbed both her arms this time, squeezing, shaking a little. "Why wasn't it me? Why didn't you come to me for help afterward?"

He looked and sounded a little out of control. Lily realized Tom Anspaugh wasn't just angry; he was perhaps even a bit unbalanced, at the mercy of the emotions that had churned within him since that night.

She stepped carefully. "Take your hands off me, Anspaugh."

Funny. The thing that completely removed the last of the agent's self-control was her calling him by his last name. Spittle flew from his lips and his grip became punishing as he snarled, "It's Tom, you fucking high-toned bitch."

"Let me go, Agent, or I'll scream."

"Go ahead. You think my men are gonna help you?"

"Jackie—"

"Is in custody." He stuck one hand in her short hair, twisting it around his thick fingers, twisting and pulling. "You break my heart, you ruin my life, you oughta at least have the courtesy to call me by my first name. Just once. Or is it not good enough to come out of your perfect little mouth?"

While he'd been growing angrier, she'd pulled her anger in. Let it simmer. Let it build. Used it, just like Sarge had taught her.

Anspaugh pushed her toward the bed until her legs were backed against it. Her knees threatened to bend, putting her on her ass with him above her. It would be no more than a few steps beyond that for him to rip her jeans off, spread her legs, and rape her.

"I bet you say 'Wyatt' easily enough, don't you? You been saying it in his ear when he's screwing you? Managing to whisper it even when your mouth's full of his cock?"

He made his move. Pushed harder, trying to force her to sit. Lily had been prepared for it and when he reached down, trying to grab her crotch, she encircled his wrist in one hand and smashed his elbow in the wrong direction with the other.

He grunted.

Lily was no longer thinking, no longer coherent; she merely reacted. Having the upper hand, she punched him in the solar plexus, then kneed him hard in the groin. When he staggered back, she spun to the right and kicked up and high with her left leg, and the agent went flying. As he hit the wall and began to slide down it, Lily was conscious of two things: the voices of people calling up from downstairs, and the look of murderous rage in Tom Anspaugh's eyes.

If he got up again before someone came through that door, he would hurt her, badly, then make up any excuse he cared to. If he didn't, and one of his goons burst in and saw him on the floor, they'd take her out, anyway.

"One option," she muttered.

She didn't give it a second thought. Grabbing the purse she had thankfully left on the dresser, which contained a fake ID and plenty of cash, she darted to the window, jumped out, crashed to the lawn one story below, and ran for her life.

"Ms. Vincent? I gotta talk to you!"

The lawyer, who'd apparently lost Jesse's number after she'd gotten him out of jail the other day, sounded really mad to be interrupted from whatever Saturday morning stuff she was doing, probably in her perfect house with her perfect family. "What is it?"

"I need to get in touch with the person who hired you!" Still unable to believe what he'd just witnessed from the front window, he added, "Right this minute."

"Why? What's happening?"

He didn't know that he could trust her. But she was his lawyer, right? Lawyer-client privilege and all that shit?

There was no time to hesitate. "It's Lily Fletcher. She's alive and she just got away from the FBI. I saw the whole thing—she jumped out a window and took off down the street."

"Damn it," the woman snapped, sounding angry. Which was when the truth sank in.

Nobody else had hired Claire Vincent. She'd hired herself. "It's you?"

"Where did she go?"

"She ran a few blocks, then jumped into a cab."

"Tell me you followed."

Incredibly pleased with himself, Jesse said, "Damn straight I did. I'm in a cab not far behind her. Bitch better not go far, though. I don't want to waste my money paying no big fare."

"I'll pay all your expenses," the lawyer said, sounding hard, bitter, and desperate.

Whatever Fletcher had done to Jesse, she seemed to have done more of it to Ms. Vincent.

He suddenly understood. "Jeez, she's after you, too, right? For defending me, getting me off?"

The lawyer hesitated a second, then finally said, "Yes, Jesse. I'm afraid both our lives are in danger. You must stick close to her."

He leaned down in the backseat, craning to peer through the front windshield at the vehicle a couple of car lengths ahead of them. His driver was some foreign dude who hadn't asked why he was being asked to follow another cab, not once he'd seen the wad of bills Jesse had flashed at him.

"We're on the GW Parkway. Looks like she might be headed for Reagan Airport."

"You follow her, tell me exactly where she goes, and I'll see to it that you are paid back for any expenses. If you have to hop on a plane, call me right back and I'll pay for the ticket."

"Well, I dunno. . . ."

"I do know. This has to be done." She hesitated, then said, "Look, I'm in the city myself. If it looks like she's definitely going to Reagan, you call me and I'll come out there. You need to see which flight she gets on."

"What are we gonna do, follow her?"

"If we have to. We can't be on the same flight, so just watch where she's going, and if we have to, we'll go over to Dulles or BWI to get the first one after that."

"This is getting a little crazy. . . ."

"Crazier than waiting around for her to come after us both and kill us? Listen, Jesse, it's kill or be killed now. We're in this together."

"I ain't goin' back to prison."

"I promise you, if you help me take care of her, so we're both safe, you will never have to worry about money for the rest of your days."

He didn't know much about lawyers, about how much money they made. But he suspected it was a lot. Enough to get him far away from this stinking state, anyway. Far from his mother's angry, disgusted eyes. Far enough to start a whole new life.

"Okay, Ms. Vincent, you got a deal."

She was headed for the beach house. Wyatt had no doubt of that. Lily was being hunted, tracked, and in her mind, there was only one safe place in the entire world—the place of Wyatt's darkest nightmares, the place where he'd taken her to recover from her darkest nightmare.

The fact that the Jeep was missing from the long-term parking lot at the Portland airport confirmed it.

"Damn it," he said as he drove his rental car toward the Maine coast. "It's *not* safe."

Crandall knew Wyatt had been traveling to Maine recently. It wouldn't take long for the deputy director's goon squad to find out Wyatt owned property there. They'd be on her doorstep before Lily managed to gain one moment of peace.

There was but one consolation in this whole mess. Wyatt truly believed he'd identified their unsub, the person who had been trying to finish what Roger Underwood had started.

His stepsister, Claire Vincent.

Wyatt had a lot of questions for the woman, and he'd ask them sooner or later, whether as an official FBI agent or not. He would not rest, would not stop, until he'd found out if she was guilty, and ensured she never got near Lily again.

Thank God the woman had no way of knowing about the beach house. She should be going about her business today, having no idea Wyatt had figured out she might very well be the one who had killed those four men.

It was crazy, far-fetched even, that a woman, a respected attorney, could have done such things. But Wyatt knew from experience that female serial killers existed, and could be just as deadly as male ones.

He had seen Judith's eyes, had seen the hint of recklessness in them, and was certain it had come from her years of marriage to a psychopath such as Roger Underwood. Claire had been wholly within his sphere of influence for decades; she had been his teenage lover, had worshipped the ground he'd walked on. What *wouldn't* she do?

He knew no details. He didn't need them. That sixth sense told him she was someone he needed to talk to. And he'd do it just as soon as he got Lily to safety, even if that safety was in custody in the Hoover Building.

"Come on, Lily, call me!"

He glanced at his personal cell phone, not the one he used for work, which lay open on the passenger seat. He already knew she didn't have her cell phone with her; it was still at his place in Washington. He'd dialed the beach house several times since landing, getting no answer, but didn't read anything into that. The evening was a windy one, with dark clouds gathering to the east. Phone service on the beach was notoriously unreliable.

It was also possible she wasn't even there yet at all. He had no idea which flight she'd been on out of D.C. Maybe she hadn't beaten him by much. He'd heard about her escape from Brandon more than an hour after it had occurred, but it hadn't taken too long to get to the Richmond airport, and then to get on a flight to Maine. She might not be more than minutes ahead of him.

But it was also possible she had already arrived at the house and walked into an FBI ambush. He had been out of touch with Washington for several hours and had absolutely no way of knowing.

He still couldn't wrap his mind around what had happened this morning. Brandon hadn't known a lot, just the brief details he was able to get from Jackie before they took her away for questioning. Then Brandon and the others had been taken in, too. Anspaugh's doing, no doubt.

"Anspaugh, you son of a bitch," he growled, filled with such rage, he knew he'd do something violent the next time he saw the man. Because he had no doubt Anspaugh had done something to make Lily panic like she had. From what Brandon had told him, she had been cooperating even when Anspaugh had insisted he accompany her while she changed.

When the phone rang, he started, felt his heart race. Grabbing it, he saw a familiar name. Not the call he was waiting for, but a person he trusted. "Hello?"

"It's Christian."

Christian Mendez, one of the new members of the team. One of the only two members not currently being questioned by a raging Deputy Director Crandall, or so Wyatt suspected.

"What is it?"

Christian was a pro, an excellent agent who'd worked with the DEA in south Florida trying to put a crimp in the drug trade. He was a man of few words, and he never wasted them.

"They just let me go. Anna, too. The others are all still being questioned, and every one of you is on suspension."

"As expected."

Christian didn't ask questions, didn't want to know why he and Anna had been excluded. He didn't even call Wyatt a stupid son of a bitch for being so reckless and leading his team with him into total destruction. He simply said, "What can I do to help?"

"There's nothing. I'm on my way to find Lily, and I'm going to bring her in."

"You know where she is?"

"I think so."

Christian didn't ask, as if knowing Wyatt would never tell him. Wyatt trusted the man, but that didn't mean he would let his guard down completely. Not when it came to Lily's safety.

"All right. Call me before you bring her. I'll make sure there are plenty of witnesses this time, though I don't think there's going to be any trouble."

"Why?"

"I know the truth. We all know. Once it got so serious, one of Anspaugh's own men admitted that he'd gone upstairs to see what was taking so long, and heard Anspaugh attack her."

Wyatt's hand gripped the steering wheel so hard, the leather pattern imprinted itself on his skin. "He's a dead man."

"I didn't hear you say that," Christian said coolly. "The point is, everybody's on this thing—it goes well above Crandall. Nothing is going to happen to Lily—she'll be treated with kid gloves—as long as she turns herself in. And once we clear her of these murder charges, this should all go away."

Maybe for Lily, the only innocent party in all this. Not for Wyatt or his team, however. He wasn't foolish enough to imagine they'd all escape unscathed.

That, however, was the decision they'd made. He only wished the rest of them wouldn't have to face the consequences. He didn't care about himself—as long as Lily was all right, he would pay any price the bureau asked him to. As much as he liked his job, and knew he did it well, it wasn't as though he actually needed to work.

But the others deserved so much better than to be punished for hard work and loyalty.

Hopeful, given what Christian had told him, he took a chance and said, "Look, let them know I'm going to bring her in, all right? They don't need to come at her guns blazing, even if they do figure out where she is. I'll have her back in Washington by tomorrow."

"I'll do what I can," Christian said, not making any promises he couldn't keep. Damn, Wyatt liked the man. It was too bad he'd just ruined his own career before they really had a chance to do much work together.

"Actually," Wyatt said, knowing that if there had ever been a time to call in the favors he had accumulated over the years, or reach out to one or two friends of his late father's, it was now, "I'm going to give you a phone

number. Dial it, tell the person who answers you're calling on my behalf, and ask him to see what he can do to
help the others. I don't want Dean, Jackie, Kyle, Alec, or
Brandon getting crucified over this."

He rattled off the number, waiting while Christian repeated it back.

"Do I want to know who's going to be answering?"

"No," Wyatt replied. "That would probably make you
too nervous."

"Huh," Christian said, reminding him that the man
seemed to have no nerves at all.

"All right, not nervous. Let's just say it's for discre-
tionary reasons."

"Got it."

Disconnecting, he resumed the drive, riding the gas
pedal hard, despite the gathering storm clouds and the
cold drops of rain that began to stab the windshield. The
drive took half as long as usual. Soon enough he reached
the private driveway, half-hidden from the road, and
swung onto it. His heart was in his throat as he drove
around one curve, then another, peering through the
rainy darkness, trying to see if the Jeep was parked at
the base of the steps.

"Thank God," he mumbled when he saw it there.
Alone.

Pulling up beside it, he hopped out, felt the dwindling
warmth of the engine, and knew she hadn't beaten him
here by too long.

"She's fine," he reminded himself as he headed for the
steps, his head down against the spitting rain. By habit,
he glanced toward the motion sensor, certain it had
alerted her to his presence. She was probably watching
him right now on the surveillance cameras. Reactivating

them would have been the very first thing she did when she arrived.

The red warning light was not gleaming in the near darkness. Neither was the green one that said he was free to proceed up the steep stairs.

The system had not been activated.

Tense, Wyatt glanced at the security camera on the garage. No sensor light there, either.

"Lily," he whispered.

The car engine hadn't been *that* warm. She hadn't arrived here such a short time ago that she hadn't had time to set the system. And no way would she have walked into that house and not seen to her own protection immediately.

Gripped by worry now, Wyatt began to jog, then to run up the steps, taking them two or three at a time, slipping a little on the wet wood surface. Reaching the top of the cliff, he darted to the porch, but hesitated before entering the house. He tested the knob. Unlocked.

*This is not good.* Wyatt reached down and removed his .40 Glock from its holster, then pushed the door open. It slid noiselessly, allowing him to creep into the darkened house. A few feet in front of him, he saw Lily's purse, lying on the floor, its contents strewn around. Along with everything else, it told a terrifying story.

He almost strode forward, but Wyatt suddenly remembered those crime scenes, all those lures that had to have drawn the victims inside those hotel rooms.

Instinct made him spin just as the person who'd been behind the front door lunged forward. He saw a blade, heard it whistle as it rent the air. *An ax.* Sharp metal bit into his shoulder, but he got off one shot, seeing a face as his attacker was thrown back.

*Claire Vincent.*

Blood dripped down his arm, pain eating him alive as his muscles and tendons gaped open. Thinking only of making sure the psychopath didn't get past him to the woman he loved, he ignored it, stepping closer to the lawyer who lay on the floor.

Claire wasn't dead; she was still wriggling, conscious. The bullet had hit her in the middle, above her right hip, and she bled profusely. Wyatt lifted the weapon again, not to finish her off, of course, despite how satisfying it might have been. He merely needed to cover her until he found out how badly she was hurt. "Don't move," he said, "or I'll send you where you belong, into a grave right beside your fucking brother's."

The woman stared up at him, insanity and rage warring in her eyes. Then she looked just past him, as if seeing the ghost of her twisted lover, and managed a weak smile laden with evil.

She whispered, "You first."

Her tone gave him a second's warning and he tried to get out of the way. But his responses were slowed by blood loss, his reactions a split second off due to the pain. He moved too late.

By the time he realized she hadn't been alone, pain, bright and intense, exploded in his head and he was lost.

# Chapter 18

Lily heard the shot. Not violently explosive, not like in the movies, but unmistakable to someone who'd been alert for that sound, or any other threatening one, every night she'd been in this house.

She didn't panic. Didn't even reach for the shower handle to turn the water off. Instead, she stepped out in silence, grabbed her shirt, and pulled it on over her wet, naked body. Underwear, too. The jeans and shoes she'd taken off in the bedroom, on the other side of the closed bathroom door, not that she'd have wasted time with them, anyway.

She inched closer to the door, listening. Who would fire a gun? Not the FBI, not the police—whom would they be shooting at? They'd be bursting in here, ordering her to get down, arresting her.

*Anspaugh?* He might be enraged enough, but he wouldn't have the brains to track her down so quickly.

The killer, then. She'd been followed here. Either that or he'd figured out where she'd been hiding and he'd come here to wait for her return, as if knowing she'd be drawn back to this one safe place at some point. He must have disabled the alarm system while she'd been taking her leisurely shower, not even realizing how close danger had come.

*But who were you shooting at?*

A horrible possibility came to mind. *Wyatt.* Though her first instinct was to race into the bedroom, to get the gun from her dresser drawer, she did nothing, pulling all her thoughts into one tight, blazing point in her brain.

A sound somewhere in the house. A voice. A thump.

She edged toward the window. It was small, high. But doable.

Standing on the toilet lid, she eased the sash up, pulled the screen in, and wriggled through the opening, one foot, then the other, shimmying out on her belly. Rain assaulted her, sharp and cold, flecked with hints of ice. One story above the patio, with no way to break her fall, she slowly slid down, dangling there, trying to keep her grip on the wet frame. Then, praying she'd forgotten to pick up the exercise mat after her last workout with Sarge, she let go.

The surface on which she landed was soft, wet, squishy. *The mat.* So at least one thing had gone her way today.

Lily immediately crouched down on her belly, peering through the sliding door into the kitchen. The darkness within surpassed even the nighttime sky, and she had to wait for her eyes to adjust.

She saw movement beyond the kitchen, in the cavernous living area. A man was bent over a shape on the floor. A few feet away lay another dark form, crumpled and lifeless. The man turned his head slightly, so she caught a glimpse of his profile.

Jesse Boyd.

She almost vomited, being this close to the man she'd once wanted to rip apart with her bare hands. *You son of a bitch, you monster, I'll kill you.* The words screamed in her head, but didn't pass her lips in even a whisper, for she knew the very faintest sound could betray her.

And she greatly feared she knew what those shapes on the floor meant. People, unconscious, injured. *Dead?* Her heart constricted, the air thick in her throat, threatening to choke her.

Her attention was drawn from the monster. The person Jesse had been checking on began to sit up, the child murderer lending a hand. They both rose to their feet; then Jesse moved a little to the right, enough for Lily to get a better look. She saw silver glasses, a pinched face.

The lawyer. Claire Vincent.

She wasn't entirely surprised. Ever since this morning when Jackie had pointed out Claire's name on the background report, identified as Roger Underwood's stepsister, she'd been curious to learn more. Now, seeing her here, Lily began to put things together. Was it possible the attorney was the lily murderer, and Boyd now her accomplice?

Wanting to hear their plans, she risked making a sound. She slid her fingers into the crevice of the door, tugging it open one inch, no farther, glad she'd left it unlocked when she'd gotten home a half hour ago.

"Get upstairs," the woman inside was saying. "The shower's still running. With the thunder, she probably didn't even realize she heard a gunshot." She pointed toward the floor with one hand, the other clutching her right side, which was coated with blood. She'd been hurt.

God, did Lily wish she could see more. Like who that other dark shape crumpled on the floor could be. Whose gun Jesse was bending over to retrieve.

*Please, please, not him.* But she already knew it was. Wyatt had come looking for her and walked right into an ambush.

"Shoot her the minute you walk in the bathroom. Don't say anything—just shoot right through the shower curtain or the door. Take her down."

"I don't know how," Boyd said, his voice whiny, weak. "I never shot a gun in my life."

"You stupid fool!" Claire snarled, her face twisted with rage, her eyes sparking with an insane light. "Go shoot her or I'll do it—then I'll come back down here and kill you myself."

That would be convenient, but she couldn't hope the woman would kill her accomplice before he found out Lily was not upstairs in the shower.

"It wasn't Fletcher who killed Will Miller, was it?"

Lily had no idea who Will Miller was.

"It *was* you. You set this all up, wanted me to kill her for you. Do your dirty work, right?"

"Your genius is staggering," the woman said. "Now get up there and finish the job before I bleed to death. You do want her dead, don't you?"

Boyd nodded. "Yeah. But I don't like being used."

The woman swayed, but her condescension was clear. "I apologize; do forgive me for my bad manners. Now *go*."

Jesse went, trudging slowly, step by step, as if dreading his deadly errand. The man held the gun out to his side, as if he was afraid it would go off by itself and kill him.

If only Lily were that lucky.

In a moment, Claire Vincent was wounded and alone, but she was also psychotic. Like a trapped animal, she might be even more dangerous right now. If Lily hadn't been damn sure that was Wyatt lying unconscious—*not dead, please, God, not dead*—on the floor, she would have slipped over the railing, down to the beach, and escaped the two killers. But she couldn't, not without Wyatt.

She eased the door farther, never taking her eyes off Claire. The woman had sagged against the wall, bent over, blood dripping freely from between her splayed fingers.

Four steps to get past the kitchen table. Two more to reach the knife block on the counter. Second one from the right was the biggest, but the one on the far left was sharper, utterly wicked. Twelve steps across the smooth wood floor to the base of the open staircase. For seven of those, she would be blind to anyone descending, but entirely visible to the wounded woman at their base. Those last five would be the most critical. Either of the two murderers could see her and warn the other.

Lily crept in, cautious. She counted her footsteps. Reaching in the darkness for the knife block, she unerringly withdrew the one she wanted.

She turned and walked again. Ten steps. Eight. Six. All the time eyeing the stairs for Jesse's return, then past them to focus on Claire Vincent.

Risking one quick, confirming glance at the body on the floor, she recognized Wyatt. Her heart raced when she saw the wound on his shoulder, the blood on the back of his head. But she also saw his chest moving as he breathed. *Not dead.* Yet she couldn't help him until she eliminated both threats.

She'd reached the danger zone. No way to see if Boyd was coming down, no way to hide from Claire's gaze. Steeling her will and gripping the knife, she flew forward, aided by the element of surprise, and had the knife under the lawyer's throat before the other woman could even gasp.

The lawyer's eyes rounded with shock. "You . . ."

"I'm finished with my shower," she whispered.

Lily looked up and saw nothing. Jesse was apparently still standing in her bedroom, trying to grow a big enough set of balls to burst into the bathroom and kill her. Or figure out how to turn the damn gun safety off.

Claire opened her mouth as if to scream.

"Don't or I'll slit your throat. I swear to God I would take pleasure in doing it."

The woman whimpered. She appeared dazed, in pain, and, judging by the amount of blood at her feet, badly wounded. Yet she'd still managed to orchestrate Lily's murder, to cock her weapon—Jesse—aim it, and send it up the stairs to finish the job.

Lily should have shoved the woman down, grabbed Wyatt, and dragged him out of here. But he was badly hurt. The steps down to the driveway were long, to the beach even longer, and Jesse had Wyatt's gun. He could catch up with them and shoot them down easily. So instead, she grabbed Claire by the front of her shirt and pulled her, hard, to the floor. She reached for the phone, which sat on the closest table, lifted the receiver, and heard nothing but dead air. The cut cord on the back of it explained why.

"Thanks. I can use that," she snarled, yanking the longer part of the cord out of the wall. Moving quickly, she wound it around Claire's hands, binding her tightly.

A quick glance up the stairs confirmed Jesse's continued indecision. Lily took the opportunity to check on Wyatt. His shoulder gaped open—she could see the bone—but the blood loss wasn't critical yet. A quick check of the bloody lump on his head led her to believe he'd been struck, not shot.

"You're going to be okay," she whispered. "This will all be over with in a couple of minutes." She considered rooting through his pockets to look for his cell phone, but didn't want to risk moving him, and also didn't want to keep her back to the stairs any longer. "I'll take care of Boyd, then get you some help." She reached down to gently brush his dark hair off his brow. "I love you."

Returning to the base of the stairs, the knife in her hands, Lily crouched and listened for any sounds from above. When Jesse pounded down those stairs, he was going to get one heck of a surprise.

"I need an ambulance," Claire whispered weakly.

"Fuck you."

"I mean it. I'll die. It was never personal, you know, never against you."

Lily ignored her, unable to believe the gall of the woman who'd come here to kill her.

"Roger called me for help that night," she whispered. "Me, of all people, I was the one he turned to. I'd loved him all those years and he was finally turning to *me*."

Okay, the woman was obviously sick.

"I didn't know about you, or that other agent. He just told me he'd gotten in trouble and needed help getting rid of the van. I knew nothing else until I saw the news the next day. He'd made me an accessory after the fact to murder and I had no idea."

"Poor you, now shut up." Lily cocked her head, listening, still no sound from upstairs. What the hell was Jesse doing, taking a nap on her bed?

Claire continued speaking, her whisper weak and pathetic. "I tried to talk to him all week, then finally ended up following him. He went to the old shack on the beach."

Her whole body recoiling, Lily finally gave the woman her full attention. "And you saw me?" *Saw me and did nothing?*

The woman nodded. Her eyes held no apology, only anger. "We argued."

The unknown woman. Had Lily heard Claire and mistaken her for the ghostly voice of her twin sister?

"I told him to kill you, but he refused. He was keeping you. He wanted you for himself." Claire sniffed, as if heartbroken. "There was always someone else. Why were you so special?"

"I wasn't exactly thrilled about it," Lily snarled.

"He told me we'd talk later, that we had to act normal. That night, after dinner, I snuck into his house and confronted him. Asked him why. Why everyone else? Why Judith, why children, why you? Why not me anymore?"

The very twisted nature of the question—why did he want children and not her?—didn't seem to occur to the woman. Nothing did. Claire Vincent was crazy. Maybe it wasn't the technical term, but as far as Lily was concerned, the woman was just fucking nuts.

"I told him I would satisfy him more than anyone else if he'd only let me." Her eyes narrowed and for the first time, she began to show some sign of normal emotion. Anger toward the man who'd caused all of this.

"What did he say?" Lily asked, drawn almost against her will into the woman's story.

"He told me he'd used me. That my own brother had been a better lay than I was."

God in heaven.

"I don't much like Philip anymore, but I did when he was a little boy. And when Roger told me what he'd done, I just lost it. I picked up the wine opener, stabbed him with it, shot him with compressed air. I guess it hit a vein and an air bubble went to his heart."

Lily didn't follow, but she didn't need to. The woman had just confessed to killing Roger Underwood. It was the first thing she'd said that actually made Lily's opinion toward her go up a notch.

"I went back to the beach to finish you off, sure you'd seen me or heard me that afternoon, but you were gone. I've been waiting ever since for you to show back up."

"Which is why you started killing those other men, hoping to make me look like a killer."

The woman shuddered, her eyes closing as she whispered, "Yes. And because those other men were all just like him, and killing Roger only once hadn't been good enough. He raped my baby brother. And he broke my heart."

None of the rest of the evil things he'd done seemed to matter to this woman, who let out a guttural groan as she appeared to drift into unconsciousness.

"Hey! Ms. Vincent? You there?" a voice called from above. "She's gone—the screen's inside the bathroom— she musta climbed out the window and run down to the beach!"

Thankful Jesse hadn't grown a brain since she'd last seen him, Lily tensed and prepared to attack. Jesse's footsteps pounded as he came down the stairs, and Lily, the small knife in her hand, knew she had to disarm him the minute he came into view. She could take the bastard, but not if he kept the gun.

"Ms. Vincent?" His foot appeared.

*Now.*

She launched, hoping to either stab him in the arm or else surprise him into dropping the weapon, but she wasn't that lucky. The swipe of her knife missed him by no more than the width of a single hair. He was bulkier than she'd remembered, but his reactions were faster than she'd expected, and he spun out of her reach. Lily followed, throwing herself at him before he could bring the gun up and aim it.

They both fell to the floor; she landed right on top of him. Jesse drew back his arm to punch her off his chest, but Lily curled in a ball and rolled off by herself, kicking with all her might as she avoided his fist.

He grunted in pain. "Bitch," he snapped, out of breath from the foot she'd just jabbed into one of his lungs. But instead of fighting back, he slid forward, his fingertips finding the gun he'd dropped. He snatched it up and swung it around toward her before she could get at him. And for the second time in her life, Lily found herself literally staring down the barrel of a gun.

This time, there was no way the shot would miss.

She swallowed, not closing her eyes, glaring at him with all the hatred she felt for the man. Steeling herself for the impact, she was shocked when there was a flash of movement, low, to Jesse's right. Then something swung up from the floor. A thud, a crunch of bone, a man's scream, and then a gunshot.

It missed.

"Wyatt!" she cried, seeing him kneeling beside Jesse

Boyd, who was writhing around the floor, screaming about the pain in his leg.

Small wonder, considering an ax protruded from it. The murderous duo had apparently stopped to gather supplies from the garage.

"Lily?" Wyatt whispered.

She launched toward him, wrapping her arms around him to catch him before he could topple over. His arm dangled at his side, the wound bloody and vicious, and she couldn't imagine the pain he was in. Yet he'd still managed to swing that ax, to save her life.

"It's going to be okay," he mumbled, sounding dazed, barely conscious.

"I think that's what I'm supposed to be telling you," she replied, unable to stop kissing his face, stroking his hair. "Let me get your cell phone so I can call an ambulance." Glancing at the two other people who lay on the floor, she muttered, "Or three."

Considering Claire Vincent had stopped moving, had stopped whispering, and hadn't reacted at all to the brief but violent confrontation, maybe one of those would be a hearse instead. Meanwhile, Jesse's screeches had diminished to low whimpers, and when he looked down and saw the ax, he actually passed out. Lily took the precaution of tying him up with a lamp cord.

"Come on," she told Wyatt, not wanting to leave him here, close to the couple who'd nearly killed them both. "Let's call 911. I need to get some pants on, and then we'll wait for the ambulance on the patio." Shaking her head, she admitted, "I could really use a cigarette."

Though the local police wanted her to stay at the scene to answer their questions, Lily insisted on riding with

Wyatt in the ambulance. Good thing. Wyatt didn't think he'd be able to let her out of his sight anytime soon. Not without descending into the shakes at the memory of seeing a gun pointed directly at her face.

"You okay?" he asked.

"I think I should be asking you that."

"I'm fine. Hurts, but I'll be fine."

She reached up to wipe at her eyes, not for the first time. "Thank you for saving my life."

"Are you joking? You saved mine, too."

"Does that mean we're now responsible for each other, for the rest of our lives? Isn't that the old saying?"

He turned his head, looking away. Because as much as he wanted her to be part of his life from here on out, he knew she shouldn't be. She'd been thrown into a pit of darkness and tragedy a couple of years ago, but all that was coming to an end. Now she should be with someone who smiled and laughed, someone who'd give her kids, then toss a football around with them in the backyard. Someone who'd charm her and tease her out of an occasional bad mood. Romance her. Grow old together happily.

That wasn't him. None of it. He was serious and intense, didn't want the life he envisioned her having. And while he loved her enough to give it a shot, knowing he would never be what she wanted, or what she really needed, he just couldn't put off the inevitable.

"You're okay; it's all over," he whispered. "You can go now, be free, start over. Live like the past couple of years never happened."

Her voice strained with sorrow, she said, "The past couple of years have changed who I am forever, Wyatt.

They've defined the woman I'm going to be for the rest of my life."

He gripped her hand. "They don't have to. You don't have to let them."

"I can't wave a magic wand and go back to who I once was. Nobody can."

"You deserve some happiness."

She kissed his hand. "As long as I'm with you, I'm happy."

Though it pained him, both physically and emotionally, he slowly shook his head. "No. You don't need to be stuck with me."

"You're not getting rid of me."

He leaned up a little, wishing his head would stop spinning. And while there were better times and better places to have this conversation, he knew he had to tell her the one thing that might convince her that he wasn't the big, wonderful hero she'd painted him to be in her head.

"It's my fault, Lily. All my fault."

"Are you crazy? You saved my life. Not just tonight, not even just back in January. But every single day since." Her voice shook. "You gave me the motivation to get out of bed each morning, to keep working out with Sarge when I thought the pain would drive me insane. Even fighting with you, being mad at you, sending you away, treating you like crap when you came back—all of those things happened because you made me *feel*, Wyatt, when I once thought I would never feel anything again."

Maybe. That didn't mean she needed to live the remainder of her days based on feelings she'd had during her darkest ones.

Swallowing, his mouth dry, he told her what he'd been unable to tell her before. "When I say it's my fault, I mean, I am responsible for Boyd's release."

She stared down at him, confusion swimming in her blue eyes. "He got out because I wasn't around to testify and keep him in."

"The evidence that was thrown out," he insisted, "was tossed because of me. Because I exposed what was going on in the crime lab."

She sucked in a small, surprised breath.

"The DNA, the fibers, everything. It was all processed in the FBI lab right before I blew the whole place wide-open."

Her mouth in a small circle, she whispered, "Oh."

It was obviously sinking in, but he made it even more clear. "He never would have gotten off, could never have come after you, if not for that. Lily, I am entirely responsible for the release of your nephew's murderer."

"Ma'am, we're about to pull up to the emergency room. You'll need to move out of the way," a man's voice said before Wyatt could even hope for a reply.

"I'm sorry," he murmured. "So damn sorry."

Then a paramedic appeared above him and he could no longer see Lily's face, couldn't gauge her expression.

And had no way of knowing if she'd be there when he woke up.

He was trying to push her away.

Now that she was safe, now that they would, hopefully, be able to return to Washington and take up their lives again, Wyatt had decided she was better off without him.

Lily couldn't pretend surprise. She'd known this day

would come. Wyatt had told her many times that he was a loner, an intense man who had never had room in his life for anyone else and liked it that way.

"Well, too bad, mister," she whispered as she paced the waiting room of the hospital. He'd been in surgery for a couple of hours, the doctors trying to save his arm, repair all those ripped muscles and tendons. Her heart broke when she thought of the pain he'd been in and all the pain yet to come when he had to rehabilitate that arm.

She knew a really good therapist. And she'd be right by Sarge's side in urging Wyatt on. Because Lily wasn't going anywhere.

If he had told her he didn't care about her, didn't love her, maybe she'd have thought twice. But since she wouldn't have believed him, maybe not. She probably would still have argued it with him.

He hadn't said that, however. He'd merely tried to drive her away by confessing something that had obviously been racking him with guilt. How utterly Wyatt. Tormenting himself because he'd done the right thing and it had just happened to have an effect on her life.

He just didn't get it. Doing the right thing despite all the obstacles, and the possible repercussions, was one of the things she loved most about him. Just like he'd done the right thing in saving her life, hiding her, keeping her alive all those months when he had known what it would eventually cost him.

A lot.

But they'd deal with that later, with what would happen to Wyatt for the decision he'd made to help her. For now, she was doing as much as she could to lessen the impact. Lily had already managed to get a message to the director's office, going over Crandall's head entirely. Though of course she hadn't spoken with the director himself, especially late on a Saturday night, she had gotten a few assurances from one of his assistants. With the local police backing every word of her story, she'd been promised her case would be handled fairly and that she could return to Washington to turn herself in tomorrow.

Tonight, she had other things to do. Namely, keep a quiet vigil during the long hours when Wyatt was in surgery. Finally, at around four a.m., a doctor came in to inform her it was over. Lily, who'd been dozing on an uncomfortable couch, leapt to her feet immediately, asking only the most important question. "Is he going to be okay?"

"Yes, fine. Time will tell how much use he will regain of his right arm."

"Fortunately, Doctor," she said, already heading for the waiting room door, "he's a lefty."

Not letting anyone get in her way, Lily headed to the recovery room. A nurse pointed to the curtain, and Lily yanked it back, seeing him lying in the bed. Bandages covered his neck, arm, and shoulder. And while he should probably have been woozy from anesthesia, his blue-eyed stare was sharp as he watched her enter.

"You stayed."

She walked to the bed and kissed his forehead. "Of course I stayed. And I'm going to keep on staying."

"I'm not the right man, Lily."

"You are the *only* man. The only one, ever."

"You're so young."

"You're crazy—I'm thirty years old. Definitely old

enough to know what I want, and that is you, Wyatt Blackstone. Only you."

He shook his head wearily. "It's a bad idea. I can't give you what you need. A normal life, a family . . ."

She frowned. "I want you to be my family. *Just* you, nobody else, ever. And you should be aware of that up front."

He stared up at her, and she knew he realized what she meant.

"I'm not kidding, not reacting hastily. I know what I want and what I don't." She lowered her voice, reaching to tenderly brush his dark hair back from his handsome face. "And what I want is you and me, forever. You are the only one who sees me as I really am. Not the pretty, gentle girl I was, but the strong, tough woman I've become."

He lifted a shaky hand and touched her cheek, then slid his fingers through her hair to the scarred ear. "You're beautiful."

She tilted her cheek into his hand. "I know I am, in your eyes. What's even more important, you can see the darkness in me and still think I'm beautiful. And I know you can help me live my life *around* that darkness, not expecting to plow straight through it, but always skirting it, careful and alert to its borders, respectful of its dangers. But not mired in it. Do you understand?"

He hesitated, then nodded once. Of course he understood. He'd been living his life the same way since he was a little boy.

"I love you," she said simply, baring herself entirely. "I love you and I want to spend the rest of my life with you."

He closed his eyes briefly, and when he opened them

again, she saw pure, unguarded warmth. Tenderness. Emotion. "I love you, too, Lily."

Carefully, so carefully, she bent to him and brushed her mouth against his. "We'll find our own kind of happy, Wyatt."

"I know we will."

# Epilogue

Wyatt remained in the hospital for three days after his surgery. Three long, irritating days during which he had climbed the walls, especially after one of the nurses had taken his cell phone.

Staying in Maine when he most wanted to be in Washington, dealing with the fallout from everything that had happened, was the most difficult part of the whole ordeal. Far worse than the pain. He needed to go in and face the music himself, get his team out of trouble, put in his resignation—or accept his termination. He was also desperate to make sure they didn't try to pin anything on Lily. Like her assault on Tom Anspaugh and her subsequent escape.

Instead, he'd been stuck here. Lily had left the morning after they'd been attacked. Though it had been hard to let her go, he knew that with the calls he and the local police had made, plus the help of Christian Mendez, who'd picked her up at the airport, she would be safe turning herself in. And according to her phone calls, she was.

But she hadn't said much more than that, insisting that everything was fine and she'd explain it all in person when she came back. She didn't tell him if she was facing charges, if his team was still employed, if everyone accepted the almost-crazy-sounding truth that attorney Claire Vincent was, in fact, a serial killer. Nothing.

She was there handling everything, all on her own. He, meanwhile, was just supposed to lie in bed and wait.

Waiting had never been one of Wyatt Blackstone's favorite things to do.

"Stop thinking about it," a voice said from the doorway to his room.

Lily.

As she entered, his eyes devoured her, looking for any sign of fear or sadness, pain, or anger. There was nothing, just an easy, laid-back expression as she sauntered over to his bed.

"You're back," he said.

"For such a smart, literate guy, is that the best you've got to say?"

He grabbed her arm and pulled her down, catching her mouth and kissing her deeply, wanting to inhale the very essence of her after being deprived of it for three long, difficult days.

When they separated for air, their faces remaining close together, she said, "That was a much better greeting."

"Wait till you see how I say good-bye."

She shook her head. "I never want to."

"Agreed."

Lily slid onto the bed, curling up next to him, on his good side. He hadn't even begun to ask her the many questions racing through his head, just enjoyed having her back here, free and happy.

Finally, though, she began to tell him. All of it. She started with the issue he most wanted to know about.

"I swear to you, Wyatt, Tom Anspaugh is never going to bother me again. I am not being charged for assaulting him and fleeing, because he finally broke down and admitted what he did, acknowledged he had physically threatened me, and apologized. He also admitted he has a drinking problem and is on leave, trying to get himself straightened out, and knows it's his last shot at saving his job."

Not good enough. Someday that bill would come due and Anspaugh was going to pay it. Their paths would cross again; of that, Wyatt had no doubt. But he didn't want to worry her about it, not when she was so pleased at the way things had worked out.

She should be. She'd done a magnificent job, judging by what she told him about the meeting with Crandall and so many others. "Crandall kept wanting me to say you knew I was alive from the start," she said with a deep frown. "That you faked my death from the very beginning. As if you would have actually left me there in that shack . . ."

"Don't." His hand tightened on her shoulder. "Please don't."

She was silent for a moment, then continued. "I didn't give in. Told the truth and nothing but. And what it all came down to is, I'm not facing any charges, I'm alive, and I'll be declared so, sooner or later. I'll get my identity back, though not my job, not that I want it."

He lifted his head and looked down at her. "What will you do?"

"I was thinking of trying live-in girlfriend for a little while, then going to work as a computer-security consultant. I think I'd be good at teaching companies how to prevent hackers like me and Brandon from getting into their systems."

Girlfriend. That might do for now, though eventually Wyatt knew he'd want her to try on the title of wife. They were going to make one incredible team.

"Sounds good." He managed a teasing smile. "I suspect you're going to need to get a good job to support me in the style to which I've become accustomed."

"Okay, but the fifteen-hundred-dollar suits have got to go."

"Deal." Growing serious again, he sighed and said, "Enough. Let's just get to the end. Tell me what I'm going to find when I go back in to face the music."

She raised one pretty brow. "Well, I think you're going to find you're on suspension, without pay, as is Brandon. The others got official reprimands."

"Suspension?" he asked, surprised. He'd already assumed he would be fired, and had been thinking more along the lines of prosecution.

"Crandall wanted you fired, but he didn't get his way. He's still trying to get you stripped of your title, downgraded, and the hearing isn't going to be pretty. I don't know whether the Black CATs will even exist anymore once you get back."

He nodded once, disappointed. But also already thinking, forming his arguments, mentally listing all the reasons his team should be kept intact. Starting with the fact that every one of them was damn good at his job, and together, they were utterly brilliant.

"I can deal with Crandall," he muttered.

"I'm sure you can. Besides, I hear you have a friend or two in high places." Her tone pleased, she added, "They very loudly reminded the director of all that you've done, not just with the crime-lab mess, but in being instrumental in the capture of several notorious serial killers in the past year."

Damn. He hadn't wanted that. "I didn't call in favors for myself," he said. "I just wanted the others to get out of this mess with their jobs and their pensions intact."

"Well, first off, I don't think anybody did you any favors, Wyatt, since you're eventually going to have to go back to work under Deputy Director Crandall."

Good point.

"Besides, they weren't doing it out of friendship." She gently ran the tips of her soft fingers over his palm, every stroke reminding him of how much he needed her hand to be wrapped in his. "It was about nothing more than the fact that you do an excellent job. Eventually everyone had to acknowledge that you saved my life." She shrugged modestly. "I made a very good witness, if I do say so myself."

He laughed deeply. "I'm sure you did. You're very good at arguing your case. I can't imagine anybody refusing you anything."

She shifted a little so she could look up at him; that beautiful face, made even more so by trauma and grief, now shone with warmth and happiness.

"Does that mean if I ask you nicely, we can get another beach house, maybe on the Maryland shore this time?"

Knowing what she was saying, what she was offering, he tenderly brushed his fingers through her hair. "We don't have to get rid of the Maine house. I know you love it."

Serious, intent, she said, "Yes, we do. It was my crutch, and it was your cross. Neither of us needs it anymore."

"No, I suppose we don't," he admitted. "Absolutely the only thing we need is each other."

In the final moments of her life Lisa Zimmerman realized she knew her killer.

With his black-cloaked form illuminated by moonlight, it took just one particular, whispered expression to send the truth flooding into her pain-numbed consciousness. Her slowing brain cells jolted back into awareness.

*"You?"* It hurt to push the whispered word across her swollen lips, which were caked with blood and dirt, and flecked with bits of dug-in gravel. Despite the pain, she added, "Can't be."

But it was true.

She knew who had tied her to this tree, her arms stretched painfully above her head, leaving her to dangle from wrenched shoulders and balance on the tips of her bare toes. Knew who had slashed the vicious blade across her abdomen, until she'd felt warm, sticky blood spill down her legs onto her own feet. Knew who watched her from behind the black hood, his dull eyes reflecting no emotion, as if her agony didn't exist.

Knew him.

Until this moment, she'd been floating, dazed, and nearly disappearing into a world she created in her own head, one in which this was happening to someone else, and she was merely an observer. Now, though, shock sent her blood-deprived, slowing heart back into overdrive, until it thudded in a hard, desperate rhythm. Her shallow breaths, each of which caused a strange whistling sound in her chest, grew more rapid.

Knowing made it worse. That *he* could do such a thing . . .

Knowing didn't, however, ease the pain that had begun with the first sweep of the knife. She'd tried to escape it by giving in to the slow lethargy of blood loss. Now the terror she'd felt when she'd realized she was being kidnapped came rushing back like a bullet hitting her dead center.

Feeling capable of moving again, she expended what little energy she had left in a vain effort to pull back and evade the next slow, deliberate stroke, meant to torment more than wound. He'd wounded her deeply the first time. Now he was just playing.

*I've known you most of my life. How* could *you?*

His identity offered no glimmer of salvation. Sent no ideas of how to escape through her half-dead brain, which seemed ready to shut down, with one final prayer that it would be over soon. It didn't give her courage or make her want to put up a fight, as she had when he'd grabbed her as she'd stumbled out of Dick's Tavern. That had been . . . days ago? Weeks? *Centuries?*

No. It might have seemed like an eternity, but it had probably been an hour or two since she'd left the crowded bar. She'd been so drunk she had at first thought some guy who'd bought her a drink was hoping for some payback in the dark shadows of the gravel parking lot. Or that the one real friend she had left in this town had come to drag her home, safe and sound, whether she liked it or not. *Safe and sound . . . at home?*

The merciless crunch of his powerful fist on her jaw had quickly killed those ideas. Her kidnapper had dragged her across the ground, half-conscious, unable to whimper, much less call for help. Not that anybody else had been outside to hear.

He had thrown her into the back of a covered pickup and driven her out here into the middle of nowhere, where she'd assumed she was going to be raped. But every minute since, he'd made it clear he didn't want to fuck her. He used to—*God, why did you laugh at him?*—but now he wanted only one thing: to watch her die.

The pain, so sharp at first, had dulled into a deep burning. She begged for mercy, knowing it wouldn't come. "Please let me go. I won't tell. I know how to keep secrets."

"Just stay quiet," he said. His words were a little choppy, as if, despite his still, calm demeanor, he was finally feeling some emotion about what he was doing to her.

*Maybe . . .*

As quickly as it had arisen, the hope that he might actually have some glimmer of humanity that could be appealed to disappeared. Because through swollen, half-closed eyes, she saw him reach down and rub his crotch.

Yeah. Definitely feeling some emotion. "You sick motherfucker," she spat.

"Shut up, filthy slut!" He swung his arm back, but this time, instead of the blade, he used his fist to quiet her.

He didn't want this to end too quickly. There would be no goading him into making it quick. "You're dirty and you deserve what you get."

The blow flung her head back and she saw stars. Not the figurative kind, but a blanket of real ones filling the midnight blue sky above. So many they'd take a thousand nights to count, a lifetime to appreciate.

She had minutes, at most. Seconds if she was very lucky.

Trying to distance herself from it, she kept staring upward, focusing on the full moon, the heavens. "Daddy," she whispered, pleading for something she'd lost long ago.

How could the world still be turning and life continuing everywhere else when she was being tortured to death? Beneath all that light, that immenseness, she was entirely and completely alone with the monster who wanted her dead.

"I'm sorry." Tears oozed from the corners of her eyes to mingle with the blood and dirt on her cheeks. She didn't know who she was talking to—some God she'd long since stopped believing in? Herself for getting caught in this trap?

Maybe she was trying to say the one thing she'd never said to the one person who truly deserved to hear it. *This will break her heart.*

The vision of her sad, weary mother, who'd been so loving, yet so impossibly blind, brought her head forward. She again focused on her attacker.

He was no demon. Just a vicious, awful human being.

"Why?" A weak whisper was all she could manage. She had to have lost a lot of blood. It no longer gushed, but still dripped slowly down her front. Its warmth against her bare skin contrasted sharply with the cold air of the March night. *Not long now.*

"Because you're a whore and nobody will miss you," he said with a shrug.

How had nobody ever noticed he was insane?

"Wait here." As if she had any other choice.

He glanced to his right, shook his head, then strode to the edge of the small clearing in which he'd imprisoned her.

That was when she saw the video camera.

Standing on a tripod, it was pointed directly at her. A small red light pierced the darkness, indicating the camera was on, recording this. He was capturing her pain, casting her final moments into a bloody sequence of two-dimensional images.

"You're gonna be famous," he claimed as he adjusted the thing.

He tilted it down a little. A whirring noise told her he'd zoomed in closer.

"Sick pig," she mumbled, though the words were so soft she barely even heard them. She wasn't able to breathe well, barely had the air to make any audible sounds.

"We're both gonna be famous."

*Both famous.* Lisa's eyes drifted closed. Her muscles unable to support her any longer, her legs slowly went limp. She hardly felt the agony of her shoulders pulling from their sockets under the full pressure of her nearly dead body weight.

*Famous.*

The word zipped through her mind, making her suck in one last desperate breath of hope. Even as she heard the crunch of dried leaves beneath his feet as he returned to finish what he'd so brutally started, she couldn't help feeling a tiny moment of triumph.

He was on that tape with her. Disguised, yes, in a black cape and a hood. But she had recognized him. Somebody else would, too. Long after she was dead and gone, someone would see that video and catch him. Small comfort, but it was something.

The footsteps stopped. Lisa didn't have to open her eyes to know he was again beside her. The warmth of his breaths emerging through the opening in his hood brushed her cheek. If she had any strength, she'd turn her head and sink her teeth into his throat. But strength had long abandoned her. As had dreams of escape. Justice, though, that fantasy hadn't disappeared yet.

"Ready for your close-up?" he whispered.

*Close-up of you, too, bastard.*

He touched her cheek with one black-gloved finger. "Don't be sad. Lots of people will see this. They'll love you and they'll never know what a cheap whore you are."

The arm swung. A kiss of steely fire. And a few random thoughts before oblivion.

Why was he making this video?

Who would see it?

*Don't let Mama see. . . .*

Then blackness.

# LESLIE PARRISH

## *FADE TO BLACK*

### A Black CATs Novel

After transferring out of violent crimes and onto the
FBI's Cyber Action Team, Special Agent Dean Taggert is
shocked to encounter a case far more vicious than any
he's ever seen. A cold and calculating predator dubbed
"The Reaper" is auctioning off murder in the cyber
world and is about to kill again—unless Dean and
beautiful sheriff Stacey Rhodes can stop him.

## "CRACKLES WITH DARK, EDGY DANGER."
—*New York Times* bestselling author JoAnn Ross

# LESLIE PARRISH

## *PITCH BLACK*

A Black CATs Novel

Alec Lambert desperately wants to catch The Professor, a serial killer who lures his victims with Internet scams. Now working with scam expert Samantha Dalton, he finally has his chance. But as they draw ever closer to discovering The Professor's identity and stopping his murderous rampage, they realize Sam is the killer's new obsession—and possibly his next target...

**"COMPELLING, HOLD-YOUR-BREATH ROMANTIC SUSPENSE."**
—*New York Times* bestselling author JoAnn Ross

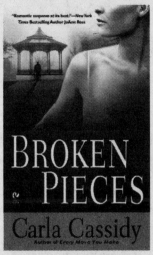